Crimson Dreams

Crimson Dreams

The Crimson Series

Book One

"Blood-drinking Dhampir, werewolves, time travel, and more!

Crimson Dreams has something for everyone!"

–Raven Hart, author of "The Vampire's Seduction."

Crimson Dreams

The Crimson Series
Book One

Georgiana Fields

ISBN: 978-1726036474

Cover Design: Gina Dyer
Photography: Gina Dyer
Photo Credits: Depositphoto
Interior Design: Melba Moon
Editor: Mary Marvella

Dedication

To my husband, John, and my sons who have encouraged me, and to my family who has supported me.

To my sister from another mother, Gina for never letting me give up and always keeping me on track.

To my many friends who have encouraged my imagination. And a special thanks to my fairy godmother, Mary. Thank you all for pushing me toward my dream.

Chapter One

"If I had your brother here, Simon, I'd cut out his heart and serve it to him on a platter." Rose Kelly didn't care if everyone in the restaurant stared at her. How could this happen!

Sitting across from her in a Versace suit he probably found at a consignment shop, Simon snickered. His dark brown eyes sparkled with humor as he leaned across the table.

"That's the problem. My dear, Scott isn't here, to be honest with you, I don't think he has a heart. Besides, if he were here you'd have to get in line to kill him, right behind the FBI, his investors, his creditors, and me. Now stop being so damn dramatic. It's not like you won't be able to find work elsewhere, Rose. You're the best I know in this business. Hell, the economy is bouncing back. You'll be fine. You always land on your feet. But the simple fact is my brother is an ass who stole everything he could from the company. Baby, Victorian Dreams is bankrupt. We're broke! Shit! I wouldn't be surprised if he didn't steal the damn coffee maker."

She slammed her hands on the table, jarring it. The red wine in her glass splashed onto the white linen tablecloth. "How could this happen, Simon? Didn't you know what he was doing? I have to go into work tomorrow and tell everyone what's happened. My God, Simon, these people have families."

He released a heavy sigh. "What can I say, he is my brother. Now, tomorrow you're going into work to tell everyone what's happened, and you're going to divide this up as you see fit." He tossed a manila envelope toward her. "It's all I could come up with for severance pay."

Rose studied Simon's face. Gone was his ever-present grin. "Where will you be?"

He stabbed the air in front of her nose with his finger. "Hopefully, not dead."

"I'm serious, Simon." She stared at him across the table. *He has the nerve to tell me I'm overreacting.*

"So am I, Rose." He motioned for the waiter. "Another whiskey."

Rose rubbed her forehead to ward off the headache she felt coming. "What about my ten o'clock appointment with Mr. Madoc? He's flown in from England, you know."

"Right now, Rose, he is the least of my problems." Simon glanced at his watch. "I would love to discuss this more with you, but I have another meeting with someone who may be able to keep my ass out of jail."

Rose tossed a twenty on the table.

He handed the bill back to her. "Keep your money. Oh, and make sure you and everyone get all your shit cleared out tomorrow. Once the auditors get involved, you won't be able to keep as much as a paperclip."

"Good night, Mr. Becker." Rose tucked the envelope into her purse, then pushed away from the table to stand, and bumped into the waitress. Rose cringed at the sound of breaking glass and turned. The waitress had spilled her entire tray of drinks on a customer.

Scarlet-faced, Rose handed the drenched man a napkin. "I'm so sorry about this."

She looked up and into the most compelling pair of pale green eyes she'd ever seen.

"It's all right, Miss."

Behind her Simon laughed loudly and clapped. "Rosie, you always know how to make me laugh."

More heat rose in her cheeks. Rose snatched her purse and ran out of the restaurant. Dodging people, Rose made her way through the hotel lobby and toward the elevator.

Every time she found happiness, it seemed the universe threw her a curve ball. Rose pressed the button and waited for the elevator doors to open. How would she tell her co-workers they didn't have jobs anymore?

"Tough break." A man's deep voice came from beside her and jolted her from her thoughts.

She peered over at him but didn't recognize him. "Yeah, it is," she said, keeping her eyes on the elevator door. What was taking it so long?

"Can I buy you a drink?"

She faced him. He was tall, dark, and rather handsome, despite the eye patch covering his left eye. "No, thank you."

"At least permit me to escort you to your car, you look upset."

As pleasant as he seemed, something warned her not to be alone with this man. "Someone's picking me up. Thank you," she lied.

"Then I'll wait with you until *he* comes."

The elevator doors opened, revealing a group of people who appeared dressed for a formal wedding. She stepped into the elevator, followed closely by the stranger. As the doors closed, she pushed them open and quickly exited. Rose took the stairs to the parking garage.

The parking deck smelled of exhaust and gas. The dim lights cast eerie shadows on the walls. Loud footsteps echoed behind her. Rose peered over her shoulder. No one.

Her heart pounded, and the tapping of her high heels echoed with each step she took. This was a perfect place for a mugging or worse. Instinctively Rose yanked her Taser from her purse.

She wasn't usually paranoid, but with the recent killings in the area, she wouldn't take any chances. She looked over her shoulder again to make sure she wasn't being followed.

Rose drove home with her windows up and car doors locked. Instead of going her usual route, she took the long way. Something about the man at the elevator gave her the willies. Neither his scarred face nor his mannerisms put her off. She didn't think he was the serial killer plaguing the city, but something threatening emanated from him.

Rose pulled into her building's parking garage and checked to see if anyone had followed. Feeling confident no one had, she ran to the elevator with her keys in hand. Once inside her apartment, she locked the doors.

Rose flipped on the lights. Normally the dark didn't bother her, but she felt more at ease as if the light would keep the bogeyman away.

Weary to the bone, she flopped onto her couch then dug around in her purse for her phone. Denny had called four times. As much as Rose cared for the old man, she just couldn't bear to talk with him. Tomorrow would be soon enough to deliver the bad news.

She flicked her finger across the screen, searching for her news app, catching the latest podcast.

"A man's body was discovered late this afternoon, making it the fifth homicide this month. FBI agents working with the Atlanta Police Department Task Force have little information about the killer or killers. And now for the weather."

Rose saved the file to her SD card before exiting the program and set her phone on the table beside her. "That's not what I wanted to hear. I know about weather in June, hot, hazy, and humid." Sighing, she picked up the photograph of her late husband from the coffee table. "Richard, if I learned one thing from your death, it's that I'll survive no matter what life throws at me." She replaced his photo next to their wedding picture. "I'll get through this, too."

Life had handed her another kick in the teeth.

Resting her head on the back of the couch, she took in her studio apartment. Her employment with Simon would have been her stepping-stone to starting her own business.

Why was she such a damn jinx? No. Negative thinking wouldn't solve her problems.

She wouldn't permit Scott to snatch away her dream. She'd start her business now! After all, she ran the company, not Scott or Simon. Heck, they thought gingerbread was only something you ate. She was the one with the contacts and the knowledge. "Yes!"

Rose shoved from the couch and headed straight for her roll-top desk. Logging onto her laptop, Rose opened her files for last year's tax forms and bank statements. She examined the numbers. Rose stretched, she'd gotten numb from sitting so long. She rubbed her hands over her face before she took a second look at the numbers. As crazy as this was, it just might work. Time and a miracle were what she needed. A huge miracle. Rose drew in a deep breath. "It's a gamble." She sent the file to her phone before strolling toward the shower.

~ ~ ~

At eight, the bell over the office door rang. Rose looked up from packing up her desk and out into the lobby. Denny strolled in. He carried a white paper bag and two cups of coffee. This wasn't the worst day of her life, but it would be for so many.

Denny pushed open her door then plopped the bag on her desk. "Tried calling you last night." He gave her a mock frown. "You know they found another body. You didn't kill Simon, did ya?"

"I heard." Rose smiled up at the tall black man who'd been both friend and confidant over the past ten years. His gray hair hinted at his advanced years. How in the devil would he find work at his age? Over the years, he and his wife Nancy became family. Damn, she'd let them down. "And no, I didn't kill Simon—he isn't the one I want, anyway."

Denny handed Rose a cup. "Double shot of espresso, black, no cream, no sugar. I hate to tell you, but you look like hell."

She took the cup, then gulped the hot liquid. "Thanks, I needed this. I've been up all night. Close the door, please."

5

He pushed the door closed with his foot. "No one's here but us. Must be something pretty bad for you to want the door shut."

She nodded and stared at the wall behind him, focusing on her degree from Savannah College of Art and Design.

"Let me guess. Pretty Boy finally got caught with his hand in the cookie jar."

Tears burnt her eyes, but she blinked them back. She'd sworn long ago not to let anyone see her cry, and she'd be damned if she'd start now. "How'd you find out?"

"I could lie, but I won't. Maggie and I heard Simon talking on the phone. He sounded pretty scared. I kinda feel sorry for the guy."

Rose exhaled and met Denny's gaze. "Our fearless leader gave me the job of telling everyone the news." She glanced at her phone on her desk, then back to Denny. "I've got an idea. But I know it won't be a solution to our imminent situation."

A smile curved his lips. "You never do stay down long. What is it?"

"I want to start my own company. But Denny, I'm worried about you and Nancy."

"There's no need for that. Nancy and I are going to be fine. We paid off the house, we don't have any bills, and we have insurance through her job. Besides, this will give me time to go down to Cypress, Georgia and look in on my dad. Don't like him living in that swamp, but, hell, he's lived there all his life." He looked at the empty boxes by her desk then back at her. "Feel like eating? I got us some biscuits. If you need help packing, I'm here."

She shook her head, her jaw tensed.

At nine-thirty she stood in her office, staring into eight sets of eyes. "I know you've all heard rumors. Well, I hate to tell you they're true. Simon's brother has allegedly embezzled from the company. As of last night, Victorian Dreams ceased to exist."

"Allegedly, my ass," someone said as the room erupted with curses.

She held up her hands. "I know you all are pissed—Hell, I'm pissed, but Simon, I don't know how he did it, and I'm not sure I want to know, but he came up with a month's severance pay for all of you."

One of the carpenters, Tim, stood and stepped forward. "I know I can find work anywhere, especially with the growth going on around this town. But I need insurance. What about our 401k and that stuff?"

Rose clenched her teeth. She willed herself to remain calm. "From what Simon's told me, it's gone. It's all gone. There is a warrant for Scott's arrest, and, from what Simon told me last night, the Feds have frozen all of Scott's bank accounts, including the accounts here."

"You mean the accounts the Feds know about, but what are they going to do for us?" another man asked.

"Not a damn thing," someone else replied. "Ever realize Becker rhymes with pecker?"

Rose felt their pain. Damn, she hated Simon even more for not having the balls to do this himself. "I don't know. I realize you have families, and I'm sorry I don't have more information for you."

Maggie, the office manager, pushed her hand through her black hair. "Honey, I don't blame you for this mess." She looked around at the others. "I don't think any of us do."

When the bell over the door chimed, Rose looked out into the lobby. Her heart dropped to her stomach. She'd expected her ten o'clock appointment, but in walked the guy she'd dumped drinks on last night. Simon must have told him where to find her. She stared at the stranger through her office window. He looked around the lobby like he owned it. An air of self-confidence and authority emanated from him. "Let me see what this gentleman wants."

Rose opened her door then strolled into the lobby. Good grief, the man was a giant. He had to be at least six foot nine or taller. Surely, he had to be a professional athlete or something. Her gaze traveled over him. Last night she hadn't noticed his devilishly handsome good looks or his height. Strolling toward him, she took in his broad shoulders and trimmed waist.

Her eyes traveled back to his face. The square set of his jaw suggested a stubborn streak. She forced a smile and stared up into his pale green eyes. They seemed to penetrate her soul. "I'm sorry about last night. If you give me the bill for your cleaning, I'll be more than happy to pay it."

The man cleared his throat and ran his hand over his short blond hair. "That's very courteous of you, but I'm not here about my dry cleaning. I'm here about my home."

Rose bit her lower lip, not believing what he'd just said. The man looked more Scandinavian than British. "You're Mr. Madoc. From England?" Duh, as if his accent didn't give it away.

He inclined his head. "The same. And you are?"

So totally screwed. Rose had an office full of people to worry about and now this. She wanted to kill Simon, but orange just wasn't her color. "Rose Kelly. Sir, I'm sorry, but Victorian Dreams will not be able to restore your home."

"What?" He didn't raise his voice, but it rang with irritation.

Rose squared her shoulders and looked him in the eyes. "Victorian Dreams is bankrupt. It no longer exists. I'm sorry for your inconvenience."

"Inconvenience—Madam, you call flying from London to Atlanta a mere inconvenience? What about the money I've already paid?"

The doorbell rang again as Simon entered. "I had thought you, and everyone would be gone by now."

"Simon, Mr. Madoc to see you." She nodded toward the sexy giant, then marched back to her office. She slammed her door, rattling the glass. "Let them deal with each other."

8

Rose met the eyes of the people she'd worked with for the past five years. "If there are no other questions, I suggest you pack-up your belongings as quickly as you can."

She stood fighting back the tears for what seemed an eternity before Denny gave her a bear hug.

"I'll give you a call later." He kissed her cheek, then picked up his envelope. "Keep in touch," he said to the others. As he opened the door, Denny smiled over his shoulder at her and left.

The others in the office shook her hand and followed him out the door.

Maggie lingered behind until she was the only one. She clasped Rose's hands. "Thank you for giving me a chance."

Maggie's simple expression of thanks nearly broke Rose's self-control. She pushed the door closed and turned seeing the boxes on the floor. Anger swept through her, pushing aside her sadness. Snatching up a box, Rose propped it up with her knee and raked everything on her desk into it. Her coffee cup broke. She picked out the broken pieces and tossed them into the trash. The sound of smashing glass surprisingly comforted her.

Someone banged on her door. She looked up and moaned. Simon glared at her and pounded again on her door. Reluctantly Rose opened it. "What now, Simon?"

"That bastard is planning to sue me. Me, for breach of contract."

"Can you blame him?" She didn't have the patience for Simon's whining and heaved the box from her desk.

"If I knew where Scott was I'd beat him to a bloody pulp, then chuck his ass into the Hooch." He flopped down into her chair.

"Don't say that to the FBI when you talk to them, or they may dredge the Chattahoochee River."

"They wouldn't find him. Hell, he's probably lying on a beach somewhere." Simon leaned back in her chair and propped his feet on top of her bare desk. "Look, Rose, we both know who really ran this company. Yeah, it was mine and my

9

brother's, but you were the brains and the backbone. Shit, Scott, and I saw this business as a way to make a quick buck. You were the one who made us successful. What I'm trying to say is why don't you do this guy's house? Take it on freelance."

"Maybe." Rose kicked the door open with her foot. There were more important things to consider, like the next chapter of her life.

Once outside, she set the box beside her jeep. Someone touched her shoulder. She jerked around and came face to face with Mr. Madoc. Or rather face to chest. The man was huge.

"Let me help you." He reached for the box.

She stepped back. "That's all right. I can handle it. Thank you."

"Look, I'm sorry about losing my temper in there. After all, Mrs. Kelly, your day hasn't been a bed of roses, either."

Rose worried her lower lip. "Don't worry about it."

He withdrew his wallet, then handed her his card. "I would like to speak with you concerning renovating my home."

She noticed the white band on his finger where a ring had once been. "I don't think you understand. There is no company."

"You are the person I want—not Victorian Dreams—not the company. You come highly recommended. And from what I've been told, you're the person I need to restore my place. Please, call me. I'm staying at the Swiss. I've written the number to my room on the back." He smiled at her, then turned and strode down the sidewalk.

Rose took in his tempting physique. He moved his muscular body with strangely familiar ease.

She read his card. "V. Madoc. Hmm." She'd always wanted to see England, but she had more important issues to deal with first. She shoved the card into her pocket and went back into the office. Simon sat in her chair, waiting for her.

"I saw you talking to the Brit. Are you going to do him?"

"What!"

"His house." Simon grinned.

She lifted the last box from the floor. Drawing in a deep breath, she left for the final time.

Six hours later she soaked in her tub. After she'd left Simon sitting at her desk, she'd driven to the gym and worked out for two hours, which did nothing to relieve her stress. To make matters worse, she'd stopped by the bank. Her banker informed her she wouldn't qualify for a loan as large as she would need, not enough collateral. Rose moaned and closed her eyes. Another bump in the road.

At times like this, she wished she wasn't on her own. God, what she wouldn't give to be able to pick up the phone and talk to her parents. Everyone she'd ever loved had died, her brother, her parents, her grandparents, and finally Richard.

Enough of this pity-poor-me crap. Hadn't her grandmother always said when life slammed the door shut crawl through a window?

Rose opened her journal. She stared at the blank page. The day from hell, part two she wrote.

Her phone rang. She should ignore it...But. "Hello."

"Mrs. Kelly, please?" inquired a male voice with a heavy British accent.

"Who is this?" As if she couldn't tell from his accent it was tall blond and sexy calling.

"Vaughn Madoc. I hadn't heard from you and wondered if you'd thought about our conversation."

"You don't give up, do you?"

"Not when it's something I want. Will you have dinner with me? I'd like to discuss my offer."

"Your offer?"

"About my home? It's five o'clock now, say seven?"

"I didn't say yes, yet."

"But you will, if for no other reason than to repay me for last night's drenching."

She laughed. Very well, she'd meet with Mr. Tall and sexy. Maybe she'd found her open window. "Where shall I meet you?"

"I've heard the Abby is a nice place."

She swallowed. "It is." Expensive, too.

"Good. I'll meet you there at seven."

At seven-ten Rose walked up the stairs to the Abby. She spotted Vaughn dressed in a black suit, sitting at the bar. She also noticed the looks she received from the other women in the bar. Pure envy was plastered on their faces when he came over to her.

~ ~ ~

Vaughn let his gaze travel from her light reddish-brown hair swirling about her shoulders, to her full breasts, and down her long legs to the sandals on her dainty feet. The teal sleeveless dress she wore set off her hazel eyes. Damn, the mere sight of her affected him in ways he hadn't experienced in over a hundred years. He ran his tongue over the tips of his fangs and offered her his arm. "I'm glad you decided to join me."

Confident, she took his arm. "I was curious about this offer of yours."

The host showed them to their table.

Getting control over his beast, Vaughn admired the luxuriantly decorated restaurant before ordering their wine. He hadn't been this nervous in centuries. He met her gaze. "As I see it, we can help each other. I have a home in desperate need of repair, and you are unemployed."

Her hazel eyes sparkled in the candlelight. "True. But aren't there qualified restoration designers in England."

"Yes, there are, but I want you. As I have told you before, I have done my research. Restore my home. If your work is as good as your reputation, and from what I know about you it is, I'll help you start your own company. Isn't that what you want, your own business? I have the resources to get your business started."

12

He knew he'd surprised her. She chewed on her bottom lip. A habit of hers he knew so well.

"Just what do you know about me? And how did you know I wanted to start my own company?"

Vaughn's heart pounded. Rose's curiosity was doing the work for him. But how could he get Rose to commit? "You're capable. You're honest." He shrugged. "I simply deduced you wanted to start your own company after seeing your distress about Victorian Dreams closing." He motioned toward her. "Your turn. What do you wish to know about me?"

The waiter brought their wine.

He watched as Rose ran her fingers slowly up and down the stem of the glass, imagining her doing the same to a particular part of his body. "I noticed the white band on your hand, were you married?"

Vaughn glanced at his hand. The ring had not been off his finger since their wedding day. He felt naked without it. Why did she have to ask about that? "A long time ago, next question."

"How did you get my number?"

"Simon. It was the first thing he offered me when I threatened a lawsuit."

Rose nodded. "Tell me about this home of yours. I understand all old English houses have a resident ghost."

"No ghost, I can assure you. However, there have been rumors of a vampire or two."

A faint smile pulled at her lips. "Vampires? Well, if they look like Alexander Skarsgård, Stuart Townsend, or Brad Pitt, I think I can deal with them."

Vaughn laughed. "I can assure you they are not as mundane as Hollywood vampires."

"Vampires don't frighten me."

"No?" He remembered her reaction when she'd first discovered his true nature and tried not to laugh. "So, you will take my offer?"

"I'll be honest. You make it very tempting, but I can't afford to go over to England for who knows how long. And just a little FYI, I hate flying."

He laughed. "I will pay your roundtrip fare to England, plus provide housing for you and all expenses while you are there. As for your fear, I promise to help with that as well." Another argument countered.

"I need time to get my personal life in order. Also, I'm not familiar with the building codes of your country. It may take quite some time to restore your home."

"I have spoken with contractors who are willing to assist you. Fly back with me. Give the place a look and give me your opinion on what repairs should take priority. You can then fly back here and take care of what you must, then return to England and stay until you complete the job."

"You've thought of everything."

"When it comes to obtaining what I want, yes."

During the delicious meal of roast lamb, Vaughn described the house and the visions he had for it. He wanted to restore the place to its original splendor. He smiled at Rose. She'd listen to him ramble on about his home just as she'd listened to him ramble on about the case, all those years ago. His plan had to work. He would get her to England one way or another. He would not take no for an answer.

Vaughn sipped his wine, then lowered the glass. "How did you get started in this business?"

She looked as if she were weighing his question. "I became interested in restoration and preservation while researching my family roots. I fell in love with the pictures of some old homes and dreamed about living in one someday."

"Simply from pictures?" He asked, wanting to put all the missing pieces together.

"My grandmother loved to travel during the summer. She called it our road trip vacations. Anyway, simply put, I fell in

14

love with the Victorian homes I saw across the country. . . Some were in complete disrepair. I felt a need to save them."

After their meal, he walked her to her car. "I have a favor to ask you. I would love to see Stone Mountain and other areas of this great city, but I don't know anyone here. Would you mind showing me around, if you're not doing anything?"

A faint smile curved her lush lips. She opened her car door, then slid into her seat. "Call me in the morning, and I'll give you my answer."

"About my house or showing me around your city?"

"Both." She winked at him, closed her door, then started her engine.

He stood in the dark and watched as her car's taillights faded from his sight. He'd waited over a hundred years to see her again. He could wait a few more days.

A cold shiver ran down his back, a feeling he'd not experienced in a long time. He narrowed his eyes and turned to the shadows.

Philip was here.

Chapter Two

Vaughn stood in front of his hotel window, watching the sunrise. He could sense Philip out there somewhere. He had to be the one behind the killings and, no doubt, he was after Rose.

Vaughn couldn't leave her unprotected or do anything that would change the past. He had to keep Philip from her. She had to remain safe.

Vaughn picked up the phone and dialed, impatiently waiting for Alan to answer. "Philip is here in Atlanta."

For the next hour, they discussed the situation and the best action for the family to take. Philip had eluded them all these years, but not this time. This time, they would stop Philip. This time, Rose would stay safe. Vaughn agreed with Alan the Wolfes should be the ones to go after Philip.

After ending their call, Vaughn stared out into the gray morning. He only had four days to get Rose to accompany him back to England. If she wouldn't—he didn't want to think about the consequences. His plan had to work. He deserved— No, they deserved another chance. He glanced at the book on the bed. If they no longer had the past, at least they could have the future.

Rose was stubborn. He turned and staggered over to the bed. He hadn't slept in weeks. The anticipation of getting her back had overwhelmed him. He stretched out on the bed. Unable to sleep, he picked up the aged and worn leather-bound notebook. Everything she'd written had happened to the smallest detail. For over a hundred years he'd thought out this plan. It had to work. It would work. He studied at the date on the yellowed and aged page, today's date.

He'd read her journal every day since she vanished from him. He knew every word by heart. The journal had been his only link to her. He closed it and rested his head against the headboard. According to her writing, she would return his calls. He wished she'd written down how long she'd waited until she had. He hated waiting. He'd already waited too long.

~ ~ ~

Rose sat in the Waffle House down from her apartment, sipping her coffee. Denny sat across from her. He'd phoned early this morning, waking her. He wanted her to have breakfast for no other reason than he'd gotten up at his usual time to go to work.

Rose told him of Vaughn's offer. "What do you think?" she asked.

Denny shook his head. "Hell, I don't know what to tell you. This opportunity could be the chance of a lifetime. Then again, it could be the biggest mistake you've ever made. Baby, I don't know what to say."

"Gee, with advice like that it will be easy for me to make up my mind."

Denny laughed and took her hand. "Look, from the first time Richie introduced us you struck me as a lady who knew her mind." He squeezed her hand. "I think you already know what you're going to do. Just bring me back a model of a double-decker bus."

"Denny, I'm scared to death, what if I fail? Hell, what if this guy is some crazed killer?"

He gave her that look that said she was foolish. "I don't think the man is a crazed killer. As for you failing, well, then you come back with your tail tucked between your legs and start over. Rosie, if I've told you once I've told you a thousand times. Life is what you make of it. You can sit on the sidelines and watch the parade go by, or you can march in it. The choice is yours."

"You know I hate being called Rosie." She slid out of the booth. "I should check my voicemail. Mr. Madoc may have already tried to call."

Denny laughed. "If he hasn't, he will. Let me know when you're leaving so Nancy, and I can take care of your place. Glad you haven't got any critters we need to tend to."

17

"If I did, they would all be dead."

"Will you stop thinking crap like that? Hell, Nancy, and I love you. We aren't dead."

"Only because I never lived with you."

He rolled his eyes at her. "Go check your messages."

Rose stared at her cell phone. Four missed calls. She had to hand it to Mr. Madoc he was tenacious.

Oh well, what did she have to lose? She hit redial.

"Hello," he answered.

"Mr. Madoc, this is Rose Kelly."

"Have you decided to show me around your town or give me an answer on my offer?"

"Both."

Four hours later Rose strolled through the plantation grounds of Stone Mountain Park. In all the years she'd lived in Georgia, this was the first time she'd been to the park. She peered up at him. "What do you want to see, next?" she asked.

He returned her smile, revealing perfect white teeth. "I don't know. How about we ride the cable car to the top?"

"Give me a few minutes to get my nerve up." Standing so close to him she noted the attractive laugh lines about Vaughn's mouth and eyes. They added character and strength to his already handsome face. She guessed he was in his mid to late thirties.

Vaughn lowered his sunglasses. "If you are afraid of heights," he pointed to the trail. "we can hike if you'd like."

"Thanks. I hate heights and flying. Let's walk. It will give you a chance to tell me about your house."

With his long strides, she had to jog to keep up with him. Finally, she gave up trying and slowed her pace. She liked the view back here anyway. Rose watched Vaughn's butt muscles bunching and relaxing as he walked up the path. The man made his tight jeans look good.

He grinned at her over his shoulder. "Apologies, I forget my stride, I will slow my pace. The view is great from here though, isn't it?"

She blushed. If she didn't know better, she'd swear Vaughn could read her mind. "I was keeping up." Rose took off her cap and wiped the sweat from her brow before she tucked her ponytail back under it. Taking a deep breath, Rose leaned against a tree. This hike was better than any work out she'd had in a long time. A refreshing cool breeze blew. "Is anyone living in your home, now?"

"No one has lived in the place for over a hundred years. Some plaster has fallen, wallpaper is faded and torn, and there's water damage. However, the structure is sound."

She pushed away from the tree and started back up the trail. "Why has no one lived in it for so long?"

His expression sobered. "Some say the house is cursed. As the story goes, a woman vanished from there without a trace. Her husband searched for her, but never found her. Consumed by grief, he boarded up the house and moved. There's also a hidden room."

A hidden room heightened her interest. "How can a room be hidden? Someone must have knocked down a few walls."

He shook his head. "There are ten windows upstairs on the outside of the house, but only eight windows on the inside of the house. They didn't knock down walls. They boarded up the room."

She stared at him. A ray of sunlight struck his hair, making it shine like gold. She fanned herself. "You haven't attempted to tear down the walls yet to find the room?"

"I figured that would be your job."

"Oh, thanks, leave it to me to find the room along with the corpse of your vanished woman. Her husband probably walled her up inside."

Vaughn chuckled, and his eyes twinkled with spryness. "We can leave tomorrow."

"Wait a minute." She gasped. "I have to make arrangements first. I can't just travel to England as if I were traveling to Florida. There are things I have to do. The soonest I could leave is at least a week."

He frowned. "I already booked tickets."

She stared at him. "Without even knowing if I would agree to this? Mr. Madoc, you are a very presumptuous man. Even if I did agree, I still have to pack. I'm sorry, tomorrow is out of the question."

"Mrs. Kelly, when I made arrangements to come over here, your employer assured me you would be accompanying me back to England. I understand now your employer neglected to inform you of this. However, I don't see why you can't fly over for a few days. All you have to do is go over the place and tell me what must be done to keep it from falling into further disrepair." He sighed. "Come back to me, Rose."

She stopped in the middle of the trail and peered over her shoulder at him. "What did you say?"

"Come back to England with me, Rose."

Rose bit her lower lip. There was no reason for her not to go. She needed the work. Simon had already checked both Vaughn's personal and professional references. There wasn't a single reason not to go with him. "I guess taking a nice slow boat is out of the question?" she teased.

He ran his hand over his short-cropped hair. The muscles in his jaw twitched as lips pulled into a smile. "Completely out of the question." He motioned her to move ahead of him. They were finally at the top.

Rose walked along, deep in thought. He'd presented the perfect opportunity to her. She peeked over her shoulder at Vaughn. He stood, staring at the panoramic view. She repositioned her cap, then eased forward. This would be good a time for her to attempt to deal with her fears. She marveled at the breathtaking view. The crystal clear sky dipped and kissed the emerald green sea of trees that encircled the city of Atlanta.

Rose stepped closer to the edge. Her heart pounded. Anxiety made her tremble. She would overcome this silly fear.

Vaughn smiled. "You'll be home in four days, a week at best."

Rose turned around and faced him. "Okay. I'll do it."

"Excellent!" He clasped his hands behind him. "Wait until you see the place, Rose. I know you'll love it." His face lit with excitement. "Wait until you see the tub."

"Oh, don't worry. We can replace the fixtures if you want."

"You misunderstand. The bloody thing is a good seven-foot-long brass tub with lion paw feet. It had to have been custom made. Someone tried to steal it, thieves, vandals, perhaps another contractor. Who knows?" He paused. "I've already had it repaired."

Rose tentatively stepped forward. Trembling, she stared over the edge. She paled and stepped back. "If you want to see more, I'll wait here for you."

"No, that's all right." He motioned to the trail again. "Ready to start back?"

"Sure. The sooner I get home the sooner I can pack and the sooner you can show me this magnificent tub. You said you had it repaired."

He directed her to a rock and motioned her to sit. "Yes, the bounders dented it up pretty badly trying to acquire it. I had a metal-smith repair it. He did an excellent job."

Rose smiled at him as she crossed her arms over her chest. "Don't understand why I can't take a boat."

"You may find yourself getting seasick." He chortled.

"I hate flying."

"So I've been told."

~ ~ ~

Rose sat next to Vaughn as he drove his BMW sedan through London. The Dramamine was finally wearing off. The knots in her stomach were untying. Thank goodness Vaughn had sat by the window. She would have been a nervous wreck if he'd insisted she'd take the seat. A perfect gentleman, he hadn't even flinched when she'd squeezed his hand during take-off.

Rose opened her notebook. She briefly read over her checklist, passport, driver's license, cell phone, and all her credit cards. Denny would pick up her mail and check on her apartment. At this point, she was out of luck if she'd forgotten anything.

Rose fingered the photo taken of her and Vaughn at Stone Mountain, then closed her leather-bound notebook and set it on the backseat. Vaughn insisted on her keeping the picture. "How long before we reach the hotel?"

"Not long. Do you want to stop by the house first? It's on the way."

"Sure." She sat back and gazed out the window of the car. The rain drizzled down the glass. She'd dreamed of coming to England someday. A thrill ran through her. She couldn't believe someday had finally arrived.

The car slowed, then turned onto a road.

Rose read the name on the signpost, Cardigan Park. She stared mesmerized out the window at the Edwardian homes. The houses were in various stages of restoration. Some houses appeared restored entirely, while others were barely standing.

Vaughn slowed the car. "My house sits on five acres, so even in the city, there is a bit of country."

He drove through an open wrought-iron gate. "Last year I had the driveway paved to make it easier for the workers to get their vehicles onto the property. Originally, the drive was cobblestone.

She drew in a deep breath, seeing the gables of the house peeking through the branches of oak trees. "Oh my gosh, it's gorgeous."

A faint smile curved Vaughn's lip. He pulled up to the house and stopped. "Do you want to go inside?"

"Yes." Rose reached in the backseat, grabbing her notebook and purse. Standing up, she tilted her head back.

"One, two, and three. . ." She counted the windows as she walked around the house and jotted down the information. "Nine, ten. You're right there are ten windows on each of the three floors. Is there an attic?"

He stepped next to her, holding an umbrella over her. "Not anymore. The second owner converted the third floor into a study."

Rose made a rough sketch of the house as raindrops splattered on the page. "I see. The owner must have loved this garden. The balconies back here were not standard for this style of house." Rose surveyed the well-kept garden. "These rose bushes look as if someone has been tending them."

"I have no idea when or who added the balconies." Vaughn inclined his head slightly. "As for the roses, I've tended to them. I couldn't let them die."

She looked at him, seeing him in a different light. As big and intimidating as he appeared, he possessed a gentle soul. "You like roses."

He nodded. "Shall we go in before the storm hits?"

Rose perused the outside of the house as she followed Vaughn up the front steps. The porch seemed sturdy enough, but she wouldn't know for sure until she examined the wood better. The brick exterior appeared in good shape. She'd have Danny contact her masonry expert just to make sure. The oak door needed refinishing. Hmm, what was that? An intricately engraved plaque next to the door caught her eye. "May all who dwell here find their destiny," she read the words aloud. "Do you know who had this made?" Rose traced her finger over the plaque. "Usually, aphorisms are in old English or ancient Latin."

"I don't." He glanced over his shoulder at her and smiled. "But I like it."

"I do, too."

He unlocked then pushed opened the door. Vaughn flicked on the lights. Overhead, a converted gaslight illuminated the room.

23

"You told me no one had lived here in over a century." Rose looked around the empty and dusty room. "Are these reproductions or did you retrofit the original light fixtures."

"I had electricity installed because I assumed you would need it to do your job."

"You've also started replacing the stair railing."

"For safety reasons. I've only replaced the rotten or broken pieces. I didn't want to do too much without your approval. I'm not the expert here. You are."

She examined at the floors, then went down on her hands and knees. The wood pegs caught her attention. Rose dug in her purse for a tissue then rubbed it over the wooden flooring, wiping away the dirt. "These floors are mahogany. Look here. Did you know the wood pegs are in the shape of playing card suits?"

Vaughn offered her his hand. "I noticed the pegs on my first visit. As far as the mahogany floors go, they are only here in the entry hall. The floors are red oak throughout the rest of the house."

The warmth of his hand eased up her arm as she stood. "Thank you," she whispered and proceeded into the room to her left. "This looks to be the dining room."

Vaughn shook his head. "It was a music room or parlor. The dining room is over there." He motioned to his right. "Through this door is the kitchen."

Rose gasped and ran over to the white Queen stove standing against the far wall. "I can't believe this." She ran her hand over the appliance then looked over her shoulder at him. "Where did you find it? This stove isn't a reproduction."

Thunder rumbled through the house. The lights flickered.

He grinned at her. "Believe it or not, it came with the house. Follow me before we lose power, I'll show you the bathtub."

24

With notebook in hand, she followed Vaughn up the stairs. Pausing on the landing, Rose tried to imagine the house in its earlier splendor.

She pictured the bright colors of the now faded wallpaper and noticed the outlines on the wall where pictures had hung once. Rose bet a dark oak or mahogany hall-tree once stood in the entryway. Rose smiled. Yes, this house would have achieved the cluttered look of the Victorian era with elaborate curtains in a heavy fabric hanging over every window.

She had her work cut out. The plaster would need replacing with drywall. The wallpaper was stained with smut from the gaslights of long ago, but at least she could salvage a piece of the wall covering for her collection. The wood floors need sanding. In general, the house wasn't in bad shape. With time and work, she could bring this place back to its original elegance.

She turned back to see Vaughn watching her. "Where is this infamous tub?"

"In here." He pushed open the door to a bedroom. "This house has a bath for every bedroom, a luxury even for today."

She stepped around him and strolled to the other side of the room. Peering into the bathroom, Rose couldn't believe her eyes. Damn the tub was big enough for three people. The massive brass lion paw tub gleamed against the right wall. She knelt down, running her hand over the tub. "I can't see the repair. The craftsman did a wonderful job. You're very lucky to have found him. Now let's find this missing room of yours."

She followed Vaughn from the room wondering where they were going next. He pointed to the flight of stairs ahead of them. "There's one thing for sure you'll get your workout living here."

He laughed as he ascended the steps. The man had a nice ass that was so tempting. She wanted to reach out and grab it.

A loud boom of thunder echoed through the house followed by the sound of pounding rain. "Just my luck I'd be in a house with a missing room during a thunderstorm."

"You're not frightened, are you?" Vaughn stopped in front of a door, and she didn't miss his hesitation before opening it. "The room should be in here."

"I'm not afraid." Rose walked into the room, studying her surroundings. The room stood empty except a large oak desk and a wingback chair near the double windows. She understood why the desk remained. It was too large to get through the door. As for the worn, faded green baroque chair, why it remained was a mystery. "If you wanted I can reupholster that chair."

"Yes. I would like that." Vaughn eyed her curiously.

The dark paneling covering the walls made the room feel smaller than it was. The dirty windows provided efficient light. So where was that missing room?

Rose paced off the footage of the room. It was an odd size. The windows were in front of her, behind her was the hallway, and to the left was the front of the house. The hidden room had to be to her right. "The room should be somewhere behind this wall."

"I agree." Vaughn leaned against the desk then picked up an object.

"What's that?"

He raised his tawny eyebrow. "A knife I used as a letter opener. I thought I'd lost it a long time ago." He placed the knife back on the desk.

She strolled over to the wall and tapped on it, hearing a definite thud. "Did you hear that?"

"Yes. It sounded hollow to me."

Rose ran her hand over the paneling. "This section is loose." She stepped back and bumped into Vaughn. Damn the man was a brick wall.

He leaned over, using the knife to pry loose the paneling. "Let me see if I can pull this from the wall." He handed her the knife, then pulled the paneling away with little effort, revealing a door. "My dear, I believe we've found the missing room."

Rose tucked the knife and her notebook into her oversized purse, then turned the knob. She pushed opened the door and peered into a dark, dusty, and empty room. Bookcases covered the walls. Even the wall with the double windows had shelves. Whoever created this room loved to read.

Vaughn touched her shoulder, stopping her from entering. "Do not go in there. Let me get a flashlight first."

"Why, think your vampire is hiding inside?"

Hardly," he chuckled.

Rose watched as Vaughn left. She didn't need a flashlight, enough light filtered in through the dirty windows for her. She stared at the empty doorway and started to call him back. Her curiosity got the better of her.

Rose shivered as if she'd entered a tomb.

A hundred years of dirt and grime coated the windows. Cobwebs hung thick as curtains from the ceiling and draped across the double windows. She breathed in the musty smell and coughed.

Lightning flashed. The room vibrated with the rumble of thunder. Rose turned and peered back at the doorway she'd just walked through.

A flash of light blinded her, and the room spun out of control. She tumbled to her knees, scattering the contents of her purse across the worn wood floor. Dear God, the flooring was giving away!

Rose held her breath as the room spun out of control. Familiar sounds assaulted her. Old radio broadcasts and music blared in her mind. Bright lights and images from history books blurred before her eyes. The chaos made her head hurt as the spinning continued. Dizziness overwhelmed her.

Suddenly the room stopped spinning and felt like an elevator free-falling. Seconds stretched to hours. Her screams were lost in a soundless void.

The falling sensation ceased. Rose lay on the floor and willed herself to open her eyes. She gasped. The room had changed completely.

Chapter Three

Bright sunlight lit the room through sparkling windows. The thunderstorm had moved away. Rose gathered her belongings and placed them back into her notebook.

Rose pushed to her knees, trying to gather her wits. When her head didn't spin as much, she stood, her legs trembled. Her eyes were blurred, and she blinked to clear her vision.

Rose couldn't believe her eyes. She turned around in utter shock. This wasn't the same room she'd been in five seconds ago. Had she lost consciousness? Had she been drugged? She studied the room closely. Either someone carried her while she was unconscious into a different room, or someone cleaned the windows and filled the bookcase with what appeared to be first editions of some very rare books. She looked down at her feet. The lush Aubusson rug hadn't been in the room moments ago. No, this had to be a different room that was the only answer that made any sense.

But why? Why would Vaughn bring her here to pull such a lavish ruse? Had she misjudged him? Was he trying to make her think she was crazy?

On shaky legs, Rose walked toward the open door. Vaughn had some explaining to do, and he'd best do a damn good job. She wasn't in the mood for any more fun and games. His fun house had left her with a splitting headache.

She narrowed her eyes. Another practical joke. Vaughn sat at a now polished, immaculate oak desk. He'd even changed his clothes. Instead of a sage green shirt and jeans, Vaughn now wore a dark green velvet smoking jacket and white collar-less shirt. He'd parted his hair in the middle. He had gone so far as to glue on a bushy mustache and Mutton chop style sideburns. What in the hell kind of game was he playing? "All right! I want to know what's going on here."

Vaughn lifted his gaze from his book. "Who are you and how did you get in here?"

That did it. Rose had held her temper long enough. "Oh, for crying out loud. Where do you come off asking me who I am? You brought me here. I have better things to do than to be a guinea pig for your fun house. I don't like playing games, Vaughn. How the hell did you get all this furniture in here? Did you rig this house for the walls to move? Don't answer that!" She threw her hand up, palm facing him. "Just show me to the exit and let me get out of here?"

~ ~ ~

Vaughn studied the woman standing before him. Recognition stabbed him, but not of the woman herself. His people had an instinctive response alerting them to their true mates. She was his mate, the very person he'd thought he would never find.

She appeared slightly older than the marriage-minded women of the day. She did have quite a figure, even in men's clothes. Her light reddish-brown hair hung loosely to her shoulders, and the fire glowing behind her hazel eyes bewitched him.

Shaking his head, he closed the book he'd been reading and met the woman's furious glare. "My dear. I can assure you we have never met."

"That's a bunch of bullshit!"

He struggled to keep his composure. Though this woman had spunk, her language was far from amusing. "Madam, you have me at a disadvantage. You know my name, but I do not know yours. If you will tell me your name, and please refrain from such obscenities, I will try to figure out how we know each other."

Her lips thinned. "I've just spent ten hours on an airplane with you and another two hours going through Customs. Not to mention the time, you spent persuading me to fly over here with you, and you, can't remember my name is Rose? One of us is crazy, buddy, and it isn't me."

"Vaughn," Sara called, from the doorway. "To whom are you speaking?" She stepped into the room, eyeing Rose. "Oh, my."

"She just appeared out of nowhere." Vaughn beheld Rose. He'd finally found his mate and the woman was a bloody lunatic. "Madam, I don't know you. I have no idea as to what you are speaking about or how you have entered my home."

"Oh, good grief. I can't believe this." She snatched something from inside the book she held. "Take a look at this." She tossed the card at him. "Now, tell me you don't know me."

He caught the item and looked at it. His heart skipped a beat. *A colored photograph.* The photograph was of him dressed rather oddly, standing with his arm around this woman's waist. He ran his tongue over the tips of his fangs. She wore the briefest of underwear. The bare skin of her legs and arms shocked and aroused him. He lowered the photo. "When was this photograph made? How was it made?"

"Yesterday, no, actually, two days ago. And it was taken with a camera."

"Impossible."

"Oh yeah? You were with me at Stone Mountain Park in Atlanta, Georgia. You hold the picture to prove it. Or do you have an evil twin?"

He studied the photo. Impossible. However, something strange was going on. This woman was so confident he'd brought her over here and on an airplane. Was it possible? He ran his hand over the cover of his book. The title glared at him. H.G. Wells,' *The Time Machine.* "An aeroplane? Do you mean an airship, a dirigible?"

"No! Not a blimp, but a metal Boeing 747 jet airliner. We sat in first class."

Sara took the photo from him and gasped. "Vaughn, how did this woman get in here?"

He took his eyes from the book and met Sara's bewildered expression. "I have no idea. I was reading. It lightened, and suddenly she stood before me."

Rose gripped the edge of the desk. "Will one of you tell me what's going on here? What day is it?"

He forced a smile. "Today is the second of June 1900."

Rose paled. She stumbled back from the desk. Shock and disbelief crossed her face. "1900? You're joking."

He shook his head, studying her. "I can assure you I am not."

Rose glanced over at Sara, then back to him. "This can't be." She hurried to the window, taking deep breaths of air. "If I look out this window, I should see the car you drove us here in, unless you've moved it."

She pushed the curtain aside and peered out the window. Rose drew in an unsteady breath. "The trees were much smaller. This isn't the same house it's completely different." The curtain fell back into place as she faced him again. "It's different. This driveway's cobblestones, not asphalt. Dear God, what's going on here?" Her eyes widened. "Somehow you rigged things so the room would turn. Either that or somehow you drugged me and moved me to a completely different house. That would explain the different view from the window. I've got to hand it to you. You're clever. Now, tell me why in hell I'm here! Why go to all this trouble? Why me?"

Sara reached her hands out and stepped toward Rose. "My dear, I can assure you no one in this household has done any of those things to you. Where is your home, your family?"

"I told you I'm from Atlanta, Georgia. I flew over here in an airplane with him." She thrust her finger at Vaughn.

He raised his eyes to Sara. "Man cannot fly. There has not been a successful attempt."

Rose bit her lower lip. "I can prove to you I flew over here." She opened the satchel, withdrew a scrap of paper from it, then slammed it on the desk in front of him. "This is my boarding pass." She pointed to the date. "This is the date I left Atlanta."

He stared at the strange paper before him and read the date. Impossible! The date was over a hundred years in the future. How could this be?

Rose reached back into her satchel. This time she pulled out a card and a small book. "Here are my driver's license and my passport." She handed him the items.

He took the strange looking items. The card was made out of unusual material and had a color photograph of the woman in one corner. He read the information printed on it. Rose Kelly, height: 5 foot 7, weight: 155, date of birth: October twentieth. His sight fell to the year.

Dear *Yeva*! How could this be? What kind of trick did she play? She was born in a time beyond when doomsayers predicted the world would end. He turned the card over, then handed it to Sara. He'd held the proof in his hand yet what he saw could not be possible. This woman could not have traveled back in time. He peered at his book again, or could she have? After all, his kind was not believed to exist. "H.G. Wells', *The Time Machine*." The words slipped from his mouth.

Sara frowned. "What did you say?"

He held up his book. "I was reading this when the young lady appeared." He looked at Rose. "Your strange paper and picture card do not prove you came from the future."

Rose took a step back from him. "Look, I've played your game long enough. I even like the turn-of-the-century clothing you and your partner are wearing." She motioned to Sara. "But enough is enough. I'm calling it quits. I'm calling a taxi to take me back to the airport. The longer I stand here arguing with you, the dizzier I'm getting." She pulled a small white box the size of a deck of playing cars from her pocket, tapped it with her finger. She grimaced. "Great, no service!" She slammed the small white box on his desk.

He picked up the odd object. The material was extraordinary, smooth like glass, but not made of glass. The fascinating thing about the contraption was the glowing light emanating out from it. "Madam, this isn't a game. The year is 1900. What is this contraption?"

"A cell phone—Oh and here, explain these, too." She removed her bracelet and tossed it to him. She then flipped the pages of her book, removed another small card. She tossed this at him as well. "Digital wristwatches, cell phones, and calculators weren't invented in 1900. So tell me how I have these?"

Disbelief washed over him. He'd never seen such things as he now held. This woman could not be from his future. Nevertheless, he could not deny the proof he held. "I believe you should have a seat, Madam."

She planted her hands on her hips. "I'll stand. Thank you."

"This house was owned by a gentleman who disappeared three years ago. The property fell into foreclosure. I paid the taxes and purchased it. However, while I have lived here, nothing out of the ordinary has ever happened, until now." He motioned with his hand toward the woman. "Today is the second of June 1900."

"I don't believe you. You're suggesting I've traveled back in time! Are you suggesting that I opened the door to your library and walked through the space-time continuum? Is it? Is that what you're implying? Because if it is, it's impossible." The angry tone in her voice faded as she looked around the room. She strolled to the wingback chair near the window and ran her hand over the baroque fabric, her fingers trembled. He'd had the chair moved in here for Sara's benefit. "That would explain the furniture and the clothes," she whispered. Her eyes no longer held anger, but disbelief. "I can't stay here. I have to return home. I've had it with this nuthouse."

"I have to believe this is what has happened. Perhaps one of your cards or your cell phone is a time machine." He looked at her possessions on his desk, then back to her fear filled eyes.

Rose clutched her book to her as if it offered her security. "This is impossible. No one can travel through time, because there is no such thing as time travel." Her voice quivered. "I don't belong here. I have to return home."

Compassion showed in Sara's eyes. She stepped toward Rose. "Perhaps, if you repeat what you did, the action will send you back."

Rose gave a faint nod. She staggered back on shaky legs into the library.

From where Vaughn sat, he could see Rose turning around in a circle. She then paced back and forth through the doorway. When she didn't return to her time, she leaned against the doorframe, her eyes cast upward, she said, "It's not working. Why isn't it working? Why can't I go back?"

His heart ached when he saw her eyes well with tears. She blinked them back and swallowed great gulps of air. *Such strange behavior for a woman, why not go ahead and cry?*

He stood and walked around the desk. The book Rose held slipped from her fingers, her eyes rolled back, and she slumped forward.

Vaughn caught her around the waist and pulled her lithe body against his. He looked up at Sara. "She does not belong here."

"It's quite obvious she cannot go back to her time the way she came here. Unless you plan to build a time machine for the child." Sara's lips pulled, and she sighed. "That is impossible. Even our ancestors with all the technology they possessed, did not have the ability to time travel. I'm afraid this poor child cannot return to her time. She will have to stay with us." Sara had a determined look in her eye.

"Rose will remain with us, but I'm concerned she may be ill."

Sara knelt beside him and touched Rose's forehead. "She isn't feverish. Perhaps she fainted from the shock."

He looked at Rose's pale complexion. She hadn't fainted from the shock. She was ill. Rose didn't strike him as the type to succumb to the vapors. She seemed a stronger woman. "What of her family, what if she has a husband? Surely, someone must be worried about her."

"I'm sure her family is worried about her. But, Vaughn, you look so happy in the photo. Our Creator, *Yeva*, sent this child here to you for a reason." Sara retrieved Rose's book from the floor.

He scooped Rose up into his arms then stood. He carried her from the room. "Why would the Creator send me a mate from the future?" He willed open the door to a guest room with his mind.

"It isn't for us to question the wisdom of the Creator, our Mother. She has plans for us all."

Vaughn placed the unconscious woman on the bed. She was so beautiful. He brushed her silken hair from her cheek. His hand lingered longer than it should against her soft skin. "I will find a way to send her back to the time where she belongs."

Sara pulled the covers over Rose. "If you cannot? Then what will you do?"

"Protect her." He walked to the door. "I will send Penny to help you." He turned, and his gaze fell to Rose. "What are we to tell people? We cannot tell them the truth."

"We will tell them Rose is my friend from America. That is all anyone needs to know. Vaughn, I think it would be best if only you and I knew the truth."

"I believe you're right." He pulled the door closed behind him.

Vaughn strode to his study. He sat at his desk, then dropped his head in his hands. As much as he wanted to keep Rose with him, as much as he wanted to woo her, in his heart, he knew it would be wrong. Rose needed to go back to the future. His heart felt much lighter, knowing he did have a mate. He would find her again.

Someone knocked on the door.

"Enter." He looked up as Andrew, his butler, stood in the doorway.

"I understand we have another guest, sir."

"The young lady is Sara's friend."

"Is the lady part of the family, sir? The young woman I mean."

"She is human."

"Understood, sir. Will the young lady be dining with us?"

"I do not believe so. Have Mrs. Brown prepare a tray, please."

"Very well. Anything else, sir?"

"No, that will be all, Andrew." Vaughn focused his eyes on the book. He picked it up and flung it through the open doorway. The force of his throw embedded the book in the far wall with a loud thud.

~ ~ ~

Sara slipped a cotton nightshirt over Rose's head, then smoothed the shirt down. "Penny, we will have to find her some suitable clothing."

Penny folded Rose's clothes then placed them on the blanket chest at the foot of the bed. "Shall I leave these here?"

"That will be fine. I shall stay with Rose if you have other duties you need to tend to."

Penny nodded. "Did you say her trunk fell from the dock? The poor girl, I think I may have a dress she can use, nothing fancy, mind you."

"I'm sure Rose will appreciate that. Thank you, Penny."

The housekeeper left the room, pulling the door closed behind her.

Sara eased down onto the rocker near the window. It seemed her stay would be more extended than she'd initially planned. Besides, Mishenka wouldn't be returning from his trip to India for another month.

~ ~ ~

Rose snuggled under the crisp cotton sheets. She was home, in her bed. Everything had only been a dream, a very crazy-ass dream, but still a dream. She stretched and opened her eyes. "No! This isn't my bedroom." She gasped. Her heart pounded in her chest. "Where am I? Where the hell am I?"

"Child, you're safe." The petite woman with slightly graying black hair sat in a chair by the window. She wore a classic turn-of-the-century navy satin dress with leg-o-mutton sleeves. A large cameo brooch accented the white ruffled collar of her blouse. She was the same woman who had been with Vaughn's look-a-like. She looked up from her needlework. Concern showed in her eyes.

"Safe! I'm not safe here. I don't know where here is," the words tore from her. It wasn't a dream. Tears rolled down her cheeks. And damn it she hated crying. She swore she'd never cry again. Rose was stuck in the past with no way of returning home. If indeed she truly was in the past.

Rose shoved the covers off her and pushed up on her elbows. The room tilted and she swallowed to keep from puking. Cold sweat coated her body. "I have to go home."

"If we knew how to send you back, we would. Know this child you are safe here."

Rose wiped her tears and met the other woman's eyes. The old woman's intent gaze pulled Rose into their depths allowing her to see the truth of the woman's statement. Rose had genuinely traveled to the past.

A strange feeling of peace engulfed Rose. Somehow, she felt the elderly woman and this Vaughn would keep her safe.

"You had us worried." The woman smiled gently.

"What happened?" Rose tried to sit up. Dizzyness assaulted her, and she fell back onto the pillows. "How did I end up in here?"

"You fainted, my dear."

"I fainted?" Despite her spinning head, Rose tried to sit up in bed. She realized she'd fainted, but how did she end up in the past? "Where are my clothes?"

"I'm Sara Lucard. Penny, Vaughn's housekeeper, and I thought you'd rest better if you were not in your trousers and slippers. Forgive us, but we took the liberty of dressing you in a nightshirt."

Rose ran her hand over the crisp cotton shirt. Simple in design, its long sleeves were folded several times to her wrist. It belonged to someone much larger than her. "Thank you. It's beautiful. Please tell whoever it belongs to, thank you."

Her head spun, and Rose closed her eyes, leaning back against the large fluffy bed pillow. If she didn't know better, she'd think she was hungover. She could hardly think.

"Are you well, child?" The concern in Sara's voice warmed Rose.

When she opened her eyes, Sara stood next to the bed.

"I feel so light-headed," Rose said. "I feel as if the room is spinning."

Sara touched Rose's forehead. "You are not feverish. Perhaps this is an effect of your time travel."

Rose moaned. "I knew I shouldn't have come over here with him." She pinched the bridge of her nose. She knew the truth, still questioned it, but knew this was real. Somehow she'd traveled back into time. Either that or she was a prisoner of some steampunk freak. Option A or option B?

No, Rose knew the truth as strange as it was, somehow she was back in 1900. And she had no freakin' way of going back home."

"Him who, dear?" Sara asked, drawing Rose from her thoughts.

"Vaughn."

"Vaughn? Was that the name of the gentleman who brought you here in the flying machine?"

"Yes, and he looked just like the Vaughn here. If I've truly traveled through time to the past, then they have to be related for them to look so much alike. I have to assume the man from my time is this gentleman's great-grandson or something."

Sara smiled as if she understood what Rose had said. "That would explain things. Do you feel like eating? I will have some food brought up to you if you do."

"The nausea is almost gone. I could try to eat a little." Rose sat up again. This time the dizziness wasn't nearly as bad. "Vaughn said he'd purchased this house from someone who disappeared?"

"William Martin, a peculiar little man who kept to himself and was always working on his inventions. The neighbors told me they could hear funny noises and see strange lights coming from the house late at night. One night the noises stopped. No one has seen Mr. Martin since.

"Who knows what experiments he performed. I only know the refuse left here was quite unexplainable." Sara strolled toward the door. She paused as she opened it. "Chicken broth and toast, I think, will do you good." She smiled pleasantly at Rose. "I shall return soon, dear."

When Sara returned, a large gray cat wandered in with her. The cat leaped onto the bed. Swishing its tail, it walked heavy-footed up the length, keeping his eyes on Rose. The cat purred as he curled up beside her.

Rose stroked the cat's thick, soft fur. "You're a big fellow." She looked over at Sara. "What's his name?"

"I don't know. Vaughn has called the cat many names, but none I would repeat."

"Sara, where is the bathroom? I need to relieve myself."

"The loo is the door to your left. Do you think you can manage alone? Wait, I will send Penny up to help you. You might faint again."

"That's all right. I can manage." She didn't feel faint, and she didn't need help to pee.

~ ~ ~

Sara left and strolled down the staircase to the kitchen. For the first time in many centuries, she had hope. Vaughn had brought the woman to the house. He'd called her his mate. A smile

39

pulled at her lips. If she had anything to do with it, she would see the birth of a great-grandchild.

Had Vaughn brought Rose to the house in her time, or had he met her in this time? Hmm, interesting.

Pushing open the kitchen door, spotting Vaughn's back. "Fancy finding you in here, dear."

"I thought Rose might be hungry," Vaughn replied as he faced her. "Mrs. Brown informed me you thought chicken broth and toast would be best. I, however, feel Rose needs more to eat."

"I feel I must inform you I used my powers to ease Rose's fears." Sara frowned, staring at the plate of pigeon pie, rice pudding, cheese, and bread. A teapot, cup, and saucer sat on the table. "I did not alter her mind. I simply cleared the doubts from it and made her see the truth." Sara peered around the kitchen before meeting Vaughn's gaze.

Concern and a tinge of anger flashed over his face. Good. "Do not press into Rose's mind, again. We do not know what affects her time travel will have on her."

"As you wish." Sara patted Vaughn's cheek, chuckling to herself. The boy already was completely smitten with the woman. "Where is Mrs. Brown?"

"Here, Madam." Mrs. Brown's stout and round figure strolled into the kitchen. She dried her hands on her apron. "I told the Mister, pigeon pie might not sit well with the young lady. Could even give her the stomach grip. 'E wouldn't hear me out. Says she needs more than broth to eat, says 'E knows what's best for the lass." Mrs. Brown tapped her foot, eyeing Vaughn. "Well, Madam, what will you have me prepare for the lass?"

"Some broth will be fine, Mrs. Brown, and a spot of tea."

Vaughn turned and flung open the kitchen door. "Bosh," he yelled, storming from the room.

"Oh, dear," Mrs. Brown clasped her hands. "Think we angered him?"

"He will get over it," Sara said.

Mrs. Brown chuckled. "The Mister doesn't like to have his orders changed."

"He will get over that, too," Sara replied.

~ ~ ~

Vaughn tapped lightly on Rose's door to announce himself. He opened it for Penny, who carried the tray of broth and tea.

He drew in his breath as his eyes fell to the V-opening of his nightshirt and the gentle swell of Rose's breasts. He would never be able to wear that particular nightshirt again without seeing her in it. He cleared his throat and forced himself to look at her eyes. "How are you feeling?"

"Much better, thank you." Rose placed the book she had been writing in on the bed beside her. "I was just jotting down what has happened in my journal." She held up the book. "Do you still have my other items?"

Penny set the tray across Rose's lap, then poured Rose a cup of tea. "Mrs. Brown made her chicken soup for you, Miss." She curtsied. "Will there be anything else, sir?"

"No, that will do for now."

Penny backed from the room, leaving the door open behind her.

"I went through your satchel, but I removed some of your items. I have them here if you want them. However, I feel they should be secured in a safe place, lest others see them." Vaughn eased into the chair by the bed. He watched Rose eat. Her coloring seemed to return, and she didn't appear so pale to him.

"You're right, but may I have my phone, so I can turn it off and save the battery?"

He stood and handed her the satchel, along with her strange object. He watched as she pinched the box before reluctantly handing it back over to him. "I will keep this safe for you."

Through the thin fabric of the nightshirt, he could see her nipples. He diverted his eyes and moved back to the chair. His

41

fangs lengthened, and his groin ached as he shifted in the chair. "I wasn't sure what you could eat. Is the food in the future much different?"

She dabbed the corner of her mouth and looked up at him. "Food hasn't changed much over the years." She worried her lip before lowering her eyes. "I don't know what I should say, what I can say. I don't want to do anything or say anything that will jeopardize the future."

Fear once again showed on her face.

"Then tell me about your family, your husband. I'm sure they are worried about you."

"I don't have anyone who would be worried."

"No one? I find it hard to believe. What of your friends, your suitors?"

A faint smile curved her dainty mouth. "My friends know I'm visiting England and don't expect me back anytime soon. As for suitors, I don't have any."

He could not believe his ears. Were the men of the future so blind they could not see her beauty? Then another thought crossed his mind. "Men and women still court and marry in your time?"

Her smile faded. "Men and women still marry. As for me, my parents and brother are dead, as well as my husband. So, you see, no one will be wondering where I am."

He wanted to comfort her. Instead, he shifted in his seat. Every question he asked only caused her grief.

"Vaughn, what is your cat's name?"

"My cat? Has that demon been bothering you?"

"No, actually I've enjoyed his company."

"I've given him the name, Beelzebub, and he does not belong to me. He came with the house."

"Beelzebub is too harsh a name for such a sweet cat."

"Sweet? Surely we are not speaking of the same creature. Give him time. He will show you his true colors."

Rose's eyes sparkled as she laughed. The sweet sound warmed him like a fine brandy.

The door creaked as Sara entered the room with a dreadful looking dress draped over her arm.

"Where are you taking that awful garment, to the rag-bin?" he asked. For that was the only place for the garment.

Sara arched her gray eyebrow at him and hung the dress on the dressing screen. "Mind your manners. Penny thought Rose could wear this until we obtain her more suitable clothing." Sara turned to Rose. "Penny is about your size, only a tad bit shorter. I hope you don't mind, but you simply cannot wear your clothing out of the house. Enquiries would be made."

~ ~ ~

Rose hadn't thought about clothes, or how she would survive in the turn-of-the-century.

She touched her ears. Her diamond stud-earrings were still there. They were the only wealth she had here in the past. "I don't have any money to pay for clothes. As it is, I don't know how I'll ever repay you for your kindness."

Compassion, tenderness showed on Vaughn's handsome face along with something she couldn't name.

He stood, then he lifted the tray from her lap. "You were sent here to me, to my house for a reason. Therefore, you are under my protection and care. Whatever you need, I will provide. Do not concern yourself." Vaughn left, carrying the tray with him.

Sara pushed the rocker closer to the bed before she sat. "As soon as you feel up to it, dear, we will have you fitted for proper attire. Let me see. You will need at least a dozen dresses. I think five skirts and shirtwaists will do you. You should also have two riding habits. Do you ride?"

"Yes, I can ride. I can even ride sidesaddle."

"But of course. How else would a lady ride?"

Rose stifled her giggles before meeting Sara's eyes. They gleamed as she counted off the outrageous amount of clothing Rose would need. Twelve pairs of drawers, eight chemises, four corsets, and corset covers. Good grief, if this woman had her way, she would cost Vaughn a small fortune.

"You will need matching shoes and hats. A cape, and we must get you fitted for a few evening gowns," Sara smiled. "for when we attend the theater. I heard Sarah Bernhardt is coming back to London. I saw her in *Fedora,* a wonderful play. Do you enjoy the theater?"

"I love the theater, and I would love to see Sara Bernhardt. But, Sara, hopefully, I won't be here long enough to need so many outfits. A few undergarments and a couple of dresses should be enough. Honestly." Rose stroked the fur of Beelzebub. He curled up on the bed beside her. "I don't want to be a burden."

Sara's mouth closed in a smile. "Very well, then. We shall order what you will truly need."

"Thank you." Rose raised her eyes, meeting Sara's kind expression. She couldn't be more than five feet tall, and Rose bet Sara wore heels. "Is Vaughn your son?"

"No. My son Alan took Vaughn and his sister Aileen in after their parents were murdered during the war. Vaughn was fourteen. Alan could not care for Vaughn's infant sister, so he sent her to be raised by my daughter, Angelique and her husband."

War? Rose wracked her brain, trying to remember which war England was involved in during the later part of the nineteenth century. England had colonized most of the world during this time. But she couldn't remember the battles fought. She'd ask later. Right now her head hurt too much for questions.

Rose closed her eyes and sank deeper into the pillows.

"My daughter and her husband live in Scotland. We will have to travel there, perhaps this autumn. Though I don't like that drafty pile of stones, Ian calls a keep."

"Does Vaughn have any other siblings besides Aileen?" Rose opened her eyes, not wanting to appear rude.

Sara shook her head. "His older sister, Katherine, died tragically on her wedding night. Aileen is all the blood family he has, but she is such a trial for him. Aileen is a strong-willed lass, with a mind of her own. I overheard you telling Vaughn you were married."

It no longer hurt Rose to speak of Richard. At times she even enjoyed it. It gave her a chance to talk about him, to remember the happy times they'd shared. "I was married a little over six months when Richard, my husband, was killed by a drunk driver. It'd been five years since his death."

~ ~ ~

Sara pushed herself from the rocker. The poor child had suffered so much in her life. "Get some sleep, child." Sara strolled to the open window. "This night air isn't good for you." As she pulled the window closed, she met Vaughn's red stare. *Eavesdropping isn't very gentlemanly.* She sent her thoughts to him and locked the window.

But it is a wonderful way to learn more about our guest. He smiled as he easily floated to the ground.Sara pulled Rose's door closed, then walked down the stairs.

Vaughn handed Sara a glass of blood mixed with sherry as she entered the parlor, then he drew his cape across his bare chest. "I wasn't eavesdropping. I was enjoying the night air and happened to be passing by her window."

"A second floor window? You should be more careful. Even though it is only a quarter moon, it is still a cloudless night. There was enough light for someone to have seen you."

He shrugged. "No one saw me. At my age, I know how to be careful."

"What would have happened if Rose had closed the window instead of me?" Sara's temper flared, and her eyes flashed a brilliant red. "Answer my question. What would you have done if it were Rose who had shut the window?"

Vaughn tossed the contents of his glass down his throat. He poured himself another drink. "Rose did not see me, so I have no reason to answer your question. Why did you give her my nightshirt? Could you or Penny not find something more suitable for her to wear?"

"What Penny had would not do, and Mrs. Brown's gowns and mine would be too short for the girl." Sara swirled the red liquid in her glass. "Rose informed me she does not wish to be a burden on us."

"I have already informed her she is my responsibility. What did you say to give Rose the idea she'd be a burden?"

"I did not give her the idea. Your Rose is an independent woman from the future. I fear this will be more of an obstacle for you to overcome than your true nature will be for her to accept."

He poured himself another glass, then drank it. "Take Rose to the seamstress and order whatever she needs. Watch her and see what she likes, whatever the price."

Sara placed her glass on the tray. "I will make sure she is dressed in the finest garments."

"Good. I informed Andrew that Rose would be staying with us. He asked if she was part of the family."

Sara twisted her thin lips. "You called Rose your mate. She will have to be told our secret sooner or later."

He stared at the deep red liquid Andrew had kindly supplied. It satisfied his blood hunger, but not his lust. He took his eyes from the contents of the glass and looked over at Sara. "But in what time shall I claim her, here in my present or my future? And when I do tell her? Rose may not accept me for what I am. Then what?"

Chapter Four

Someone was humming. Good grief, who could be so cheerful this damned early in the morning? Rose opened her eyes. Next to the wardrobe stood a redheaded woman wearing a simple, long, black skirt, and white blouse. Her copper colored hair was swept up into a French twist.

The woman turned around and curtsied. "Morning, Madam. I pray you slept well?"

"Yes, I did, thank you." Rose stifled a yawn. "You don't have to call me madam. I'm simply Rose."

The woman, who appeared to be in her late twenties or early thirties, smiled warmly. "I'm Mr. Madoc's housekeeper, Mrs. Thatcher. When it's just the two of us, if you wish, you may call me Penny."

"It's nice to meet you, Penny." Rose slid to the edge of the bed and stretched.

She'd slept in a large room. Ivy printed wallpaper covered the walls. Heavy curtains of hunter-green velvet hung at the window and around the mahogany bed were pulled back with gold tassels. A large mahogany armoire graced the far wall, and a matching vanity with washstand stood against the left wall.

Beelzebub leaped onto the bed next to Rose. He nudged her with his head and purred loudly.

"Well, good morning to you, Beelzebub." She scratched behind his ear. "Your name doesn't fit you. You're such a sweet kitty."

"He is. To everyone except the Mister," replied Penny.

"Why?"

"I think it's because the cat believes he is the master of the house and not Mr. Madoc." Penny winked at the cat and smiled.

"When we moved to this house, the cat was already here. Thin and sickly he was. Mr. Madoc's heart is as big as he is, so he tended to the cat." She nodded for emphasis. "Nursed him back to health, Mr. Madoc did."

Penny picked up the large cat that was mostly gray with a little white on his chin., Penny stroked the cat's fur. "And he repays Mr. Madoc with his devilish ways. It's a wonder the Mister hasn't tossed the scamp out."

Penny set the cat down. She strolled over to the door to the bathroom. "Madam, would you like to bathe this morning or wait until later?"

"If I'm to call you Penny when we are alone, then you should call me Rose." Rose slid from the bed.

Penny blushed. "Rose, then."

"I could use a hot bath, and I need to brush my teeth, but I don't have any of my items with me. I don't even have a hairbrush." She followed Penny. A hot bath would be fantastic. She ran her tongue over her teeth. She had to brush them.

"Her Grace told me last night about your frightful ordeal. My heart goes out to you. To think of all the awful luck you've suffered. I'm sure you're happy to be here." Penny opened a cherry-wood cabinet door in the bathroom. "Ah, here we go. I knew we had several of these." Penny held a crude looking toothbrush in her hand and a tin of toothpowder.

Rose gratefully took the items from Penny. "Yes, I'm glad to be here." Rose hoped she hadn't said the wrong thing.

"It's a bloody shame the way the dock workers treat a body's belongings. They should've been more careful with your trunks than to let them fall off the dock. I'm sure Mr. Madoc will see to it they make good for your things. He's a good man, Mr. Madoc is." Penny blushed slightly. "I'm sorry, Miss. I forget myself at times and run on."

"That's all right. I enjoy your company." Rose smiled at the woman. The servants on Downton *Abby* or *Upstairs Downstairs* don't behave like this. Penny was warm and welcoming not stuffy as the servants on those TV shows. Rose wondered who else lived here. "Penny, are there others who live here with Mr. Madoc?"

"It's only Mrs. Brown, my husband Andrew and myself who live with Mister Madoc." Penny handed Rose a bar of sweet smelling lavender soap. "I'll leave you to your bath. If you don't need me, that is."

"I'll be fine, thank you."

Penny closed the bathroom door.

The burgundy and white porcelain tiles were cold under Rose's bare feet. She pushed aside the shower curtain and looked at the three brass handles on the tub. Hot, cold, and the third operated the shower.

She'd turned on the hot and cold water. A loud guttural noise followed by gurgling and sputtering came from the faucet. Rose backed away, knowing water would soon come gushing forth.

A trickle of water dripped out of the faucet. Another sound of gurgling came, then finally a geyser of rust-colored water rushed into the tub.

Rose waited several minutes until the water cleared before she placed her foot under the running water and shivered. Well, she'd have to wait a little longer before testing the water again. After several long minutes, she checked the water. Still cold. She turned the cold water off and ran only the hot. She waited several more minutes before checking the water again. Great, the only difference between hot and cold was the name on the handle.

Braving the frigid water, she stepped into the white enameled, cast-iron tub.

After her quick bath, Rose grabbed a thick, soft white towel from the cabinet. "Welcome to the twentieth century," she said, wrapping the towel around herself.

Penny waited for Rose in the bedroom, then helped her dress.

Rose stared at her reflection in the full-length mirror. She didn't want to hurt Penny's feelings about the dress, and beggars can't be choosers and all that. But the color was dreary, and the length was a tad short, on a positive note the dress fitted in the waist.

Rose smiled at Penny in the mirror. "Thank you."

"Think nothing of it." Penny motioned to the vanity for Rose to sit.

~ ~ ~

Rose stopped with her hand on the dining room door. What would she say to Vaughn this morning? She didn't know if she wanted to apologize to him or try to explain how she got here. Squaring her shoulders, she swallowed the lump in her throat and pushed open the door.

Vaughn wasn't in the room. A sense of disappointment shot through her. Her shoulders slumped.

Sara looked up from her breakfast plate. "Good morning, Rose. How did you rest?"

"Fine, thank you." Rose took in the sight of the dining room. The burgundy wallpaper darkened the room and made it look smaller than it was. The large, elaborately carved mahogany table and chairs, and the equally large china cabinet furthered the illusion of smallness.

"I'm sure you're hungry. Mrs. Brown has prepared ham, scrambled eggs, and there is fresh fruit," Sara said, motioning toward the sideboard.

Rose took a china plate with the same Wedgewood pattern as her grandmother had. She helped herself to the eggs and ham. Her mouth watered at the delicious looking oranges. After placing an orange on her plate, she joined Sara at the table. "This does look good."

Sara rang a small bell next to her plate. A second later a tall, thin gentleman entered the room.

"Yes, Madam."

"Andrew, could you please bring some fresh tea for Rose?"

He nodded and left the room, only to return with a silver teapot and a cup and saucer. He placed the teacup near Rose then poured her tea.

"Would you care for sugar?" he asked.

"No, thank you." She smiled up at him and noted his blond hair and youthful appearance.

Andrew nodded toward Sara. "Madam, will you be going for your morning promenade?"

"Not today, Andrew. Please have the carriage made ready for us. Andrew, this is Mrs. Kelly. She's visiting from America." Sara nodded to Rose. "Andrew is Vaughn's valet. If you need anything Andrew or his wife, Penny, will see to your needs."

Rose smiled at him.

He returned her smile, revealing a dimple in his right cheek. "If you ladies will excuse me, I'll have the carriage made ready." He turned on his heel and left through the kitchen door.

Sara touched Rose's hand. "Do you feel well enough to pay a visit to the seamstress today?"

"Yes." Rose moved her hand to the pocket of the dress she wore. She could feel the tiny lumps of her diamond earrings she'd wrapped in a handkerchief. They were a full two caret in weight and should more than pay for the few items she needed.

"Good," Sara said.

Rose finished her breakfast in silence, keeping her hand over the earrings. She didn't want to intrude on these people. It wasn't their fault she'd literally dropped in on them. Rose gripped the packet in her hand, then drew in a breath and smoothed out the fabric of the dress. She was in the past and had a lot to learn, especially about this period's etiquette.

"Sara, you have not corrected me, but I realize it isn't proper for me to use your given name in this time. How should I properly address you? Should I call you Lady Lucard, your Grace, what? And how should I address Vaughn?"

Sara waved her hand. "Sara will do. My husband, Mishenka, and I do not believe in titles when we are among family or friends. In public, etiquette dictates you address me as Your Grace."

Rose met Sara's bright blue eyes and felt a warm glow flow through her. Rose reached into her pocket. She wrapped her fingers around the handkerchief, then slowly withdrew it from her pocket. She handed the small bundle to Sara.

"What's this, my dear?" Sara carefully untied the handkerchief. Her mouth slightly opened as she met Rose's eyes. "Child, these are yours. There is no need for you to give them to me."

"I've always paid my debts. I can't stay here and expect you to care for me. If I cannot go back to where I belong, then. . ." She closed her eyes and stiffened her spine. She'd survived the deaths of her brother, her parents, her grandparents, and even her husband. She'd been laid-off, and she'd been so broke she wouldn't have money for ramen noodles. If she'd survived everything else in her life, surely she could survive living in the past. "If I can't go back home, I need to make it on my own. Will you help me find employment?"

"I see." Sara sat straight in her chair and folded her hands in front of her. "Would you be willing to work for me?"

Before Rose could answer, Sara held her hand up. She pushed herself away from the table, then stood.

The kitchen door swung opened, and Andrew stepped into the dining room. He gave a quick nodded to Sara. "Madam, the carriage is ready."

Sara smoothed her hands over her pale gray satin dress. "Thank you, Andrew. Rose, we can discuss your future in the carriage."

~ ~ ~

Vaughn stood in the dimly lit back room of the local hospital where medical autopsies were performed. He knew how the man had died just by looking at the body.

52

Vaughn stared at the cloudy eyes of the man who had been his friend, James Wilcox, husband, father, solicitor, and confidant.

Clenching his fists tightly, Vaughn looked over at Inspector Hughes. "What time was the body found?"

Inspector Hughes adjusted his spectacles before he pulled a handkerchief from his coat pocket. "Around seven. Sorry about calling on you so late last night." He wiped the sweat from his wrinkled brow. "Awful mess this is, Madoc. People are saying the Ripper has returned and is responsible."

"The wounds of the victims are not like the victims of Jack the Ripper. This man was torn apart by a savage animal, not meticulously cut." Vaughn drew in a deep breath. The foul stench of death sickened him. Vaughn recognized the marks on the body. They looked all too familiar. His clawed hands were capable of making such wounds. The puncture wounds in the throat, those, also, he could inflict. He pulled the sheet up, covering his friend's body.

The door opened, and Doctor James Austin entered. He extended his hand as he approached Vaughn. "I see the Yard has asked for your help, Mr. Madoc."

Vaughn shook the younger man's hand. "The victim was my solicitor. Is your father performing the examination?"

James faintly shook his head. "No. Father's hands are not as steady as they once were. I've taken over his practice." He tossed back the sheet. "Have you noticed the wounds in the neck? It looks as if the attacker slashed the victim's throat to cover up the needle wounds. My theory is this poor man fell victim to the followers of Kali." He shivered. "Barbarians all of them. They drained the body of most of its blood, probably to drink. Thugs do that, you know."

"Thugs strangle, they don't butcher their victims, and their cult hasn't been heard of since 1840," Vaughn corrected the young doctor. "Talk like that could cause a witch hunt in the Indian community. Innocent people would be killed, and the real killer would go free."

Doctor Austin blushed as he covered the body once again. "Then who do you think killed this poor chap?"

"That, sir, is what the Yard will find out," Hughes said, eyeing the doctor.

Hughes stepped closer to the table. "The housekeeper found the victim in his office. According to her, he was alone all day. She insisted no one paid him a visit."

Vaughn turned, facing Hughes. "I find this hard to believe. I knew Wilcox. Not a day went by that someone didn't seek his advice. I'd like to question his housekeeper again. Perhaps in her shock of finding her employer, she'd forgotten some details."

Hughes nodded. "Smashing idea. We can stop by Wilcox's home on the way back to the station."

~ ~ ~

Vaughn opened the door to the cab, then stepped down from the carriage and faced Hughes. "How soon will the photographs be ready?"

"The photographer said they should be ready by tomorrow."

"Good. Hopefully, our killer won't strike again tonight. He's killed twice this month already."

"But are we dealing with one person or several people? Not one of the victims has anything in common."

Vaughn stared at Hughes. "The victims have to have a common thread, something the killer sees, but we're missing. I'd like to look over all the files of victims slain in this same manner. I've counted nine in the past three years."

"It will take time but come by tomorrow. I'll give you what we have. Get some rest, Madoc. You've been up all night and all day." Hughes shook his head. "It's almost time for tea."

After Vaughn shut the cab door, he turned, to walk down the path to his home. The bright sunlight stung his eyes. He positioned his hat to block as much of the sun's rays as possible.

54

There had been nine killings like this. No, ten with Wilcox. The murders were escalating, from three spread over the first four years, to two last year. The death of Wilcox made the fifth this year, alone.

Andrew opened the front door. He greeted Vaughn, taking his hat and coat.

"Madam is in the parlor, Sir."

"Thank you, Andrew."

Vaughn squared his shoulders. He ran his hand over his unshaven face. Perhaps he should freshen up a bit before seeking out Rose and Sara.

"Vaughn, is that you?" Sara called from the parlor.

"Yes."

He strolled into the room. The curtains were pulled back to let in the late afternoon sun. Sara sat on the ladies' chair by the fireplace. The teacart stood positioned next to her.

He bent down, brushing a kiss on her cheek. "Where is Rose?"

"Have some tea. You look like something your cat brought in. You're still in the same clothes you wore yesterday." Sara poured him a cup.

"Thank you. Where is Rose?" he asked again as he settled on a wingbacked chair.

Sara's eyes sparkled. "She's dressing. We were in luck today. Lady Winston's granddaughter decided not to marry Sir Douglas. Charlotte is about the same size as Rose." Sara handed him a plate of Bakewell tarts.

He loved the small almond cakes filled with raspberry preserves. He took four of the tarts. Vaughn stretched his tired legs in front of him. It felt good to relax a bit. "Tell me, Sara, what does Lady Winston's granddaughter have to do with Rose?"

Sara looked at him as if he were bird-witted. "Charlotte had ordered more than enough clothes for her trousseau."

"Ah, I see. Because Lady Winston's granddaughter would not need the clothes, you purchased the garments for Rose."

55

Sara leaned toward him and took his hand, placing a tied white handkerchief in it. "Rose only ordered three dresses. I did as you instructed and purchased everything she would need."

He untied the handkerchief. "Where did these come from?" He held up one of the earrings. "They appear to be real diamonds, not paste."

"They belong to Rose. She doesn't want to be beholden to us. Rose has asked to work to pay for her expenses. Vaughn, what are we to do to make her feel comfortable?"

"I have no idea. I will think of something." He rubbed his brow. His life had become more and more complicated with each passing day. He had a killer to hunt down, and a woman, who hadn't even born yet, living under his roof. What else could happen?

He opened his eyes and drew in his breath, sitting up straight, then standing when he saw Rose glide into the room. The dark green silk dress she wore fit her beautifully. The elegant dress had the fancy sleeves women were wearing. *What did Sara call them? Leg-o-lamb? What a funny name for sleeves.*

His gaze swept over her, moving lower to the fitted waist of the dress and to the skirt, which hung smoothly, accenting her rounded hips. He smiled as his eyes drifted back to her lovely neck. The tiny pearls and lace drew his eyes to her low neckline. Sara's cameo adorned a soft green ribbon at the neckline. He walked over to Rose, then offered her his arm. "You look lovely, Mrs. Kelly."

"Thank you, Mr. Madoc."

"There is no need for formalities. Please use my given name."

"Then you must call me Rose."

He walked her to the sofa. "Would you care for some tea?"

"Please, thank you."

Sara poured. "Here you go, dear."

56

Vaughn handed Rose the delicate teacup. He lowered his eyes and gazed at her full breasts before taking his seat. Bringing his desire under control, he retracted his fangs before he spoke. "Did you enjoy your day, Rose?"

"Yes, I did."

Rose blushed, taking the cup from him. "Sara and I even had time to stop by a bookstore."

Vaughn finished his last tart. "Did you find a book to your liking?"

"Oh, yes, but Sara told me you already have the books in your library."

"Do I?" He looked over at Sara. He couldn't think of any books a lady would enjoy reading. He knew he didn't have any by Jane Austen or either of the Bronte sisters. He turned his attention back to Rose. "Which books interest you?"

"I love to read Robert Louis Stevenson and Sir Arthur Conan Doyle. I'm also fond of Shaw and H.G. Wells."

~ ~ ~

Rose sipped her tea. Sara had said Vaughn had left the house late last night. He had to be exhausted.

Vaughn raised an eyebrow at her as if he didn't believe her. "I have all their books."

"Do you have any by Hawthorne?"

"As in Nathaniel Hawthorne?"

"Yes. My favorite is The House of the Seven Gables."

"You amaze me. A woman who likes to read what I do." His light green eyes twinkled. "I have the complete collection of Hawthorne. After dinner, I will show you my library where you may select a book to read."

Sara took a letter from the teacart. "Vaughn, before you go dress for dinner, this came for you today. It's from Ian."

Vaughn opened the letter. He frowned as he read. The muscles in his jaw twitched. He carefully refolded the message, then placed it into his coat pocket. He stood, said nothing, as he strode over to the bell pull. He then yanked it.

Keeping his back to her and Sara, Vaughn stood, shoulders slightly hunched and his hands balled into fists. He seemed to be reining in his temper.

"Sara, I hope it isn't bad news."

"With as much wax as Ian placed on his letter, I have a feeling it is."

Vaughn turned when Andrew entered. "I need *my* brandy."

"Yes, sir." Andrew stepped from the room. Moments later he returned with a decanter of brandy and a snifter. He offered them to Vaughn.

Vaughn poured himself a glass. "It seems my sister has taken a fancy to one of the neighbors." He drained the snifter, then poured himself another drink.

"Brian MacDonald doesn't have a son," Sara said.

Vaughn shook his head. "Glen and Royce were out hunting. They found Aileen in the arms of William Campbell."

Sara gasped, "Oh dear. They didn't kill the lad did they?"

Vaughn grumbled something under his breath.

Rose was certain it wasn't nice.

He took the letter from his pocket, unfolded it, and read, "Seeing my wife will not permit your brother the honor of killing the Campbell bastard. I'm sending your sister to you." Vaughn refolded the letter. "Aileen will be here tomorrow. It is taking both Royce and Glen to drag her here. I'll meet them at the station."

Uneasiness came over Rose. She should say something. "Is there anything I can do to help?"

Vaughn raised his head. He stared at her oddly. His mouth curved up into an almost wicked grin. He slowly stroked his chin, staring at her. He glanced over at Sara, then back to Rose. His smile widened into a broad grin, one resembling the proverbial cat that ate the canary, a very frightening sight.

"Sara has informed me you wish to earn your keep," he stated.

"Yes," Rose squeaked. Her mouth had suddenly gone dry.

"Good. You shall be my troublesome sister's companion." Vaughn folded his hand behind his back and strolled from the room. "One problem solved."

Chapter Five

At dinner, Rose breathed in the wonderful aroma. Roast beef, new potatoes, and sweet peas graced the table along with two kinds of pudding and freshly baked bread. There was enough food to feed a huge family. Her mouth watered. "The food looks wonderful."

Rose stared at the elaborately set table. Each place setting had a dinner and side plate, heavy silverware consisting of four knives, four forks, three spoons and four crystal glasses including a wine glass. She bit her lip, trying to remember in which order to use each piece. She recognized the knife, spoon, meat, salad, and dessert forks. Perhaps, if she watched to see what items Sara used, she wouldn't embarrass herself.

Vaughn handed her a serving bowl of creamed peas. "I believe Mrs. Brown outdid herself tonight. However, Andrew didn't have to use every bloody piece of silver we own."

"Vaughn, your manners," Sara chide.

He rolled his eyes and sipped his wine.

Rose tried the roast beef. It tasted divine, better than any she'd ever eaten.

Sara buttered her bread, then raised her eyes, looking at Rose. "My dear, in your time is there crime?"

"Yes, unfortunately, there is."

"A pity," Sara sighed. "I was so hoping that was not the case."

"Right now, the city I live in is plagued by a serial killer. The local papers have named him the Atlanta Slasher."

Vaughn's fork slipped from his hand. "Why do they call him this?"

"It started with some of the local media comparing his victims to those of Jack-the-Ripper. I guess the name stuck."

"I see. Are the victims prostitutes?"

Sara gasped. "Vaughn, this is not a suitable topic for dinner."

"Forgive me. I forgot myself," Vaughn said, offering Sara a smile.

Rose couldn't keep her eyes off of Vaughn. The candlelight softened the outlines of his face. However, she did prefer a smooth face to a mustached one. "Perhaps after dinner, if you are interested, I could tell you what I know about the killer in my time, or maybe show you."

"Show me?"

"I saved a couple of files on my phone to read on the flight. I may be able to pull them up for you to read." No sooner had she offered her help, than fear gripped her. What if by helping, she changed the future somehow. "No, on second thought, I shouldn't. I may change the future."

He covered her hand with his. "Please, you see, I'm aiding Scotland Yard in their search for such a killer. You might give me a clue as to how to catch this fiend."

Sara's lips twisted into a frown. "Vaughn, Rose is a young woman, not a Bobbie."

His hand lingered on Rose's. Warmth eased up her arm. She wanted to help, but what if she did something, said something that altered the future. Her future.

He removed his hand. "I guess the lack of sleep is affecting my judgment." His eyes met Rose's. "You are right. Murder isn't a proper topic for an attractive lady."

Heat rose in Rose's cheeks. "Don't be ridiculous. Have you forgotten I love to read mysteries? But. . ."

His expression grew serious. "But? Is something wrong?"

"I don't know. I'm afraid of saying something that could change the future."

He leaned closer to her. "I understand, but how will stopping a killer change the future, other than for the better?"

She didn't want to argue, but. "If you stop the murderer before he kills someone who should have died and didn't, that person could go on to do something later in life that should not have been done, thus changing the future."

Vaughn nodded slowly. His lips thinned. He sat silent for a few minutes staring at her. "If a person was the intended victim and his life spared because we captured this murderer . . . this spared victim could go on to do great good for the world."

Sara sat back in her chair, glancing back and forth between Vaughn and Rose. "Listen to the both of you. You could be up all night arguing this issue. As for myself, I believe it is time to retire."

Vaughn stood. He nodded toward Rose as he helped Sara from her chair. "Shall we return to the parlor?"

Sara covered her mouth to hide a yawn. "I think I will go to my room for the night. I'm rather tired." She glanced over at Rose. "Good night, dear."

~ ~ ~

Vaughn took Sara's arm. He walked her to the stairs, knowing Sara wasn't tired. She was giving him time alone with Rose. He bent toward Sara and brushed a light kiss on her cheek. "Good night, Sara. And, thank you."

She cupped his chin in her hand. "Don't rush her. Treat her like a fine china cup."

Vaughn smiled, then he turned. He strolled back to where he'd left Rose. She wasn't in the dining room. He concentrated on her heartbeat. She was out on the terrace. Folding his hands behind him, he strolled toward the terrace.

She turned, smiling at him. "It's so lovely out here."

"It is, but not as lovely as my Rose . . . garden."

He stared at her. The dark green of her dress accented her apricot and cream-colored skin. He remembered the image of her in the colored photo of her—slim waist flared into rounded hips, her lithe and firm looking legs.

She stepped closer to him. Despite the faint light, he saw her full breasts rise with each breath.

He lifted his eyes to the hollow of her neck filled with soft shadows. He fought the urge to take her in his arms. How would she taste on his lips?

His fangs lengthened. He purposely ran his tongue across their tips, drawing his blood. He needed to shock himself to keep from taking Rose. "Are you homesick? Silly question, forgive me. Of course, you are."

"To be honest, I'm not homesick. I'm nervous about what will happen next, about changing the future." She turned from him, then straightened her back. "I will tell you about the Slasher."

"Thank you." He lightly touched her elbow. "I understand your fear. You fear by helping me you will change your future. Perhaps that is why you were sent back to this time, to change the future. If that is the case, then I can see only good coming out of this."

Rose turned and looked up at him. "What's your first question?"

Oh, he could think of a hundred questions to ask her, and none pertaining to the case. "Do your police have any clues as to who he is?"

"No. The bodies are found mauled. When the police discovered the first two victims, the authorities thought a wild animal had somehow caused the deaths. That's what the media reported."

"What changed their minds?"

"Forensic evidence found by the crime lab, but the FBI hasn't released any more information."

"FBI?"

"The Federal Bureau of Investigation. They are like your Scotland Yard."

"I wish I could contact them."

"That would be nice, but we'll have to wait until July 1908, for The Bureau of Investigation and even then they won't be much help."

"That does create a bit of a problem. It is a shame I cannot travel to the future with you. Rose, is there anything else you can tell me about the killings from your time, anything peculiar about the victims?"

"Not really. The police are keeping tight-lipped. The few bits of information leaked to the press the police called rumors and not facts. I saved the articles because I wanted to read over them carefully. If you want I can try to access those files for you."

"Files? Oh, yes, the ones on your white box." Exhaustion was clouding his mind, and the longer they stayed out on the terrace, the more he desired her.

"You need some sleep," Rose said as she strolled back toward the house.

"True, but first, I promised you a look at my books. Shall we?" He stepped back from her, allowing her to enter the safety of the well-lit room.

Vaughn followed Rose up the stairs. With each breath he took, the scent of her blood called to him.

Lack of sleep was catching up with him. Vaughn caught his reflection in the hall mirror. *Bloody hell.* He couldn't let Rose see him like this. His fiery red eyes and fangs would send her fleeing into the night. He drew in several calming breaths. He risked another glanced at the mirror. Better. He still looked like death, but at least his human form stared back. His lack of sleep was making it difficult to control his craving.

Rose paused at the top of the landing. "I'm a little nervous going back in here."

"I will not let anything happen to you." He opened the door to the study and slid his hand to the small of her back.

~ ~ ~

Rose tingled from the warmth of Vaughn's hand. She'd only known him a day, actually a few hours, but she felt as if she'd known him all her life Strange how some people just clicked. "Sara told me you used to work for the Pinkerton Agency."

64

He turned up the gaslights, casting a warm glow over the room. "Yes, for about four years, then I grew tired of living in America. I missed England's refinement." He turned. "No offense."

"None taken."

"The most important thing I learned from working with the Pinkertons was to use all available resources." His eyes twinkled. "Right now I have very little to go on. The killer isn't selective in his victims. He kills male and female, young and old."

"That sounds like the murderer in my time." Panic rose in her. "Oh, God, you don't think he was somehow transported back to this time like I was?" Despair washed over her. "Or when I was? What if I caused him to be here?"

Vaughn's expression softened, and he tenderly took her hand in his. "You did not cause this. The man I hunt did not come from your time with you. I can assure you. The murders have been going on for five years. At first, victims did not appear to have anything in common. It wasn't until these last victims that a pattern emerged."

"Do your police have any leads?" she asked, feeling somewhat relieved.

He shook his head. "None at present."

"I'm sure you'll find him." Standing close to Vaughn, she noted his firm features and the confident way he held his shoulders. Here was a man who was sure of himself. Someone she wouldn't mind getting to know better. If she had to be transported back in time, she was glad it was here with Vaughn and Sara.Here, she felt safe.

"My, dear, you have more confidence in me than I do in myself." Vaughn opened the door leading into the library. "I believe you will find something to your liking in here."

"I think I have."

He raised an eyebrow in a questioning manner.

Heat rose in her cheeks. *Oh great, open mouth and insert foot.* "With so many books, I'm sure I'll find something I'd like to read." She hesitated, staring into the room. This was the same room she'd first appeared in, the walled-up room from her time.

Vaughn took her hand in his. His large hand engulfed hers in size and warmth. "We'll enter together."

Rose held tightly to his hand and stepped into the room. She didn't take a crazy ride to another time. Vaughn stood beside her, still in the past. So far.

"Rose, are you all right? Is something wrong?"

She looked up into pale green eyes full of compassion. It has only been a day, and she was already falling for Vaughn. "I'm fine." She looked away. "I guess I was half-frightened of being sent through time again. Who knows where I would end up next."

"We couldn't have that. I wouldn't like it if you ended up in King Henry's court."

The warmth of his breath teased her cheek. She leaned slightly into him, then straightened her back. She backed away. "It's strange to be in this room again."

His eyes met hers, and he cleared his throat. "You enjoy Hawthorne. Correct?"

"That is correct."

He strolled over to the far bookcase. "I have arranged these according to my favorites, not in alphabetical order."

"So where do Hawthorne and Doyle fall?"

"They should be close together on this shelf."

She walked over to the shelf he'd indicated and began reading off the titles. "Hmm. I see you like Dickens and Poe, as well." She bent down as she continued searching. "It would be easier if you did alphabetize them."

"For whom? They are my books."

"Ah, just what I was looking for." Rose slid the book from its place. She turned, finding herself standing between Vaughn's arms.

Anticipation pounded through her as she lifted her eyes to his full lips, wishing for some crazy reason he would kiss her.

Instead, he backed away. "Now that you have your book if you will excuse me, I believe I shall retire for the evening."

Her heart fell, all the way to the basement. She knew he'd heard it hit with a thud. "I'm sorry. I forgot you've been up all day and night." She clutched the book to her. "Thank you. I'll return this when I'm finished reading."

"Take your time." He guided her out of the study, then down the hall to her room.

Rose reached for her doorknob, as Vaughn did.

It was bad enough she'd been attracted to the Vaughn in her time, but to also be attracted to his great-grandfather. There was something that drew her to him. To them.

"Goodnight, Rose." His breath caressed her cheek.

She turned to face him and gasped. His eyes were glowing red and fangs peered from beneath his lips.

Using the book, she struck him in the head. She shoved past him, dropping the book as she ran toward the step.

"Rose, I'll not hurt you." He grabbed her arm, blocking her escape.

"Back off!"

"Rose, please let me explain." His grip eased on her arm.

Rose grabbed his hand, yanked him forward as she brought her foot behind his leg. She used Vaughn's weight and size against him, making him tumble to the floor.

Free of his hold, she bolted towards the staircase. Her foot slipped on the carpet, and she stumbled slightly before regaining her footing.

"Rose, come back," Vaughn shouted.

Come back? Yeah, right. She couldn't risk him catching her and sprinted down the rest of the steps.

"Rose. Stop."

She glimpsed over her shoulder. Vaughn raced down the steps after her. His long strides, bringing him closer and closer to her. She fumbled with the locks then yanked open the front door.

Outside in the moonless night, she ran down the cobblestone path. The dense fog made it hard for her to see the gate at the end of the tree-lined path. Her heart pounded the closer Vaughn's footfalls sounded. The gate was open. She had to get away from him.

In the distance, the sound of clopping horse hooves and the clattering of wheels echoed on cobblestones. A carriage or wagon, someone was coming. If she could flag down the driver then maybe she had a chance of escaping. The sound of its wheels seemed closer as if right behind her.

"Rose, stop!" Vaughn shouted.

She looked over her shoulder. The massive chests of the black carriage horses were inches from her. Fear froze her. She couldn't move, couldn't scream.

A hand grabbed her from behind. Rose was yanked backward with such force she fell to the ground. The horses thundered past, their hooves kicking up dirt from the road. The wheels of the coach came so close she could reach out and touched them. The driver hadn't even slowed to see if she was all right.

Heart pounding, Rose sat in the street and rubbed her hands up and down her arms. She was alive! That is if she didn't have a heart attack. Her heart pounded so fast it felt as if it would come out of her chest.

Petrified and out of breath, Rose forced herself to calm down. She wouldn't become hysterical. She wouldn't cry. It was over. She was alive.

Her rescuer lifted her onto his lap. His strong arms wrapped around her, holding her tight. She rested her head against his broad chest. The sound of his racing heartbeat drummed in her ear. His large hand gently caressed her back, rubbing up and down, soothing her.

Rose tilted her face and gazed up into the eyes of her rescuer. "Vaughn."

"Are you injured anywhere?" His hand tenderly brushed her hair from her face. "Rose," he said urgently. "Are you hurt?"

She shook her head. "You saved my life. Why?" Her voice sounded stifled and unnatural to her ears. He hadn't hurt her. Instead, he'd saved her.

Gently he tipped her chin up, forcing her to meet his green eyes. "I could never harm you. You must believe me. You will always be safe with me. Please, let me help you. Let me care for you while you are here, in my time."

Rose stared into Vaughn's eyes, brimming with tenderness and compassion. She no longer feared Vaughn the person or the creature he could become. In her heart, she knew he'd spoken the truth. She was safe with him. He wouldn't hurt her. *But by God.* "You scared the shit out of me!" Rose yelled and punched his rock-hard shoulder.

The jerk had the audacity to laugh as he stood and held out his hand. "I know your mind is full of questions. Come with me, Rose. I will answer as many as I can."

"Yes, you will." She placed her hand in his, allowing him to help her to her feet. The second she put weight on her leg, a sharp pain knotted her calf, and she gripped his muscular arm. "Ouch."

"You are hurt." Vaughn slid his arm around her waist. In the faint glow of the streetlights, his eyes widen with concern.

"I'll be fine. I think I pulled a muscle." She put more weight on her leg, and the pain seemed to ease. "Yep, pulled muscle, just have to walk through it."

He grumbled something about stubbornness then swept her up in his powerful arms as if she weighed nothing at all.

"Put me down. I can walk. I should walk." She tried to push out of his arms.

"Will you be still?" His voice contained a silken thread of warning.

Despite knowing he was otherworldly, she felt safe in his strong arms and stopped fighting him. Rose snaked her arms around Vaughn's neck and rested her head against his shoulder. If he wanted to carry her, she'd enjoy the ride. Breathing deeply, she drew in his scent. Damn, the man smelled good. Like her favorite tea, spiced orange.

Vaughn carried her up the front steps, through the still open door, pausing only long enough to kick it closed with his foot. He held her tight as he strolled into the parlor, then sat her on the couch. Vaughn eased down beside her, lifting her leg onto his lap. "Let's see how badly you're injured."

Mysteriously the lights brightened. Odd. Rose looked up at Vaughn and gasped. "I'm not hurt, but you're bleeding. You put yourself between the horses and me. Oh, my God, you were struck." She reached out to touch his face.

He jerked back. "It's nothing."

"This isn't necessary." She tried to pull her foot from him.

"Hold still. I want to see if you have fractured your ankle."

She yanked her foot from him. "I'm more worried about you, than my charley horse."

"Stubborn woman!" He wiped the blood from his cheek with his sleeve. "See, it is nothing."

"Men!" She stared at him, at his face. Reality sank in. The bruises on his face were gone. Vampires healed quickly, didn't they? "He said the house had vampires."

Vaughn's eyebrows rose. "Who said?"

"The Vaughn in my time said the house had a resident vampire, but I thought he was joking—but you weren't—he wasn't. Oh, never mind. How long have you been made?"

"Made?" He grimaced. "I do not understand."

She eased away from him and pressed herself against the back of the couch. "How long have you been like this? A vampire, I mean."

70

Understanding gleamed in his eyes. A faint smile curved his lips. "All my life." He leaned back, resting his arm along the back of the couch.

"You mean your life as a vampire?"

~ ~ ~

Vaughn shook his head. She would have read that book. "You have read Bram Stoker, I see."

"Guilty, as charged." A faint smile curved her lips

"One book I'd love to burn." Vaughn stroked his chin as he studied her. He sensed many emotions within her, but none were fear at the moment. "It pleases me you have gained control over your hysterics."

Her head snapped up. A brief flicker of anger showed in her eyes. "I don't get hysterical."

"I will have to remember that the next time you run in front of a carriage."

"I was frightened." She blushed and lowered her eyes. "I never thought of a vampire as . . . being real."

"They are not. Vampires do not exist."

Rose slowly faced him. "No offense, but to me, fangs plus red eyes equal cold-blooded, coffin sleeping, blood-sucking vampire."

He chuckled. He did like Rose's spunk. "I am not cold blooded. I do not sleep in a coffin." He met her gaze. "We are Dhampir, an ancient race who came to this planet when humans still dwelled in caves. My Father was pure Dhampir. He had no human blood in him. My mother was half-human. Humans call us Vampire, Werewolf, and Demon. I assume we are the cause of such fables."

"So what the devil is the difference between a Vampire and a Dhampir?

He loosened his necktie. It would be a long night. If he were not careful, his answers could bring a return of her fear. He smoothed his mustache as he contemplated his response. "A vampire is a reanimated corpse that has no soul and must drink the blood of its victims to live. A Dhampir is a living being,

71

with a soul. A vampire is a mythological creature of the night. We can enjoy the sunlight."

"Your mother was half human?"

He nodded. "My grandfather was Dhampir, he met and fell in love with my grandmother. They had a very long and loving life together."

Rose narrowed her eyes, staring at him as if he were a new invention.

His throat went dry. He swallowed, wishing he had something to drink. "My father told me of our world, a world with two suns and three moons." He watched Rose's face, expecting to see fear once again in her eyes. Instead, he saw curiosity. "Because of wars and pollution, our planet was dying. Our scientists built ships that brought us to this planet. But over the centuries our technology slowly died as we tried harder to fit into human society."

"You're an alien, an extraterrestrial, possibly the missing link?"

"Missing link? Extraterrestrial?" For some reason, he'd liked it better when she'd thought him a vampire.

Rose sat silently, worrying her lip, and staring at him.

He hated her silence. He hated the ticking of the clock. "Do you have any other questions?"

"You said you were not cold-blooded, and you did not sleep in a coffin, but you said nothing about drinking blood." She moved her hand to the base of her throat. He wondered if she realized she had done so. "Do you drink blood? Human blood?"

Vaughn shifted on his seat, ready to race after Rose once more. He could lie to her, but she was his mate and mates don't lie to each other.

He nodded.

The color drained from Rose's face. Her eyes darted to the open doorway then slowly panned to him.

"But not the way you think," he quickly added. He didn't wish to chase after her again tonight. "I do not hunt like Dracula, who preyed on humans to survive."

She swallowed, and her eyes grew large. "Okay, but you do drink human blood. Why?" Her words came out barely above a whisper.

He had to choose his words carefully. "My body craves it, much like your body craves water. Our kind needs to take in small amounts of human blood on a regular basis. If we do not, or if we are injured and have lost a great deal of blood, we will suffer immense pain. The loss of blood also prevents us from healing, and we can no longer maintain our human appearance. But I have never killed anyone for their blood."

"So, how do you get the blood? Do you have donors or something?"

"Yes. I will not feed my need at the expense of others."

She nodded and appeared to relax some. Her heart wasn't pounding as wildly as it had been. Rose lowered her eyes, not looking at him. "How did your parents die?"

He'd expected many questions from her, but not this one. "Why do you ask?"

"I lost my parents when I was ten. My father owned a small airplane." Her voice quivered, and tears welled in her eyes, but she blinked them back. "I watched the plane crash. Sara told me you lost your parents when you were a young boy. Were they killed because of what they were?"

Before answering her question, he touched her mind. He saw the pain she'd suffered from the death of her parents. He felt her grief at the loss of an older brother and the loneliness brought on by the loss of her husband. She thought herself the reason for the deaths of her loved ones.

He reached over and took her hand in his. His heart lifted when she didn't pull away.

"In a way, yes, my parents were killed because of my mother's human blood. They were not killed by humans, but by Dhampir."

Rose covered his hand with hers.

"In my race, some individuals believe our bloodlines need to stay pure. They do not believe we should marry humans, or even marry outside of our clans. They feel the mixing of bloodlines will weaken our abilities. They fear mating with humans will eventually make us human. One such family was named Dietrich."

"Purist," Rose said. "I guess every culture has them.

The clock chimed. How long had they been sitting, talking? He didn't want to move. He enjoyed having Rose next to him. Her fingers intertwined with his.

"Can I ask what sort of abilities?" she asked.

He looked up from their joined hands into her hazel eyes. In the firelight they appeared to have flecks of gold in them. "Some have the ability to change into animals but prefer the form of wolves. Other clans can fly, and last, there are those who can fade from sight."

"Dematerialize, changing into a cloud of mist. All the abilities described in Dracula."

He nodded, then drew in a deep breath and forged onward. "My sister Aileen was only two days old. Dietrich and his men came under the pretense of paying their respects to my mother and newborn sister. My father handed my sister to me and told me to hide in the forest. Shortly after I ran from the house, I heard my mother's screams and felt my parents' deaths in my heart.

"I hid in a cave I would play in and watched as my home burned. My parents were murdered before they named my sister." Even after all these years, the memory still pained him.

"Sara told me her son was the one who found you. Were you in the woods long?"

"Alan Lucard and his men found us several days later. Aileen was near death. Because Alan didn't have the means to care for my sister, he gave her to his sister and her husband, Ian. They named my sister and have loved and cared for Aileen

74

ever since. My sister lives in Scotland. As for myself, I joined Alan and his men in the hunt for my parents' murderers."

Rose had moved closer to him. Her finger gently caressed his hand. "You've been loyal to the Lucard's ever since?"

"They took me in, protected me, educated me, and gave me a position."

The glow of the lamplights shimmered in Rose's eyes. He didn't see scorn or hate, but understanding in them. When he breathed in the air was sweet with her scent, not tainted by the pungent smell of fear. Rose had accepted him as he was. *Thank you, Yeva.*

"What happened to the men who murdered your parents?"

"They were brought to justice." He would not tell her the satisfaction he felt as he listened to them scream for mercy, just as his mother had screamed.

~ ~ ~

Rose stared at their intertwined hands. She'd been a fool to fear him, but . . . He was still a vampire, no matter what name he called himself, as was his sister. Rose shifted keeping her hand in his. "Your sister is the same as you. Your sister and Sara need to drink blood too. Correct?"

"They do. But Sara has already proven you are perfectly safe in her company. You will be safe with Aileen. I can see you becoming more of a friend to her than an employee."

"So is anyone else looking at my throat as a tender morsel?"

Vaughn rolled his eyes and laughed, a warm, rich laugh. "Woman, you try my patience. No one is looking at you as a morsel. I will not take your blood. Unless you offer it to me freely," he added in a deep, rich, silky voice.

Rose gently pulled her hand from his then crossed her arms over her chest. "Yeah, so why were you trying to before?"

Vaughn stared at her, his mouth hung open, and his brows furrowed. He pushed his hand over his hair and stood.

"Madam, I assure you. I have never tried to take that liberty with you."

"Oh, yes, you did. Upstairs in the hall, outside my bedroom door, remember?" She tilted her head back so that she could look up at him. The man was a behemoth, but damn was he good looking.

Vaughn's face turned red, and he turned away from her. "I wasn't trying to bite your throat."

"Then pray tell, what were you trying to do?"

His blush receded, leaving two red spots on his cheeks and he rubbed the back of his neck. "I was trying to steal a kiss."

Chapter Six

Vaughn stretched and opened his eyes. His curtains were still drawn, his clothes had not been laid out, and he didn't hear Andrew preparing his bath. Vaughn pulled the sheet over his shoulders and rolled onto his side. Despite all he needed to do, a few more minutes of sleep wouldn't hinder him.

His pocket-watch chimed. He snatched his watch from the bedside table, flipping it opened. Ten o'clock? "Bloody hell." He'd slept the morning away. "Blast it all!" Aileen would arrive at three. He needed to see Hughes. Damn, he would have Andrew's head for this.

Vaughn quickly shaved, nicking himself several times in his haste. It was a bloody good thing he healed quickly. How could Andrew shirk his duties? After dressing, Vaughn bounded down the stairs.

The sweet sound of Rose's laughter floated in from outside. His mood lifted as he walked out onto the terrace. She and Sara were enjoying the morning sunshine.

Sara smiled at him as he bent down and brushed a kiss to her cheek.

"Sara, do you know why I was permitted to sleep so late?" he asked, trying to keep his tone pleasant.

"We instructed Andrew not to wake you." She patted his face as though he were a boy.

"I should have known Andrew wouldn't shirk his duties."

Sara's eyes shifted to Rose, then back to him. "After my morning stroll, I think I will speak with Mrs. Brown about tonight's dinner." She stood and went back into the house.

Rose glanced up from the book she'd borrowed from him last night and greeted him with a heart-warming smile. "Good morning."

"And to you, my lady." He slowly perused her.

Rose wore a light gray skirt and a white cotton shirtwaist. Her hair was twisted into a bun with a few loose curls framing her face and hung softly about her neck. He liked her hair unbound as she wore it when he'd first seen her, but that was not the fashion.

A gentle breeze blew her curls. He resisted the urge to wrap his finger in one.

Rose lowered her eyes to the book.

Blast it all. He wanted to see her face, not a book cover. "How is your ankle?"

"Fine. It's not even bruised." She smiled then went back to reading.

He stood beside her. Her emotions seeped into him. He felt caution and apprehension from her, but not fear. He stroked his chin and studied her for a brief second. This wasn't the same spirited woman he'd chased last night. "Rose, I can tell something is bothering you. May I inquire what it is? Has Sara said something to upset you?"

"No, Sara hasn't upset me. What makes you think something is wrong?" Rose closed the book and placed it on the table beside her.

"You would make an excellent card player. You keep your features deceptively composed. However. . ." He took Sara's empty seat beside Rose. "As you know, I have certain abilities, one of which is the fact I can sense other's emotions. Right now, I detect you are apprehensive about something."

A blush teased across Rose's pale and beautiful face. She stared at him, her mouth slightly open. "You can read my mind?"

"When your emotions are heightened, like now and the way they were last night, I can see glimpses of your thoughts. I cannot freely read your mind. I have not taken your blood."

"And you won't. Right?"

"I gave you my word." He'd always heard that blood freely given by one's mate tasted sweeter than the nectar of gods. He longed for the time when she would give herself to him completely. "Please tell me, what has you upset."

Rose opened the book. She tilted her face up, meeting his gaze. "The inscription, is to you isn't it?"

"It is my book. Nathaniel gave it to me. I met him when he was appointed U.S. Consul at Liverpool. Nathaniel was a dear friend."

"That was in the mid-1800's."

"True. Nathaniel held the position from 1853 to 1857."

"But you only look thirty-ish. How old are you?"

"I was born on March 13, 1700."

She eyed him with a calculating expression. After what seemed an eternity, she drew in a shuddered breath. "You're two hundred years old. How old is your sister?"

"Aileen is fourteen years younger than I."

Rose's eyes widened. "Why does she need a chaperone? I mean, Sara and I can go out as we please. I hope you did not offer me the position simply out of pity."

He folded his fingers together. Despite what Ian had written in his letter, Aileen was a lady. "Pity has nothing to do with it. Appearances must be kept in order to protect us. Just as I don't look my age to you, neither does Aileen look hers. She is, for all purposes, a young, unmarried woman and will need someone to accompany her to the theater and park as protocol demands."

"I'm sorry if I offended you. I forget things are much different in this time than what I'm used to." Rose bit her lower lip and lowered her eyes to her book. A habit of Rose's he noticed she did whenever she was at a loss for words or felt uncomfortable.

His harsh tone had upset her. "You didn't offend me. Aileen is—how shall I put this? She has never taken any of her suitors seriously. For her to take a sudden fancy to this David Campbell. I have to assume it is for no other reason but to shock the family. Aileen knows Ian MacPhee's feeling toward the Campbells, all Campbells." He reached over and clasped Rose's hand in his. "However, if I'm wrong about her motives, then I think Aileen will need a friend more than a chaperone."

Rose lifted her eyes. He was pleased to see the glint of humor had returned to them. "Some things don't change with time, once a big brother, always a big brother."

He laughed and stood, putting the matter aside. "Would you care to see my garden? I have time to show it to you before I must leave."

"I'd love to see it," she said, taking his arm.

As he stepped from under the terrace, he squinted. He stepped back, rubbing his eyes.

"Vaughn?" Rose stared up at him. "What's wrong?"

"The sun is bright this morning."

"I see one fact about Vamps is true. Wait here. I'll be right back." Rose turned then quickly dashed into the house.

Surely, Rose did not think the sun would burn him to a cinder. After all, she had seen him in the daylight before.

A few minutes later Rose returned carrying black wire-framed dark glasses. "Here, try these on." She handed the glasses to him.

"Eyeglasses will not help."

She tilted her chin up stubbornly. "Put them on."

"Only to please you," he said, sliding on the strange glasses. They truly blocked the sun's burning rays. Instantly his eyes felt better. "These are smashing!"

"I'm glad. They're called *Ray-Ban*." She grinned. "You can keep them. With their circular wire frames, they look like glasses from this era. No one will suspect they're from the future."

He was at a loss for words. This gift from Rose was wonderful. "Thank you, but they are yours." He could not keep them.

"Yes, and I want you to have them."

He folded her arm under his. What had he done for the Creator to bless him with such a woman?

"Vaughn?"

The uneasiness in Rose's voice was unmistakable. "Yes," he said, dreading what she would ask.

"Is it possible you are the same person, the same Vaughn I know in my time? You saw yourself or your descendant in the photo I have. You look the same."

"I have no idea. This man from your time looks like me, yes." Surely, he was the same person. But how? Why would he let his mate slip away? He covered her hand with his. Somehow, he'd lost her once. He would not lose her again. "If I am the same person, then I can only assume my future has already been altered."

"Why do you say that?"

"When we first met in your time, did I mention our meeting here?"

She shook her head. "All you talked about was this house."

"Then, you see. My future has already been changed. I would not have forgotten you in a hundred years, not in two hundred years." He stared at her full lips and wanted to taste their sweetness.

"Your roses are beautiful."

"Thank you. I tend to them myself."

She slid her hand from his arm and strolled over his rose bushes. Rose leaned forward smelling a pale pink rose, the color of her cheeks. "My grandmother had a bush like this one. She called it the Seven Sisters, but it wasn't fragrant like this one."

His heart pounded in his chest. Rose was the flower he hoped would forever bloom in his garden, a rare long-stemmed rose.

He plucked the bud, then handed it to her. "This particular bush is the Fairies." How did one go about courting a woman from the future, a woman who had thrown him to the ground as easily as if he were a toy and had the power to cloud his mind with nonsense? "May I ask you a question?"

"Shoot."

"Pardon?"

Amusement flickered in Rose's eyes, and she laughed. "Shoot means to go ahead. It can also be a mild cuss word."

"I see. I think." Would he ever fully understand everything she said?

"Whatever it is, you may ask."

"Very well, how was it you, being much smaller than I and a woman, were able to push me to the ground?"

"I've taken Judo and various other forms of self-defense classes. It keeps me fit."

"I see. You caught me off guard and used it against me. However, if I were to come at you from behind, then I would have the upper hand."

"Don't count on it buddy."

"Oh?" He might not have understood her wording, but he knew a challenge when he heard one. Smiling, Vaughn wrapped his arms around Rose.

She shifted, twisting her body, and he found himself falling over her shoulder. Once again, he ended up on his backside, looking up at her.

"How?" he asked. "I am considered a giant, a behemoth, yet you did this."

Shrugging, Rose grinned at him. "It's called a shoulder roll. I essentially used your size against you. You know, the bigger they are, the harder the fall and all that."

~ ~ ~

Rose stared at Vaughn sitting on the ground. The sunglasses she'd given him sat cock-eyed on his face. She couldn't see his eyes behind the black lenses, but the corner of his lips turned up in a faint smile.

"Perhaps you could teach my sister these moves of yours," he grunted.

Rose covered her mouth with her hand to hide her grin. "I'm sorry," she laughed.

"Madam, your apology would go farther if you were not laughing."

Hearing the chuckle in his voice, she laughed harder. "Let me help you up."

"Since I'm already on the ground, I assume it will be safe." He took her hand and pulled her down on to his lap.

"You cheated!" She pushed against his chest.

"Did I?" he whispered, covering her lips with his.

His strong arms held her to him. A surge of excitement rushed through her as her arms slid around his neck. Her lips parted, and she kissed him back.

When Vaughn kissed her tenderly, lightly, she felt as if it were her first kiss. His hand slid to the back of her neck, holding her as he deepened their kiss.

"Sir," Andrew called from behind them.

Vaughn lifted his lips from hers, then quickly kissed them again. "What is it, Andrew?"

"The carriage is ready, sir."

"Very well, I will be there shortly." Vaughn set her from him, then rose fluidly from the ground. Smiling down at her, he swiftly lifted her to her feet, then tipped her chin up with his finger. "When I return, we will have to continue our tour of the garden."

She didn't miss the double meaning of his words. "I can hardly wait."

He raised her hand to his lips, then turned, and followed Andrew out of the garden.

Rose smacked herself in the forehead. *What the hell was I thinking?* She had no business getting involved with anyone in this time. And certainly not with a vampire, correction, Dhampir.

She stopped in front of a garden bench and sat. Vaughn was immortal. He had to be to live so long, but what if he wasn't? She wouldn't go down that road. She'd made a vow never to fall in love. She would stick to it. By some twist of fate, she had another chance to live. She wouldn't repeat past mistakes by falling in love with someone and watching him die.

Rose picked up the blossom Vaughn had given her and smelled its sweet fragrance. Somehow she'd make a living in this time without the help of Vaughn Madoc. She had to do this, to keep him safe.

As Rose walked up the steps of the terrace, she met Sara.

"Did you enjoy the garden?" Sara asked.

"Yes, I found it quite inspiring."

"Andrew has informed me lunch is served. I have instructed him to serve us out here."

Lunch? Rose moaned. It hadn't been long since they'd had breakfast. Tea would be served at three and dinner anywhere from six to nine. Good grief, if she weren't careful, she'd have a fanny to replace the bustle she wore. "That's fine with me."

Beelzebub meowed as he came up the steps.

Rose stared down at him as he'd dropped a fat mouse at her feet.

"Even you are trying to feed me." She rubbed the cat's head.

After a lunch of cheese, bread, and fish, Rose picked up the book she'd left. She'd nearly finished reading the whole story when Andrew came out onto the porch.

"Madam, Her Grace is serving tea in the parlor."

Well, she could do with a cup of tea. "Thank you, Andrew. I'll be right in." She stood and stretched. This life might suit Sara fine, but Rose was a working woman. If she didn't find something to keep her busy, a job or something, she would die from boredom. "Come on, Beelzebub. It's tea time."

The cat followed her into the parlor, so closely she feared she would trip over him. She'd barely settled in a chair before the scamp curled up at her feet.

Sara poured Rose a cup of tea. "Would you care for a crumpet?"

"No, thank you."

"Vaughn should be arriving soon with Aileen."

Rose sipped her tea, eyeing the delicious looking sweets on the cart. "Will he tell his sister about me?"

Sara set her cup down. Her expression changed and became almost somber. "Vaughn and I believe it is for the best only he and I know about your adventure. We informed the staff you are a friend of mine from America."

"But Aileen is Vaughn's sister. Shouldn't she be told?"

"No. Rose, Aileen can be trusted, but the fewer people who know, the less chance for you to end up in an asylum or worst. If and when the time comes, Aileen needs to know, then and only then we will tell her."

Asylum? Rose shivered. If anyone let it slip she thought she came from the future, they'd surely lock her away. Sara was right.

Penny rushed into the room and whispered something in Sara's ear.

"Of all people," she said through her teeth and cast her eyes upward.

Rose looked up as Andrew escorted a gentleman into the room. The man looked familiar. Tall, dark, and rather handsome, despite the fact he wore the most outrageous suit she'd ever seen. Dressed in a blue-stripped cotton coat and cotton-duck pants, he looked like he belonged in a barbershop quartet. He clutched a straw 'boater' hat in one hand. Rose stifled a giggle. The way his mustache curled up, she'd bet he had enough wax on it to make a candle.

Rose cast a glance at Sara, noting her forced smile. It didn't take supernatural mind reading abilities to know Sara did not want to entertain this man.

"Philip, what a pleasant surprise," Sara greeted him.

He stepped over Rose's foot, kicking Beelzebub. "Your Grace, you look ravishing. I see your travels to America agreed with you. Did you by chance meet any savages?"

Sara slid closer to the teacart. She motioned to Rose. "Philip, I would like you to meet my friend, Mrs. Kelly. Rose, Philip Dorjan is a friend of the family."

Philip offered his hand to Rose.

Beelzebub laid his ears back and hissed. Rose didn't blame the cat one bit. She bet the jerk purposely kick Beelzebub.

Philip's smiled at Rose as if it were a chore. "Madam."

"A pleasure to meet you, sir." Not. His handshake was limp, cold, and felt like a dead fish. She withdrew her hand from his and resisted the urge to wipe it on her skirt.

"I'm sure," he said, when he took his seat next to Sara, she leaned away subtly, but Rose caught the action. "Why does Vaughn permit that beast to remain here?"

Rose wasn't up on Victorian etiquette, but she knew it wasn't proper for him to plopped down beside Sara the way he had.

Sara poured milk into a saucer. Smiling, she placed it on the floor. "Perhaps it's because Vaughn is fond of the creature. I have heard cats are excellent judges of character. Do you not agree, Rose?"

"Yes. I find Beelzebub to be a doll." As if on cue, the cat purred and rolled to his side, playfully batting at her skirt.

Philip's smile faded. "Tell me, is the news I hear true?" He moved closer to Sara on the couch.

"What news?" Sara asked.

"Aileen is coming for a stay."

"Crumpet?"

He waved his hand, dismissively. "No, thank you. Now you are keeping me in suspense. Is Aileen coming?"

"She is."

"Oh, wonderful. I will have to take Aileen to the park and fill her in on the latest news. You did hear about Lady Winston's granddaughter?"

Sara waved her hand dismissingly. "Aileen knows of Charlotte's broken engagement."

86

Rose watched Sara's expression. Though she was polite, it was obvious Sara thought little of Philip. Rose didn't think much of him, either. Anyone who would harm an animal was a jerk.

Philip set his cup on the table. He pulled his pocket watch from his vest. "Dear me, I didn't realize how very late it is. I must take my leave." He stood. "Please let Aileen know I inquired about her."

"I will let her know, Philip," Sara's monotone made Rose want to laugh.

Philip gave Rose a nod. "Madam." Then he left the room in a flourish.

A few moments later, Sara peeked out the window behind her. "I would rather Aileen marry the Campbell than that popinjay. Thank goodness, poor Aileen wasn't here when he showed up. I fear she's had a tough go at it already with Vaughn."

"Does Vaughn dislike the Campbells, too?" Rose asked. She didn't want to pry, but her curiosity had the best of her.

"He only wants what is best for Aileen."

The sound of several male voices boomed into the parlor. Vaughn's deep voice made Rose smile. She turned in her seat in time to see a young woman rush into the room, followed by Vaughn and two other men. The tall men looked so much alike Rose assumed they were brothers. The only difference between them was the color of their hair, one blond and the other's as black as ink. Both men had piercing blue eyes.

Beelzebub purred and rubbed against the men's legs. The blond bent down and gave the cat a firm petting. "Still running the house, I see."

Rose fidgeted, trying not to stare at Vaughn's sister. Aileen didn't look like a vampire in her light brown traveling dress, with her reddish blond hair tucked neatly under a hat. Aileen looked like a young woman no more than twenty.

"*Babushka*," Aileen said. "Will you please reason with them?" She pointed to the two men. "I'm old enough to choose my suitors."

Sara hugged the younger woman. "Shh-Shh, there will be time to talk about this later. Aileen, I want you to meet a friend of mine, Rose Kelly."

Aileen greeted Rose with a warm and friendly smile. "Forgive me my rudeness, Mrs. Kelly. Vaughn told me *Babushka* had a friend with her. I didn't think you would be this young."

Vaughn leaned against the doorframe and laughed. "See, Aileen. I didn't saddle you with an old and decrepit woman as a companion." He winked at Rose as he entered the room.

"Vaughn!" Aileen glared up at him. "I said nothing of the sort." She gazed over at Rose. "Mrs. Kelly, you must believe me. I said nothing of the sort."

"Oh, I'm sure your brother is teasing." Rose smile at Vaughn's sister.

Vaughn moved to Rose's chair. His tight expression relaxed into a smile. The warmth of his look sent shivers down Rose's spine.

He rested his hand on her shoulder. "Rose, I would like to introduce to you Royce Lucard."

The blond gentleman nodded and approached her. He made a slight bow, then took her hand and lifted it to his lips. "The pleasure is all mine," his deep rich voice resonated.

"And Glen MacPhee." Vaughn pointed to the other man.

Glen also took her hand and brought it to his lips, brushing a light kiss across her knuckles. "A pleasure to meet you."

"Gentlemen," Rose said with a smiled.

A wolfish grin curved Royce's lip. "Vaughn, when you told us about *Babushka's* friend, you neglected to say how beautiful she was."

"He's either blind or has been so busy workin' he didna notice her beauty," Glen laughed.

Sara tapped her spoon against her cup. "Allow Rose time to become accustomed to your teasing."

Rose regarded at the men, then Aileen. The love Rose felt from just being in the room warmed her. Aileen and Vaughn were lucky to have been taken in by this family.

Vaughn squeezed her shoulder gently. "Rose, you will have to forgive my brothers. It has been a long time since they have been in the company of a lady."

Brothers? She studied the gentlemen again.

"What am I?" Aileen asked.

Rose looked up at Vaughn. She'd like to see how he planned to get himself out of this fix.

Vaughn inclined his head a bit and narrowed his eyes at Aileen. "You, my dear, are my sister."

Aileen crossed her arms over her chest, and her eyes suddenly flashed from pale green to fiery red. "And I am not a lady?"

"I merely said you were my sister." Vaughn lowered his voice to almost a whisper.

Glen stepped in front of Aileen. "Weel, when Royce and I happened upon you, you were by na means acting like a lady." He thrust his finger at Aileen.

She knocked his hand away. "Dash it all! David was only kissing me."

"David, is it now?" Royce threw his hands up. "Kissing you? I have bedded women on less of a kiss." He lowered his head and turned, facing Rose. "I beg your pardon."

Aileen's lips quivered, and tears welled in her eyes. "Why did you have to beat him to a bloody pulp? You could have at least let me see how serious his injuries were."

"Weel, I sure as hell wasn't planning to dance with him, and as far as I'm concerned if he dies tha' weel be one less Campbell to worry abou.'" Glen sneered.

The situation was serious, but Rose bit the inside of her cheek to keep from laughing at the man's heavy brogue.

Aileen fell onto Sara's shoulder and sobbed. "I will find a way to be with David."

Rose didn't know Aileen, but the anguish on her face tore at Rose's heart.

Sara wiped Aileen's tears. "Is David your mate?"

"I never felt like this about anyone before. David makes me feel alive. He makes me feel whole," Aileen said through her tears.

"Did you tell Ian and Angelique this?"

Aileen shook her head vigorously. "I tried. Ian would not speak to me about it. He said because I have betrayed him, I am no. . . ." She cried harder. "He said I was no longer his daughter." Aileen shoved herself from the couch, rushed by Royce and Glen, and ran from the room.

Andrew entered the parlor. He purposely strode toward Vaughn. "Sir."

"What is it, Andrew?"

He whispered something in Vaughn's ear.

Vaughn's lips thinned as he exhaled. "Very well." In that very second, Vaughn seemed to age ten years.

"Trouble?" Glen asked.

"Afraid so." He looked at Sara. "I will not be dining with you tonight." He closed his eyes, then opened them. "See if you can calm Aileen."

Glen rolled his eyes. "Do'na worry abou' her. In a day or so she'll have forgotten the Campbell and have a new suitor."

Royce patted Vaughn's back. "We'll accompany you."

Both men gave Rose a quick nod, then followed Vaughn out of the room.

Rose stared at the empty doorway. Her stomach knotted. Vaughn might be immortal, but she doubted he was indestructible, too. After all, even Dracula had his weaknesses.

Chapter Seven

Cold chills ran down Rose's spine as she stared at the parlor's empty doorway. She forced her anxious thoughts from her mind and tried to think of something else. "Sara, why is there a problem with Aileen seeing this man?"

"He's a Campbell, and Ian hates all Campbells for what they did at Glencoe and Culloden."

"You're kidding, right? If I remember my history correctly, those battles happened over two hundred years ago. Talk about holding a grudge." She sat back and crossed her arms over her chest. Good grief, how could he be so prejudiced against someone for what his ancestors did, or. . . "Wait a minute. Was David there—I mean is he?"

"Is he what, Rose?"

Rose bit her lower lip. "Is David like Aileen and Vaughn? You know special?"

"No. Mr. Campbell is human, like you."

"Then why is he being blamed for something he had no control over? Personally, if the guy likes Aileen as much as she likes him, I don't see the problem."

A faint laugh slipped from Sara. "Ian is a stubborn Scot and slow to change his mind, but Aileen will be pleased to know she has another ally in you."

~ ~ ~

Vaughn glanced at his pocket watch. It was well past midnight. The carriage shook as it rumbled along the cobblestone road, shaking his weary body. He would not rest until he caught this killer. Vaughn raised his eyes, glancing from Royce's icy look to Glen's angry one. "As I explained, I feel the killer is one of our kind."

Royce nodded. "I will inform Father of this. Whoever the killer is, he must be stopped."

"I agree," Glen muttered. "Vampire, tha' is what the common man will call him. We know what tha' will mean."

"We all will be in danger," Royce answered. "Do the victims have anything in common that could point to the killer?"

Vaughn looked out the carriage window. A dense fog had rolled in, a perfect night for another murder. "All the victims do have one thing in common, *me*."

Glen's eyes narrowed. "Explain."

"The first victim was once my mistress. The next four were business associates, but they didn't know about us. However, the following five victims did know about our kind." Vaughn balled his hand into a fist. "Austin was a harmless old man." His claws dug into his hands.

"Was Austin helping you in your investigation?" Royce asked.

The carriage slowed to a stop in front of the house. Vaughn opened the door and stepped out. "Hughes and I paid Austin a visit two days ago. He told me the same weapon was used to kill all the victims. He discovered this by measuring the distance between the marks. Austin was a brilliant man."

Vaughn looked up at the house. "It seems Andrew has left a light on in the parlor for us, gentlemen."

Royce and Glen flanked Vaughn as they walked down the path.

"Father will not be pleased," Royce said. "There are so few of us left. If one of them is a rogue, it will mean trouble for all of us. You know Father will order a hunt." Royce stared at Vaughn. "I do not have to tell you what that will mean for you, nor do I have to tell you Father will be quite angry you kept this from him."

"Alan is the least of my worries." Vaughn opened the front door. "Brandy, gentlemen?"

Glen nodded. "Aye, thank you."

"That would taste good." Royce grinned. "By chance do you have any cigars?" He paused in front of the parlor door.

"Well, well, what have we here? Sleeping Beauty waiting for her prince?"

Vaughn pivoted on his heel and came to see what Royce was talking about. Rose slept on the couch. A book lay on the floor. She'd fallen asleep, perhaps waiting up for him? He smiled at the possibility.

Royce smoothed his coat and proceeded into the room. "Perhaps, I shall wake her."

Glen stifled a chuckle, pushing Royce aside. "Why you? I will do the honors."

Vaughn grabbed Royce by the scruff, lifted him, and turned him. Then he pushed Glen from the room. "Out, both of you."

Vaughn shut the door. When he turned, he stood gazing at his sleeping angel. He moved, so as not to startle her. His heart warmed as he gently caressed her cheek.

Rose's eyes fluttered open. Her warm, sleepy smile drew him as if he were under a spell. He bent toward her and covered her lips with his as he eased onto the couch beside her. His arms slid around her thin waist, and he drew her closer to him.

~ ~ ~

Rose startled instantly awake. What the devil? She shoved against a hard chest, pushing the man to the floor. "What do you think you're doing?" She demanded, sitting.

Vaughn gazed up at her, his eyes glowed red, and the tips of his fangs were visible. "I'm beginning to think you prefer me on the ground, sitting on my bum."

She bit her lip, looking at him. "Sorry about that. Look, I'll admit, I'm attracted to you. I think you're downright handsome, except for the hair on your face, but I can't allow myself to get involved with you."

He stood and looked at her intently before he strolled over to the wingbacked chair. "Is it because of what I am?"

"No. That doesn't have anything to do with it."

93

"Then it is my stature." He sighed. "My great size has always frightened women."

"Your height has nothing to do with it, either." She thought his great size made him even hotter. She shivered remembering the feel of his hard muscles. *Down girl.*

"Then do you still mourn your husband?"

"I will always think of Richard with love, but he is not the reason I will not allow myself to get involved." How could she tell Vaughn if she allowed herself to get involved with him, he'd die?

"Then why?"

"I can't stay here. I have to find my way back to my time." She pushed herself from the couch. Rose paced around the room before she settled on pacing back and forth in front of the fireplace.

"Rose, you've tried to go back and could not. whatever sent you here only works once for a person."

"How do you know?" she asked, throwing both hands up in frustration.

"It's a hypothesis. If William Martin disappeared the same way, he has not returned. Thus it's obvious you cannot go back to your time. Therefore, whatever sent you here must only work once for a person."

"I only want to be friends. I don't want to risk falling in love with you or anyone." She drew a step nearer to him. Her eyes burned, and she blinked back tears, refusing to let them fall. "I watched my brother die of Leukemia. I witnessed my parents' plane crash. I went to live with my grandparents, and my grandfather died of a heart attack. Then for six years, I watched my grandmother fight breast cancer. By marrying Richard, I sent him to his death. I'm tired of having everyone I love die. I'm tired of being a jinx to everyone I love, of being a bringer of death. I will not sentence you to death, too."

"You didn't cause the deaths in your family. Death is a part of life."

"That's easy for you to say. You don't know what it's like to have everyone you love and care about die.

A sad smile curved his lips. "No, not everyone, just my parents. Living as long as I have, I've buried countless friends. Matter of fact, I lost a dear friend tonight."

How crass could she have been? She'd forgotten about his parents. "I'm sorry, Vaughn. Please forgive me. I don't want anything to happen to you or any member of your family. I have to live somewhere else."

"I cannot let you leave, not with a killer on the loose." He leaned back in the chair and ran his finger under his stiff high-neck collar as if it were choking him.

Wrapped up in her own problems, she'd forgotten Vaughn was under a lot of stress. He was trying to catch a murderer and dealing with his family problems. If that weren't enough, she'd literally popped into his life uninvited.

She studied his face. In the faint light of the room, he looked tired and mentally drained. He seemed to have aged years in only a few hours. The last thing he needed was her dumping on him.

Rose sat on the footstool in front of him. She placed her hand on his knee. "Was that where you went today?"

"Yes."

"Was he another victim of the killer?"

Vaughn nodded, pulling on his collar once more

"I take it you are no closer in finding out why or who?"

Vaughn looked at her and drew in a deep breath. "I believe I am making some progress. Yes. I believe I even know what he is?"

"You know who the killer is?"

"Not who, but what he is."

She studied his expression. "I don't follow."

Vaughn rubbed his hand over his face. Resting his arms on his knees, he met her gaze. "The killer is one of my kind. All the victims have a common thread. Me. Someone who knows me well, who knows my acquaintances and friends, is killing

95

them off." He tenderly caressed her face. "Does this make me a bringer of death, a jinx as you say?"

"No."

"Then you should not think yourself one, either." He lowered his head. "Go to bed, Rose. You need your sleep."

"So do you."

He shook his head. "I'll sleep once I catch this fiend."

"Vaughn." Before she realized it, she sat on the arm of Vaughn's chair and slipped her arm around his shoulders. "Maybe someone is trying to frame you. You know, blame the murders on you."

"Perhaps, but people are dying." Tenderly he looked at her. He brushed her cheek with his knuckles. "That is the reason you can't leave. You have to stay where I can protect you and keep you safe."

"I don't—"

Placing his finger over her lips, he said. "I will die someday of old age, not because you live under my roof."

"Does the killer know how to—does he know how to defeat you?" She couldn't bring herself to say 'kill.'

"Yes, just as I know how to kill him." Vaughn rubbed his hands over his face and sighed. "It's late, and this has been a busy day. We both should get some sleep."

When he smiled at her, she felt her blood surge from her fingertips to her toes. There was no denying she felt a magnetism building between them. If she weren't careful, she'd be in his bed. Dammit. He was breaking down every one of her defenses, and he didn't even know he was doing it.

She slid from the arm of the chair. "Tomorrow, if you want, I'll help you go through the files you have, as well as the files on my phone. If we can."

He stood and took her hand in his. "I need all the help I can get. Thank you." He bent toward her and brushed a kiss to her lips. "Good night, Rose."

She stood frozen, staring up at him, captured by the heart-rending tenderness of his gaze. Then, as if drawn by an invisible thread, she found herself pulled to him. She went up on her tiptoes and kissed him lightly on the lips. "Good night."

The smoldering flames flickering in his eyes aroused her. She wasn't a fool. If she stayed a second longer, they'd be ripping each other's clothes off. She grabbed the book she'd borrowed and left him standing like a statue.

~ ~ ~

Vaughn rinsed the soap from his clean-shaven face, while he studied his new appearance in the mirror. He ran his hand over his smooth upper lip. A week had passed since the last murder, but he was no closer to finding the killer. Because of Royce and Glen's constant hovering, Rose had been afraid to look at the files she'd saved on her white box, until last night.

That box of hers! Amazing! If only he had something in this time that would provide it energy. What did she call it again? Didn't matter, what did matter was the information he had seen and read. Ah, Rose she had been so excited when she was able to find those files for him.

Rose. Vaughn could not get her out of his mind. He found himself thinking of her constantly. Blast it all. So, she only wanted to be friends. Very well, but she hadn't said how good of friends. He'd seen the glimmer in her eyes and smelled her desire. He'd heard her heart pounding. She desired him as much as he wanted her. She was just stubborn.

He left his washroom. Vaughn stood on the landing to go down for breakfast. No. He would have Andrew bring up a tray while he went over his files again. He turned and strolled to his study.

He was thankful for Royce and Glen's help. He'd been more grateful when they had left the day before. Vaughn stroked his smooth face. He turned the knob of his study and pushed open the door.

97

On his desk sat the box of files, the records of a killer, one he knew as well as he knew himself. If only he knew the bastard's face.

He dreaded hearing from Alan, who would no doubt ring him or send a telegram as soon as Royce informed him of the latest murders. Royce was right. His father wouldn't be pleased. Alan would no doubt order an all-out hunt.

Vaughn slammed his fist on the desk. He wasn't looking forward to being called onto the carpet for not keeping his lordship informed. Granted, Alan was now the ruling head of their people, but just once Vaughn wished, he could please the man. "God help Royce when he tells his father."

Someone tapped on the door.

"Enter," he called.

Rose stood before him, staring at him. Her eyes were wide. Her gaze roamed over his face. "You didn't come down for breakfast."

"Andrew brought up a tray." He smiled at her expression. "Is there something wrong, Rose? You look surprised."

"I'm fine. You shaved."

"A task I do daily." *So, she didn't like the hair on my face.* He lowered his eyes to the files. He knew what she meant. He'd shaved off his mustache and trimmed his sideburns.

Perhaps now he could steal a kiss without her turning from him.

She placed a stack of papers on his desk. "I stayed up last night taking down notes from the files. I still think the killer is human."

"My gut tells me otherwise." He studied the hand-written pages she'd placed on his desk. "If I'm right, then I can only assume the person I hunt in this time is the same individual in your time. So, you see my dear, your being sent back in time to me was so you could aid me in stopping him, preventing him from killing in the future."

Rose reached across and took hold of his hand. "Come with me, please. I want to show you something."

He looked down at her hands, at the dirt pushed under her nails and around her cuticles. "You have been digging?" He looked up at her. She had a speckle of dirt on her left cheek. "Are you and Aileen looking for buried treasure?"

"Don't be silly. I was weeding your roses. You've been so busy lately with the case I decided to take pity on you and weed it."

He stood, keeping her hand in his. "Let me guess. You want me to see the damage you have done to my garden?"

"Damage, my foot." A mild storm rumbled behind her gray eyes. "We may need this," she said, picking up one of the photographs from his desk.

"What does that picture have to do with my garden?" He dabbed the dirt from her face.

"Well, if you'll follow me you'll see."

Reluctantly he followed her outside. Though he wanted to woo her, he'd better things to do than to look at her gardening skills. He came to an abrupt halt, seeing the excellent job she'd done with his roses.

"Look. Do you see it?" She pointed to the freshly raked dirt.

"I see you have raked out the dirt around the plants, and you have pulled the weeds on the walk. Is that what you wanted to show me?"

She huffed and rolled her eyes. "No. Don't you see the marks? See how much they resemble the wounds in this photo?"

He stared at the dirt. The marks made by the hand-rake were similar, but not as viciously made. "I'm afraid they are not the same."

Rose picked up the small hand-rake. She raised her hand over her head, then brought the gardening tool down with tremendous force, making deep, jagged marks in the soil. Her eyes flickered. "What about now?" See, they look more like the picture. The killer may be human and using a weapon to simulate claw marks."

He stroked his smooth chin. She did have an excellent point, one he'd not thought of before. "Human or Dhampir, he poses a threat to both communities."

"How many people know about you?"

"Few, but now I wonder if too many know." He kept staring at the marks as he helped her to her feet. Something was wrong. He was missing something significant. *But what?* It hit him. "What about the blood?"

"What?"

"How do you explain the lack of blood?"

"Give me a second." Her brow furrowed and she tapped her foot, then a smile curved her lips. "Two explanations." She held up her fingers. "What if the murders happened somewhere else and the killer simply dumped the bodies where the police or whoever found them? The second and more logical explanation is that the killer is exsanguinating the victims by inserting a needle into their jugular veins, which would create the wounds in the necks. Both theories would explain the lack of blood found at the crime scene."

She was *not* like any of the other women he knew. Rose was beautiful and diabolically clever, as well. "Very good. Perhaps you should be the one working with the Yard, instead of me."

"Really? Do you think I can get a job with them?"

"No."

Her lovely mouth twisted into a frown. "But you just said . . ."

"You are a woman. They would not hire you."

The garden gate slammed. "Rose!" Aileen shouted.

Vaughn turned as his sister came into view. She wore a bright smile, one he'd not seen since she'd arrived. "What is it, Aileen?"

"Andrew just informed me my ponies are here, and Ian also sent a groom."

He smiled at his sister, then back at Rose. His sight fell to her full lips. Blast it all! He'd been a bloody proper gentleman for a week. How he wanted to taste Rose's sweet lips. He brushed his thumb across her lush lips, drawing a gasp from her. "We will continue this later."

Aileen grabbed Rose by the hand and pulled her toward the stables. "Oh, Rose, now we can go to the park, and into town and shopping."

Vaughn followed as Rose was tugged away from him by his sister. Once they were out of sight, he entered the house.

~ ~ ~

A cool evening breeze blew strands of Rose's hair around her face. She sat on the terrace listening to the sounds of the night, but not enjoying them. Her thoughts were of Vaughn. He'd not joined them for dinner. Instead, Andrew had taken a tray up to him. Vaughn refused to come down, insisting he needed to keep reviewing the files. She'd helped him this afternoon. He read, then reread each one carefully making notes. She understood the need to find this murderer, but Vaughn was pushing himself too hard.

She also worried about Aileen. She and Rose had become fast friends. However, all during dinner Aileen had talked about her ponies. She'd beamed when she'd seen them and smiled even wider when the groom, David Bell strolled into the stables.

Rose rolled her eyes. You'd think he'd be smart enough to come up with a better name. *David Bell indeed, try William Campbell.*

Rose shook her head. It wasn't any of her business. However, she'd not get drawn in between sister and brother. If Aileen eloped with David, it would hurt Vaughn. Rose didn't want to see him hurt. He deeply cared about his sister.

On the other hand, Rose didn't want to see Vaughn's temper when he discovered the charade. The man wasn't stupid. Distracted, but not dumb. Vaughn would know soon enough.

Beelzebub jumped up onto her lap. He kneaded her legs, then curled himself in a tight ball. He purred as she stroked his thick fur. *The fat fur ball.* "You think I'm your servant, don't you?"

He opened one eye and rubbed his head in her hand.

"I take that as a yes."

The evening breeze brought with it the sound of hushed whispers. She wasn't alone. Her curiosity got the better of her, and she lifted Beelzebub from her lap. He flicked his tail in annoyance before he meowed, sulking off into the darkness.

Rose followed the voices around the corner of the house. She stopped, seeing Aileen and her groom in a lover's embrace.

Yeah, not going to intrude on them. Rose eased back, stepping on Beelzebub's tail. The cat howled and darted through the bushes. Aileen whirled around.

"Rose," Aileen gasped. "Please don't tell."

Rose stood still, staring at the lovers. A lock of David's long auburn hair blew on the breeze as he held Aileen protectively in his embrace. Aileen's eyes were wide. In the faint moonlight, Rose could see a hint of blush coloring Aileen's cheeks.

Rose drew in her breath and held up her hands. "It's none of my business. As far as I'm concerned, you are old enough to make your own choice. However, if the subject comes up, I won't lie to your brother."

Aileen nodded. "Thank you."

Rose met David Campbell's eyes. In the faint light, she could see the bruises still on his face. "So what happened to the real groom?"

"I paid him off."

"Well, you do realize if either Mr. Lucard or Mr. MacPhee returns you will be exposed."

A grin eased over David's lips. "I'll be looking forward to seeing them again. I have a wee debt to repay them."

Aileen elbowed him in his side. "You will do nothing. They almost killed you."

He chuckled. "So you were worried?" He nodded at Rose. "I'm a lowly groom, Madam. They will na pay me any mind."

"I don't know about that. Well, carry on—I mean, goodnight." She turned, then moseyed through the garden gate.

"Beelzebub," Rose called. She hoped she hadn't hurt him. "Where are you?" Rose bent down and looked under a bush, but it was too dark to see if he had hidden under it. She huffed, giving up her search. She stood and took a step back, bumping into a solid form.

Slowly Rose peered over her shoulder at Vaughn's chest. She turned and looked up at him. "I'm sorry, I wasn't looking where I was going," she offered.

"I noticed."

"I was looking for Beelzebub. I stepped on his tail, and he ran off."

Vaughn took her hand and placed it on his arm. "That was the noise I heard."

"I hope I didn't hurt him."

"That devil. I doubt it. However, my dear, I don't envy you. Beelzebub will get even with you for your clumsiness. Mark my words."

"Beelzebub is a sweet kitty. He'll do no such thing."

Rich laughter rose from Vaughn, and his eyes twinkled with merriment. "Beelzebub has you wrapped around his furry paw."

"No, he doesn't."

Vaughn raised an eyebrow at her.

"Okay, maybe just a little." She wet her suddenly dry lips. "I'm glad you decided to take a break from those files."

"I'm missing something."

"You'll find what you're looking for."

"Maybe I already have." He tilted her chin up.

103

Every alarm in her mind went off.

He lowered his lips to hers.

The light touch of Vaughn's lips on hers sent shock waves through her entire body, making her knees weak. Rose pressed her hands against him for support.

"Just friends," she said in a broken whisper.

"As you wish," he responded, lowering his lips to hers again.

Rose kissed him with a passion and hunger that matched Vaughn's. His fangs lengthened as he pulled her tighter into his embrace. She instinctively tilted her head as he kissed the hollow at the base of her neck. She pressed against him, feeling the hardness of his groin. Her body responded to him. She was playing with fire, but at that moment she didn't care, she only wanted to be in his embrace, she wanted him, wanted to make love to him.

Chapter Eight

Rose moaned as she felt the heady sensation of Vaughn's lips against her neck. He kissed, licked, and sucked on the sensitive area where her neck met her shoulder.

Vaughn eased his hold on her and, drew away. He turned to the shadows, shielding his face from her.

A cool breeze chilled her.

"Vaughn?"

"Forgive me, Rose. Perhaps we should return to the house." He spoke in an odd, yet soft voice as he turned his face.

He was hiding something from her. Rose eased in front of him and cupped his face in her hands. His shoulders slumped slightly, and he met her gaze. His eyes were no longer green, but bright red. The fire burning in them should have frightened her, but she saw the tenderness in his eyes.

Gently she touched his lips with her finger, then with her lips. "There is no need for you to hide your face in the shadows, not from me."

He drew her into his embrace. "With the desire of the flesh comes the desire for blood. I want you desperately," he said in a broken whisper against her ear.

Her heart swelled with his words. She wrapped her arms around his neck, kissing him.

His tongue traced her lips. Her lips parted, and he explored the recesses of her mouth. His kisses kindled a fire deep within her she'd thought long dead.

Carefully Rose ran her tongue across the tips of Vaughn's fangs. She relished his touch.

He lifted his lips, as he set her from him. His breathing was heavy and erratic. "If I don't stop now, I will take you to my bed."

All her life she'd wanted someone to stay with her, to protect her, to love her. She thought she'd found that with

Richard until destiny ripped him from her, taking her heart, as well. Rose bit her lower lip. Could she risk being hurt again? Was it her destiny to be Vaughn's lover? She searched his face for her answer.

Vaughn's eyes were full of life, pain, and longing. He needed her as much as she needed him. At that moment she knew she could take a chance on loving him. "Richard was the only man I've ever slept with, the only man I'd wanted to sleep with."

Richard's image flashed through her mind. His smiles, his walk, even the little things that made her mad at him. Every moment of their short time together flooded her mind. He'd always told her he wanted her to be happy, to live each day of her life fully. That was how Richard had lived his life. His face appeared in the forefront of her mind, and his smile warmed her.

"Rose." Vaughn's soft voice broke into her thoughts.

Richard's image faded. She raised her eyes to find Vaughn watching her. She breathed in the sweet smell of the rose garden and took his hands in hers. "It's been five years. I'm a little out of practice."

~ ~ ~

Vaughn looked at her. His heart pounded with anticipation. He fought the urge to sweep her up into his arms and carry her to his chamber. He wouldn't claim her until she fully understood what it meant to be his mate. He covered her lips with his, kissing her tenderly. "I will not let you make your decision until you understand what will happen."

She laughed, and her eyes sparkled with amusement. "Just because it's been a while, that doesn't mean I've forgotten how to make love."

Vaughn brought her hand to his lip, brushing a kiss across her knuckles. "The night air is getting a bit chilly. Shall we go in?" He tucked her hand under his arm.

"And then what?" Her voice was deep sensual and full of promise.

He stiffened. Bloody hell, perhaps it would be safer if they stayed in the night air. He cleared his throat. "We will talk. There are things you need to know."

"I'm not a virgin. I know what goes on in a lover's bed," Rose whispered.

When they entered the parlor, he led her to the couch while he eased down onto the wingback chair. He had to put distance between him and Rose until she understood. Then…his groin hardened.

"You can sit beside me. I won't bite." She smiled seductively at him.

"But I may."

"So, I take it we're going to have Sex Ed. 101?"

He stared at her. He didn't want to seem like an imbecile, but he had no idea what she'd said. "I'm not human. I'm not like your husband, nor will I be able to make love to you as he did."

Her cheeks pinked and she lowered her gaze. "Oh. Are you impotent? Because there are other ways—?"

He shoved himself from the chair. "Bloody hell, woman! One does not ask that of a man. I brought you in here to talk. To tell you. . ." He ran his hand over his hair and paced in front of her. Blast it all. He'd come in here to explain things to her, to tell her of his needs, of his love.

He closed his eyes and drew in a breath. What was he doing? When he opened his eyes, he met hers, bright with unquenchable warmth. "I don't want you as my mistress, Rose. I want you as my mate, my wife. If I were to take you to my bed, I would make love to you, fill you with my seed, and take your blood."

All amusement drained from her face. Rose's eyes widened, and the color faded from her cheeks.

"You said you wouldn't do that," she whispered.

"I wouldn't be able to control myself. I would claim you as mine." His hands clenched. "I would drain your body of blood to the point of death. Then I would give you my blood in return. We would become as one for the rest of our lives. Our hearts would beat together. I would know every thought, every emotion, and every need you had. Come morning you would be pregnant with my child." He lowered his voice and sat beside her. This was not how he imagined telling her about his needs and desire for her blood. His desire for her. Curse his bloody temper! He drew in a calming breath and proceeded. "After you are mine, if you so much as looked at any man with desire, I would kill him."

Her eyes flashed with anger. "As if I would want another man."

His heart swelled. Rose only wanted him.

"Oh, quit grinning like a fool. Just answer me one thing. Every time we make love will I become pregnant with your child?"

"Only the first mating guarantees a child. There are many of my kind who have been together for years and had only one child while others are childless." A thought froze him. "Do you want children, Rose?"

"Very much, so." She stared up at him.

"Rose, I did not mean to raise my voice, nor was it my intention to anger you, but you had to know what would happen, what will happen when you come to my bed."

"At least you are honest."

"When I'm in your arms, I cannot control what I am. I'm sorry. I know what I promised, but I will not be able to keep from taking your blood if you come to my bed."

She met his gaze and covered his hand with hers. "You have no reason to apologize. But I need time to think about what you've told me. I also need time to come to grip with my fear of this time bomb hanging over my head. The last thing I want is to start a life with you, have children, only to have it

108

ripped away by being sent back to my period. Leaving you alone would kill me." She rose fluidly from her seat.

He caught her hand, not wanting her to leave until she knew he would never let her go. "If that happened I would search till the end of time to find you again."

A sad smile curved her lips, and she slid her hand from his. "Good night, Vaughn."

As he watched Rose leave the room, bitter despair seized his lonely soul. He'd noticed the shadows of grief cross her face when she spoke of her husband. A lucky man he was to have had her even one night in his arms.

"Good night, my love," he whispered.

~ ~ ~

Rose watched the rainbow caused by mid-morning sunlight filtering through the window of the study. She closed her journal and leaned back in the leather chair. She hadn't slept last night. Her mind had been in a whirlwind. It still was, despite her morning walk with Sara.

Rose kept thinking about Vaughn, about what he'd said. He desired her. He wanted her to be his mate and the mother of his children, but he hadn't said he loved her or that he would ever love her.

When she woke this morning, she hadn't wanted to see him. Later when she went down for breakfast, she'd discovered he'd left the house, disappointed filled her heart. The man was addicting as a drug. What was wrong with her? She knew her answer. First, she'd fallen in love with him. Second, he hadn't said he loved her. Third, according to him, making love with him would get her instantly pregnant. Fourth, and most important, having her neck bitten frightened the hell out of her. Her stomach somersaulted at the thought. No, the thought of Vaughn draining her to the point of death was what scared her. She couldn't control the full body shivers that grabbed her.

She ran her hand over the leather bound journal. She'd written everything in it that had happened to her, including the fact she'd fallen in love.

Beelzebub jumped up onto the desk. He paced in front of her a few times before he flopped down on her journal. He looked at her. "Meow."

"If you're hungry, go bother Mrs. Brown. Now, scat."

He ignored her while he proceeded to groom himself.

"Do you mind? I'd like to finish this."

Beelzebub flicked his tail, and she found herself scratching his head. "Guess Vaughn was right. You do have me wrapped around your paw."

"I heard that," Aileen said from the doorway. "Rose, what are you doing up here in this room? The sun is out, and it's such a wonderful day. We should go to the park."

"You've twisted my arm."

Aileen's eyes widened. "I have not touched you."

"I'm sorry, it's an American expression. It means you have convinced me to do something, like go to the park."

Aileen grinned. "Oh, good. Now finish what you are doing so you can change into a promenade suit." She furrowed her brow and tilted her head, looking down at the papers on the desk. "What are you doing, anyway?"

"I was working on some papers for your brother, but my mind drifted, so I started writing in my journal."

"Oh, well, hurry up and change your clothes."

"What's wrong with what I have on?"

"Silly goose, you cannot wear a wrapper to the park. Everyone will see us. What if we meet up with my brother? You want to look nice for him."

Rose rolled her eyes. *As if Vaughn notices what I wear.* Besides, it had taken her forty-five minutes to get dressed this morning. Aileen now wanted Rose to change to go to the blasted park. She didn't think so.

Aileen stroked Beelzebub's coat. "Have you taken a fancy to him?"

"He's a sweet kitty."

"Not Beelzebub, Vaughn," Aileen said.

Sara walked into the small room. "What are you two doing inside on such a nice day?" Sara frown and she narrowed her eyes. "Rose, are you ill? You're flushed."

Rose jerked to her feet. "I feel fine. Let's go to the park."

"Not until you change first." Aileen insisted.

"Are you ashamed to be seen with me?" Rose teased.

"Of course not, you are my dearest friend. I ah. . ."

Warmth eased over Rose. She was fond of Aileen, too. "I was only teasing you, you goose." Rose smiled over her shoulder at Aileen.

~ ~ ~

Rose met Aileen's gaze in the mirror as Penny finished buttoning up the back of Rose's dress.

Sara sat on the chair by the window. "That shade of green looks wonderful on you, Rose."

"Thank you. But Sara, please, no more dresses. I can't afford to repay Vaughn for this latest one."

"Posh, he has you working far too hard, as it is. You deserve the dress."

"There, I've fastened the last button," Penny said. "Rose, I think this hat will go nicely. It's simple, but the brim is large, and I love the feathers."

Rose bit her lip, picking up the huge hat and placing it on her head. "It'll certainly keep the sun out of my eyes." Good grief, she looked as if Charles Gibson had dressed her himself. The hat slipped when she turned her head. "Aileen, which hat-pin shall I use?"

"The silver one, I think."

"I don't have a silver one."

"You do, it came with the evening gowns Sara ordered for us. They arrived yesterday."

Rose turned and met Sara's laughing eyes. "Sara! Where am I going to wear an evening gown?"

"When Vaughn takes you to the theater. In a few months, the winter season will start. Surely he will take you to several balls."

Rose threw her hands up in surrender. "Like that's going to happen."

Aileen crossed her arms over her chest. "Why not?"

"Aileen, your brother is a confirmed bachelor. All he cares about is his work. Why do you think he hasn't taken a wife yet?"

Aileen's hands fell to her side, and her expression stilled. "For a long time I thought it was because of Katherine, but I guess it's because he hadn't found the woman he desired."

Rose forced a smile to her lips. "Your sister Katherine?"

"I never knew her, for she died before I was born."

Rose's gut twisted. "I recall your telling me something about her. Sara, how did Katherine die?"

Sara's lips thinned, and she turned, looking out the window. "Christian, her mate, lost control and killed her. Out of grief for what he'd did, he took his own life."

Rose gasped and sat on the bed as her knees buckled. "Dear God."

Aileen's eyes welled with dark tears. "It was a custom for a member of the bride's family to wake the couple for their first breakfast. Vaughn discovered their bodies. He was so young at the time. A child."

"How old was he?" Rose blinked back her unshed tears for the horror Vaughn must have seen.

"Ten," Aileen whispered. "I can only imagine the nightmares he suffered."

A knot formed in Rose's throat. "Is this common?" She held her breath. She wasn't Dhampir. She was human. If Katherine didn't survive her wedding night, how did Rose expect to survive a night in Vaughn's bed?

"Rose," Sara turned again to face her. "I wasn't there, but I do know what happened to Katherine . . . was rare. Christian was a troubled soul. He loved her, but there was a dark side to him, a part of him he kept hidden from everyone. I don't know what happened during their joining, no one truly does."

112

Rose didn't feel any better. If she decided to give herself to Vaughn, would she survive? Her heart pounded, and she drew in a calming breath. "Were Vaughn and Katherine close?"

"Very close," Aileen said. "From what he's told me, they were inseparable. She taught him to fly."

Fly? A little voice inside Rose's head asked. "Aileen, what do you mean by *flying*? Fly what?"

"Vaughn can fly. At night, when the moon is dark, my brother loves to soar in the clouds."

"Can you? Aileen, can you fly?" Rose asked.

"No, but when I was younger, I thought because Vaughn could, so could I. I jumped from my bedroom window and fell like a rock."

"Your brother was kind to you that day," Sara said with a grin.

"You weren't hurt?" Rose asked.

Sara laughed. "She escaped the fall unharmed. However, she screamed like a banshee when Vaughn took a switch to her backside."

"He was a brute," Aileen muttered, then planted her hands firmly on her hips. "Vaughn didn't feel so kind when he was warming my posterior."

Still laughing, Sara stood. She cupped Aileen's chin with her hands. "Did he not take you in his arms and hug you afterward?"

"Aye, but my backside still hurt."

Sara grinned and shook her head. "Be happy it was your brother and not Ian. Otherwise, you still would have trouble sitting." She opened the door and paused. "While you are out and about I think I will take a nap."

Rose looped her arm with Aileen's. "Shall we go to the park?"

Aileen's face lit. "By all means."

They were halfway down the stairs when Andrew opened the front door.

113

"I am here to see Miss MacPhee." A man's voice came from the other side of the door.

Aileen froze. She paled and grabbed Rose's hand. Slowly, Aileen stepped up on the step behind her. "Please don't let him see us," she whispered.

"Aileen!" Philip Dorjan pushed past Andrew. "When I heard you were in London I had to come and see you."

"Philip, it's a pleasure." Aileen squeezed Rose's hand, leaned forward and whispered, "Please do not leave me with him. I beg you."

"Don't worry. Philip Dorjan is the last person I'd leave you with."

Philip eyed Aileen like a cat eying his quarry. "You look even more beautiful than I remembered." He offered her his arm.

"Thank you, Philip. I would like you to meet Mrs. Kelly, my dear friend, and companion."

"We have met. Mrs. Kelly, it's a pleasure to see you again." He made a slight bow.

"Mr. Dorjan."

"Shall we go into the parlor?" Aileen asked, keeping a tight grip on Rose's hand. Aileen led Rose to the settee, then eased down beside her.

Philip took the wingbacked chair closest to Aileen. "Are you ladies planning on going out?"

"Yes," Aileen said. "We plan to go by the seamstress and bookshop."

"Then I insist on taking you."

Aileen paled. "We could not intrude upon you, thank you."

"But I insist."

Rose bit her tongue. If it were her call, she'd simply tell Philip to get lost, but Aileen wouldn't do such a thing. Rose stifled a laughed as Beelzebub strolled into the room, making a wide arch around Philip. Even the cat didn't like the man.

Philip sneezed, then pulled a handkerchief from his pocket. He dabbed his nose. "I hate cats. Especially that one."

Beelzebub flicked his tail and leaped onto Rose's lap. The rascal wedged himself between her and Aileen. Despite his loud purring, he sat rigidly, staring at Philip.

Aileen stroked Beelzebub's coat. "I love cats. And I think this one is an angel."

Philip smiled benignly at her. "Aileen, tell your man I will take you into town."

"Philip, thank you for your offer, really, but I have neither had a chance to drive my carriage nor exercised my ponies since they arrived. I was so looking forward to it. Please do not think harshly of me. Perhaps another day."

Philip twisted the end of his mustache, smiling at her as if she were a child he meant to appease. "What type of carriage do you have?"

"Ian purchased a Peter's Ladies' Phaeton for my last birthday. Vaughn gave me two perfectly matched gray Welsh ponies. At times I must look carefully at them to tell them apart."

"Only the best, I see," Philip said.

When Andrew entered, his eyes darted to Philip, then to Aileen. "Madam, your carriage is ready."

"Very well, ladies, then I will take my leave. Perhaps I may accompany you to the park on another day?" Philip stood, nodded toward Aileen.

"Perhaps you may," Aileen said.

As Philip offered his hand to Aileen, Beelzebub laid back his ears. He growled low in his throat. Abruptly, Beelzebub swatted Philip's outstretched hand, scratching him and drawing blood.

Philip jerked back his bloody hand. "That cursed beast! Someday he'll get his comeuppance. Good day, ladies." Philip stormed from the room.

The front door slammed a second later.

"Bye, Felicia," Rose muttered under her breath.

"You are a bad kitty," Aileen said, petting Beelzebub. "I shall see that Mrs. Brown gives you an extra helping of fish."

"Aileen!"

"What?" Her wide-eyed innocent look gave way to giggling. "Serves Philip right. I have seen how he treats his horses and hounds. Rose, why did you call Philip Felicia?"

Crud. "Oh, it's an old American saying from the nineties." *The 1990's.*

~ ~ ~

Vaughn sipped his wine, staring over the rim at Rose. When she was near him, all he wanted to do was hold her. The dark burgundy of her gown contrasted beautifully with the green in her eyes, making them appear paler in color. "Rose, did you enjoy my sister's driving, or did she frighten you?"

It would be so easy to know her thoughts, but he wouldn't invade her mind. He was a patient man. He could wait for her answer. He just wished she would bloody well hurry up and tell him.

She lowered her goblet. "I enjoyed the ride. The park was beautiful. Tomorrow Aileen wants me to show her how to ride a bicycle. We saw several women in the park riding them."

Sara's eyes widened. "Certainly not. Those things are too dangerous. Besides a proper lady should not be seen on one of those contraptions."

Rose lowered her eyes to her plate. Her face clouded with uneasiness as she bit her lower lip. He didn't need to read her mind to know she was ill at ease being in the middle of Aileen and Sara's disagreement.

Vaughn looked from his sister's stormy glare to Sara's unyielding eyes. "Rose, do you know how to ride one of these bicycles?"

She lifted her gaze to his. Her face was full of strength. "Yes, I do."

"Then I see no harm. However, I would prefer you teach Aileen here, rather than in the park."

"What do you plan to wear to ride on a bicycle, your riding habit?" Sara asked.

Aileen's mouth quirked with humor. "If I can ride as well as I handle my ponies, then Rose and I will order bicycling outfits."

"And I will receive the bill, correct?" He chuckled.

"But, of course, dear brother."

Rose placed her napkin on the table. She nervously rubbed the fabric between her finger and thumb. "Vaughn, about the evening gowns, I'll repay you for them." She frowned at Sara. "And I promise there won't be any more bills from me."

"I told Sara to order you and Aileen the gowns. Lord Lucard is having a gala in honor of his wife's birthday. I would like very much for you to accompany me."

Aileen pushed away from the table and stood. "If you will excuse me, I want to check on my ponies." She glanced at Rose, then left.

Sara eyed Aileen as she left the room. "I think I shall retire to the parlor. I'm reading a book I borrowed from you. Quite interesting."

"Oh, which book?" He helped Sara from her seat.

The Time Machine." She patted his cheek, a habit of hers that made him feel like a child.

He met Rose's smile then helped her from her seat. "Would you like to sit on the terrace? We have a few nights left when the weather will still be warm enough."

"I'd like that. Did Aileen tell you about Philip's visit?"

He chuckled, taking her arm, and leading her to the wicker settee. "Yes, and I believe Aileen even asked Mrs. Brown to give Beelzebub fresh fish for his dinner, the scamp."

"I haven't seen him since we returned from the park. He's usually sleeping on my bed."

"He is more likely out courting a queen. He will return once he has won her over."

A faint, mournful sound came from the darkness. In the shadows, the outline of a cat came into view. It moved slowly, almost dragging itself across the lawn.

"Beelzebub?" Rose pushed from her seat. She ran down the steps. "No!"

Vaughn ran after her, stopping at her side. He stared at the poor creature. His wounds were all too familiar looking. The cat had been in a fight and had lost. There was nothing else to do for him. It pained Vaughn to see the hurt in Rose's eyes.

She knelt and tenderly touched Beelzebub's bloody face, then looked up at him. Tears welled in her eyes, and for the first time in his presence, she allowed them to fall. "This is my fault. I told you I shouldn't stay here. Everything I love dies. Everything!" She swiped at her tears. Rose pushed to her feet and looked up at him. Her tears streamed down her face. "Please, put him out of his misery," she cried as she ran into the house.

~ ~ ~

Rose ran up the stairs, shoved open her bedroom door, then fell on her bed. She hadn't cried like this since Richard's funeral. Why had she let a cat with an attitude weasel his way into her heart?

Several minutes, an hour later, she didn't know how long she'd cried, someone knocked on her door, then opened it and entered.

"Go away," she ordered.

"Rose," Vaughn's voice whispered behind her.

The bed dipped with his weight, and he drew her into his arms. He held her against his broad shoulders. After a long moment, he tipped her chin up, then wiped her tears with the pad of his thumb. "Do you think me a killer?"

"No. How can you ask me that?"

"There was a time I thought that of myself. I found my sister and her mate dead. I opened the gates for Dietrich and his men who killed my parents. Even now I feel as if I have caused the deaths of innocents. You see, the killer I have been hunting, his first victim was once my mistress."

She shuddered inwardly at the thoughts. "I know what you are trying to do, but it isn't the same."

"It is. Did you give your brother the illness that killed him?"

"No."

"Did you do something to cause your parents' plane to crash?"

"No!"

"I did open the gates for the men who killed my parents. I am to blame for their deaths."

She touched his face, meeting his tender gaze. "But you said you knew them. You didn't know they meant your family harm."

"Just as you had nothing to do with the deaths of your loved ones. You are not a bringer of death, nor a killer Rose."

She shoved out of his arms. She didn't want to hear his 'I know how you're feeling' story. "Nice try. But I know what I am. I had thought my curse hadn't followed me, but I was wrong. Tonight proved it."

"How did your husband die?"

"He was killed by a drunk driver." She threw her pillow across the room. "The son-of-a-bitch didn't even know what he'd done."

"Did you buy this man his drinks?"

"Please get out and leave me alone!"

Vaughn shook his head. "Answer my question first."

"No, I was working when the police told me."

"So how can you honestly tell yourself you caused Richard's death?"

"What about Beelzebub?"

Vaughn bent down. He cradled the cat in his arms, then placed Beelzebub on the bed. "You told me to put him out of his misery. When I bent down to snap his neck, the scamp bit me." Vaughn regarded at his hand. "Ferociously, I must say."

She couldn't believe her eyes. Beelzebub was alive. He looked like he'd been in a fight, but not as bad as he had in the garden. "What have you done?"

Vaughn stroked the cat's fur. "Had you not asked me to put an end to his suffering, he wouldn't have bitten me. It appears my blood can heal animals. However, I don't know what other effects it will have on him."

She swallowed the lump in her throat then wiped her eyes. "Are you saying Beelzebub is like you, now?"

"I'm saying you saved his life." He took hold of her hand, pulling her to him. "Since you have been here you have brought only happiness to me." He lightly brushed her lips with his. "You've made me feel alive."

Chapter Nine

The hallway light cast strange shadows on her bedroom walls. Rose sniffed back her tears as she watched Beelzebub lick his coat. The cat paused and looked at her, then rubbed his head against her. He was alive.

She shook her head to clear her mind. The legend of the vampire's blood was true. It did have the power to restore health. She stared at the cat. Was he now like Vaughn? Was Beelzebub bound to Vaughn as Renfield had been to Dracula? "So, will Beelzebub be able to fly, too?"

Vaughn's shoulders shook while a faint smile curved his lips. "Dear Lord, no bird would be safe if that happened. However, Beelzebub could not fly before, so he cannot fly now." His gaze roamed over her face. "I see Sara has been telling you things."

She nodded. "Aileen told me you could fly. Do you fly as a bird does?"

He dried her cheek with his handkerchief. "No. To be honest, I cannot think of a creature that flies as I do."

Rose brought her feet up onto the bed and rested her chin on her knees. "Is there anything else you can do, like walk through walls or turn into a bat?" She couldn't remember him telling her if he could, but then again Vaughn didn't tell her he could fly either.

Chuckling, Vaughn leaned against the bedpost and crossed his arms over his chest. "I'm afraid I cannot turn into a bat. Even if I could change, bats are small creatures." One side of his mouth turned up, and his green eyes seemed to shimmer. "As for walking through walls, I tried once when I was a lad, bumped my nose, so I've not tried it again."

"Learned your lesson, did you?" The thought of Vaughn running into a wall on purpose made her laugh. And the feeling was wonderful.

"Quite so." He rubbed his nose.

Rose stroked Beelzebub's coat. She was sitting in a dark bedroom, petting a cat that should be dead. "So how do you fly? Is it like Superman?"

Vaughn furrowed his brows. "Who?"

"Oops. Sorry, Superman is a cartoon character from my time."

"How does he fly?"

"Well, he puts his arms out in front, shouts 'up, up and away,' then leaps into the air. See, he's from this planet that blew up—oh, never mind."

Vaughn stood and extended his hand to her. "Come with me."

She slid from the bed and took his hand. "Where are we going?"

He scooped her up into his arms. "For a breath of fresh air." He stepped through the open window.

Fear seized her. "Put me down!"

"That would hurt."

She looked down. Way-way down to the garden below. She squeezed her eyes tightly closed and buried her face in Vaughn's shoulder. "I'm afraid of heights. Please take me back inside."

"Rose," he breathed against her ear. "Open your eyes. Look around. I will not let anything happen to you. Trust me."

She opened her eyes. They were flying, but it didn't feel as if they were moving at all. Oh God, she was flying! The cool air swirled around her and blew through her hair. Now she knew how birds felt, totally free.

She clung tightly to Vaughn while she took in the view below. "You do love Beelzebub. The garden is in the shape of a cat's head."

"I didn't design the garden. The only way for me to know the shape was to see it from above."

She gripped the fabric of his coat as he dipped toward the garden. "Vaughn!"

"Relax, Rose, I will not drop you." His breath caressed her cheek. "Do you trust me? Would you like to see the city?"

She nodded. "Sure." What was she saying? She was flying over England in the arms of a vampire. She'd left her common sense behind in the future.

Drawing in a breath, she tried to squash her fear of heights, but her other fears only replaced it. What would happen to her in this foreign country, this foreign time? Vaughn said he'd take care of her. Was that what she wanted? She'd always taken care of herself.

His aftershave teased her with its spicy fragrance. She took a deep breath and rested her head against his broad shoulder.

The scenery blurred and everything around her became white as a cloud. Her fear of heights forced its way into her mind. Her fear had kept her from joining her parents on their disastrous flight. She tightened her arms around Vaughn's neck and buried her face.

"Rose, look how beautiful everything is from up here."

"I'm frightened. I want to go back."

"Very well, but at least open your eyes. Enjoy the view of the city as we return home."

She fought her fear and did as he asked. Thankful she had. Rose marveled at the beautiful sight. Far below her, she saw the faint glow of gaslights. The outlines of houses and buildings, filtered through the fog below them. "It's beautiful." She gasped and pointed. "Big Ben, I didn't get a chance to see it when we flew into the airport."

Vaughn grinned. "Then I'm glad to be able to show it to you."

The air grew thick as they entered a cloud. Vaughn's breath teased her cheek, and she wasn't sure, but she swore he'd brushed a kiss against her hair.

"Vaughn, where are we?"

"Home," he said and landed.

"You can put me down now."

He set her down and released his hold on her. "As you wish."

She stared up into his red eyes. The tips of his fangs peeked from his lips. She reached up, tracing the outline of his mouth with her finger. His cheekbones were more angular and pronounced and his brows more ridged. Despite his form, she still found him desirable. The man was sexy as all hell.

"I have to be in this form to fly," he offered. "It pleases me you no longer fear me like this."

She cupped his face in her hands. "I find you very attractive."

"Fascinating." He closed his eyes and relaxed. "In this form, my senses are at their most sensitive. I can hear people speaking miles from here. I can distinguish the different scents of the roses in my garden." He opened his eyes and gazed into hers. "I look forward to sharing my gift of flight with you again. Perhaps I can help you overcome your fear of heights."

She nodded, and her arms slid from around his neck. She took his hands. "How do you do that? Fly, I mean."

He laced his fingers with hers. "I showed you."

"Yes. I know you did, but how did you do it?"

"I think it, and it happens. I cannot explain how I fly, because I don't fully understand it myself."

She smiled.

"I honestly don't know. When I was six, I wanted to soar with the birds. The next thing I knew, I was in the air. I was frightened and excited at the same time. Katherine, my sister, stood on the ground and watched me. The next day she showed me how to control my thoughts so I could go where I wished." He touched Rose's lips with his finger. "I'm happy you are smiling again."

"You are sure, Beelzebub won't be able to fly?"

A deep laugh erupted from Vaughn. "My blood did heal him. I doubt it will give him the gift of flight. But perhaps I should not speak so definitely."

Rose looked up into Vaughn's face. The look in his eyes melted her heart. She lowered her gaze. "I guess we'll have to wait and see what changes happen to Beelzebub."

"With my luck, that blasted cat will have nine hundred lives instead of nine and all spent under my feet."

"Admit it. It bothered you to see Beelzebub hurt."

"His wounds bothered me. They appeared similar to those made by our killer."

She exhaled. Vaughn's mind was back on the case. "You don't honestly think the killer attacked Beelzebub, do you?"

"No. Maybe. I don't know. But I do have an idea which animal could."

"But the killer is a man."

"Is he?" Vaughn turned and tipped her chin up, forcing her to meet his gaze. "I feel the killer is Dhampir. There are some of us who can change form."

"I know. You've told me this. But what if the killer is a human? He could be some mental case thinking he's a vampire or something."

"This is the twentieth century, Rose. No one believes in vampires or werewolves. They are only creatures of folklore."

"I'm still going with my psycho option."

"The killer is a rogue and will be stopped."

"You know something. All right, I'll bite."

He raised his brow. "You will?"

She dropped her head against his chest. "Bad choice of words."

"Not for me."

"Not going down this road." She liked this jesting side of him. "So, getting back to the killer, what's his motive?"

All the humor left Vaughn's eyes. He ran his hands over his hair. "For the love of God, I would give my right arm to know the answer."

Rose cupped his face with her hands and looked at his handsome face. Worry and stress had etched lines around his eyes and mouth. "You've been pushing yourself too hard. You need to take a day off. You need to relax before you kill yourself."

"I cannot!" He turned from her. His shoulders sagged, and he hung his head. "Forgive me, Rose, for grousing. I shouldn't worry you with my problems." Though he faced her, he didn't meet her gaze. "For me to catch the murderer, I must become him. That is my problem. I cannot figure out the force behind him. What drives him to kill? The victims are all different. The only common thread is me."

"Okay, you said you thought he was one of your own. What about the desire for blood."

"If he were only feeding his hunger, why mutilate the bodies?"

"He's a predator. Maybe he's like a cat and likes to play with his food."

Vaughn's mouth pulled into a sour grin. "Is that how you see me?"

She winced. "No! I see you as a very strong and wonderful man. And before you ask, I don't see you as the killer, either. But you have to face it. This guy is completely deranged. He's a few French fries short of a happy meal. Hell, he could be after you."

Vaughn raised his brow. "How so?"

"He could be killing off your associates to get to you."

He shook his head. "But why? Why not come after me directly?"

Hell if she knew. "Perhaps to make you suffer." Something clicked in her mind. "Could the men who killed your parents be after you?"

"No. The ones responsible were all killed."

"Are you sure?"

The faint smile on his lips and the gleam in his eyes answered her question.

"Okay, then what about their families? Did Dietrich have any children?" His life was in jeopardy so she was going to

126

look at every option she could. Damn it! She would not let Vaughn suffer. She wasn't going to lose him, too.

"Yes, they had children. Your theory is a possibility but a doubtful one."

"But still a possibility." Rose reached out and took his hand. "Let's find a place to sit and think about this."

"No, you should go to bed. I will ponder this on my own."

"Like hell, you will. Damn it. We're in this together."

His head snapped up, and he pointed his finger at her.

"Do not give me that look. You asked for my help. You're going to get it. Like it or not, bud."

Vaughn huffed. "Very well, I accept your offer. Speaking of offers, have you made your decision about mine?"

She'd been thinking about Vaughn's offer ever since he'd made it. If only her decision were simple to make, but it wasn't. Despite what Vaughn thought, she still was a jinx.

"You are not this jinx thing you keep referring to yourself. When you stop this foolish thinking and make up your mind, you can come to me at any time. There are no locked doors between us."

"May I ask you a question?"

"Rose, you should know by now you can ask me anything."

"Why did Katherine die?"

Vaughn's mouth fell open, and he gasped. A shocked look crossed his face. "Aileen told you?"

"Yes, and Sara, and you, tonight you said you found your sister and her mate."

"Please, don't think I was keeping her death from you. I was not."

"I never thought you were, Vaughn. Why did Christian kill her? Sara said he lost control."

"That is a question I have asked myself. But Christian is the only person who could answer it. Is that the reason you have not made up your mind about my offer? Are you afraid you will perish in my bed?"

127

"It is one of my many doubts. I'm not Dhampir. Katherine was. I need to know what my chances are of waking up the next morning if I go to bed with you."

He drew in a shuttered breath and met her gaze. "There have always been stories of tragic unions. As a youth, I thought these stories were made up by mothers wanting to keep their daughters innocent. I cannot give you the answer you want."

"Vaughn," she whispered. "Will you hold me?"

"You ask me this even after what I've told you?"

She stepped into his embrace. "With you, I feel safe."

"You said Katherine was one of your many doubts about becoming my mate. What are your other doubts? You have said my height and size did not frighten you, were you being honest?"

She leaned back in his arms and ran her hands up his chest. "Yes. I find you very sexy and desirable. I look forward to seeing these muscles. But I will be honest. The thought of you drinking my blood scares the absolute crap out of me."

"I will not lie to you. If you come to my bed, I will take your blood."

"Until I get over that fear, I can't give you my answer."

His arms dropped, and he stepped away. His heated gaze fell to Rose's throat. "Then I think, we should part company for the night."

She looked into his glowing eyes and nodded. "Good night."

As Rose turned to leave, a part of her wanted to stay with him, no matter what the consequences.

~ ~ ~

Rose pulled the bed-sheets up and rolled over onto her side. She closed her eyes. The horrific sight of Vaughn finding his sister entered Rose's mind. She sat up and pushed the thoughts from her mind, only to remember scenes from horror movies. Tom Cruise and, Bela Lugosi had portrayed their vampires well. They'd made the vampire a desirable lover, though a deadly one. However, Vaughn wasn't a vampire since he was alive.

Rose slid from the bed, then strolled over to the window. She wrapped her arms around herself and gazed out into the night. She'd felt safe flying in Vaughn's arms despite her fear of heights.

She pushed open the window. The cool air chilled her. When she was with Vaughn, she hadn't noticed the cold.

Vaughn wanted her to be the mother of his children. Would their children be like their father and have the gift of flight? She would be grounded. What if they got into trouble? She wouldn't be able to go to them. Her eyes blurred with tears. She'd thought her dreams of having children had died with Richard.

Beelzebub purred at her feet, causing her to look down. "Come here, Vampire Kitty." She scooped him up into her arms. Rose rubbed her cheek against his soft fur. "Are you going to suck my blood?"

Beelzebub purred, rubbing his face against hers.

~ ~ ~

Vaughn relished the warmth of the mid-morning sunlight on his face. He pushed the wonderful eyeglasses Rose had given him up on his nose. They were a bit small, but he'd adjusted them to fit. "Rose," her name slipped from his lips.

When the garden gate shut, he turned to see her stroll toward him as if he'd summoned her. "Good morning, my lady."

"Good morning." An approving smile curved her lips and wrinkled her eyes.

"You appear quite jubilant this morning."

"I'm glad to see you're not hovering over your desk, wracking your brains out, and going blind staring at those files."

"Oh, I see. Well, it should please you I have eliminated the major populous of England as my suspects."

She took hold of his hands. "So you're going with your gut feeling. You think it's one of your kind. A Dhampir."

"I cannot ignore the evidence at hand, Rose. I could not sleep. Before the sun rose, I started writing down all the names of those who were not in London at times of the killings. Before coming out here, I telephoned Royce to ask him for his assistance. He should be here in a day or so."

Rose pulled her mouth into a thin tight line. "Here I thought you were taking a day off."

He didn't like the expression on her face. "What do you and my sister, have planned for today?" he asked.

"A picnic in the park. Will you join us?"

He shook his head. "The park is where people gather and parade around like peacocks showing off their plumes."

"What better place to watch people than at a park? Who knows, you may even spot your elusive killer," she snapped and stomped away.

Four hours later Vaughn strolled through the park with Rose on his arm. How the bloody hell, had she persuaded him to join her?

Sara and Aileen had paused to speak with Lady Winston.

Vaughn glared at a passing gentleman, not liking the fleeting thoughts he gleaned from the man's mind. The black and white striped outfit Rose wore hugged her well-rounded body. He'd noticed the looks she received from the passing gentlemen. He heard their whispered thoughts as if they'd spoken them. They were lucky he didn't kill the lot of them. Rose was his. "Shall we wait here by the fountain for Sara and Aileen?"

"Fine with me." Rose shifted her parasol from one shoulder to the other, nearly hitting him as she did. He caught the tip, protecting his face.

"Sorry." Her eyes grew wide, and her cheeks blushed. She bit her lip as she glanced up at him. "You know, this thing could be a lethal weapon."

130

"In your hands, yes." He laughed, seeing her gray eyes dancing with amusement.

"Teasing me, are you?" She turned and nearly struck him again. "Here come Aileen and Sara."

"Bloody hell, Philip Dorjan is with them."

"Poor Aileen," Rose whispered.

Vaughn bent close to her ear. "All of us should be pitied." He straightened and extended his hand. "Philip, fancy meeting you here today."

He shook Vaughn's hand. "I didn't expect to see you, old man." Philip then nodded to Rose. "Mrs. Kelly."

Rose took his outstretched hand and shivered. "Mr. Dorjan."

"Not working Vaughn? Do tell me you have solved London's latest mystery," Philip sneered.

"The case is not solved, but I do know the killer."

Was it his imagination or had Philip flinched? It was wishful thinking. The man was a flop.

Philip turned to Aileen and Sara. "How do you put up with him, ladies?"

Sara glanced at Vaughn. "Rose listens to his ramblings about this entire dreadfulness. Please, could we discuss something more pleasant than these horrible killings?"

Philip's eyes narrowed at Rose. A fake smile creased his lips as his attention shifted to Vaughn. "I heard you purchased a new thoroughbred."

"A chestnut, yes."

"Then would you consider racing him against my black? We can make the stakes interesting. Say, if my black wins, I get your horse and vice versa."

Vaughn's eyes darkened, and his lips thinned. "I think not."

"Admit it, Madoc. You *fear* being bested by me." Philip puffed out his chest and raised his voice. "You are a coward when it comes to such challenges."

131

Sara looped her arm with Aileen's. "I believe I see Lady Mayfield. Good day, Mr. Dorjan."

Aileen peered over her shoulder. "Rose, are you coming?"

~ ~ ~

Rose shook her head at Aileen, not wanting to leave Vaughn. It wasn't that Rose didn't think he could handle Philip, but the fact Vaughn shouldn't have to put up with the ass.

Her attention swept from Philip's smirk to Vaughn's stony expression. A muscle worked in Vaughn's jaw as he stood still, clenching his fist.

Vaughn was many things, but he wasn't a coward. Why was this little twit of a man baiting Vaughn? *Asshat!*

"Philip, I have seen what you do to your animals. You beat them and run them to the point of death. I will not be a party to the destruction of any creature." Vaughn held out his arm to Rose.

Philip stepped in front of them. "Vaughn, honestly, the way you go on one would think these beasts have souls."

"I will not race you."

Philip turned, grinning at her. "Mrs. Kelly, your opinion please, what do you think of a man who backs away from a challenge? Do you find him a man or a mouse?"

Rose fumed. She didn't know what the slimy, frog-faced ass-wipe was trying to prove, but one thing was certain, Vaughn was much more a man than Philip would ever be. She drew in a deep breath and forced a smile. "Mr. Dorjan, I find a real man doesn't have to prove his masculinity. It is the puffed up toad who croaks in vain about his manhood."

Vaughn arched eyebrow and a faint smile curved his lips. Apparently, her response both humored and surprised him.

"Gentlemen, if you will pardon me." She turned abruptly. The sound of someone behind her falling into the fountain made her cringe.

Rose looked at Sara. She held her hand over her mouth. Aileen was laughing and pointing to something behind Rose.

Dreading what she would see, Rose turned slowly. *Please, God, don't let it be Vaughn.* Rose burst out laughing at the sight of Philip sitting in the fountain. His hat floated beside him.

He snatched his hat from the water and plopped it on his head. His eyes narrowed at her. For the briefest of seconds, she swore they flashed red. "Madam, this is not funny!"

"Please forgive me, Mr. Dorjan." Try as she might, she couldn't stop laughing. Philip looked hilarious sitting in the fountain with that soaked hat on his head. She bit the inside of her cheek to help with her giggles. "It was an accident, I assure you."

A small group had gathered around them. Laughter filled the air.

Vaughn offered his hand. "Here, Philip. Let me help you out."

Philip pushed Vaughn's hand away. "I don't need your help." He stood, splashing water as he stepped from the fountain. Philip stormed off, speaking to no one.

A laugh slipped past Sara's lips. "I say, that is one wet toad."

Vaughn offered Rose his arm. "Madam, I'm at your service for defending my honor with your trusty parasol."

"After this, Philip probably thinks more of Beelzebub than me," she told Vaughn through her giggles.

His smile faded and his eyes grew dark. He did not like the thought that entered his mind.

Chapter Ten

Sara stepped back and watched Rose run behind Aileen, holding her up on the bicycle. The bicycle wobbled, then fell, pulling Rose and Aileen down with it.

Laughing, Rose pushed the contraption off them. "You almost had it that time."

Aileen sat up. She pushed her tousled hair from her eyes. "I hope no one saw us. I would hate to be teased by Royce or Vaughn."

"I don't think they're watching us. Vaughn was in too much of a hurry to discuss the murders with Royce." She helped Aileen up from the ground. "Do you want to call it quits?"

"No. I want to be as good as you are on this thing. Let me have a go at it again."

Sara held her breath as Aileen tried the bicycle once more.

Rose ran behind the bicycle. She stopped and turned loose. Aileen peddled, keeping the contraption upright. She was riding it. Sara stifled her cry of jubilance. She turned and sauntered back toward the house. "Oh to be young again."

Beelzebub sat on the top step of the terrace. He looked at her and purred as she ambled up the steps. She bent down and scratched him behind his head, then patted his large stomach. "You are getting fat. Rose has been feeding you too much."

As Sara entered the house, Penny hurried to her.

"Good afternoon, Madam, the capes you ordered for Mrs. Kelly arrived a few minutes ago. I have placed them in her wardrobe, to the far left-hand side as you instructed. Do you think Mrs. Kelly will believe the dresses have been hanging there all this time?"

"No."

Andrew came around the corner. "Madam, Mr. Dorjan to see you. He insists it is of utmost importance."

Sara moaned. She honestly didn't want to listen to Philip's complaints or his latest gossip. "Everything with him is of utmost importance when he fears he will not be seen. Very well. Andrew, show Mr. Dorjan into the parlor, if for no other reason than to placate the man."

Sara forced a smile as she entered. "Philip, what is so important?"

"Your, Grace." He made her a bow. "I have come to speak with you about Aileen."

"Oh. What about my granddaughter?"

He motioned to the settee. "Shall we sit?"

"By all means. Now, tell me what brings you here?"

Philip ran his hands around the brim of his hat and lowered his eyes. He drew in a deep breath before meeting her gaze. "I have come to ask for your help. I'm smitten with Aileen, and I wish her to be my mate. It has become obvious to me she is avoiding me. I hope it is because she is shy."

Sara was too startled by his announcement to offer any objection. The situation was worse than she'd imagined. Though she didn't particularly like Philip, she didn't want to hurt his feelings. "I see."

Philip's eyes glimmered, and a smile curved his lips but didn't touch his eyes. "Will you speak to her, persuade her to have me?"

"No."

His smile dipped into a frown. "Why not?"

There was no other way to tell him but, to be honest. "Aileen has found her true mate."

"May I inquire as to the identity of this gentleman?"

"You don't know him."

"Another friend of yours from America, I assume."

Beelzebub leisurely strolled into the parlor. The fur on his back rose as he spotted Philip.

Sara lifted the cat onto her lap. "Had enough sun, have you?"

"Your Grace, please, the name of Aileen's so-called mate. I would very much like to meet him."

"As I told you already, you don't know him, so his name will be of no use to you." She stroked Beelzebub's coat, smoothing it.

Philip sat rigid, staring at the cat. After a few long minutes of silence, he sighed. "Very well. If you do not help me in my quest, I will pursue Aileen on my own."

For the first time, Sara felt sympathy for the young man. He was blind to Aileen's indifference. He was truly smitten. "Philip, you know no one can come between one of our kind and our true mate. To do so would have a tragic outcome. Please, try to understand. You need to stay away from Aileen. I'm certain you too will find your mate, but it's not Aileen."

Philip's eyes blazed with fury. "It will not be tragic for me, but for Aileen, and her chosen."

Sara jumped to her feet. What sympathy she had for him anger quickly replaced. How dare he threaten a member of her house? "Heed my warning, Mr. Dorjan. If you interfere with Aileen, you will deal with me. I do not think you want to do that."

He rose swiftly and grabbed her upper arm. Philip's claws cut deep into her flesh, hitting bone. "Old woman, I will not be denied."

In over a thousand years, no one had challenged her. She wouldn't let this insolent man think he would get away with his impertinence to her or her status. Her fangs lengthened. Her horns erupted, pushing from her forehead for the first time in over two hundred years. With her free hand, she pried Philip's claws from her arm. Sara squeezed his fingers until his bones crushed. With a swift motion, she grabbed Philip by his throat and forced him to his knees. "Never, threaten me."

She released her hold and shoved him to the floor. Keeping her sight on Philip, Sara rang for Andrew.

Andrew entered the room. "Madam?"

"Mr. Dorjan is leaving."

Philip snatched his hat from the settee as he stood. "You will regret this day."

"Do I hear a challenge from you?" She tilted her head up defiantly, meeting his glare.

The coward backed away from her.

"I thought not."

~ ~ ~

Vaughn leaned back in his chair, looking across the study at Royce. Bright sunlight flooded the room, and a cool breeze blew the curtains. It was a perfect day to be outside and not in here going over the case. "So, what are Alan's orders?"

Royce turned from the window. "Not only is your Mrs. Kelly quite intelligent but also very athletic." A grin curved Royce's lips. "Is she accompanying Aileen and you to Father's birthday celebration?"

Vaughn folded his fingers together and drew in a deep breath. He knew that look of Royce's well. "We are not here to discuss Rose . . . ah, Mrs. Kelly, but what Alan said."

"Is she your chosen? I have only been here a day, yet already I have noticed the way you look at her. During breakfast, you were alert to her every movement."

"Mrs. Kelly is a friend, nothing more." He could not look Royce in the eyes.

"You cannot lie to me. I know you. I also noticed how Rose looks at you."

"We are not here to discuss Mrs. Kelly. Royce, what the bloody hell did your father say?"

"No need to get upset, old man, you know very well what Father said. He has ordered a hunt. This rogue is to be found and stopped, as well as all who have aided him." Royce slid into the chair across from Vaughn. "Do you have any suspects, other than yourself?"

"Very funny, Royce. Your humor amuses me, as always." He withdrew his notes from the desk. Shrugging, he handed them to Royce. "As you can see, ninety-three Dhampir live in London."

"After you eliminated the obvious, how many are suspect?"

Vaughn rubbed his hands over his face. "Twenty-four."

"How many do you think capable of committing such merciless acts?"

"Not counting you, Glen, and myself? Twenty-one."

"Twenty, you forgot Philip Dorjan," Royce added.

"I didn't forget him, twenty-one."

Royce lifted his brow. "Come now, Vaughn. You cannot honestly suspect Philip. The man had a bloody fit the other day at the theater. A potboy spilled beer on Dorjan. I thought he would throttle the lad. No, I cannot see Dorjan splattered with blood. He would not soil his hands."

"But he can be cruel, and Philip does have a temper."

"I see your point. However, the man is still a fop."

"Even a fop can kill." Vaughn massaged his temples. "When I catch this killer, whoever he is, I will make him pay. The Queen's courts will not try him. I will."

Royce folded his arms over his chest. "I have not known you to get this emotional over a case before."

"For the last week, I have awakened full of rage from disturbing dreams."

"Have these murders rekindled your nightmares of Katherine?"

"No."

"You answered too quickly, Vaughn. Perhaps you should let Glen and me hunt the killer."

"You can hunt him, but I will not stop because of a few restless nights. My problem is the fact I'm no closer to catching this fiend than I was five years ago. Now, he is killing more frequently. It's almost as if he is playing a game with me."

"Perhaps he believes you will never catch him."

"He will be caught, and when I catch him. . ."

Rose's laughter along with Aileen's drifted in through the open window.

Royce pushed himself from his seat and strolled to the window. He leaned against the frame. "Mrs. Kelly is quite a woman."

Vaughn looked out the window. He'd prefer to be outside with Rose rather than locked in here going over this case. "That, she is."

"Have you asked her to be your mate?"

Vaughn sighed. Royce knew him too well. "I asked."

"And?" Royce prodded. "Turned you down, did she?"

"No."

He slapped Vaughn on the back. "She said yes?"

Vaughn shook his head.

"Well, if she didn't say yes or no, what did she tell you?"

"She has *yet* to give me her answer. I asked her almost a month ago. I do not know what the bloody hell is taking her so long to make up her mind." But he did know. She feared him taking her blood. Until he did, they could not be as one.

"Have you courted her, taken her to the park, the theater? Have you done anything to woo the lady?"

Under Royce's icy blue gaze, Vaughn winced. He'd been too wrapped up in the case to do any of those things. When he and Rose were alone, they always ended up discussing the murders. "I accompanied Rose, Aileen, and Sara to the park just the other day."

Royce dropped his head into his hands. "The woman has been living under your bloody roof for nearly two months. That is *all* you have done?" He looked up. "My God man, it's the middle of October! In a week Father will be celebrating Mum's birthday, then it will be Christmas and the winter season. Are you daft? I have it! You should take her to the theater. I will give you my box for tomorrow night's performance."

"I hate the theater. The seats are too hard and far too uncomfortable for my stature."

"What is more important, your discomfort for a few hours or luring this woman into your bed?"

~ ~ ~

Rose stared at her reflection in the vanity mirror as she slid her black gloves on. She wore a gown of luxurious rose charmeuse overlaid with black chiffon. The luster of the black pearls sewn on the bodice reflected in the light. Gossamer tulle, organza rosettes, and golden cording accented the gown's skirt. The low-cut theater gown and wrap, another of Sara's ideas made Rose feel elegant.

Penny pulled and twisted Rose's hair into a topknot.

"Which of these combs do you like best?" Penny asked, holding up two combs, one encrusted with diamonds and the other with black pearls and feathers.

Rose looked in the mirror, meeting Aileen's gaze. "They are both gorgeous. Which one do you think, Aileen?"

"I like the pearls," Aileen said.

Penny slid the comb in place.

Rose jumped at the sound of a knock.

The bedroom door opened and Sara entered. She carried two small black velvet boxes. "Oh, Rose, you look beautiful. I was afraid the dress would be too dark for your coloring."

Rose studied Sara's pale blue eyes. "Thank you for everything." She smoothed her hand over the gown. "When Penny showed it to me I couldn't believe my eyes. I feel like Cinderella."

"All done, miss." Penny held a hand mirror so Rose could see the back of her hair.

"It's beautiful, Penny. Thank you."

Rose stood and turned, facing Sara and Aileen. "Well, what do you think?"

Sara smiled as she placed a long black velvet box in Rose's hand. "I want you to wear this. I believe it will go nicely with your gown."

Rose lifted the lid to the box and gasped. Inside, a diamond and black pearl bracelet glimmered against the velvet of the box. The bracelet had to be at least three inches wide. "I can't wear this. What if I lose it?" She closed the box and handed it back to Sara.

Sara took the bracelet from the box, then reached for Rose's hand. "You will not lose it, and if you do, it is only a piece of jewelry." She fastened it around Rose's wrist. "Besides, I have not worn it in years. What good is it to have something if you never use it?"

Rose held her breath as Sara opened the second box. It contained a matching choker. Never had Rose worn jewelry this expensive. Her hand shook as bad as she removed the choker from the box she feared she would drop it.

Aileen took the necklace from Rose. "Here, let me fasten it."

"Thank you." Rose fingered the necklace, then took a deep breath, turned, and opened the door. She stepped into the hall with Aileen behind her.

Rose paused halfway down the steps as Vaughn came into view wearing tails, and white gloves.

Rose's voice came out breathless. "Man, you look sharp." She appreciated every inch of the man.

When she reached the bottom of the stairs, he took her hand in his and brought it to his lips. "Madam, you look very lovely." He offered her his arm. "Shall we?"

Andrew clicked his heels together as he handed Vaughn his top hat. "Sir, Madam." Andrew gave them a quick nod and opened the door.

Vaughn helped her into the carriage. He sat beside her. "I hope you do not mind my sitting next to you, rather than across from you. With my long legs, I feel we would both be uncomfortable."

She glanced around the inside of the carriage. Vaughn's legs were long, and he was a large man, but there would have been enough room. "I rather like having you sitting beside me."

"Sara's necklace looks lovely on you. It accents your beautiful throat."

Rose brought her hand to her neck and raised her eyebrow. "My beautiful throat? Are you vamping out on me?"

"No. I meant it as a compliment." He scowled. "Bloody hell, Rose, I want this evening to be special." His eyes met hers. "My dear brother made me realize that instead of wooing you I have been picking your brain for solutions to my case. Not a very gentlemanly way to act, if I do say so myself."

When she placed her hand on his thigh a sense of power came over her as his leg muscles quivered under her touch. "Wooing me? Is this what tonight is about? And here I thought we were doing the town."

Vaughn stared at her hand on his thigh. His groin hardened and he lifted her hand to his lips. "I do hope you enjoy the play tonight. It's by a playwright of the name George Bernard Shaw."

"Oh! I love his works. My favorite is *Pygmalion*, but I think he writes that later."

"How do you like *Candida*?"

"I love that one, too. Is that what we are going to see?"

He nodded. "Royce insisted we use his box."

Rose turned in her seat, facing him. "You realize he would do anything for you."

He studied her face. Her lips parted in a smile, and her eyes shone brightly. "I do, and I would for him."

"You probably spoiled him as a child."

Vaughn laughed, remembering the numerous times he had saved Royce from the switch. Perhaps, too many times. "I felt for Royce as a lad. Alan, Royce's father, was much like mine, always busy with the estate or with matters of importance. Royce's only playmates were the children of the servants, but

142

they treated him as the lord's son and not as their true friend." Vaughn slid his arm around Rose's shoulders. "I want to help raise my children. I want to be more of a father to them than my father was to me." He held his breath. Rose was from a different time, and perhaps men in the future didn't do such things. Very few men in this era spent time with their children.

She tilted her head up and met his gaze. "When I have children, I want their father to play with them, to read them bedtime stories, and be there for them. I don't want him to work nine to five, go to the gym, and only see his kids on weekends or when he comes home for the evening. I want him to be a daddy."

He hadn't understood everything she'd said, but he understood enough to know she wanted the same things he did. "That is what I also want, Rose." He lowered his eyes to her full lips. Vaught lowered his lips to hers, but before he could deepen his kiss. The carriage stopped. He lifted his lips from hers. "Perhaps we can resume this later."

~ ~ ~

Vaughn watched the play with one eye and Rose with the other. Perhaps tonight she would come to him, give herself to him as his mate. His groin hardened at the thought and he shifted in his seat.

Rose leaned toward him. "Are you uncomfortable?" she whispered.

He was thankful the theater lights were dim. "Stretching my legs," he told Rose, taking her hand in his.

Finally, the house lights brightened, and the actors took their last bows. Vaughn helped Rose from her seat.

"I instructed Aileen's Mr. Bell to have the carriage wait for us on the side street. It will be quicker for us to get out of the crowd," he explained as he led her to the side door.

Rose stopped and looked up at him. Her eyes were wide. "Why do you call him, Aileen's Mr. Bell?"

Vaughn laughed as he placed Rose's hand on his arm. "Just because I do not comment on certain situations, it does not mean I am blind to what goes on in my own home. I know who Mr. Bell is or should I say, Mr. Campbell? I have known who he was from the first time I laid eyes on him." He bent over and brushed a kiss to her lips, then opened the alley door. "My sister is lucky to have such a friend as you."

~ ~ ~

Dumbfounded, Rose followed Vaughn into the dimly lit alley. A fog had settled in while they enjoyed the play. About five other couples had the same idea as Vaughn and had used the side doors to escape the crowd out front. "Great place to be mugged," she murmured, then stumbled on the steps.

"Rose!" Vaughn slid his arm around her waist and helped her to her feet. "Are you all right?"

"I'm fine. The hem of my dress caught on something." She yanked on her skirt, pulling it free. The concern showing in his eyes warmed her. "Let's go home."

Vaughn took hold of her hand. They strode down the dark and now empty alley toward the street. She'd always avoided dark alleys at all cost, but she was with Vaughn and safe.

The fog tonight had an eerie yellowish hue about it. The sound of her heels clicking on the cobblestone only added to the spookiness of the alley. She tightened her grip on Vaughn's hand. "I'm ducking behind you if I see Jekyll and Hyde."

"I believe they are the same person." Vaughn's chuckles drowned out the sounds of carriages and voices ahead of them.

Three men moved toward them. The larger man tilted his cap at her as he strolled past. His two companions paused to light cigars.

"Evenin', gov'ner," the men said.

Vaughn leaned close to her. "When I say run, run."

She looked up at him. "But."

"Never mind," he said through clenched teeth.

The two men who'd paused, stood in front of Vaughn and Rose, blocking their way. Each man held a knife. The burly

144

man stepped away from the shorter, fatter man, who wore a dark wool cap. He motioned with his knife to Rose's necklace.

Her heart pounded. She wanted to turn around to see where the first man stood, but she didn't. Her instincts told her he was directly behind her and Vaughn.

Vaughn placed his arm protectively around her. "Gentlemen." He stared at the men in front of them.

The burly, rough-looking man stepped forward. He smoked the stump of a cigar. "Me mither would like this sparkly." He reached toward Rose's neck.

Vaughn knocked the man's hand away. "Then I will tell you where you can purchase one."

The loud breathing of the man behind them sent chill bumps down Rose's spine. Fear gripped her tighter as the man stepped closer.

The short fat man snickered. His gaze raked over her, making her feel as though he stripped her with his eyes.

He stroked his chin, keeping his eyes on her. "Kill 'em."

Vaughn jerked forward, a knife protruding from his side. He turned, grabbed the man behind them by the throat, snapping his neck. The man fell to the ground, dead. Vaughn whirled, facing the other men.

"Mother of God, protect us," the larger man wailed.

Vaughn hissed. His eyes were bright red, his long white fangs glistened, and his normally short, well-manicured nails grew into long, deadly claws. He was every bit the vampire of lore. He pulled the knife from his side and stabbed the man in the chest.

Distracted by Vaughn's appearance, Rose let her guard down. The third man grabbed her, using her as a shield.

"I'll cut 'er pretty throat," he warned.

Rose rammed her elbow into his stomach, turned, and using the palm of her hand, struck him in the nose.

"Bloody whore!" He slashed at her, missing her, then turned his attention to Vaughn. "You're the one! You're the killer. Well, you'll not get me." He charged at Vaughn.

145

Vaughn pushed her out of the way and blocked the attack. The mugger ran into the far wall and fell to the ground. He groaned and rolled onto his side. He'd landed on his knife.

Without a word, Vaughn took her by the hand. They hurried from the scene.

He opened the carriage door then hastily helped her inside. Vaughn glanced up at David. "Home and be quick about it." Vaughn fell with a moan against the seat.

In the faint light from the street, Vaughn appeared pale and his face tense in pain.

Rose stared at Vaughn's blood-soaked shirt. He wasn't a vampire, and he wasn't immortal. She'd be damned if she'd lose another loved one. She stared at his wound. "What can I do?"

"I'll be fine once we get home."

"How bad is it?"

"Not terribly."

She reached down and tore her petticoat, then met his gaze. "Lean forward and let me see."

"I'll be fine." His voice laced with pain.

"Don't pull this macho-bullshit on me. Now, lean forward and let me have a look at your side."

He mumbled something under his breath and did as she'd asked.

There was too much blood. Carefully, Rose pressed the cloth to Vaughn's wound. "It looks as if he got you in the kidney, or maybe your spleen. Hell, I'm not a doctor, but I know this is bad."

~ ~ ~

Vaughn shook as the hunger gnawed his stomach. To heal he needed blood. "The wound is deep."

She touched his forehead. "You're cold."

He met her worried expression and smiled.

"You need blood or you're going to die, aren't you?"

He closed his eyes.

146

Rose stroked his cheek. "Take my blood. If it heals you, Vaughn, take it."

"No."

"Vaughn Madoc, if you die, so help me, I'll kill you for lying to me."

He laughed and winced from the pain. "You said you don't get hysterical."

Rose cupped his face in her hands. "I give you my blood willingly."

He could not fight the pain or the hunger anymore. "Do you understand I will know your every thought? You will be mine."

Rose unfastened her cape, pulled off the choker, then with trembling hands, drew him to her throat.

When his fangs pierced her skin, her sweet blood trickled into his mouth. Instantly he was engulfed with her memories, visions of men riding in strange automobiles, and metal ships flying in the skies, people trapped inside boxes. He started to retract his fangs when her emotions flooded his mind. Her love for him wrapped him in a warm blanket, and he clung to her. She loved him. His fangs dug deeper into her neck, and he fed.

Rose's hands fell limp. She sagged against him.

Vaughn lifted his mouth from her throat and stared at her pale complexion. He'd taken too much.

Chapter Eleven

Vaughn tapped lightly on Rose's door. No answer. Afraid of what he would find inside, he could barely hold his hand as he turned the knob. He pushed open the door and peeked in. Relief washed over him, and he exhaled. Rose slept with Beelzebub curled against her. The lazy cat lifted his head and growled.

"Don't fret, my friend. I'm not here to harm her. I'm only making sure she is out of danger," he whispered.

Careful not to make a sound, he approached her bed. He didn't want to wake her. He stared at her throat. His marks were healing, but the wounds in his heart gaped. He reached out and smoothed her silken hair from her face, then bent down and brushed a kiss to her lips. "Forgive me, my love, for I will never forgive myself."

A faint smile curved Rose's lips, and she moaned and rolled toward him.

As tempting as it was, he resisted the urge to enter her dream. "Sleep well, my love. I will never allow myself the chance to harm you again." He backed out of the room. "Take care of her, Beelzebub."

Vaughn closed the door. He turned coming face to face with Sara. "I had to make sure Rose was out of danger. Her color has already started to return to normal."

"What happened tonight?"

Guilt, anger, and shame filled him because of his lack of self-control. "Rose offered me her blood, and I was too weak to resist. Once I felt her love, I could not control myself. I wanted to take her into me, to make her part of me. I almost killed the woman I love."

Sara's eyes welled with tears. "Oh, Vaughn, Rose is your true mate. If she were not, her emotions would not have affected you."

148

"But a mate I can never claim."

"Don't make this decision in haste. So few of our kind are lucky enough to find someone to love us, and even fewer of us find our true mates. *Yeva* handed yours to you. There is no other explanation as to why and how Rose came to be here. Do not push away what the Creator has given you."

"The hell with the Creator! I'm beginning to think she is a vicious bitch who enjoys playing games with our lives."

"You should not speak that way."

"I have asked Andrew to pack my things. I plan to stay in London for a few days."

"What of Rose? You need to stay here. You need to speak to her. She will be worried about you."

"No."

"But—"

"I said no."

"What do you want me to tell her?"

He tightened his fists as he walk toward his room. "Tell Rose I'm a monster."

~ ~ ~

Sara stared at his retreating back. His shoulders hunched with the heavy burden of guilt he'd piled on himself. "You are not a monster."

"I'm as much one as the killer I hunt," he said, continuing to his room.

She wouldn't argue with him. He was a stubborn man, and in his current state of mind, she doubted he would listen to her anyway. "Very well, run off to London. In a few days when you have come to your senses, then I will speak to you."

He slammed his bedroom door.

The morning sun hadn't broken the horizon when Sara watched Vaughn's carriage disappear down the street. She pushed the door closed. He was a fool. *Very well, if he wants to act like a child, then he will be treated as a child.*

149

Sara gripped the banister rail and stared up the stairs. She took the steps at a slow pace as she tried to think of what to tell Rose.

As Sara entered the room, Rose opened her eyes and smiled. She started to sit up but fell back against the pillow.

"How do you feel, Rose?" Sara asked. The poor dear didn't look at all well.

"Dizzy. How's Vaughn? Is he all right?"

"Yes, he's fine."

Rose tossed back her bed covers. She attempted to sit again, but instead, she squeezed her eyes shut. Sara caught Rose as she slumped over the side of the bed. "I have to see Vaughn. Why do I feel so funny?"

Sara eased Rose back into bed. "What you have to do, young lady is stay in bed. Vaughn is not here. He has gone to London for a few days."

"Why? He was stabbed last night and lost a great deal of blood. He shouldn't be gallivanting all over England."

Sara pulled the covers up over Rose, then tucked her snug in bed. "I believe he wanted to speak with Inspector Hughes."

"He didn't say good-bye," Rose whispered. She smiled weakly. "I guess I shouldn't worry about him, but I do."

The love shining in her eyes filled Sara with sympathy for Rose and anger at Vaughn. He should not have run off in the wee hours of the morning and definitely without telling Rose good-bye. "My dear, no matter how intelligent a man is, sometimes he doesn't think. I'm certain you were on his mind when he left. He will return before long. In the meantime, you need your rest. You lost a great deal of blood last night, too. Now, stay put, and I will have Penny bring you breakfast."

Sara stepped from the room and nearly ran into Aileen, pacing in the hall.

"How is Rose? Will she be all right? I can give her my blood if it will help her."

150

Sara hugged Aileen. "She is healing and will not need your gift. Right now the poor dear is worried about your stupid, stubborn, asinine brother."

"Why has he left for London? He should be here with Rose."

"He fears he will kill her as Christian did Katherine. I wish I could make your brother understand he is irrational." She took hold of Aileen's hand. "Let us go down for breakfast. I told Rose I would have Penny take her up a tray."

"What is wrong with my brother? The first time I took David's blood, I didn't want to stop drinking, but I did."

Sara tripped on the steps and grabbed the banister. She stared at Aileen. "You have taken David's blood? Have you given him yours? Are you breeding?"

Aileen paled and lowered her eyes. "He will not claim me until we are properly wed."

"Well, that is one thing in his favor." Sara exhaled. She proceeded down the stairs. "Does Ian MacPhee know you have marked David?"

"No, and neither does Vaughn."

"If I know your brother, he knows."

Aileen bit her lower lip, a habit she'd learned from Rose, and lowered her gaze. "*Babushka*, what are we to do about my daft brother and Rose?"

"For the time being, nothing. We cannot let Rose know the real reason Vaughn left the house. It would break her heart. As for you, I think it is time I had a conversation with Mr. Campbell. Alone."

Aileen's eyes widened, and she grabbed Sara's arm as they entered the dining room. "Please, *Babushka*. I love him."

"I know you do, my dear. Does Mr. Campbell understand he's not only taking you as his wife? He is getting all of us including your guardian, Ian MacPhee as family? Mr. Campbell will for all purposes be Ian's son."

Aileen groaned and sank into a chair.

~ ~ ~

Vaughn sat in the smoke-filled room of his club. On his lap rested the morbid photo of Dr. James Austin's mutilated body. Vaughn stared at the photograph of his old friend.

A shadow fell over him. Vaughn didn't need to look up to know Royce loomed over him.

"What?" Vaughn asked.

"I should ask you the same thing. A few days ago, I sat in your study helping you make plans to woo a beautiful woman. Today I find you hiding. What happened?"

"Do you plan to stand there or are you going to take a seat?"

"Testy are we?" Royce sat and drew a cigar from his jacket. "Would you like one?"

"No."

"Just thought I would ask. Now, tell me why you are here and not back home making plans for a wedding or better, making me an Uncle?"

"I almost killed her." He lowered his eyes to the hideous picture. "Any more questions?"

"Shall we go to your room and talk of this in private?"

"Have you forgotten how to use your mind? I thought I taught you better." He sent his thoughts to Royce.

Royce chuckled. *"No. I have not forgotten. Now, tell me what you mean you almost killed her. When I saw Rose yesterday, she seemed joyous."*

"You saw her? Did she look healthy?"

"What's going on?" Royce asked, eyeing Vaughn.

"I believe this discussion *does* require some privacy. Perhaps we should retire to my room." Vaughn slid the photograph into its file then stood. "After you."

Once inside his room, Vaughn fell on the bed. He crossed his arms behind his head. "Have a seat and tell me about my Rose."

A sly grin appeared on Royce's lips. "Your Rose? So you do love her."

"Yes, but it's a love I will never consummate."

"Are you a bloody fool? The woman is in love with you. But here you are acting like a frightened schoolboy. I saw your marks."

"Did Rose tell you she loved me?" Vaughn's heart pounded in his chest as he anxiously awaited Royce's answer.

As if Royce knew this, he blew a smoke ring from his mouth and watched it float across the room.

"Damn you. Will you bloody answer me? Did Rose tell you she loved me?"

"No. Rose did not, but then she didn't have to tell me. I saw it from the way she acted whenever anyone mentioned your name. Her eyes lit up, and her lips twitched with a smile. I heard the pounding of her heart and smelled her desire whenever she spoke your name."

Vaughn swung his legs over the side of the bed. He rested his arms on his thighs. He stared at the floor, avoiding Royce's gaze. "I fell asleep in Rose's room the night of our attack. I was worried about her, you see, and didn't want to leave her side. I dreamed."

"Most people do dream when they sleep."

Vaughn closed his eyes and tried to force the misery he suffered from his heart. "I guess they do, but not like this. I dreamed I was ten again and entering Katherine's and Christian's marriage chamber." When he'd opened his eyes, Royce no longer sat in the chair. He'd crossed the room and stood beside Vaughn.

Royce's hand gently gripped Vaughn's shoulder. "Go on."

"When I opened the door, it wasn't Katherine I saw, but Rose, lying in the pool of blood." He looked up at Royce. His mouth hung open, and his eyes were wide. His cigar dangled from limp fingers.

"Dear Lord. No wonder you are acting like an ass."

"I will not let this premonition become a reality. I will not permit myself to harm Rose in any way."

Royce sat on the bed. He leaned forward, resting his arms on his legs, and allowing his hands to dangled between his knees. "I understand your dilemma. However, you cannot permit her to leave the inner circle of the family. Though I doubt Rose would betray us, we must ensure she doesn't, which means we have two choices. The first choice is to keep Rose under a watchful eye. And the second choice—I don't have to tell you what that is."

"She will stay with Grandfather and Sara."

"You have marked her, which means no man can ever touch her without facing your wrath. Rose will wither and grow old as a spinster, not a very promising life for one such as she. You, my brother, have also damned yourself to a life of celibacy.

~ ~ ~

Rose pulled the brush through her hair. It had been four days since Vaughn left. Four days, but he was home. For the first time in years, she felt alive. He'd arrived with Royce while she and Sara were out for a walk.

Rose sat at her vanity, staring at her grinning image. She looked like the Cheshire Cat. Her stomach fluttered as she pushed away from the vanity. Slowly she pressed her hands against the flat of her stomach. Tonight, after dinner, she would go to him and give him her answer. Hopefully, by the morning, she would be carrying his child. Before she left her room, she snatched Beelzebub from her bed and hugged him. Today would be the best birthday ever! Beelzebub glared at her as if she were crazy, then pushed out of her arms, and sauntered from the room, flicking his tail in annoyance.

Royce met her and offered his arm as she entered the parlor. "You look ravishing tonight, Mrs. Kelly." He winked "Your smile makes me wonder if you are keeping a secret."

"I don't think I'm keeping any secrets, Mr. Lucard."

Royce chuckled. His deep blue eyes glowed with laughter.

Rose turned her attention to Vaughn, no one else in the room mattered to her, but him.

He glanced at her but didn't smile. "Mrs. Kelly, you look much better than you did the last I saw you. I'm pleased you have recovered."

Mrs. Kelly? Why did he call her that? Maybe he was mad at her for not giving him her answer. It wasn't her fault he'd left. She took a seat beside Sara. Then again, Vaughn could be acting this way because of Royce. Yes. That had to be the answer. Vaughn wasn't a shallow man. "Vaughn, did you accomplish a lot while you were with Inspector Hughes?"

He cleared his throat loudly and glared down at her. Without answering her question, he motioned to the door. "Shall we go in for dinner?"

He was mad at her. Dammit, she should have told him sooner. Well, she wouldn't wait any longer.

She lingered behind as Aileen, Sara, and Royce went in for dinner. "Vaughn, may I have a word with you?"

Sara glanced over her shoulder, then smiled and took Royce's arm.

~ ~ ~

Vaughn closed the door behind Sara, leaving them in the room alone. The dull ache of foreboding knotted his stomach. Keeping his back to Rose, he closed his eyes. *Yeva, Creator of us all. Give me the courage to do what I must. It pains me to have to hurt the one I love, but hurt her I must to keep her safe.*

He turned and met Rose's smiling face. "What do you wish to discuss with me, Mrs. Kelly?"

Her smile faded from her eyes, but not her lips. "What happened to Rose?"

"For me to address you as such is too personal. After all, you are my sister's companion."

"If you're pissed because I waited until now to give you my answer, you can get over it."

He held up his hand to stop her. He didn't want to hear what she would tell him. It would be too painful for him to

155

bear. "Your answer to my proposal is no longer necessary. I no longer wish it. While I was in London, I came to the realization a union between us would be impossible."

The color faded from her cheeks, and her lips trembled. "Why?"

He hated to be cruel, but he saw no other way to protect her from himself. He wanted so much to grab her and pull her to him, to kiss her, but it could never happen again. He lengthened his fangs, threw his head back, and gave a choked, forced laugh. "Why, you ask? Look at me. Look at what I am. Tell me what you see."

Tears welled in her eyes. "The man I love."

"Love! That, madam, is an emotion I cannot give you in return. Lust perhaps, but never love."

"What have I done to cause you to act like this? Please tell me. I'm sorry for whatever it was."

He had to deliver the final blow. He had to jab that last barb that would send her fleeing from him forever. He had to make her hate him. Trapped by his lies, he would forever lose his one true love. "Madam, the truth is I do not want another man's castoff. It is burden enough to have to provide for you. I will not share my bed with you."

Despite the tears rolling down her cheeks, Rose squared her shoulders and looked him in the eye. "Go to hell." She threw her words at him like stones. "And, Mr. Madoc, if I happen to return to my time, stay the hell away from me."

Vaughn sneered and forced the words from his mouth. "I will never seek you out."

She opened the door and marched away with dignity.

He stared at the place where she'd stood. His heart ached with grief and pain. He'd succeeded. Rose hated him.

Drained and lifeless, he opened the door to the dining room. Sara sat alone.

She glared at him. "You realize you have ripped Rose's heart from her chest and today of all days."

"Telling her that lie was the hardest thing I ever had to do."

"Which lie are you speaking of, the lie about not loving her, or the one of not seeking her out if she happens to go back to her time? Knowing the guilt and pain she suffered for the loss of her family and husband, did you have to call her another man's castoff? You also know very well she is trapped here and you dared to call her a burden."

"You heard our conversation."

"How could I not hear? However, I don't think Royce and Aileen heard. They ate in the kitchen, not wishing to listen to your lies. Now if you will excuse me, I need to see to Rose."

"*Babushka*, my Rose is a proud woman. She will not want to stay here." Guilt-ridden, he lowered his eyes, unable to face Sara's harsh stare.

Sara sat still. "You have not called me *Babushka* since you were a child. Fitting, since you are behaving like one."

He knew his words to Rose were sharper than the carving knife on the table before him. But he did what he had too. "I have not felt this much grief since the day I watched my family's home burn. What I am feeling, however, is not important. What is important is Rose. She must stay within the inner circle of the family."

"Don't fret. I will care for Rose. You can inform your household staff Rose, and I will be leaving tomorrow, providing I can persuade her to stay the night."

"*Babushka,* what is special about today?"

Sara pushed away from the table and stood, glaring at him. Her eyes burnt brighter now than ever. "It's October twentieth, Rose's birthday. You should be even happier with yourself, making today so special for her."

~ ~ ~

Moments later, Sara knocked lightly on Rose's door. Hearing no reply, Sara pushed open the door. The gown Rose had worn lay tossed on the bed, along with her undergarments. She wasn't in the room. Sara closed the door and concentrated. She sighed, locating Rose.

Sara strode down the hall toward Vaughn's study. Her heart ached at what she saw. Rose wore her mannish clothing. The child sat on the floor with her back against the doorframe of the library. Her eyes were red and swollen from crying. Vaughn had torn Rose's heart from her chest with his words as viciously as if he'd used his bare hand.

"I can't go home. I tried again, but I can't. I'm stuck here alone. Oh, God! What have I done to deserve punishment like this?"

Sara sat on the floor and drew Rose into her arms. "God is not punishing you, child. I am here with you and will always be here for you. You are not alone."

~ ~ ~ ~

Rose shook her head. She didn't want to be dependent on anyone, especially Sara, but with no money and no means of support, Rose had no other choice. Karma truly hated Rose to trap her in the past with a man she loved and who wanted nothing to do with her. How could Vaughn think she lied about Richard? That bastard!

"I can't stay here another second." She pushed herself from the floor and offered Sara her hand, then helped her to her feet. "Sara I have to get away from here, from him, tonight."

"There is no place, but I will have Andrew prepare the carriage, and we will leave at first light. But for now, perhaps some fresh air will do you good." Sara wiped the tears from Rose's eyes. "I will inform my son we are coming."

Rose nodded. "Thank you." She started down the stairs, then paused. "I don't want to risk seeing him. I think I'll go to my room."

"You are *my* child now." Sara slid her arm around Rose's shoulders, squeezing them. "Come with me, and I will tell you about my cottage in Wales, my stubborn husband who travels the world, and my seven brothers and six sisters. The fresh air will help relax you."

Sniffing back tears, Rose nodded. "Your parents had fourteen children?" Rose asked as she and Sara stepped outside.

"Yes, but my husband Mishenka and I were only blessed with two though we tried for many more." She wiped another tear from Rose's cheek. "I'm sure Mishenka will adore you when you two meet. Shall we go to the garden?"

"No—please. That's Vaughn's garden. I can't."

Sara patted Rose's hand. "I understand. Then let us go this way." She pointed toward the lane.

Rose breathed in the brisk October air. She had been in the past nearly four months. Was Denny getting worried, had he tried to contact her? Maybe when she'd been sent back in time, she'd been completely erased from her time, with no memory of her existing from peoples' minds. *It doesn't matter anymore. There is no way for me to return.* Rose straightened her back. It was time to pull up her big girl panties and make the most of the new life she had. She peered down the lane. The gas light cast an eerie glow on a hansom cab parked beneath it.

Besides the sound of their shoes on the cobblestone walk, the only other sound was the clanking of the cab's wheels as it slowly rolled down the lane.

Sara slowed her pace. "Rose, have you ever been to Russia?"

The crack of a whip and the sound of horse hooves pounding on the cobblestones interrupted Rose's reply. She turned.

The cab driver hid his face beneath a red muffler. He whipped the horses, driving the animals onto the walk toward her and Sara. Rose shoved Sara back through the gate opening.

Everything happened so fast. Sara's screams echoed in Rose's ears as the horses knocked her to the ground, their hooves cut into her back. The metallic taste of blood filled her mouth with every breath she drew. The pain made her gasp.

She couldn't feel her legs, only pain. She closed her eyes briefly.

Someone lifted her head and pillowed it on a soft lap. Rose barely lifted her eyelids, focusing on Sara's face. Dark tears stained her cheeks.

Shh, child, you will be all right."

Vaughn appeared from nowhere and knelt beside Sara, almost as if he materialized from the fog. Dracula could turn in to mist.

"Rose," Vaughn whispered.

She gasped, trying to breathe. She was dying. But she wasn't afraid. She welcomed it. She would finally be with her parents and all the people she loved, but most of all . . . "Richard," his name slipped from her lips as she succumbed to the darkness.

Chapter Twelve

Rose opened her eyes. So where was the bright light? And what the devil was that roaring sound?

Beelzebub placed his paw on her chest. The cat then nuzzled her cheek. Her head hurt, and her body ached, but she wasn't suffering the excruciating pain she'd felt before. "I'm not dead," she sighed.

"No, you're not," Vaughn's voice came from the darkness of the room.

She tried to roll over onto her side to see him, but a sharp pain stopped her. "The last thing I remember was being knocked to the ground by the coach."

"Stay still," he ordered. "Your body has not finished healing." He turned up the lights, then stood next to her bed and gazed down at her.

"The driver steered the horses onto the walk intentionally, trying to run us down," she said, shifting to get comfortable.

"Did you see his face?" The words fell coldly from Vaughn's mouth, and his face was a blank, emotionless canvas.

"No. The driver had a red muffler over his face."

"Did you notice anything strange, anything that could lead me to his identity?"

"Everything happened so fast." Why was Vaughn questioning her? Her head hurt.

"Think, Rose, try to remember."

She was trying to think. Didn't Vaughn understand that? "He wasn't trying to stop. He whipped the horses mercilessly."

"Is that all you remember?"

"At the moment, yes." Her head throbbed too much for her to think.

She started to sit, but Vaughn placed his hand on her shoulder.

"Please, Rose. Lay still. Your body needs to heal itself."

"So, I'm Rose now and not Mrs. Kelly?"

He flinched. "Listen to me."

Something about his tone of voice frightened her. She leaned back against the bed pillows. "What?" Even in the faint glow of the gaslights, she could see his serious expression.

"When you were struck down, you were mortally injured."

"Mortally? But I don't understand."

"I gave you my blood to heal you. You will now live a much longer and healthier life because of it."

"You did what? You made me like you and Beelzebub. Oh, God. How could you, Vaughn?"

"You were dying, and I could not let that happened. I gave you the gift of life."

"Not a gift, but a curse."

"Is that what you think?"

"I wish you had left me in the gutter to die."

"How could you choose death over life?" His voice was barely above a whisper.

"I would think you would relish the chance to be rid of me once and for all, as I'm such a burden on you..." She paused. "And another man's castoff. But I see you couldn't resist the chance to play God. At least in death, I would have been with someone who loved me, my husband. Instead, I will be tortured, trapped here with someone who despises me." Closing her eyes, she turned her face to the wall. Rose's grief overwhelmed her, and she allowed her tears to fall, not caring if Vaughn saw them. He'd won. Other than her sobs, the only sound she heard was Vaughn's long sigh, followed by the closing of her door.

~ ~ ~

Vaughn tried to shake off the numbness that weighed him down as he entered the parlor, but he could not. He forced a smile for Aileen and Sara. Royce paced in front of the fireplace.

Royce stopped in mid-stride. "*Babushka* has informed me the driver of the cab was one of our own."

162

Vaughn turned. "Do you know who it was?"

She lowered her teacup. "No. I was too concerned about Rose at the time. Had she not pushed me out of the way, the cab would have struck me as well. Vaughn, do you think it was the murderer you are hunting?"

"Possibly."

"Why attack Rose and me?"

Vaughn stared into the flames. "Rose and you were attacked because of me." Rose's words echoed in his mind. *I wish you had left me in the gutter to die.*

He whirled at Sara. "This is your fault. You have caused this." He pointed at her. "What was your reasoning for putting Rose in danger? No respectable woman walks the streets at night."

"Before there is any more bloodshed." Royce poured a glass of brandy, then handed it to Vaughn. "Did Rose see the driver's face?"

"No."

"How is she? Aileen asked.

He shook his head. "She wished I had let her die. How could Rose prefer death to life?"

"If I were dying," Sara said. "And given the choice of living a loveless life or being with my deceased husband who had loved me, I too would wish to be with those who loved me and would welcome death. Why do you think so many of us follow our mates in death?"

Vaughn threw his glass into the fire, smashing it against the fireback. "Women!"

~ ~ ~

Sara watched him leave. He might tell himself he would not have Rose as a mate, but by the exchanging of blood, they had become bonded for eternity.

Sara's mind burned with the vision of Vaughn rushing from the house seconds after the accident. His face contorted with fear as he knelt beside Rose's broken body. He'd scooped her up into his arms and carried her into the house. His blood-

163

tinged tears rolled from his eyes and mingled with Rose's blood.

Sara stared into her cup, before taking a sip. She remembered how Vaughn had paced the room while she and Aileen washed the blood from Rose's body. A moan from Rose's lips had sent Vaughn rushing to her side, shoving Aileen away from Rose. He'd refused to leave Rose until she woke.

Foolish man to think he would harm Rose as Christian had Katherine. Perhaps Alan and Mishenka could convince Vaughn of this. They both knew of Christian's dark side. They had even tried to prevent the union.

Very well, if Vaughn wanted Rose out of his life, so be it, Sara thought. She'd take Rose to Wyvern House, then see just how long it took Vaughn to follow. "As soon as Rose has healed properly, we will be leaving. Aileen, please go sit with Rose."

Once Aileen left, Sara looked at Royce. "We need to plot. Close the door."

~ ~ ~

Bright sunlight flooded the room. Rose stretched. The pain wasn't as severe today as it had been last night. She wiggled her fingers, then rolled over onto her side.

Beelzebub hadn't left her all night. He'd slept with his head resting on her pillow. His pink nose was inches from her face. He opened his eyes. "Meow."

"Good morning to you. I guess you and I are blood brothers." She stroked his fur. "Cat lovers all over would call me lucky to share the same blood as you, but I don't think I'm lucky. I get to live forever, knowing the man I love doesn't love me." She tossed back her bed covers and slid from the bed. Her legs gave out, and she fell to the floor. "Nooo!"

"What are you doing?" Aileen entered the room and rushed to her side.

Rose tried to push herself up. "I was trying to go to the bathroom." Fear and anger twisted inside of her. Not only was she trapped in the past, but now she was crippled. How much worse could her life get?

Aileen slid her arms under Rose.

"What are you doing? You can't lift me."

"I'm a lot stronger than I appear to be, besides, Rose, I don't think you want my asinine brother to carry you to the loo."

"You're right about that."

"Your body has not healed completely. Until it does, you need to stay in bed." She carried Rose to the bathroom. When she'd finished, Aileen took her back to bed. "By tomorrow you should be able to walk, and in a few more days you will be completely healed."

"Why can't I walk today? Vaughn said I was mortally injured?"

Aileen pulled up the covers over Rose, then sat on the edge of the bed. "The cabs' wheels rolled over you, crushing your body. Even after Vaughn gave you his blood, we were not certain you would live."

"Crushed?" Rose stared deep into Aileen's eyes. "How did Vaughn give me his blood?"

"After he carried you into the house he bit into his wrist, then pressed it to your lips. Because you had already given your blood to him, he could enter your mind and encourage you to drink. I was frightened I'd lose you. You are my dearest friend."

"Next to David, right?" Rose teased.

Aileen lowered her eyes.

"What is it? You and David haven't broken-up?"

"No. When you and Sara leave, I will be going with you."

"But what about David?"

"He asked me to marry him."

Rose threw her arms around Aileen's neck. "I'm so happy for you. When? Are you eloping?"

165

"After we leave Wyvern house, David will join us in Wales. *Babushka* said she would help us."

"What about your brother? Are you going to tell Vaughn?"

"That would not be wise. You know I have lived with the MacPhees all my life. They are my family, and I think of Ian MacPhee as my father. If I tell Vaughn about David and me, Vaughn would feel honor bound to inform Ian. You know what would happen then."

"Yeah, World War Three."

"Pardon?"

"Sorry, just another American expression."

"Rose," Aileen said, taking hold of Rose's hand, "I hope you will stay with *Babushka*. I cannot bear the thought of you going back to America."

Warmth spread through Rose, and she squeezed Aileen's hands. "I've already made up my mind. I'm going to take Sara up on her offer. Besides, from what your brother has told me, I'm going to be around for a while. He told me he'd given me a long and healthier life. Aileen, just how long will I live?"

"With as much blood as Vaughn gave you, you may live to be several hundred years old. However, I'm not sure how long you will live. When you become Vaughn's mate, then you will live as long as he does. That is unless something happens and you die prematurely, but you need not worry. Vaughn would not let anything happen to you."

"Your brother doesn't want anything to do with me. He certainly does not want me as his mate. He made that point absolutely crystal clear to me. Now, let's talk about something else, like when are we going to leave? Do you know where Sara wants to go? Last night she said something about Russia."

"*Babushka* loves to visit her sister Alisa, who lives in Saint Petersburg. I remember when I was younger Sara would take me there. It's such a beautiful city."

A sinking feeling came over Rose. In a few years, Russia would be involved in a bloody revolution. So much would happen in the next ten years. "I can hardly wait to see it. Until I came here, I'd never left America."

"You will love traveling with *Babushka* and Papa. They will take you places you can only imagine. Last night when we watched over you, *Babushka* mentioned something about visiting Egypt."

Rose relaxed. "I'm getting excited just listening to you talk. When I was little, I dreamed about traveling all over the world. I've always wanted to see the Sphinx, the Taj Mahal, and the Eiffel Tower."

"Oh, Rose, you have plenty of time to see Eiffel's Tower before it's dismantled. Royce said the city of Paris wouldn't start taking it down until 1909. I can't understand what all the hoopla is about concerning an ugly mass of metal beams."

Rose bit her lower lip, knowing the Eiffel Tower would never be taken down. It's the pride of France. "Aileen, when your brother showed me London. . ." She looked away and gazed out the window. Tears stung her eyes. "It was wonderful," she whispered. Well, she wouldn't have to worry about mastering her fear of flying. Vaughn wouldn't be taking her on any more magical trips. Dammit, she wouldn't cry over him.

Aileen placed her hand on Rose's shoulder. "I know Vaughn will come to his senses."

"When pigs fly."

"Rose, trust me. He does care for you."

"No, he doesn't. The truth is your brother doesn't want anything to do with me. According to him, I'm nothing but your companion."

"You mean more to him. I can see it in his eyes. I know he loves you. I saw how he acted when you were hurt."

Rose's whole body became engulfed in such a tide of grief she didn't want to talk any longer.

"I didn't mean to upset you."

"I'm okay," she lied. "I'm a little tired. I think I'll take a short nap before you try to teach me to play chess again. It looks as if I'll finally have time to learn. It's not like I'm going anywhere today."

"Penny should be bringing you a breakfast tray soon."

"I'm not hungry right now, maybe later."

"Very well." Aileen left, pulling the door closed behind her.

As soon as the door clicked, Rose punched her pillow. He'd called her another man's castoff. He knew what had happened to Richard. Vaughn Madoc could burn in hell for all she cared.

Beelzebub purred and rubbed against Rose. *My constant companion.*

She hugged him, then buried her face in his soft fur and fell asleep.

~ ~ ~

Rose stared out the window at the rising sun. She'd finished writing about her injuries and her heartache. She'd even jotted down all the important dates in world history she could remember. She'd make sure Aileen and Sara were not in Europe when Hitler came into power.

Rose grinned. She'd even made a list of all the stocks and bonds to purchase in the future. She might as well take advantage of her knowledge.

She closed her journal and sighed. Three days were long enough for her to stay in bed. She needed to get up and move around. Carefully she eased her legs over the side of the bed. Trying to stand would probably be one of the stupidest things she'd did. Didn't matter, she'd do it anyway. *Consequences be damned.* She grabbed hold of the bedpost and pulled herself up. Sharp pains shot through her legs, but she could stand.

Cold sweat beaded her forehead, and her knees wobbled as she eased her hand from the post. Hesitantly she took a step, then another until she finally made it to the bathroom without face planting. Exhausted and out of breath, she sat on the side of the tub. Maybe a bath would help her sore muscles.

The bath had made her feel much better. The more she moved around, the less stiff she felt. Dressing took a bit longer, but she'd managed it on her own. However, she discovered her ribs were still too sore for her to wear a corset. She smoothed her hands over the simple flannel wrapper. No one would notice she wasn't wearing a corset.

Beelzebub purred contentedly, watching her from the bed. He stood and reached out a paw toward her. She petted him, then left her room and found Royce walking down the hallway. "Good morning. I didn't realize you were here."

He cocked his left eyebrow. "Do you feel well enough to be out of bed? You look a little pallid."

"I feel fine, other than stiff." For some reason, she suddenly felt quite warm.

"Mrs. Kelly?"

"I'm dizzy."

Royce caught her and swung her up into his arms. "I believe you need to be back in bed."

She pushed against his chest. "No. Please, give me a few minutes, and I'll be fine. Honest, the dizziness has passed."

"Perhaps what you need is some nourishment, as I have heard you have not eaten at all since your accident." He carried her downstairs.

"I can walk," she protested.

"I'm sure you can." Royce laughed. "But I'm enjoying the feel of you in my arms." He paused on the landing and clicked his tongue. "Such a rebel you are, Mrs. Kelly, no corset."

Aileen's voice drifted from the dining room followed by a comment from Sara.

Rose pushed on Royce's chest again. "Mr. Lucard, I think you can put me down now."

"Call me Royce, and I think I will put you down when I'm ready." He carried her into the dining room, then set her in the chair beside Aileen. The cad then made a flamboyant bow.

Vaughn lowered *The Daily Express* he'd been reading. His eyes flashed a blazing red as he glared at Royce.

169

Royce's ice blue eyes twinkled as he met Vaughn's glare. "Is something wrong, old man?" A faint trace of laughter rang in his voice. "Has *Babushka* completed the crossword puzzle again?"

Vaughn crumpled the paper and muttered something under his breath as he pushed away from the table. Never once did he look at Rose. He kept glaring at Royce.

Rose lowered her eyes, unable to look at Vaughn. He hated her so much he couldn't stand the sight of her.

Aileen passed a bowl to Rose. "Would you care for some eggs?"

"No, thank you." Her appetite had left her.

She could feel Vaughn's angry glare on the back of her neck as he paced behind her.

Aileen turned in her seat. "Vaughn, what is wrong with you, you are so testy this morning."

Vaughn stormed from the room.

Her eyes welled with tears one splashed on her plate. Rose pushed from the table. "Please, excuse me."

"Rose," Sara called, "you need to eat if you wish to get well."

"What I need is to pack my things. It's quite obvious, Vaughn doesn't want me in his home."

"Vaughn does not know what he wants." Sara's tone was sharp. She rang the silver bell beside her. A second later Andrew entered the room.

"Your Grace?"

"Andrew, please inform the staff we are leaving immediately for Wyvern house. I want all of our belongings quickly packed."

"Yes, Ma'am." He gave a quick bow.

"And Andrew." A sly grin spread across Sara's lips. "I want all evidence of us, especially of Rose, removed from this house."

"Understood."

170

~ ~ ~

Vaughn started up the stairs to his study, then changed his mind. He needed to get away from Rose. He needed to sort out his emotions. It pained him to see how fast she had replaced him—and with his brother Royce

Grabbing his overcoat and hat, Vaughn opened the front door. Inspector Hughes was coming up the walk.

"Good morning, Hughes. What brings you here?"

"There has been another murder."

"Who."

"A Cabby. Early this morning a stable boy discovered the cab. He'd opened the door and found the poor chap inside. I came straight away. I want you to see the crime scene. Disgusting sight."

"Has the body been removed?"

"No."

"Good." He followed Hughes. "You walked?"

"Yes."

Vaughn's mind kept wandering back to Royce carrying Rose into the dining room and the sweet sound of her laughter.

"I say, you seem to be deep in thought today," Hughes commented.

"Three nights ago Sara was nearly run down by a runaway coach. I wonder if there is a connection."

They hiked a few more blocks before turning down an alley leading to the stables. A black hansom cab stood guarded by two bobbies.

Vaughn inspected the horses. Scabs covered their flanks where someone had whipped them. No other marks were on the horses, he noted.

A photographer from Scotland Yard approached the Inspector. "Do you wish for me to get pictures of the victim's eyes? I understand they are open."

"Yes. Some say the eyes capture the last thing a person sees before death."

Vaughn glanced over at Hughes. "You don't honestly believe this, do you?"

"At this point, I will try anything to catch this madman."

Photographing a dead man's eyes was the most ridiculous thing Vaughn had ever heard. Next Hughes would be forcing air into the dead man's lungs to see if he would speak his killer's name. "Do whatever you must." He opened the cab door and swallowed down nausea that overcame him. "Dear God!"

Hughes patted Vaughn's back. "I should have warned you. Horrible sight. Poor chap, by the look on his face he suffered a painful death."

"This is not like the others." The victim's blood coated the inside of the cab, unlike the other scenes where there had been a lack of blood.

The victim's hat, coat, and muffler were tossed into the cab after the coachman's murder.

Vaughn held the coat up, examining it. "Hughes, look. There is hardly a drop of blood on this coat."

"Only a few splatters on the hat. What do you make of this?"

Rose's words pounded Vaughn's brain. The driver was hiding his face. Rose. Bloody hell, she invaded his mind even here.

The garments confirmed Vaughn's suspicions. The killer was the one who ran down Rose. Because of the unseasonably warm weather, Rose and Sara had been taking evening strolls. The murderer had to have been watching and waiting for them. But why?

After the photographer took his pictures, Vaughn reached over and closed the victim's eyes. "I think I have seen enough."

"Can I give you a ride back to your home? My carriage is over there." Hughes pointed to the end of the alley.

"No, thanks, walking will give me time to think." Vaughn squinted as the mid-morning sunlight stung his eyes. Instinctively, he reached into his coat pocket, pulling out the glasses Rose had given him. He fingered the thin wire frames, then crushed them in his hand and shoved them back into his pocket.

He had to harden his heart to her or else he would rip out Royce's throat. Damn him to Hell.

Rose. Vaughn slammed his fist into his hand. He'd let his desire for her interfere with his investigation, and because of it, another poor soul had suffered. His feelings for Rose would not hinder him anymore. Yet, every time he saw her, his heart yearned for her.

He slowed his pace as he moved down his street. The gables of his home peeked over the tops of the oaks, and the leaves had changed. He could not live there anymore with her, nor could he send her away. Rose had no other place to go. He would leave. He would tell her he needed to spend all his time investigating the murders. He could move to his club, only a few blocks from the Yard.

When he strode through the gate to his home, a chill came over him, and he pulled his coat tight. He could not sense Rose's presence, nor could he sense Sara's or Aileen's. Perhaps they had gone to the park. He ambled up the steps as Andrew opened the front door.

"Good day, sir." He took Vaughn's coat and hat.

"Have the ladies gone to the park, Andrew?"

His servant lowered his eyes. "No sir, they packed and left with Mr. Lucard."

"Left? When? Where?"

"Shortly after you departed this morning. Her Grace ordered their belongings packed."

"Thank you, Andrew."

His house felt cold and empty as he wandered into the parlor. The room was clean. The books Rose had borrowed no longer sat in a stack by the couch. Sara's teacart sat empty.

Even the lace doilies Sara insisted on adorning his furniture were gone. The ticking of the mantel clock echoed in the quiet room. His Rose had gone. She'd left him.

Vaughn paced from the parlor into the hall. He stared up the stairway. The house was silent, empty, and cold. Finally, he sat on the steps. His guilt for the way he'd treated Rose and the pain of her leaving him had created devastating loneliness. He dropped his head into his hands. Wasn't that what he wanted?

Beelzebub strolled in front of him, paused, and hissed.

Chapter Thirteen

After a three-hour train ride, Rose sat across from Royce and Sara in a carriage. The train ride was an adventure Rose thoroughly enjoyed. The car they rode in was elegant and the seats comfortable. Not so much this carriage ride. The bumping over the uneven road was torture on Rose's still tender and sore ribs. They were on their way to Royce's parents' home. A humble little cottage on the border, he'd said. She wondered how much longer she had to endure the rough carriage ride.

Sara and Aileen slept. Sara's head bobbed with the rocking of the carriage while Aileen rested her head on Rose's shoulder. Every so often Aileen's lips pulled back in a faint smile. She must be dreaming of David.

Royce sat across from Rose. He glared out the window. He'd been unusually quiet. He caught her staring at him.

"What?" he asked. He arched his eyebrow

"When we left London, you looked angry. I saw it in your eyes."

"I am angry at Vaughn. For one who can be so intelligent, he can be so stupid. A good thrashing would not bring my brother to his senses, but I have a feeling I know what will."

"Don't waste your time or energy, Royce. Vaughn has made it quite clear he wants nothing to do with me."

Royce's blue eyes turned cold and calculating, and for the first time, she felt uneasy in his presence. She didn't think Royce would hurt her, but the longer he stared at her, stroking his chin the more apprehensive she grew. After several agonizing minutes, he held up a finger. "One question, Rose. Do you love Vaughn, knowing the monster he is? Knowing what he is capable of?"

No. Rose wanted to scream out her denial or laugh, but that would be a lie. She met Royce's icy gaze. He already knew the answer, and even if he didn't, she couldn't lie. "Yes."

"Then trust me." The ice melted from his eyes, and he comically jiggled his eyebrows, grinning like an idiot at her. "Trust us."

"Are you sure your parents won't mind my coming along? If they don't have enough room, I can stay at an inn. I don't want to intrude." She'd been intruding on everyone since this crazy adventure began.

For the first time since early morning, a warm smile curved Royce's lips. "I'm sure my mother will be able to find a place for you to sleep, even if we must put you in the attic. However, if you look out your window, you may be able to see my parent's humble abode off to your left. It's the only house in the valley."

She pushed aside the curtain and peered out. "Dear Lord! You call that a cottage?"

Deep, rich laughter erupted from Royce. "As you can see, my dear, I think we can find a place for you to stay, though it might be difficult."

"Is your father royalty?"

"No, but you must call him your Majesty."

Rose swallowed the lump forming in her throat. "Your Majesty?"

Sara slowly opened her eyes. "Royce, you should be ashamed of yourself, teasing Rose as you have been doing?"

"*Babushka,* I thought you were asleep."

"Just because my eyes are shut, does not mean my ears are." She winked at Rose. "My dear, our family has a long line of blue blood, but we are not nobility. My husband carries the title of Duke of Dacia. Royce and his father have the title of Lord."

"Then you're a Duchess."

"As I told you before, I like the use of my given name."

Rose glanced back to Royce. "Majesty, huh?"

"I rather liked the sound of it."

176

"Why doesn't that surprise me?" She twisted her lips and shook her head. "Sara, tell me more. What or where is Dacia?"

"It is now part of Romanian. At one time, it was once called Walachia, and ruled by Vlad Dracul."

"That name, I know."

A sly grin curved Royce's lips and he looked over at Aileen. "Oh, he was demented, but he was not as evil as people will have you believe. Many came before him and after him who were worse. Unfortunately, the country has a history of bloodshed."

Aileen stirred, her eyes fluttered open. After a few moments, she licked her lips, then covered her mouth to hide a yawn. "Are we almost there?"

"Almost Sleeping Beauty. You've awakened in time to hear me tell Rose about our family's little secret."

"Royce," Sara warned.

His grin widened. "It's so ironic how things happen in life."

"Royce, Rose has been through enough this day." Aileen's voice lowered in warning. "She does not need your teasing."

Rose eyed him. In the short time, she'd known him she'd learned Royce was a practical joker. He was not one to be taken seriously.

He reached across and took her hands in his. "Have you not wondered why my family adopted my beloved sister here and the overly large jackass that is her brother? After all, they are blood sucking vampires." He shuttered. "Hell's demons."

Rose pulled her hand free of his. She crossed her arms over her chest, meeting Royce's smiling eyes. "I believe the proper term is dhampir, as vampires do not exist." Rose enjoyed taking all the wind out of his sails. "As I stated earlier, I saw the angry red glow in your eyes.." She raised an eyebrow at him. "I assume you are also Dhampir. I'm going to go out on a limb here and say, so is your entire family. But I have a question. What do you call your human mates? Are they also considered Dhampir as well or just human mate?"

177

Sara winked at Rose, before pushing up on Royce's chin. "Close your mouth, dear, you may swallow a fly."

Royce glanced at Sara, then to Aileen, then back to Sara. "You told her or did Vaughn?"

A faint laugh escaped Sara. She leaned forward and patted Rose on the hand. "I consider Rose my child. And as such, she deserves to be trusted. She knows our secrets. We all have secrets." She winked at Rose. "However, some secrets must remain just that, secrets," Sara added.

Rose nodded, understanding Sara's meaning. Her time travel had to be kept quiet. She knew too much information that could change the future. But she would still use her knowledge to protect her new family. She'd always wanted a lasting relationship, had dreamed of a family that would always be there for her. *Always.* The word just took on an entirely new meaning. With Aileen and Sara with her, Rose found it satisfying.

The carriage came to a stop then rocked as the driver climbed down. The door opened, and the footman helped Sara from the carriage.

"I will help you, Rose. You may still be sore from your accident." Royce lifted her from the carriage then offered her his arm. "Shall we?"

With each step, she stared in awe at the huge house. The place had two wings that she could see, possibly three wings. She counted five stories, including the basement, and attic. Rose craned her head back to get a better look at the central triangular pediment and dormers. From the roof design and the other Queen Ann style elements of the house, the sweeping steps, and carved stone door-case. She estimated the house was built around the early 1700's. Hmm. More likely construction started around 1702. "This house is gorgeous. Do you know what year it was built?"

"Grandfather started construction on it around the early 1700's. I'm not sure of the precise year. Mum and Father moved here after the mated."

"I hope I don't get lost."

Royce laughed. "You have to get inside before that can happen. Come on, Rose. Everyone is waiting for us inside."

"Is there a third wing?" She doubted it.

"No, Father wanted to build one for Grandfather and *Babushka*, but they are never here long enough to warrant it." Royce led her up the rest of the stone steps to the front door. "Rose, if you are this taken with the outside, you will be even more impressed once we enter," he said and motioned toward the open door.

"Sorry. I'm just awestruck." Rose followed Aileen into the vast entryway of polished white marble. Above hung a beautiful sparkling crystal chandelier lit the room. Spots floated in front of her eyes, and she blinked.

A tall, handsome man with ebony black hair and a young blonde woman came toward them. "Mother, Royce, we were not expecting you until later in the week. What a wonderful surprise," the gentleman said.

Royce hugged the woman. "Mum, Dad. I would like to introduce you to Rose Kelly."

"She is so pretty Royce, is she your chosen?" his mother asked, causing heat to rise in Rose's face.

"No, Mum. She is Aileen's friend."

"I see."

Rose couldn't get over how beautiful Royce's mother was and young looking. She had to be Dhampir too.

With Royce standing close to his parents it was easy to see he got his looks from both of them. He had his mother's blond hair, but his piercing icy blue eyes he got from his father.

Royce held his hand out to her. "Rose, I like to introduce, my parents. Lord and lady Lucard."

Good grief. How did one address a lord and lady? Did she curtsey? Oh, well. She offered her hand. "Your Lordship."

179

Royce's father warmly smiled as he took her hand. His gaze seemed to linger on her throat. "We do not hold formalities within these walls. You may use my given name, Alan." He tucked her hand under his arm. "My wonderful wife, Emma."

Royce's mother smiled warmly at Rose. "Welcome, my dear. I will have you placed in the room next to Aileen."

"Thank you."

The doors to her right flew open. An older man rushed toward them. He grinned brightly, and his eyes seemed to shimmer with joy. "My Sara." He held his arms wide as he hurried toward her.

"Papa! Mother didn't tell me you would be here," Royce exclaimed.

The older man swept Sara up into his arms. He spun around several times then kissed her passionately.

"Mishenka put me down." Sara laughed. "You old fool."

"You missed me. Yes?"

Sara patted his cheek. "You know I did, dreadfully. How was India?"

He grinned wickedly at her. "I'll tell you all about it tonight. I even brought you back a gift. It is a fascinating book. I'm sure we will have pleasurable nights reading it."

Rose sighed, watching Royce's parents and his grandparents. Seeing the three generations together, she could see the very strong family resemblance. Royce and his father were the same height and of similar build. His grandfather was slightly shorter, but only by an inch. He was also stockier, with salt and pepper hair. Royce's grandfather also had an elegant air about him.

Any apprehension Rose had, slipped away as the warmth and love of this family engulfed her.

Sara led her husband over to Rose. "My dear, this old goat is my husband, Mishenka."

Mishenka bowed, then took Rose's hand. "A pleasure." He lifted her hand to his lips and brushed a light kiss to her knuckles. "My Sara has written wonderful things about you, my child." He lightly brushed a stray lock of hair from her face. His piercing blue eyes glanced at her *throat* "I even have a gift for you. It is a very lovely necklace."

"Thank you," she whispered.

The footmen brought in the trunks.

"Take them to the east wing," Emma instructed the men. "Ann, show our guests to their rooms, please," she told a female servant. "Rose, Aileen, Ann, and Molly will serve as your maids. You may follow them. I know you will want to freshen up after your long journey."

~ ~ ~

Sara watched Rose as she ascended the staircase. If the child kept stopping to look at her surroundings, she would never make it up the stairs before dinner. Sara grinned and looped her arm through Mishenka's. It had been too long since they were together. She had issues that needed to be dealt with before she and Mishenka could retire to their room. "Alan, a word."

Her son raised a questioning eyebrow. "Mum?"

"Royce, will you join us?" She had to inform them of Vaughn's behavior. "Can we go someplace private?"

Alan pushed opened the door to his study. "I noticed Vaughn had marked Rose. Why did he not accompany you? Have there been some developments in this dreadful case?"

Royce took a cigar from his father's desk. "Marked her, yes, but he does not want to embrace her."

"What?" Mishenka roared.

"Papa, Vaughn fears he will harm her if he claims her." Royce snipped the end of the cigar, then lit it. He puffed several times before blowing a cloud of smoke from his nose.

"Why is Vaughn so imprudent? He has already exchanged blood with her. I can smell him on her! The girl reeks of him. Has she rejected him?"

181

"No. Rose has taken Vaughn deep into her heart. She has accepted all of us for whom and what we are, without question, without fear. Rose is an exceptional woman." Sara lifted a decanter from the shelf. "No, it is Vaughn who is being an—"

"Ass," Royce blurted.

"Thank you for that observation." She poured herself a glass of the thick dark liquid. "Sit, and I will explain everything. We have a campaign that requires careful planning."

"Mother, you sound as if you are going to war," Alan teased.

"No, son. Not me. *We* are going to war."

~ ~ ~

Rose stood in the huge bedroom assigned to her. Against the left wall sat a magnificent walnut bed with a half tester. She ran her hand over the cutwork bedspread, then sat on the bed. "This thing is big enough for three people."

Someone knocked lightly on her door.

"Come in," she said.

A maid entered and curtsied. "I'm Molly, Miss, and will be serving you while you are here." She unpacked Rose's dresses and started putting them away. "Dinner will be served at eight. Do you need help dressing?"

"Yes, please. I think I will wear the brown velvet gown."

After Rose was properly dressed and her hair coiffured Molly curtsied, then left.

Rose's mind drifted. "How will I get over him?" She stared at herself in the mirror. Finally, she shoved from the vanity then strolled over to the French doors. The heavy doors swung open easily, and she walked out onto the balcony. There were so many stars in the night sky more so than wha she could see in Atlanta. Of course, she could see moe, no light pollution. Vaughn probably enjoyed it up here. He could fly around without detection. There she went again, thinking of him. He was probably glad she was out of his life.

182

Faint sounds of laughter and music floated in the night air and lifted her spirits. Coming here was the right thing to do.

It's Vaughn's loss, not hers. He blew his chance. "Dammit! I don't need a man, and I sure as hell don't need Vaughn Madoc."

"Rose," Aileen called from behind her. "You didn't answer when I knocked."

Rose slowly turned. "Sorry, I was deep in thought."

"Because of my brother?"

"Yes. I'm a fool, Aileen. I've lost everyone I've ever loved." She blinked back her tears.

Aileen placed her hand on Rose's shoulder. "You have not lost everyone. You still have the rest of us." She looped her arm through Rose's. "What you need is something or someone to get your mind off my stupid brother. This gala will be perfect to help you heal." Aileen's eyes held a mischievous glint. "Shall we go down for dinner?"

"You're right. I do need something to distract me, but not a someone. And before we go down, do you think this neckline is too daring?"

"No. I like that gown. But I think it needs a necklace."

"Another one of Sara's surprises. When Molly was putting away my garments, I noticed I have another six new outfits, besides this one." And it didn't bother her one damn bit Vaughn would get the bills, either.

"*Babushka* believes new clothes will perk up any woman's spirits." Aileen's eyes sparkled mischievously. "Once Quaid and his brothers get a glance at you, especially in this gown, I believe they will keep you so occupied you will not give my blooming brother another thought."

"Who is Quaid?"

"Quaid is a physician. He's a cousin from America. He and his two other brothers are here from Texas." Aileen gave a little sigh. "If I wasn't in love with David." She laughed wickedly. "I might flirt with him. The Wolfe brothers are extremely handsome." Aileen shivered, then cleared her throat.

"Morgan is the oldest, but very shy. Quaid, he's too serious for me, but from what I've heard, he's as much a rake as Royce. Tristan is a boy, who I fear, Royce will quickly corrupt if he hasn't been already. Tristan absolutely worships Royce."

Rose closed her eyes and shook her head. She'd been ripped from her place in time and thrown into the past. She'd had her heart broken. No, not broken, ripped out, then smashed into a million little pieces. The last thing she need was Sara or Aileen playing matchmaker. Of course, if they are as handsome as Aileen said— No-no-no! She didn't need a man!

Rose took the ebony box from the vanity. Sara and Mishenka had come to her room earlier and given her the box. Mishenka had explained the simple gold necklace was a gift welcoming her to the family as his and Sara's child. He'd told her it was also as a thank you for saving Sara's life. The gold basket weave necklace would be perfect with this dress.

Rose lifted the lid and gasped. The box contained more than the gold choker Mishenka had shown her. She discovered her diamond earrings, a sapphire necklace, along with three other pairs of earrings. Tears threatened her eyes as she stared at the pearl choker and bracelet she'd worn the night Vaughn had taken her to the theater. That had been both the happiest and saddest night for her.

"None of that, now." Aileen reached into the box and removed the gold choker. "*Babushka* and Papa would not have given these to you if they did not want you to have them." She placed the necklace around Rose's neck. "I think this will look wonderful with your gown." Aileen reached back into the box. "These diamond earrings will be perfect."

Rose fingered the heavy gold necklace. It did go well with the dress. "Aileen, why did Alan and Mishenka stare at my throat? Don't get me wrong. I'm not frightened anyone will bite me, but it was obvious."

Aileen lowered her eyes. "They were staring at the marks Vaughn placed on you."

Rose felt the color drain from her face. "What marks are you talking about?" She looked at her throat in the mirror. "I don't see any marks."

"Here," Aileen said, touching Rose's throat. "See those tiny white marks?"

"Those? That's where he—they happened the night he was stabbed."

"When Vaughn took your blood that night, he marked you. His marks let others of our kind know you are. . ." Aileen bit her lower lip.

Rose stared at Aileen in the mirror's reflection. "To know I'm . . . What?"

"You are his."

"Bull shit!" She twisted in her seat. "Your brother told me he didn't want me. He made no bones about it. And now you're telling me he's branded me! That son-of-a-bitch!" She stared at Aileen. All the color had drained from her face. Aileen's eyes were wide. "I'm sorry Aileen. I didn't mean to take my anger out on you. Your brother is a demented asshole."

"No. Do not apologize." Aileen sauntered over to the bed and sat. "I understand your anger. I'm angry at him as well. I do not understand my stupid brother. He is what you call, a hat of an ass."

Rose grinned at Aileen's words. Perhaps she needed to watch her language better when she was around Aileen. "What exactly do these marks mean?" Rose prodded. "I'm Vaughn's how? Like under his protection? What?"

"They let others of our kind know you belong to him. No other Dhampir male or any human male knowing you are marked will have you."

"Oh, hell with the no! We'll see about that! I'm not his property." The anger rushed through her, and she stormed over to her trunk. She lifted the lid and removed her handbag and reached inside, then pulled out a small tube of concealer. Rose looked in the mirror and applied the makeup to Vaughn's handiwork. She turned back to Aileen. "Better?"

Aileen shook her head. "They are no longer visible to humans, but we can still see them, will always be able to see them."

If Rose had Vaughn Madoc in front of her right now, she'd castrate him. "Aileen, so help me, I'm going to wring your brother's neck the next time I see him."

Aileen covered her mouth and giggled.

"Who gave him the right to brand me?"

"You did."

"Only because I thought he was dying."

"Because you love him," Aileen whispered.

"Loved. Past tense."

"If you say so."

Rose wasn't going to argue with Aileen, not tonight, anyway. "Shall we go down for dinner? I think I'd like to meet these cousins of yours."

Rose hesitated before entering the drawing room. Music and laughter floated out from the room.

"Aileen, am I the only human here?"

"No. To be honest, there are more humans than dhampirs. Why do you ask?"

"Just curious as to how many will be staring at your brother's handiwork."

"Oh, Rose, you silly goose."

The door opened, and Royce smiled at them, offering an arm to each woman. "I'm a lucky man to have the two loveliest ladies on my arms." He led them into the room, nodding at his father and grandfather.

Aileen took her hand from Royce's arm. "Rose, shall we go and sit with the ladies? I want you to meet my sisters, Caitlin, and Victoria. They have informed me Ian feels terrible about how he acted."

Royce covered Rose's hand with his. "You may steal Rose away after I introduce her to the male members of our family."

"Very well, if you two will pardon me, then." Aileen bussed Royce's cheek before strolling to where his mother and Sara sat with several women.

"My lady." Royce offered her his arm and led her to where a group of five men stood.

If any of them looked at her throat, she would—Dang. She didn't know what she'd do. Trying to think of an idea, she looked at the men and groaned, seeing Philip Dorjan among the group. She quickly perused the other men's faces and recognized Royce's cousin, Glen MacPhee.

The men all stopped talking as she and Royce approached. Each man greeted her with a nod and smile, except Philip. He eyed her strangely as if something was wrong with her dress.

Royce squeezed her hand. "Mrs. Kelly, you already know Mr. Dorjan and Aileen's brother, Glen MacPhee. I would like to introduce you to three of my cousins." Royce motioned to three men. Aileen had been right. They were very handsome. Their bronze complexions and high cheekbones gave her the impression they were of Native American lineage. The two older men could pass as twins despite the difference in hair coloring, while the third was a boy of about fourteen. Royce first nodded to the man with salt and pepper hair and steel gray eyes. "Quaid Wolfe, his brothers." Royce turned to a gentleman with jet-black hair and amber eyes. "Quaid's older brother, Morgan Wolfe."

Odd. Shouldn't Royce have introduced the older brother first? She'd ask Aileen later.

"I'm Tristan Wolfe, Ma'am," the boy drawled, thrusting his hand at her.

Rose bit her lip to keep from giggling. She hadn't expected to hear a heavy southern accent. "A pleasure to meet you, sir." She stared into his honey gold eyes.

The oldest of the Wolfe brothers smacked Tristan hard on the back of the head. "Your manners, boy."

Philip rolled his eyes. "Americans," he muttered and sashayed away.

Glen bowed and offered his hand. "My dear Mrs. Kelly, a pleasure to see you again." He leaned close to her ear. "Please ignore Mr. Dorjan."

Smiling, she said, "I always do."

Glen laughed, then took her hand and raised it to his lips.

"Morgan, isn't she fetching?" Tristan whispered in a loud voice.

Royce glared at the young man. "Rose, you will have to forgive this young pup. He is seldom permitted out of his kennel, and thus, does not know how to behave around a lady."

Tristan's face reddened, and he lowered his golden eyes.

"Royce, you shouldn't be so hard on him," she said. "It's not every day I'm told I'm fetching."

Tristan's brother laughed and ruffled the boy's black hair.

Morgan smiled at her. "Do I detect a slight southern accent?"

"Yes," she said, "I'm from Georgia. Atlanta, Georgia."

"Mother would love to meet you," Quaid said. "She's from Georgia, as well. Dahlonega to be precise. Now our family lives in Texas. Tumbleweed, Texas." As he spoke, he perused her and his mouth pulled in almost a wolfish grin.

Rose scanned the room. "Is your mother here?"

Tristan met her gaze. "No, ma'am. She and Pop stayed home with our two younger brothers. Our mother is. . ." His face reddened, even his ears turned red this time.

"What the lad is trying to say is his mother is expecting," Royce whispered in her ear.

A butler entered and rang a bell. "Dinner is served."

Both Morgan and Quaid offered her their arms.

She sat between Royce and Tristan and across from Aileen.

"Mrs. Kelly, do you feel well enough to ride around the estate in the morning?" Royce asked.

"Yes. However, it's been a long time since I've ridden."

"Royce, do you still have that gray gelding?" Aileen asked. "He would be gentle enough for Rose."

"Yes we do, he's a favorite of Mum's. That gray would be perfect for our Rose."

~ ~ ~

Rose smoothed her hands down the dark green riding habit she wore and breathed in the crisp fall air. She felt wonderful. Coming here had been just what the doctor ordered. Rose strolled out into the early morning sunlight. She'd enjoyed herself last night. After dinner, the ladies retired to the drawing room while the men went off to smoke and have their port or brandy.

Rose smile grew as she remembered how welcome Royce's mother had made her feel. Rose especially liked Glen's mother and sisters, Caitlin, and Victoria. They had Rose laughing, telling her about Royce and Glen's antics as boys. Rose laughed so much last night she felt alive again. Laughter did indeed purge the soul.

Rose tilted her head back, relishing in the clear blue sky. It reminded her of Royce's eyes. They were the same color as his father and Sara's. Pale eyes must be a Dhampir trait.

"Good morning," Royce said, coming up beside her. "You look chipper."

"And good morning to you, Royce. I feel good." And she did. Coming here was what she needed. She followed him through the gate and toward the stables. As they crossed the courtyard, a large black dog ran toward them. As the dog drew closer, Rose realized it wasn't a dog at all but a young wolf.

"Royce." She jumped behind him.

The animal wagged his tail and sniffed her skirt.

"Is he your pet?"

Royce chuckled. "He is not a pet, but he will not bite."

She lowered her hand, palm side up.

The wolf sniffed her palm, then licked it.

189

Rose petted him. His thick black fur was smooth as silk. His legs appeared too long for his body. "Does he have a name?"

"Useless," Royce answered.

The wolf tilted his head and growled.

Rose jerked her hand away, but the wolf gently nuzzled her hand with his nose, encouraging her to pet him again. "I don't think he likes the name Useless, Royce."

"That's just jolly too bad." Royce looked at the creature. "All right, you can come with us, but behave yourself."

The wolf wagged his tail and followed them. Surprising enough, none of the horses seemed bothered by his presence.

She mounted the beautiful gray. Taking the reins, she nudged him forward. They rode across the pasture and through a grove of oak trees. Their brilliant colored leaves had already begun to litter the ground.

"Thank you, Royce."

"For what?"

"Bringing me here. I wouldn't have survived another day if you hadn't."

They pulled their horses to a stop on a ridge top, looking down at the estate. Bright sunlight danced on a lake to the left of the house, making the water shimmer like millions of diamonds covered the surface. The orange and red autumn colors of the trees made the view even more breathtaking.

"Rose, you would have survived, because you are a survivor." He looked at her, and his blue eyes seemed to smile. Royce dismounted, then helped her down. "I want you to know you have a friend in me."

"Right now I feel as if I need all the friends I can get."

Tenderly he lifted her chin, forcing her to meet his gaze. "You have more than friends here. You have people who love you. I love you, but you are not my mate, so you do not have to fear me coming to your bed."

She backed away. "Royce, please. I'm not looking for a rebound."

He shook his head. "I care about you and think of you, not as a dear friend, but as a sister. I know you are hurting and feel alone, but you are not. There are people here who love you as much as Aileen and Sara do. You have more family here, my dear than you realize."

The wolf barked and wagged his tail.

"I think this pup has taken a liking to you, as well."

"Honestly? Is his name Useless?" She patted the wolf's head.

Royce chuckled. "No, sometimes I refer to him as a half-wit.

"That isn't nice. He seems to be such an intelligent creature. I can't believe you have him as a pet."

"Intelligent—you bloody bastard!"

Shocked at Royce's outburst, she peered down at the animal and giggled. He was urinating on Royce's boot. "I don't think he liked being called half-witted," she said, trying to control her laughter.

Royce glared at the wolf, which she swore was grinning.

"He may not, but he will make an excellent rug for my room."

"You wouldn't dare."

Royce sighed, staring at his wet boot. "The thought is tempting." He looked pointedly at the wolf. "Just for this, Tristan, you will polish all of my boots or I will inform your grandfather, about the incident with the Headmaster."

The wolf lowered his head and whimpered.

She stared at the wolf. "Tristan? Tristan Wolfe?"

Royce laughed. "Yes, this is Tristan. He has two spirits, two forms, and the ability to shape-shift if you would. Shall we head back?"

They mounted and started down the ridge through a thicket of trees.

She watched Tristan pacing beside her mount. "Wolf. Wolves have a hierarchy, don't they? I mean they have an alpha. Is that why you introduced Quaid first before his older brother last night?" She angled her head to see Royce better.

"Beauty and brains." Royce laughed. "Yes. Quaid is the Alpha of their family when their mother is not with them. Their father is human."

"Wow. Can you change into a wolf?"

"No. And I cannot fly, like Vaughn, either. But I can shift through walls. Do you feel like trotting?" Royce glanced over at her.

Grinning, Rose urged her mount into a canter. "Of course, can you keep up?"

A shot rang out, spooking Rose's horse. He reared, then bolted through the trees.

Another shot pierced the air. Keeping a level head, she pulled back on the reins. Nothing. She wished she sat astride rather than sidesaddle.

The gray wove between the trees, scraping her arms against some of the lower branches, and tearing her dress.

She could hear the pounding of Royce's mount galloping behind her.

Rose pulled back on the reins, trying desperately to slow her mount. He jumped a creek. Surprisingly, she managed to stay on. Her horse stumbled, losing his footing as he attempted to run up the muddy bank, tossing Rose from his back. She landed hard on rocks, knocking the wind from her. When she opened her eyes, Royce was kneeling beside her. Tristan sat on his haunches next to her. His cold nose tickled her cheek.

Another shot struck a rock near her head.

Royce fell across her. "Stay down." He pinned Rose to the ground, preventing her from sitting.

"I think I landed on some rocks," she whispered.

"Hush, he may be close." After what seemed an eternity, Royce eased off of her. His smile seemed forced as he perused her. "Can you feel your legs?"

"Yes. I think I can even stand."

He gently helped her. "Is anything broken? Do you hurt anywhere?"

"Honestly, I think I only got the wind knocked out of me. I guess someone thought we were deer."

Royce's cold eyes searched the landscape. Without uttering a word, he glanced at the wolf. Tristan ran off in the direction of the shots.

"No one is permitted to hunt here, not even our servants." Royce brushed leaves from her hair.

Chapter Fourteen

Royce held Rose across his lap as they rode back to the estate. His arm gently circled her trim waist. Vaughn was a fool for not taking Rose as a mate. She was intelligent, beautiful, and brave. Hell, Vaughn was more than a fool. He was an imbecile to turn her away.

Royce scanned the horizon, searching for signs of Tristan. He'd sent him to find the culprit who shot at them. Perhaps Rose was right, and someone had been poaching and didn't know they were in the line of fire. But every nerve in his body told him otherwise. "Are you comfortable, Rose?"

"I'm fine. Do you think my horse will be all right?"

"That gray is probably already back in his stall."

"You know I could have walked," she said.

"I would be flogged by every man who witnessed me permitting you to do so. Besides, you sitting on my lap will make me the envy of every one of them." He winked at her. "Think what it will do for my reputation with the ladies. They will all think me a knight in shining armor."

"Instead of a wolf in sheep's clothing?"

"You have me confused with my cousins." He laughed.

"Oh." She shivered.

"Are you chilled?"

"No, a rabbit just hopped over my grave."

"We say a goose walked on ours." He stared across the lawn at one of those new-fangled automobiles sitting in front of the house. Rose had sensed Vaughn's presence. Their bond was stronger than his idiot brother had admitted. Royce had expected Vaughn to come after Rose, but not this soon. He must have immediately left once he discovered their departure. Royce chuckled. He would enjoy himself immensely.

~ ~ ~

Vaughn stepped from his automobile and pushed his driving goggles up. He was amazed at how short a time it took him to arrive. A year ago he wouldn't have spent his money on such a vehicle, but since Rose entered his life his opinion of modern technology had drastically changed. *She's here.* His Rose was here.

He looked up. His mood veered sharply to anger, seeing Rose riding double with Royce. His arms were around her waist. Vaughn perused Rose, and his fangs lengthened. She carried her riding hat in her hand, hair mussed, hanging about her shoulders. My God, he'd torn her dress. Damn Royce. The bastard had so little self-control.

Leaving his trunks, Vaughn crossed the grounds to where Royce and Rose had dismounted. "Would you explain the meaning of this?"

Rose's face flushed and her hazel eyes grew large. "Ah, Vaughn, nice wheels." She looked back at Royce. "I can honestly say, you know how to show a girl a good time. Thank you."

Royce glanced over Rose's head at Vaughn. "Explain what, old man?" The grin on Royce's face only added to Vaughn's anger.

"Don't play games with me, Royce. I'm not in the mood for it."

"Very well, if you insist, Rose and I went for a tumble in the meadow."

Vaughn punched Royce, knocking him to the ground. "Get up!"

"So you can hit me again? I think not." Royce rubbed his jaw. "Nice hook. I think I swallowed a tooth. Yes. You knocked a tooth lose, not that I'm worried.

Rose knelt beside Royce. She wiped the blood from his mouth with her finger before turning her stormy eyes to Vaughn. "It wasn't his fault I was thrown from my horse, you jackass. If you want to beat the crap out of someone, then find the bastard who shot at us."

"What?" Fear gripped Vaughn.

Royce chuckled. He took Rose's hand and licked his blood from her finger.

She snatched her hand from his grip. "I'm not a damn chafing dish."

Royce threw his head back and laughed. "If you were, I'd lick you all over."

"Royce!" Vaughn clenched his fists. "One more word and I will kill you."

Rose shoved to her feet. She glared down at Royce. "Everything with you is a joke." She then turned on Vaughn. "And you! You son-of-a-bitch. You have no right to question anything I do with anyone." Rose turned on her heels, and with long strides, marched toward the house.

Vaughn reined in his temper. He stared at Royce, still sitting on the ground. "What do you mean, shot at?"

"As in someone taking a gun and firing it in our direction."

"Was it an accident?"

Royce raised his eyebrow and pushed himself from the ground. "The first time, possibly. The second time, the shot came so near to my head I felt the heat of the bullet. The third time the bullet struck a rock near Rose's head after her horse had thrown her. So no, I do not think it was an accident."

"Bloody hell! Then the killer is here, and he is after Rose, not Sara. None of this makes sense. Why would he change his method of killing? He slashed his earlier victims. Now, he's shooting at Rose, and the other night he tried to run her over with a carriage. Why?"

Royce dusted the dirt from his clothes. "When you catch him, ask him."

"Royce," Vaughn warned. "Do not push me."

"Perhaps we are dealing with two people, your killer and the cad who is after *our* Rose. Does the lady have a past?"

Vaughn bent over and picked up his hat. A past? Rose was living in her past. "Rose doesn't have anything in her past that would put her life in jeopardy."

Royce stared at him and shook his head. "And you are not jealous, either?"

"My feelings for her are not important. What is important is her safety. I need to inform your father of this incident."

"By all means, go tell Father. Oh, Grandfather is here as well. He has taken a liking to Rose. He told me so last night. Right after Rose bested him, and all of us, at a game of Poker."

"Rose is a very likable woman."

"As our cousins from America have discovered. Even Tristan has taken to her. He joined us on our morning ride. So you see, my jealous friend, we were chaperoned."

Vaughn glared. "Oh, so where is this chaperon of yours?"

"I sent him to find the bounder with the gun."

"Send him to me when he returns." Vaughn turned and headed toward the house.

As he started up the steps, Aileen rushed toward him. He opened his arms, smiled, and looked into her eyes. "Have you missed me that much?"

Aileen's lips thinned, and she grabbed him by the hand, pulling him along with her. "You have done some foolish things," she muttered through clenched teeth. "But this, I hate you for."

He stopped and turned her to face him. "This isn't the first time I've knocked Royce on his bum, nor do I think it will be the last."

"I do not care if you punch Royce every bloody time you see him, but bringing David here? You knew Ian would be here."

He now understood his sister's anger. "Aileen, forgive me. I didn't think."

"It is quite obvious you did not. Do you hate love so much you would deprive me of my true mate?"

197

"David is the one who chose to accompany me. I didn't ask him to come."

"You could have stopped him."

"David is his own man. I think you are making much more of his being here than you need."

"The hell I am."

"Aileen! I see you have picked up on some of Rose's colorful language."

Aileen's eyes blazed with fury. "If anyone harms David, I will never speak to you or utter your name again. You will be dead to me." She stormed away.

He watched as she headed toward the stables. Ice gripped his heart. In less than a week he'd lost Rose and now risked losing his sister, as well.

~ ~ ~

When would this heartache end? Tears blurred her vision, and she stumbled upon entering the stable. She was tired of crying. It was past time to move on with her life. At home, in her time, she'd be at the gym, sparring with someone. But she wasn't home. Rose drew back her fist and punched a bale of hay.

Damn, that felt good! She punched it again and again. Her knuckles split, but she didn't care. She punched the bale repeatedly. Her fist hurt, her heart not as much. Blood covered her hands, but her tears had stopped. She didn't need Vaughn. Hell, she could get along very well on her own. Rose stared at the bloodied bale of hay, visualizing it as Vaughn's face. She threw another punch.

Strong hands rested on her shoulders, and she swung around. Royce clenched his jaw and pulled her into his embrace, holding her while she finally let go of her anger.

"He is not worth you bloodying your hands over," Royce said against her ear. After her sobs stopped, he forced her face up and wiped her eyes. "Better?" He asked.

Rose nodded. "Royce, I'm sorry. I just—I needed to let off some steam. How can Vaughn be such an ass? What is it with him? He doesn't want me, but good God, he acts like that," she motioned toward the front of the stables. "If he thinks I'm going to live like a nun, he can think again." Tears rolled down her cheeks again. "I didn't do anything wrong." She crumbled against Royce's chest.

"No. You did not do anything wrong, my dearest Rose. As you have pointed out, my brother is an ass, a very big ass." When her tears had stopped, he took her hands. "First let me heal your wounds." Royce tenderly kissed each bleeding knuckle before smiling again at her as he nonchalantly licked his lips. "Secondly, come with me."

Royce took her hand and led her out of the stables and across the yard. They entered the main house, but instead of taking her back to her room, he led her down a hallway, then stopped in front of a set of large oak doors. Royce pushed open the doors and pulled her into the room. "I believe you will find this room more suited for you to practice punching my brother than the stable. At least here you will not likely be discovered, as we seldom use it." He chuckled.

"Thank you." Rose surveyed the Victorian gymnasium. There was a punching bag, a pommel horse, and a set of still rings.

"May I ask, Rose, who taught you to box?"

"My grandfather, he was a lightweight in his time. Do you box?"

He grinned and tossed her a set of gloves. "So as not to raise any questions, I suggest you shut the doors and pull the blinds before you begin."

~ ~ ~

Vaughn gazed out into the darkness. Clouds shrouded the moon, making the night dreary and cold. His fingers wrapped around the glass he held. "Damn her to hell." He threw the glass against the far wall of his room. The crystal snifter shattered into tiny slivers, splashing its contents on the wall. All night Rose had entertained Royce and his American cousins. *What the bloody hell happened to her hands?* They were bruised and scraped. Royce should have protected her better on their ride.

Vaughn paced. He knew Rose was from the future, but it wasn't proper for a lady to play cards with men! Then she gulped Royce's glass of whiskey as if it were water!

Staring at the broken snifter, he shook his head. Wasn't this what he wanted, for her to find another love? Of course, it was. Why the hell, did she have to show an interest in Royce or one of the Wolfe brothers? She deserved better than any of them. Vaughn turned out his lamp, then slid between the bed sheets. Perhaps in the morning he would speak to her and tell her she deserved better. Much, much better.

~ ~ ~

The couple hugged each other in a lover's embrace, kissing, caressing, touching, and bringing each other to the peak of desire.

The scene changed and became hazy. Blood dripped from the bed hangings. The man cried out in anguish. What had he done? He stared at his bloodstained hands, then shoved his hand into his chest and tore out his heart.

Rose bolted up from her nightmare. She sucked in a deep breath trying to get her heart to slow. She was awake, but she could still see the image of the child standing in the open door. How could this be? She was awake. Did she see a ghost? Or was she going insane? No. Somehow she was experiencing Vaughn's dream. His nightmare.

Grabbing her robe, she slid out of bed. She didn't know how, but she knew Vaughn needed her. Carefully, she opened her door. No one was in the hall. Good. Barefooted, she ran to the west wing, to Vaughn. She couldn't explain how, but she knew where to find him. It was as if he pulled her to him.

Without knocking, Rose eased into his room. Faint moans coming from the large cherry bed tore at her heart. Vaughn thrashed about, his body glistening with sweat.

"Vaughn," she whispered. She grabbed his shoulder and shook him, trying to wake him. He threw his arm back and knocked her to the floor.

Vaughn cried out in agony and bolted upright. He gasped, rubbing his hands over his face.

Rose pulled herself up and sat on the bed behind him. "Do you want to talk about it?"

He jerked and turned. "What are you doing here?"

"You were having a nightmare."

"You happen to be in the bachelor's wing and walking by at the same time? Or were you visiting a new lover?"

His words were a physical slap, and she jumped from his bed. "No, actually I was enjoying a pleasant dream of my own when you decided to wreck my sleep. Mind shedding some light on this?"

"Not at all." Vaughn stared at the bedside lamp, and the light grew brighter. "Is that better?"

"That's not what I meant. Why am I sharing your dreams? Why was I still seeing your dream when I was fully awake?"

The color drained from his face. "I had not counted on this happening. Because I gave you my blood, we will share the same dream when we are near each other. After you leave with Sara, my dreams will not haunt you. Go back to bed."

"Not until you explain to me what I saw."

He left the bed, his muscular bare backside toward her. If she weren't so mad at Vaughn, she might enjoy ogling his fine muscular ass. Damn, the man was fine.

Vaughn picked up his robe, slid it on, then tied the sash, and strolled to the window. "What you saw was my sister's wedding night, or rather the morning after."

"But it wasn't your sister who was lying in the pool of blood. It was me. When you told me Christian killed your sister, I thought he took too much blood, but that wasn't how she died. Was it?"

He squared his shoulders and stepped out onto the balcony. "No, my sister was torn apart. Just as the killer I hunt

201

rips apart his victims. Katherine's throat was laid open and her entrails scattered over the bed. Christian lay on top of her. He'd torn his own heart from his chest moments before I entered. Too shocked to scream, I watched their bodies crumble to ash."

As she stared at Vaughn, everything became clear. "That's why you've been acting as you have. That's why you said those vicious things to me. You're afraid if we make love the same thing will happen to us."

He didn't answer her, just stood with his back to her.

"Am I right?" She waited. "Dammit, answer me."

"It does not matter if you are right or not. I have made my decision."

They had a chance! If only Vaughn listened to reason, their relationship would work. "I didn't know Christian, but I know you. I know your heart. Vaughn, you are a tender man. A caring man. You are not a killer, my love."

He threw his head back and laughed, mocking her as he faced her. "You know me? Oh, please, madam. Do not delude yourself. I'm as much a killer as Christian and the one I hunt."

"Liar! You're only saying that because you're afraid you'll hurt me."

He strode purposefully toward her, backing her up against the wall then trapping her between his arms. "Let me tell you how much of a liar I am. When we caught up with Dietrich and his men who murdered my parents, I. Killed. Them."

She balled her hands into fists, forcing herself not to look away. Her nails cut into her palms, forming small red crescents. "Things were different. They murdered your parents. You were carrying out justice."

"Justice? I punished them, and I enjoyed it. I relished gorging myself on their blood. I loved the feel of their hearts beating in the palm of my hand. I shoved my clawed hand into their chests. I wrapped my fingers around their beating hearts. Then, Rose, I slowly pulled their hearts from their bodies. I laughed as I held them up so they could see. I enjoyed watching the glimmer of life die in their eyes. Then I wagered how long it would take for their corpses to crumble to dust. When a gust of wind scattered their worthless ashes, I saw it as a sign from *Yeva*, of Our Creator removing their evil from me. You see, Rose, humans, can survive a hell of a lot of pain. Dhampirs can survive even more." He pushed her toward the door. "Get out."

All of her determination fled, leaving her cold. "You're not Christian," she said through clenched teeth.

"Keep telling yourself that. But remember, you're still alive. Katherine is not."

Rose jerked the door opened and walked away from Vaughn. This was the last time she would allow him to hurt her. The last time she would allow herself to be anywhere near him.

~ ~ ~

Vaughn glared at his empty doorway. With her back straight, Rose left the room. She didn't falter or look back. He flopped on his bed, pulling the sheets over his shoulders. In the morning, he would speak to Alan. Rose should remain here. She would be safe here. Then once the killer was apprehended, Rose and Sara could go on to Wales. However, the thought of having Rose and Royce under the same roof ate at his gut. Perhaps he could persuade Royce to return to London and aid in the investigation. Vaughn rolled to his back, folded his arms behind his head, and waited for sleep to take him.

Sleep eluded him.

He spent hours thinking of Rose. His mind should have been on the killer. She distracted him from the moment she entered his life. It had been a mistake for him coming here. His place was in London with his mind on the case. He opened his pocket watch. At this hour of the morning, Vaughn knew he would find Alan in his study.

Vaughn paused at the door. He hated the room. The reprimand room from his youth. Even now, the thought still caught him of the many times he was summoned to this room.

As a child, he'd looked upon the man who rescued him as a god. Alan had done everything to show Vaughn love, trust, and respect. He shook his head. As a child, he'd always seemed to make a mess of things, and Alan always forgave him. Vaughn drew in a deep breath and knocked on the door. He'd mucked it up good this time.

"Enter," Alan's voice boomed from the other side.

He looked up from his desk as Vaughn strode into the room. "I understand you are leaving today. You just arrived."

"I must return to London."

"Whether you realize this or not, your sudden change of plans has hurt Emma deeply."

Vaughn had hurt many people lately. "It is not my intention to hurt her, but it would be for the best if I take my leave."

"I know you did not intentionally set out to hurt her, but Emma considers you our son. She was joyous when she saw you, and now you are leaving."

"I must."

"I called for this gathering to celebrate my beloved's birthday." Alan's tone was reminiscent of past lectures. "Will you be returning in the next fortnight for her ball, at least?"

"It pains me to have to leave so soon, but even more so the fact I find it very doubtful I will be able to return for the ball. I am sorry."

"Yesterday when you arrived you informed me the killer might be among us. I do not understand what could be more important than catching him. Will you explain your sudden change of plans? Or is this some red herring of yours to throw the killer off guard?"

"I want nothing more than to catch this monster. However, I fear my very presence will endanger someone's life."

Vaughn sank into the burgundy leather chair in front of Alan's desk and glanced around the room. The balcony doors were opened, allowing the sweet smell of tobacco to fill the air. He recognized the smell of his Grandfather's pipe.

"I think there is more to your leaving than you are telling Alan and *yourself*," Mishenka said, as he strolled in from the balcony.

"Grandfather, it is very complicated."

Alan cleared his throat, causing Vaughn to glance up at him. Alan's eyes seemed almost compassionate. "Does your leaving have anything to do with Rose?"

Vaughn briefly closed his eyes, trying to shut out the ache in his heart. "It has everything to do with her."

Alan nodded. He leaned back in his chair and looked up at the ceiling. "I see. Royce told me your nightmares have returned. He also informed me about the sudden change in your manner, as well as everything else that has taken place concerning Rose and yourself." Alan steepled his fingers and narrowed his eyes. "Including the theater incident."

"Royce has no right discussing my sleep or my affairs."

"He does because you are his brother. Despite the fact you do not carry my name, you are a part of this family. Is Rose your mate?"

"A mate I will never claim."

Alan's eyes blazed with fire, and his lips thinned. "I am sorry to hear this."

Mishenka withdrew his pipe. He stared into its bowl. "A pity. I liked Rose. She has an aura of strength about her that would have made an excellent addition to our family. All of the children she bore would have been strong-willed." He tsked, shaking his head. "I was so hoping for another game of cards with her."

Vaughn glanced at his grandfather, then to Alan's furious stare. He did not want to discuss Rose, not now, not ever. He'd made his decision. "Grandfather, as hard as it is for me, in my heart I know it's for the best."

Mishenka shook his head. "Best for whom? By not taking her as your mate you have made her an outcast. You have marked her. None of our kind will have her. No human male in our circle would dare risk your wrath. You have condemned her to a life of a spinster. You have given her your blood, but you do not want her living under your roof. She has to stay with the family. What do you propose to do with her?"

"I was hoping Rose could live with you and Sara."

Mishenka shook his pipe at Vaughn. "Saddling her to us should prove to be an exciting life for Rose. Why do you not want her as your mate? Or does she not want you?"

"It's my love for her that will not let me embrace her."

"For the love of God!" Alan cracked his knuckles. "Why?"

"I fear of killing her like Christian did Katherine."

Mishenka dropped his pipe. "Tell him, Alan. Tell him the truth about Christian, about his fits." He mumbled something in the old language as he leaned over to retrieve his pipe.

"His fits?" Vaughn asked. He'd never seen Christian in the throes of spasms.

Alan sighed. "Christian served under me at the Battle of Ramillies. During the battle, Christian suffered a severe head wound. The humans in our battalion thought him dead. By the time I found him and was able to heal him, I fear the damage to his mind had become irreversible. Once he returned home, Christian would have fits of uncontrolled rage. He was not the man he once was. I tried to prevent the marriage between Christian and your sister until Christian had completely healed. Your father would not see, not listen. I failed."

"You think Christian's wounds caused him to kill Katherine?" Vaughn stared across at Alan. "Why am I only hearing of this tale now?"

"I did not believe the past was worth dredging up. You already had so much taken from you. You were ten when you lost your sister and Christian. Then you lost your parents four years later. I did not wish to taint your good memories. Christian wasn't the same man he'd been before he went to battle. I told your sister this, but she would not listen. She called me a liar and insisted Christian would not harm her. Your parents would not listen."

Vaughn balled his fists. His nails cut deep crescents into his palms. "So, now you blame my parents?"

Alan leaned his head against the back of his chair. "No, I blame myself. I have always blamed myself for not finding Christian sooner."

"We are a cursed lot," Mishenka said. He relit his pipe and took several long puffs. "We are driven by a primal force to find our one true mate. When we do find that person, we desire to keep them safe, to bear children with them. Many of our kind never find that individual.

Some of us find them too late. Your sister believed the mate bond between her and Christian would prevail."

Vaughn stared out the window. "When Rose gave me her blood, it tasted so sweet. It was like nothing I had tasted before. Better than the finest wine. I wanted to consume every drop. I could not stop myself from gorging. Only after she slumped against me did I realize what I was doing. She nearly died in my arms, because she wanted to save me." He met Alan's gaze. "I will not risk her life, again."

Alan slammed his fist on his desk. "You have not listened to a word I have said. You have not listened to a word you've said! Damn it to hell, Vaughn, you are not Christian. You will not harm Rose. What you experienced were your mating instincts." Alan cast his eyes upward. "Ah *Yeva*, give me strength."

"Christian was my sister's true mate as Rose is mine. Katherine is dead."

Alan's eyes blazed. "Vaughn—"

Mishenka held up his hand. "No, son, Vaughn is right. He knows better than we do what is best for him and this woman." Mishenka stood. He stretched then strolled over to the bookcases. After searching, he pulled an ancient tome from the shelf and opened it. "Vaughn, do you know why we made

207

these laws that have strictly governed our people for thousands of years?"

Vaughn drummed his finger on the chair arm. Mishenka had always deeply loved all of his grandchildren, even ones not of his blood, he deserved all of Vaughn's respect. But what the bloody hell did archaic laws have to do with what they were discussing at this moment? "Yes, Grandfather, the laws were written after the witch-hunts nearly destroyed us."

"We once numbered several thousand. Now we are but a few hundred." His lips thinned, and his eyes took on a dark glow. "A scorned woman can be more dangerous than the rogue you hunt. She could expose us all."

"Rose would not betray the family." Vaughn sighed. He knew Rose. She wasn't a vindictive person.

Mishenka slammed the tome closed. "Never-the-less, heartache can turn to anger, then to revenge. I will not risk the safety of our family on an outsider, especially one who is doomed to live a loveless life. If you do not want her, kill her and be done with this issue."

Vaughn bolted to his feet. "What!"

Alan stood. He walked around to the front of his desk and leaned against it. "Father, I am certain we do not have to take such drastic measures, so soon. Perhaps we can deal with this issue in a month or two, after Hogmanay."

Mishenka shook his head. "No. The quicker this problem is resolved, the better."

Alan nodded. "Father, as always, you are correct."

"My decision is final." Mishenka turned back to Vaughn. "You created this situation. I expect you to see to it. If you cannot, I will."

Vaughn's blood boiled. He could not believe what he was hearing. How could Mishenka even consider harming Rose? Vaughn bared his fangs. His attention darted back and forth between Alan and Mishenka. "I will never harm Rose. If you try, I will fight you both, to the death."

Mishenka chuckled and clasped Vaughn's arms. "Do you hear yourself, now? You love Rose so much you would challenge Alan and me. You would consider fighting me, an ancient, knowing how easily I can kill you."

He stared into Mishenka's eyes. "I would gladly give my life for hers."

Alan clasped Vaughn on the shoulders. "Son, how could you believe *you* would harm Rose when you give her your child? Vaughn, you could not. Your fear is understandable, knowing what you saw as a lad, but illogical."

Mishenka laughed. "Oh, my boy, if you were going to kill Rose, you would have the night she first gave you her blood. Instead, you stopped feeding." He shook his head. "All this heartache has been for not."

The truth washed over Vaughn in waves. He had stopped that night. The moment Rose slumped against him, he had stopped taking from her. He'd cradled her in his arms and given her his blood. Oh what an ass he was. She'd come to him and told him she loved him, and he, like an ass, ruthlessly hurt her. Even as horrid as his actions had been last night, Rose had not feared him. "I have been a bloody ass. Rose told me I was a fool. I pray she will forgive me."

He sighed and stepped out onto the balcony. The sunlight stung, and he squinted. He stepped back into the shade. How he wished he had those marvelous glasses Rose had given him. Like an ass, he'd broken them in a fit of rage.

Because of his enormous size, women feared him. But not his Rose. She thought him desirable. *Oh, how much of a fool he'd been.* Last night when he'd desperately needed her, she came to him. Why hadn't he listened to her? Why had he acted like a bloody ass and shoved her from his room? He stared up at the sky. "*Yeva*, I pray I have not shoved Rose from my life."

The cheerful sound of laughter rang in his ears, drawing him into the sun. Aileen was playing croquette on the lawn with Rose and Tristan. Beelzebub chased merrily after the balls.

209

Vaughn stepped closer to the rail. From this distance, he could see the smile on Rose's lips. It held as much life as one painted on a doll. Even the antics of that fiendish cat could not rekindle the slightest flicker of joy in her. Vaughn turned away. Because of his foolishness, he'd drained the life from Rose. He *was* a vampire.

He wiped his eyes. The bright sun was making them water.

Only he could undo the harmful words he had spoken. By George, that was what he would do. He would go to Rose and tell her she was right. He would explain everything to her, and she would understand. Knowing Rose as he did, she would probably laugh, and find some humor in all of this.

Vaughn marched through the study. "Alan, you may inform Emma I will be staying for the remaining festivities, as well as for her ball."

Alan nodded. He grinned and placed his hand on Vaughn's shoulder. "I will give you the same advice I was given once by my father. Groveling would not be inappropriate at this moment."

~ ~ ~

Rose shivered as a familiar chill ran down her spine. Vaughn must be near. She looked up and moaned, seeing him marching directly toward her.

She took in his attire and wanted to snicker. Despite the fact, he looked like a golf caddie in turtleneck, knickers, and argyle socks, his stone expression told her she was in for another fight. He could be such a demented asshole.

"Aileen, Tristan, I'm calling it quits."

"Why? You're winning, Rose?" Tristan asked.

"Because sometimes it's best to flee than fight." She handed him her mallet.

"Rose," Vaughn called.

She glanced at him.

"A word with you, please."

Holding her head high, she stared directly into his eyes, then gave him her back and marched away.

~ ~ ~

Vaughn stopped next to Aileen. How could Rose walk away from him? He wanted to talk, to apologize, and to ask for her forgiveness. "Did you see that? Rose cut me."

Aileen tapped her ball, sending it through the wicket and striking the peg. "I believe I just won, Tristan."

"Only because Rose walked away."

Vaughn touched his sister's elbow. "Aileen, did you hear me?"

"Do you hear the buzzing of an annoying gnat, Aileen," the impish pup dared to ask.

"Aileen," Vaughn tried to keep the hurt and anger from his voice.

"Yes, Vaughn, I heard you. Rose cut you, and she did it quite well, I dare say." Aileen shoved her mallet at him, turned on her heels, and with back straight, she too, marched away.

He looked after Rose. He had succeeded. She hated him.

Chapter Fifteen

A bloody fortnight, for two weeks he'd tried to speak to Rose. Vaughn shivered, staring out the balcony doors. The sun would be up in a few hours. The ball tomorrow for Emma would climax the month-long party. Then most of the guest would leave. Hopefully, the Wolfe brothers would be among them. He pulled the covers over his shoulder. Perhaps once the house cleared of guests, he'd have a better chance to speak with Rose. He had hoped she would be on his arm at the ball. Where in the devil did she always disappear? Vaughn punched his pillow. Damn Royce, damn Glen and damn those cursed Wolfes! If they did not stop sniffing around her skirt hem, Alan would have three wolf skin rugs for his study.

"Royce, are you up?"

Vaughn glared at the door. What the devil was Tristan doing here at this hour of the morning?

"Lower your voice," Royce whispered. "Do you want to wake up Vaughn? Now, go tell Rose I'll meet her in the gymnasium."

Vaughn slid from the bed, then quietly crossed the room. He slowly opened the door, careful not to make a sound and peered out into the hall. Royce tiptoed toward the rear staircase. Vaughn closed his door. If he took the passageways, no one would see him. Though, he shouldn't spy on Rose. Hell, he wouldn't be spying on her. He'd be ensuring her safety.

He quickly dressed. Perhaps this would be his chance to speak with her. If he were lucky, she would forgive him for all the pain he has caused her. Tonight she'd be sharing his bed. He smiled at the thought.

Quickly and quietly, Vaughn made his way toward the gymnasium, the stopped and glared at the mangy dog. Across the door entrance, Quaid lay in his wolf form, guarding whatever was going on inside. The large gray wolf lifted his head and sniffed the air, then snarled. Vaughn glared at Quaid. A mangy mutt would not keep him from finding out what was going on in there.

Vaughn stepped back, ran his hand along the wall. He pushed open the hidden panel. He knew every concealed priest hole and passageway in this old pile of stones. Cobwebs no longer filled the inside of the dark passage, making it obvious someone had used this priest hole recently. He moved quickly through the passage until he came to another hidden door. Cautious, he pushed on the panel just enough to see movement in the room.

"Ah, there's my Rosie." Royce grinned, dressed in boxing shorts and white undershirt. "Have you forgiven me for besting you last night at cards?"

Vaughn watched as Rose came into view. She wore dark gray athletic bloomers and a dark blouse. She'd pulled her hair back into what his sister referred to as a ponytail.

"You cheat, and you're a man-whore, but I still love you." She blew Royce a kiss. She might as well have plunged a knife to Vaughn's chest and twisted the blade. "Give me a minute to stretch before we start." Rose began bending her body in ways God did not mean for it to bend.

"You know, love, I will miss watching how you move in the morning." Royce stared in Vaughn's direction. "I may have to make plans to visit you and Sara often on your travels. Perhaps even accompany you on a few."

She stopped her unnatural contortion and looked up at Royce. "Oh, I would love that. Thank you for this. It has made it so much easier for me to get through these past two weeks. I owe you."

"No, my sweet Rosie, you do not owe me anything."

"You ready?"

Royce nodded. "Tristan, get her gloves."

"No gloves, not today." Rose grinned. "No shoes, either."

Royce raised his eyebrow.

Rose vanished from sight. When she returned, she was in her stocking feet, but it appeared she'd wrapped her hands as well as her feet in bandages. What was she about?

Vaughn pushed open the panel more to get a better view.

Royce stepped to the punching bag. He pressed his body against it firmly. "Any time, Rosie."

"You know I hate that." Rose punched the bag, keeping her shoulder level. Vaughn watched as she punched the bag repeatedly, amazed at her perfect form. Rose mentioned she had taken self-defense classes. The only reason she'd been able to toss him to the ground. But he had not predicted she could box. Vaughn leaned against the wall, watching. It would be more enjoyable if he witnessed Rose accidentally missing the bag and punching Royce.

"Ah, come on Rosie," Royce jeered. "You hit like a girl."

"But a pretty one at that," Tristan added.

"Damn straight." Rose jumped and kicked the bag, sending Royce stumbling back and falling on his rear. "What happened Royce? Did a girl knock you on your arse?"

Sweat ran down Rose's face. She paused to wipe her brow. Royce stepped from behind the bag, drew back his fist, and lunged at Rose.

Vaughn shoved on the panel. A hand grabbed his arm, stilling him. He turned.

"If she knew you were here you would lose her forever." Emma smiled up at him. "Be still, my son. Your Rose is a warrior. You should be proud of her."

Vaughn turned back, only to see Royce on his backside, again. He glared up at Rose.

"Think you cracked a rib that time, Rosie."

"Boo-yeah! Girl power one, vamp power zip." She swiveled her hips, then motioned to Royce with both her hands for him to come to her.

Royce leaped to his feet. He threw another punch at Rose. Who slipped to her left, allowing Royce's incoming blow to pass harmlessly next to her head. Rose threw an uppercut, connecting to Royce's chin. Without hesitation, she jumped and kicked Royce squarely in the chest.

Royce stumbled back. "So, that's how you're going to play today. Very well." Royce faded, vanishing into air, only to reappear and grab her from behind. He'd wrapped his arms tightly around her. "Now, what are you going to do?"

Rose threw her arms down and away from her body, breaking Royce's hold on her. She spun around and threw a right hook, only to have Royce block her punch. Rose followed through with a left jab that connected with Royce's ribs. Their sparring continued until the first rays of light broke through the gymnasium windows. Through it all, Vaughn marveled at the grace and beauty of Rose's movements. Watching her was like watching a graceful dancer.

Royce held up his hand, as he pressed his other hand to his side. After a few moments, he sat on the floor. Royce had changed into his Dhamphic form, eyes glowing red, fangs fully extended and his nails had clawed. Even his horns had emerged. He reached up and pulled Rose to the floor. "There is no thinking about it. I know you cracked a rib today." He pressed his hand to his side again.

"Did not," Rose huffed, trying to catch her breath, "wuss."

Tristan came into view. He handed Rose and Royce each a towel, then each a glass of water. "Know, Royce, if we bobbed Rose's hair and bound her, ah, woman parts. I bet she could fight in some real bouts."

Royce shook his head. The man laughed as he swept his leg, knocking Tristan to the ground. "Tee, they are called breasts—not woman parts. And no sane man would want to bind them." Royce winked at Rose, then ruffled Tristan's hair. A wicked glint shimmered in Royce's eyes. "I know what I will do for you on your sixteenth birthday." Royce grinned even wider. "Go on. Escort our lady to her room."

215

Tristan stood and offered his hand to Rose, then pulled her to her feet. "We can go back through the priest hole. No one sees us."

"Not today," Royce said. He cast his glare toward Vaughn. "I fear there may be a rat in the walls. A very large, ugly, plague-carrying rat."

Rose stood and looped her arm with Tristan's. "We'll see you later, Royce, after I freshen up my woman parts." She laughed. Loudly and not at all ladylike.

The boy's ears were redder than Vaughn thought possible.

When Rose vanished from sight, Vaughn faced Emma. "You've known about this, and you permitted it?"

"Yes, and I permitted it because Rose needed something to get her mind off her heartache." Emma patted his chest. "I'd rather for Rose to take her frustrations out on Royce than take a battle ax to you." She strolled back through the dark passageway.

Royce wiped his face with the towel he'd draped around his neck. "Are you going to stay in the shadows or are you going to join me?"

Vaughn pushed open the panel and entered the gymnasium. "I've never known you to rise so early."

Royce pushed from the floor. "I haven't been to bed yet. After the card game last night, for which I must praise Rose, she is an excellent card player, I had a very pleasurable encounter with two charming ladies." He grinned, leaning against the pommel horse. "But enough about my pleasures, I have a request of you, old man."

Vaughn studied Royce, he seldom asked for favors. He usually manipulated people to get what he wanted. "This must be serious. What is it?"

"Leave Rose alone. For the past fortnight, you have hounded her unmercifully. At first, it was easy to over-look your action, because in a way I hoped you would come to your senses. But this morning you lowered yourself to my level, spying on Rose like this. What were you hoping to see, Vaughn, something else you could use to hurt her with, or, perhaps you expected to catch Rose and me in a lover's embrace?"

"No, that's not why I followed you."

Royce laughed. "No? Come now, Vaughn. Every night you've switched the place cards at supper. On Guy Fawkes Night when we gathered around the bonfire, I laughed at your antics. You seemed like a lovesick lad. But last night I realized the only purpose for your actions the past fortnight has been to taunt and punish Rose. And for what? Hmm? She did what you wanted her to do. She got on with her life, leaving you alone."

"Then it was you who rearranged the place cards every night, sitting Mrs. Westmoreland next to me. I thought as much. Royce, all I have been trying to do is speak to Rose."

"Vaughn, are you not tired of hurting her? You are more sadistic than that demon cat of yours. Do you not know the pain you are causing her? My God, man, can you not see her anguish?"

Vaughn leaned against the pommel horse beside Royce. "I do care. I have been trying to speak with her for the past two weeks, to beg her forgiveness, but you and the bloody Wolfes have guarded her as if she were the Crown Jewels." As much as it pained him to admit it, he needed Royce's help. "You must plead my case to her. Tell Rose I need to speak with her. Convince her."

Royce shook his head. "No! I refuse. You have put her through enough hell."

"Don't you think I realize how much I've hurt her? Dammit, Royce, I'm begging you for your help."

Royce narrowed his eyes and glared. "I'm curious as to why you have yet to inquire about all this." He made a swiping motion with his hand."

Vaughn sighed. He honestly did not care at the moment why Royce and Rose were sparring. All Vaughn cared about was getting Rose to forgive him and welcome him back into her arms. "Very well, Royce, why were you and Rose sparring?"

"The day when you arrived in your automobile I went to see if the gray Rose had ridden returned. Instead, I found Rose punching a bale of hay. I watched until her fist bled. I thought this would be a better solution."

That explained her hands. Oh, God, what had he done? Vaughn knew how much he'd hurt Rose. He saw it every time he looked at her bleak eyes or the forced smile on her lips. "I have to make her understand. I love her, Royce. I know if I could get her alone she would listen to me."

Royce slid down to the floor and drew his knees toward him. "She may not, my friend. Two nights ago, I found her in the garden, holding that cursed cat of yours. She was crying. I've caught her weeping a lot lately. According to Aileen, Rose has not been eating. When I first met her, Rose did not strike me as a woman who wept easily. You, old man, have extinguished her fire. Quaid, Morgan, and I," Royce threw his head back, laughing. "Even Tristan have simply been trying to fan that fire back to life. I fear there is no spark left."

Vaughn's knees buckled under the weight of his guilt. "I caused this," he whispered. He'd purposely hurt Rose to drive her from him. It may be impossible to win her back. "We dream shared the first night I arrived here. Rose came to my room. I told her I was as much a killer as the man I hunt." He eased down into the floor next to Royce. "I spoke with Alan and Mishenka. Because I refused to mate Rose, they ordered me to kill her. I have mucked up royally. I have to make things right."

Royce rubbed his hands over his face and groaned. "I knew about the dream sharing. I followed Rose from your room." Royce cast his eyes up and steepled his fingers, so much like his father. "This will not be easy for you. Vaughn, you first told Rose you might kill her if you claim her. Now you tell me, Grandfather ordered you to kill her because you would not claim her. To add to this, your killer wants to kill her, too. Hmm." Royce tilted his head, looking at Vaughn. "Are Tristan and I the only ones who do not want her dead? Make that, Tristan, his brothers, Glen, and I."

Vaughn rested his head against the pommel horse and closed his eyes. He'd made such a mess of things. "Mishenka is as shrewd as he is old, which means he's bloody brilliant. Grandfather only said what he did to make me realize how much of a fool I have been. I pray Rose will forgive me."

"What do you plan to tell her?" Royce asked.

"That I love her."

"Do you still fear harming her?"

"Yes and no. At times, I think I have gone daft. I dream of having her in my bed for all time then the dreams turn to nightmares. Bloody hell, Royce what am I to do?"

"The best laid schemes of mice and men. Go often askew. And leave us nothing but grief and pain, for promised joy! So wrote Robert Burns," Royce said, shaking his head sadly. "You have truly mucked things, you know."

"I know. I know." Vaughn sighed. Never had he been so frustrated. The Creator had blessed him with a mate who was well read, intelligent, and more beautiful than any woman he'd ever seen. How could he have turned her away when she looked at him in his monstrous form and told him she loved him?

He pushed himself from the floor, then offered his hand to Royce, helping him to his feet. "My pride be damned. Today at lunch, I will speak to Rose and make her understand. I will make her listen to me, even if I have to throw her over my shoulder and carry her off somewhere secluded. And if you or your flea-bitten cohorts interfere I will draw and quarter the lot of you." *Dear Yeva, please let Rose forgive me.*

Royce followed, laughing. "And when she bashes you, I promise not to laugh too loudly."

~ ~ ~

Rose sat at the vanity, studying Aileen's expression in the reflection. Her mouth twisted and her brows furrowed.

"Rose how on earth, did you receive those hideous bruises? Did that gray throw you again?"

Rose turned around to face Aileen and winced. Perhaps Royce got in a few more punches than she'd thought. "Aileen, you worry worse than a mother hen." Rose held out her arms. "See, my bruises are already faded, and besides, my long sleeves will cover any still visible."

"It's not your bruises that worry me, Rose. In the past weeks, you have lost so much weight all of the dresses *Babushka* ordered for you now require altering. Promise me you will eat today."

"I promise. Now, which skirt should I wear for the picnic?" Rose smiled. It was already the second week of November.

"I think the light brown would be perfect. Now, hurry, or we will be the last ones to arrive."

Rose quickly finished dressing with Molly's help and Aileen's critical eye. Soon Rose and Aileen strolled out onto the lawn where Emma had decided to have an autumn lunch instead of dining indoors. Quilts and blankets covered the lawn, and a long buffet was set up under the veranda. The table was laden with carved ham, apples, freshly baked bread, and cheeses of every description, along with other delightful foods. To drink there were hot ciders, tea, of course, and several types of wine. Pastries, including cakes, tarts, cobblers, and bread puddings, covered the last table. Rose glanced up at the bright crystal blue sky. A cool breeze blew a faint scent of burning pine.

Aileen handed Rose a plate. "You promised," she whispered.

"Promised what?" Royce asked.

Rose turned. "Where did you come from?"

"Well, on my father and mum's wedding night—"

"That's not what I meant." She punched his arm.

Royce's eyes crinkled with his devilish grin. "I've been standing here while you gawked at today's offerings. Now, what are we promising? I hope it's naughty."

"Rose promised me she'd eat something." Aileen stabbed a slice of ham and placed it on Rose's plate. "Look at her, Royce, she's practically wasting away before our very eyes."

"Honestly, Aileen, I've not lost that much weight."

Royce's eyes narrowed as he took in her appearance from head to feet then slowly back to her face. "Yes, you have Rose. I've noticed you were thinner but had not noticed just how much weight you have lost before now." He grinned at Aileen. "But do not worry about our Mrs. Kelly, for today we shall fatten her up." Royce then reached across the table, grabbed two glasses, then took a bottle of wine from the wine steward's hand. He studied the label. "Hmm, father brought out the good wine." Royce then tucked another two bottles under his arm.

Rose finished preparing her plate, noticing a few items Aileen had placed there. "Where shall we sit?" She glanced at Aileen, who was scouring the grounds.

Royce strolled back to them, this time carrying a loaf of bread and a small block of cheese. "Ladies, if you'll follow me, we have a blanket under the oak, close enough to all to be considered sociable, far enough away to be alone."

Rose and Aileen followed Royce to where Glen, Tristan, and his brothers stood. They each offered greetings, then Tristan took Rose's plate as Royce helped her to the blanket. Quaid and Morgan helped Aileen. Glen handed Rose a glass of wine, then one for Aileen while Royce cut a chunk of cheese from the block. He then offered it to Rose.

Rose took the piece of cheese, staring at the knife Royce held. The knife looked vaguely familiar to her. A cold shiver ran down her back. She looked up spying Vaughn strolling toward them.

"May I join you?" Vaughn asked. "Please."

Royce's hand gently circled her wrist, then slid to her hand. He laced his fingers with hers. "The decision is up to Rose."

She placed the cheese on her plate and nudged it away. Rose considered the people with her. They were Vaughn's friends and family long before she'd arrived. It was selfish of her to keep him from their company. And besides, she wasn't hungry, anyway. "By all means, Mr. Madoc, please join them. I'll leave." She moved to stand, but Royce held her firm.

"Not until you have eaten," Royce whispered in her ear.

Glen glared up at Vaughn. "Be warned."

Vaughn gave a quick nod and eased down between Royce and Tristan.

Royce grabbed Vaughn by the wrist. "We have decided to form a conspiracy to get our dear Mrs. Kelly to eat. You see, ole man, she has lost a great deal of weight these last couple of weeks. So much so, Mum's seamstress has worked late in the night with the alterations."

Giving a quick nod, Vaughn took the knife from Royce. "I wondered what happened to this."

"Apologies, I've meant to return it.

"Liar." Vaughn quartered an apple, then placed the slices on Rose's plate.

Tristan handed her a linen napkin. "You know, Rosie, what would taste really good, a nice big juicy piece of deep-fried chicken, and buttermilk biscuits, and white gravy. But this ham is delicious, too. Don't you think, Rosie?"

"Yes, it is." Rose stared at her plate. Just being here with Vaughn was like lemon juice on a cut. She should leave. Perhaps if she ate a little, they would let her leave. She picked up the piece of cheese and popped a small chunk into her mouth. The cheese was so soft and creamy and tasted so good she had to have another bite.

Royce took a drink from the bottle of wine, then passed it to Vaughn. "Quaid, I've meant to ask you and Morgan if you suffered any damage from that big storm that hit Galveston in September."

"We had a lot of wind and rain, but where we live the storm just scooted to the east of us. Damn shame, Pop said they estimate between six and eight thousand dead. Morgan was lucky. He'd left Galveston the day before it hit."

Morgan nodded. "By the time I left on the afternoon of the 7th, I could see huge swells in the Gulf, and ominous black storm clouds dominated the northeastern sky. If you watched the horizon, now and then you could see flashes of lightning." Morgan took the wine bottle from Vaughn, tilted it back, then looked at it before handing it to Quaid. "They can lay telegraph cables across the floor of the Atlantic you'd think they'd be able to predict storms better."

Rose reached over and touched Morgan's arm. "They will someday. I know it."

Vaughn cleared his throat. "Well, ladies and gentlemen, I, for one, am excited about what our new century will bring. Just look at the inventions and advancements we've seen in our lifetime already."

Aileen handed Royce her wine glass. "Well, all I care about is the right to vote." She looked at her empty glass, then shook it in front of Royce. "Do we have more?"

Royce searched around the blanket they sat. "There is no way we finished three bottles. I only opened one." He frowned staring at the three empty wine bottles behind Vaughn, then glared at him. "Wine is a mocker, my friend. Wine is a mocker."

Vaughn arched his platinum eyebrow and frowned.

Philip Dorjan sauntered up then sat down so close to Aileen his knees brushed against hers. She scooted closer to Rose. "Why do you want to vote, Aileen?"

Glen glared across at Philip. "Please, Philip, join us, by all means."

The other gentlemen snickered.

223

Aileen scooted even closer to Rose, then turned and faced Philip. "Because decisions are made in parliament that I would like a voice in deciding." Her eyes glowed.

Morgan and Quaid stood. They nodded to Rose and Aileen. "Ladies, if you will excuse us. Tristan, are you coming?"

"I think I'll stay," he slurred his words.

Rose knew Royce shouldn't have allowed the boy to drink with them, but apparently, there was no age limit at this time. Still, Tristan was a boy even if he thought himself as old as Royce.

Glen pushed from the ground. "Ladies." He nodded toward Aileen and Rose before he jogged after Morgan and Quaid.

"Vaughn, Royce, what do you think about this silliness, women's suffrage?" Philip asked. "Mark my words," he continued. "It will mean the downfall of the Empire if women get to vote."

Vaughn shrugged. "Women deserve the right to vote. Why should all the blame for putting imbeciles in office only be shouldered by men?"

Philip glared at Vaughn then at Royce. "What do you have to say on the matter?"

Royce looked up and grinned. "Father, you brought us another bottle, care to join us?"

Alan leaned against the oak. "Rose, correct me if I am wrong, but don't women in some U.S. territories already have the right to vote?"

Nothing like being put on the spot. She turned to see Alan better, then racked her brain, remembering her history. "Mostly in the western states, I'm not completely sure which ones. Quaid and Morgan would know for sure. What I don't understand, is this great empire is ruled by a woman, possibly the greatest monarch so far, and yet women here cannot vote. It doesn't make much sense to me."

Alan nodded. "A very good question, sadly, Her Royal Highness does not feel women are equal to men."

Aileen turned her face up, smiling at Alan. "Do you think someday we will vote?"

"Perhaps sooner than any of us know," Alan replied.

Philip scoffed. "Women do not have a place in politics. They shouldn't worry their little minds with such things they cannot fully comprehend."

Alan drew in a deep breath and shook his head. "What would you have, Philip, our women dressed in shifts, and chained to the bedpost, prohibited to speak unless spoken too? If that is the way you see women, then I pity you."

Philip's face reddened, he stood and gave a quick nod to Alan. "Your lordship, we could spend all day and night discussing this and never would we agree. I bid you good day." He turned and stomped toward the main house.

"Bloody hell, I thought he'd never leave," Tristan said with a hiccup. He then reached for the newly opened wine bottle and tilted it back.

Alan glared at Tristan, then turned to Vaughn. "I tremendously enjoyed driving your vehicle. It's a splendid piece of machinery. I shall have to acquire one someday."

Vaughn inclined his head. "You're quite welcome, but I didn't realize you knew how to drive."

Royce snatched the bottle from Tristan. "Yes, Father, when did you learn?"

Alan offered his hand to Rose. She took it, remembering Alan sitting in Vaughn's car, wanting so much to drive it but not knowing how. Rose grinned. Alan had been so eager for her to teach him after she told him she knew how to drive. That was the second time she'd genuinely laughed since she'd arrived at Wyvern house.

"I learned the other day," Alan said and helped her to her feet. He then offered his hand to Aileen. "Are you joining us?"

"Of course." Aileen took Alan's hand.

Tristan grinned at Rose. His eyes were glazed, and he leaned against Vaughn. "Mrs. Rosie, when are you going to teach me to drive?" he slurred, his eyes rolled back, and he fell face down into Vaughn's crotch.

Rose laughed. She did not envy Tristan the hangover he would have. "Royce, you are such a bad influence on that boy."

His laughter filled the air. "Rose," Royce called. "did you teach father to drive?"

"Yes. I did." She smiled at Royce, then laughed harder at the expressions on Vaughn's and Royce's faces.

Chapter Sixteen

Rose glided across the crowded dance floor in Alan's arms. She would always cherish the time he'd spent teaching her the waltz yesterday. "How can I ever thank you for this wonderful time I've spent here."

Alan smiled warmly at her. "Seeing a true smile is enough."

She lowered her eyes and concentrated on Alan's lead. The dance soon ended, and he placed her hand on his arm.

"Would you care for something to drink? Lemonade, perhaps?"

"Yes. Thank you."

The cool tart drink quenched her thirst. "This is a beautiful celebration."

"I am glad you are enjoying yourself. In a few weeks, we will be hosting Royce's birthday celebration. Emma is planning a masquerade. I am sure you will enjoy it as much."

Tristan sauntered over to them. "My, you look gorgeous in that dress, Mrs. Kelly."

"You look quite handsome yourself. How's your headache."

"Much better, thank you." He blushed.

Rose smoothed her hand over the midnight blue velvet of her ball gown. She'd been hesitant about wearing the gown, with its off-the-shoulder design and plunging neckline. She thought it too risqué. She was glad Aileen had convinced her to go for it.

"Rosie—I mean, Mrs. Kelly, can I have the next dance?" Tristan offered her his arm.

"May I have the next dance?" Alan corrected.

The tips of Tristan's ears turned red, and he cleared his throat. "May I have the next dance?"

Rose took Tristan's arm. "I would be honored, sir."

"When it comes to a waltz, I'm not as good a dancer as my Uncle Alan, but I sure can do the two-step." He whirled her around the dance floor.

She looked up into the boy's honey brown eyes. "Where did you learn to do the two-step?"

"From watching my brothers at the barn dances back home. Rose, we've been talking amongst ourselves and, well, we'd be honored if you go back to Texas with Morgan and Quaid next week. Quaid has already sent a wire to Mom and Pop." The gleam in his eyes softened. "Please, go back with them. It will give you time to heal and a chance to be free from Mr. Madoc. Besides, they're sailing back on the *SS Majestic.* It's one of the White Star Lines fancier ships. At least that's what Quaid said. You can write me at Eton and tell me all about it."

"I promised Aileen and Sara I would stay with them, at least until spring." Tristan's smile slipped. "But I would love to visit your family then."

He grinned. "So, you'll come then? You'll love our spread. Wide open plains for as far as the eye can see. Maybe you can sail back with me in the summer."

Tristan's excitement was so catching. Rose couldn't help smiling along with him. "That would be something to consider."

A foreboding shiver ran down her spine, and her step faltered. She stepped on Tristan's foot. "Sorry."

"Rosie?" The concern in Tristan's voice warmed her.

She glanced to her left in time to see Vaughn zigzagging around couples and coming toward her.

He tapped Tristan's shoulder.

"Shove off, Brit," Tristan snarled. His eyes glowed, and his teeth became canine.

The muscles in Vaughn's jaw twitched, and his eyes turned an unholy red.

"Tristan," she said, "I'll dance with Mr. Madoc."

Tristan paused and studied her. "Are you sure, Rose?"

She nodded, then looked up at Vaughn. "Mr. Madoc."

Vaughn took her hand, then slid his arm around her waist and held her close. He guided her across the dance floor. "You are beautiful tonight."

"Thank you."

When he smiled, her heart fluttered. She had to fight her emotions. After yesterday's lunch under the oak, she realized she still loved him, would always love him. Like the sun burning away the clouds, Rose's mind cleared. She had two choices. She could either return to America with Tristan's brothers, living out her life never seeing Vaughn again, or remain in Europe and forever suffer this pain whenever she was near him. Her chest tightened and a lump formed in her throat. "Tristan's brothers are returning to America next week. They've asked me to join them."

"You will not."

She tilted her face up and met Vaughn's smoldering gaze. "Yes, I am. I plan to tell Sara and Aileen tonight."

"It's quite warm in here," Vaughn mumbled, then waltzed her out through the open balcony doors.

Before she could react, he'd led her down the steps and into the garden.

Rose yanked her hand from his. She'd be damned if Vaughn would manhandle her and she was finished, listening to any more of his hurtful words. "I don't know what you're up to, Vaughn, but I'm not sticking around to find out." She turned and started back toward the house.

Vaughn grabbed her hand, yanked her back against him. "You are not traveling to America, and certainly not with the Wolfes. You will stay in England."

"When pigs fly." She tried to hook her foot behind his leg and throw him off balance, but her formfitting skirt prevented her. "Damn it!" She tried to pull away. "Let go."

"Rose, please."

"Let go of me." She brought her heel sharply down on his foot.

He turned her, wrapped his arm around her waist, and imprisoned her. His massive hand covered her mouth. "I know your tricks," he murmured against her ear.

Vaughn only thought he knew. Rose gritted her teeth and thought about her next move.

"I will take my hand away if you promise to keep your voice down. You do not have to yell—Rose!" He jerked but kept his hand firmly over her mouth. "If you want to bite me, there are more pleasurable areas." He eased his grip on her.

She whipped around, facing him. She should run, scream, but anger took over her better judgment. "You're one sadistic butthole. You tell me you want nothing to do with me then you hound me to death. Now, you dare to tell me I can't do as I please." Her voice cracked. She wouldn't cry. She balled her hands into fists, digging her nails into her palms. "I'm tired of your sick mind games. Leave me the hell alone."

"I'm not playing games." Vaughn stared at her but didn't look her directly in the eyes. "For the past two weeks, I have been trying to speak with you. I brought you out here to talk."

"Give me one good reason why I should listen to anything you have to say."

Vaughn met her eyes, his arms hung limply at his sides, his shoulders slightly slumped. "I love you."

His words were soft, barely a whisper, but they struck her so hard she stumbled backward.

Her tears spilled from her eyes and rolled down her cheeks. "How can you stand there and tell me that after everything else you've said to me? After all, I'm just another man's castoff."

He flinched. "I should have never said that. Forgive me."

"You're right. You shouldn't have."

"Rose." He took a step toward her. "I am a coward and a fool. You were right. I was . . . I am afraid of myself."

230

She rubbed her hands up and down her arms. She had to remain strong.

Vaughn reached for her. "You're cold."

Rose stepped back from him, shaking her head. "Tonight you tell me you love me. What about tomorrow, next week, or next month, will you love me then? What about next year or next century, will you still love me? I don't know what to believe, Vaughn. One second you tell me one thing, the next, something else. I wish I could wake up from this freakin' nightmare and find myself in my bed, in my apartment, instead of trapped here."

Vaughn eased closer to her. "I have always loved you. I will . . . always love you."

"I'm not a damn daisy you can pull off petals. You love me. You love me not. I'm human. I have feelings. I cannot ride this frigging roller coaster of yours anymore."

"Rose, I hurt you because I." His eyes welled and voiced hitched. "I was frightened of what would happen if we made love." He sighed heavily, his voice filled with anguish. "I feared you would die at my hands as my sister had at the hands of her mate. Alan and Grandfather showed me the truth. I could never harm you."

So desperately she wanted to go to him, throw her arms around him, and hold him, but she didn't move. "I don't know what to say."

"Tell me you forgive me. Tell me you will give me another chance. Tell me. . ." A tear trailed down his cheek, and his voice cracked. "Tell me you still love me."

She stared at him. His usually bright green eyes were dull and lifeless. The single tearstain on his cheek broke her heart. She'd seen him happy, angry, confident, and so involved in his case, he didn't know what day it was, but she'd never seen him like this. Vulnerable.

"Rose, I beg you, please give me another chance."

She closed the distance between them and wrapped her arms around him, pressing her face against his chest. "I forgive

231

you," she whispered. "I've seen your dreams, lived the horror with you. I know you would never hurt me." She looked up into his eyes and framed his face in her hand. Slowly she lifted herself on tiptoes. She pressed her lips to his.

He caressed her face with his gloved hands, then her shoulders. He slid his hands down her arms until his hands circled her waist. *I love you so much.* Vaughn's voice resounded in her mind. He drew her tighter into his embrace.

"Rose?" Royce's voice broke through the haze in her mind.

"Rosie, we know you're out here," Tristan called. "Come out. Come out, wherever you are."

She leaned back in Vaughn's arms. "I should answer them."

"I think not." He tenderly pressed his lips to hers again. His tongue teased the seam of her lips until she parted them. He delved into her mouth. His tongue danced with hers, and he tasted of everything good. The heat of his kiss sent tremors racing through her body. Her stomach spiraled, and she clung to him. He made her feel as if she were standing on air.

When Vaughn lifted his lips from hers, it was as if he'd stolen her breath.

Rose opened her eyes, looked around, and blinked. "Where are we? We're not in the garden anymore."

"No, we are on the balcony outside my room."

As casually as she could, she asked, "Why?" Her voice quivered.

Vaughn's hands slipped from her, and he stepped back. "I wanted to finish our conversation without being interrupted. I guess I presumed too much. I will take you back."

Her defenses subsided, and she took his hand in hers. "We don't have to go back just yet." Rose lifted his hand to remove his glove.

The question in Vaughn's expression made her smile.

"I prefer the feel of your skin, rather than cotton."

He grinned and removed his other glove then slowly, and tenderly, caressed her cheek. "Better?"

"Much." She shivered.

"You are cold." Vaughn motioned to the opened balcony doors. "Shall we?"

Rose followed him into the dark room and caught sight of the massive cherry bed. She looked away. The memories of her last time in here were too fresh.

When he waved his hand in front of the fireplace, a fire roared to life.

She jumped and looked up at him. "I didn't know you could do that."

A slight smile curved his lips. "There is much about me you have yet to learn."

Her gaze roamed over him. He was handsome in his evening attire. "I'm looking forward to learning everything I can about you." Like if he had a hairy chest or a smooth one, or if he were cut or uncut, with luck, she'd find out tonight.

His eyes once again sparkled. "That could take a lifetime . . . or two."

There was no going back. Rose closed her eyes and drew in a deep breath, clearing her mind. Vaughn wouldn't hurt her. She knew it in her heart. She opened her eyes, meeting his heated gaze. "No time like the present to start." She stepped into his embrace.

He groaned as her hands slid up his chest. She pushed his coat off his shoulders and down his arms until it fell to the floor. Vaughn raised an eyebrow at her. Next, she slowly tugged on his bow tie, untying it. Rose pulled it from his collar, held it between her thumb and finger for a second, then dropped it to the floor. Rose licked her dry lips as she unbuttoned his vest. It soon joined his tie.

~ ~ ~

Vaughn stifled a groan. Rose's actions were going to be his undoing. He'd never thought to have a woman, his mate, undress him could be so seductive and arousing. He brushed kisses to her hair, her eyes, the tip of her nose before finally kissing her mouth. It was divine ecstasy. *Thank you, Yeva. Thank you for granting us another chance.*

Lifting his mouth from hers, he gazed into Rose's eyes. Despite his desire to carry her to bed and make her his mate, he could wait. He did not want to rush her. "Do you wish to return to the ball?"

Rose shook her head then smiled seductively at him. His groin hardened as Rose's nimble fingers began tortuously unfastening his shirt studs one at a time.

His heart pounded, and his knees suddenly felt weak. He struggled to remain in control. Rose couldn't know what she was doing to him. "Rose," he breathed, "do you know where this could lead?"

When Rose peered up, a mischievous glimmer showed in her eyes. "What do you mean could?" She pushed open his shirt and frowned at his undershirt.

His breath caught and hoped she didn't notice his knees buckling. "Are you sure?"

"Yes," she sighed, then unfastened his cuffs. She slipped his shirt down his arms. Her light touch caused gooseflesh to form on his skin. Rose tugged his undershirt from his trousers. He took pity on her and lifted it over his head. If she wanted him bare-chested, so be it.

Her eyes burned with a passion he'd not seen in them before. He drew in a deep breath, and the smell of her heat nearly undid his control. "You do not fear me taking your blood?"

"Been there, done that. I'm not afraid." She lifted up on her toes and pressed a kiss to his lips. "I know I'm safe in your arms."

The shadows across his soul vanished. He let go of his passion and pulled her into his arms. The taste of blood filled his mouth, and he drew back from her. Dark, rich blood pooled on her lower lip. His fangs had pierced her.

"Forgive me." Vaughn looked away, his heart pounded. He'd hurt her, the very thing he'd swore he would not do. "Perhaps we should take this much slower." He bent to retrieve his undershirt from the floor.

Rose grabbed his arm. "Oh no you don't, I will not have you push me away again. Vaughn, look at *me*."

He faced her. "I am not pushing you away." He turned his back to her again and retrieved his other garments. "Go sit in the chair. I should only be a few minutes." He'd never been this clumsy with a woman in his entire life. Even the night he lost his virginity he had more finesse. What was wrong with him? Why, with Rose, did he fumble around like a schoolboy?

"There you go again, telling me what to do and not giving a damn about what I want." Rose wrapped her arms around him and pressed her body against his bare back. Her tongue traced the shell of his ear. "Do you know what I want tonight? I want you." She flicked his ear with her tongue.

By, God, Rose was going to be the death of him, but what a wonderful way to die. Vaughn looked over his shoulder at her. "Tonight I'm the proverbial bull in a china shop."

Rose laughed, and her warm breath teased his neck. "No, you're not."

"I feel as clumsy as a lad." He turned in her arms then he ran his fingers through her hair. It was so tempting to pull the pins and watch her hair tumble down her shoulders. "Are you sure you do not wish to return to the ball?"

He sucked in his breath as she ran her hands through his chest hair. Then with her finger, she lightly traced the thin line of hair down his stomach. His muscles quivered under her touch. She continued her downward movement until her hand covered his groin.

"I want to make love to you," she said in a low, silky voice. "I want to feel you deep inside of me, filling me."

"From this night on you will be mine. You will never sleep with anyone, but me. You will be my mate." He traced her lips with his finger. "The mother of my child. Forever, even past the grave, you will be mine."

"I wouldn't have it any other way." She kissed him with a hunger that matched his.

Vaughn pulled the pins from her hair, then ran his fingers through her tresses. Silk, pure silk. He swept his tongue through her mouth in a slow sensual dance. He couldn't wait to be inside of her, feeling her warmth surrounding him. He wanted her nude. His fingers fumbled with the tiny buttons on the back of her dress. Try as he might, he couldn't get the bloody things undone.

Rose laughed and leaned back in his arms, grinning up at him. "Having problems?"

"Of course not," he lied, looking at his hands. Hands that could crush stones, that could hold a delicate teacup without breaking it, but could not manage to unfasten this blasted dress. Why did she have to wear a dress tonight with so many godforsaken buttons?

Vaughn glared over her shoulder at the long, ominous line of buttons. He gripped the back of her dress and tore the damn thing, sending those godforsaken buttons flying across his room. "See, no trouble at all."

Her soft laugh rippled through him. "I hate to see what you do to my corset."

He raised his eyebrow at her as he slid his clawed fingernail under her laces. "I shall buy you another," he offered, before reclaiming her mouth.

Soon their clothes lay on the floor. Vaughn's hands skimmed over her silken body. "Rose," he growled when she rubbed against him. He swung her up into his arms and carried her to bed.

Tenderly he placed her on the bed, then stretched out beside her.

He inhaled when her fingers circled his cock. "Rose," he gasped as her light touch stroked him. "Woman, if you do not stop I will spill my seed in your hand." How he managed to get the words out, he didn't know.

"We wouldn't want that now, would we?" She placed a light kiss on his chin.

Rose was bare before him. He slid his gaze over her. *By, God, she's beautiful!* She fervently parted her thighs for him, as he eased between them, keeping his weight from her. Fighting to keep control, he eased into her warm body. He clenched his jaw, his fangs pierced his lip, and he stopped to allow her body time to adjust to him.

She moaned, grabbing his shoulders. "No."

"I don't want to hurt you."

She thrust her hips up, taking him fully inside of her.

He lost the battle he'd waged with himself. Instinct took over, and his fangs sank deep into her throat. Her blood flowed into his mouth as he filled her womb with his seed, giving her his child.

Vaughn pressed his lips tightly over the wounds he'd made in Rose's throat and drank deeply. Warm, sweet, glorious blood filled his mouth, Rose's blood. He clung to her, taking her essence, and absorbing the memories of her life into his heart. His throat tightened as he watched her cry as a child over the loss of her brother, then her parents. He shared her emotions when she married Richard and felt her heartbreak when he'd died. From now on only tears of joy for her, Vaughn vowed.

The more he witnessed of Rose's life, the more he loved her. He lifted his mouth from her throat, and his gaze fell on her pillow. Dark red blood had dripped on the white cloth case.

Vaughn withdrew from her body and rolled from her. He'd taken all, but the last life-giving drop of blood. Cradling Rose in his arms. He felt her body grow cold.

Quickly he drew his fingernail across his neck, cutting into his flesh. His blood stained the bed linens, mingling with Rose's blood as a symbol of their union.

He lifted Rose's head and covered his wound with her mouth. *Drink my love, drink, and become one with me.*

She began suckling, arousing him.

"My sweet," he sighed, feeling her skin grow warm under his hands. "From this moment on I will keep nothing from you. You will know my past, my deepest secrets. I will share all my fears, my dreams, my desires with you."

When she'd taken enough of his blood, he lowered her onto the bed. He spread her hair on the pillow. She was his. His marks on her throat had already healed.

Vaughn turned on his side, drawing Rose into his embrace. He wrapped his arm protectively around her and whispered, "Sleep and grow strong, my dearest."

He could not sleep. The music from the ball filtered into his room. The cool night air fanned the curtains, causing the fire in the fireplace to flicker. He watched the flames dance in the darkness. He had been a cad, a blundering idiot. No, he had been worse. He'd acted like a bloody fledgling, a schoolboy, taking Rose as he had and not giving her a woman's pleasure. He was an ass.

~ ~ ~

Rose snuggled closer to Vaughn. She found his thoughts amusing, but she couldn't let him think so badly of himself when it wasn't his fault at all. She'd thoroughly enjoyed making him lose control. "Don't worry. I'll let you make it up to me. The sun's not up yet."

He bolted upright. "You're awake! How do you feel? Tell me, how you feel."

She rolled onto her back then placed a finger on his lips. "If you will quit asking questions. I'll tell you." She lightly tugged on his arm, pulling him down next to her on the mattress. "I feel ecstatic and very much in love."

"You are not tired?" he asked, stroking her hair.

238

"No, not yet, but I expect you to make me that way." She rolled over on top of him, straddling him. Her hands roamed over his chest. "Why should I feel tired?"

"It's normal for a human mate to succumb to the dark sleep while her body heals."

"I don't know about a dark sleep, but I did have a little nap and had the most wonderful dream."

Vaughn's eyes shimmered in the firelight. "Tell me."

"I dreamed I was you. I was flying, soaring over a large meadow." She ran her finger lightly down his stomach, watching his abs quiver. "Then I dreamed I was running for my life." She closed her eyes and shivered. "I was frightened, but the fear soon gave way to joy." She opened her eyes to find Vaughn intently watching her.

"You saw my life. When I gave you my blood, I opened my mind to you. I kept nothing from you."

"When you took my blood, did you see my life?"

"Yes." He caressed her cheek with his fingertips. "And fell deeper in love *with you*." His other hand inched up her thigh. "I will no longer have to send my thoughts to you. With a few lessons, you will be able to hear my thoughts freely. If you would like, I can teach you how."

She kissed his palm. "I think I've already heard your thoughts."

His eyes grew wide. "What did you hear?"

"You were thinking you were a cad and a fledgling for not pleasing me. So we can't have you feeling like that, can we?"

He chuckled. "No, we cannot. What am I going to do about it?" Both his hands rested on top of her thighs.

"Oh, I have a few ideas." She smiled, drinking in his muscular chest.

"And I like them," he moaned.

"Will I always know what you're thinking?"

"Yes. I will never block my thoughts from you." He reached up and cupped her breasts in his hands. His fingers lightly teased her nipples. "Tell me what I'm thinking now."

"That should be easy." Her hands roamed over his body. His skin was like satin pulled tautly over steel. She kissed his jawline, then his neck. She nibbled on the area just above his shoulder, and he moaned. Vaughn leaned his head to one side, allowing her better access.

Vaughn growled low in his throat, and his hands moved down her back, then firmly cupped her bottom.

"I think I've found an erogenous zone." She blew over the area she'd nipped.

His hand skimmed over her thighs. He smiled as his fingers caressed her. "And I believe I have found yours." He flipped her to her back, spread her knees, then quickly buried his face between her legs. His tongue teased her as his very talented fingers pushed deep into her.

"Oh, God," she whimpered. When Vaughn hit her G-spot, she moaned louder. He chuckled and repeated the motion with his finger, he added another finger to her, sliding into her, stretching her. He stroked her spot, making her arch her back with pleasure. Vaughn moved his talented thumb, massaging her clit with his thumb pad.

Rose fisted the sheets. The urgency grew until an explosion of pleasure surged through her in waves. She moaned as his mouth laid siege to her. The man was relentless. Her body shook, and she yelled his name as he brought her to climax a second time. Vaughn held her until the last of her tremors eased.

When he lifted his head, a purely masculine smile curved his lips. "That's two." He kissed her stomach, swirling his tongue around her bellybutton. "Mmm." He kissed his way up to her chest.

"Vaughn," she gasped.

He rolled to his back, pulling her back on top of him. The heat in his eyes made her clench with the need for him. His hands eased back up her thighs. "I know your thoughts, my love."

He guided her down on his cock, filling her. He set their steady rhythm, keeping his hands on her waist.

Rose leaned down and brushed her breasts against his chest. "I want to drive you wild as you did me," she said against his lips.

His eyes glowed with a fire that excited her.

She drove him wild by changing their rhythm, moving slowly at first, then fast, then slowly again. She tightened her muscles and took more of him into herself, bringing them to climax.

A feral sound came from Vaughn, and his eyes snapped open. His large eyes met hers. Sweat beaded his forehead. He turned his face and ripped the pillow with his fangs, sending feathers flying.

His action startled her. "Vaughn?"

"Sorry," he gasped, then gripped her around the waist, taking control of her movements.

Vaughn sat up and thrust deeply, giving her yet another powerful climax. His body shook with the force of his release, and he cried out her name.

She hungered for the taste of blood, her blood. Rose opened her eyes. These were not her feelings, but Vaughn's. His emotions washed over her. He would not drink from her again. He feared draining her.

She leaned down, pressing her throat against his mouth. *Take what you want.*

"Too soon," he gasped, turning his head.

Exhausted but depressed she'd not satisfied all of his needs, Rose snuggled against Vaughn's chest. His hands roamed over her back.

"Did I make up for my earlier blundering?" His voice was deep and raw, but it held a trace of laughter.

"Yes, you did, and quite well, I must say." She reached and pulled the sheets up, then quickly pushed them away when she saw the bloodstains.

Vaughn eased from her, sat up, and positioned her on his lap. "A few hundred years ago I would have hung this sheet out our window. Proof of our mating."

"You mean your marks on my throat aren't enough proof?"

"The way Royce and that pack of hounds have been sniffing around your skirt hem, no."

She shouldn't find joy in what Vaughn said, but she did. "You don't have to be jealous. You're the only man I want or need." She rested her head against his chest. They had never spoken of the fact she wasn't a virgin and Vaughn did know she'd been married. Nevertheless, she wondered if it bothered him that he wasn't her first.

"Rose." He tipped her chin up. "When I took your blood I saw your memories of Richard. I hope I will be as good a husband to you as he was." Vaughn pressed his lips to her forehead before trailing kisses down her face to her throat. "It is not the taking of one's virginity but the taking of first blood that is important. In that single act, we bind ourselves to each other, making us one."

When he smiled at her, his eyes sparkled brightly with mischief.

"I don't think I like that look," she said, sliding off his lap.

His smile turned into a full toothy grin, and he stood. "Just because this isn't the 1500's doesn't mean," He snatched the sheet from the bed. "I cannot still display this."

She grabbed the sheet, tugging it. "Vaughn! Don't you dare."

His rich laughter filled the room when he yanked the sheet from her hands, then leaned toward her and quickly kissed her. Vaughn flipped the sheet around, hanging the bloodstains over the foot of the bed. "Is that better?"

She crossed her arms over her chest and glared at him, trying not to laugh. "You enjoyed that, didn't you?"

"You should know I would not have done such a thing. Do you think I want Royce and his cohorts standing under our window, serenading us all night? Especially, when I have other plans." His heated gaze roamed over her. He licked his lips.

Trying to act nonchalant, Rose crossed her legs at the ankles and stared down at the feather-covered mattress. She took a feather from the bed and placed it in the palm of her hand and blew on it. The feather floated in the air before landing on Vaughn's shoulder. "What sort of plans do you have?" she asked.

He twirled the feather between his fingers. "Are you ticklish?"

"Yes. So you can get that thought out of your mind." She slid across the bed to the other side, scattering feathers everywhere. "Why did you kill the pillow?"

"With the desire for your flesh comes the desire for your blood." He strolled around to the foot of the bed. "Your body hadn't recovered from our mating."

"But I felt your pain."

"You do not have to feed my hunger every time we make love. Until your body adjusts to its change, I will have to be very careful, not to harm you."

Rose tipped her head back, looking up at him. "Stop being foolish. I know you will not harm me."

Vaughn's expression softened. "I love you. Let me be foolish."

She allowed her gaze to roam over his body, tracing every line, every muscle. She slowly retraced his body back to his face. "When you first told me you drank blood I was repulsed by it. Now I want to satisfy both your desires."

"Do you?" He grinned at her as he dove over the foot of the bed.

She screamed and tried to roll out of his way, but she wasn't fast enough.

Vaughn pinned her under him and playfully nipped her neck, then kissed it.

Rose ran her fingers lightly down the center of his back.

Vaughn jerked, and a faint laugh escaped his lips.

"You're ticklish," she said.

"Only a little." He gripped her hand and pulled it over her head, then placed tiny kisses along her throat down to her collarbone, then to her breast. "Mmm," he moaned.

Something creaked, and with her free hand, Rose pushed against Vaughn's shoulder. "Did you hear that?"

"No." He wedged between her legs.

"Stop," she whispered and tried to wiggle out from under him. "I heard something. It sounded like—I don't know like something groaning."

Vaughn pushed to one side and looked down at her. "This is an old home. Something is always creaking." He bent down and kissed the tip of her nose. "Or are you afraid it was a ghost?"

"Ghost, vampire, what's the difference?"

"This," he said, claiming her lips.

Okay, she was silly. All old homes have strange noises. She wrapped her arms around Vaughn's neck and her legs around his.

The mattress fell with a crash.

"Rose!" Vaughn rolled from her. "Did I hurt you?"

She couldn't answer him. She was laughing so hard she was crying. They'd broken the wooden slats holding the mattress.

"Rose?"

She shook her head. "I'm—I'm fine. Oh, Lord, we've made a mess of this room." Feathers floated everywhere. "How are we going to explain the bed?"

Laughing, Vaughn pulled her into his arms. He rained kisses on her face, then kissed her lips. His kisses turned sensual, and he made love to her slowly and thoroughly.

Rose lifted her head and stared at the man beside her. Vaughn smiled in his sleep with his arm draped across her waist. She carefully lifted his arm and slid out from under it. Sitting on the edge of the mattress for a few moments, she watched him. She loved him and hoped she could be the mate he deserved. After brushing a light kiss to his lips, she pushed herself up and padded into the bathroom.

~ ~ ~

Vaughn shivered. He scooted over to get closer to Rose, then scooted over some more. His bed was big but not so big he could not touch his mate. He opened his eyes. "Rose?"

Wrapped in his robe, she sat at the writing desk. "I didn't want to wake you." Her voice shook.

The tears in her voice had him out of bed and at her side. He tenderly cupped her face and stared into her tear-swollen eyes. "Why are you crying?"

Her bottom lip quivered. "I love you."

"And I love you." He wiped her tears with his hand.

In her mind, he saw the images of her parents, her brother, and Richard, but did not understand her grief. "Tell me what is wrong, Rose, please."

"Every time I find love . . . I'm always left alone."

"I have told you, we will both live to be very old, together. I will never leave you." He tipped her chin up, forcing her to meet his gaze. "We are mated, and the bond lasts forever, married if you would like, for all eternity. Nothing will separate us. Nothing can separate us, Rose. Nothing. Not even time."

"But what if I'm taken from you? What if I'm sent back to my time?"

Vaughn lifted her from the chair and held her. "You are my mate, my wife. Our hearts connect us. No matter the time or the place, I will find you. I will search for you, and we will be together forever. I promise."

He scooped her up into his arms and carried her over to the bed, placing her on it, then slid under the covers beside her. He pulled her close and closed his eyes. *Please, do not ever leave me.*

~ ~ ~

Rose woke with the slamming of the bedroom door and the echoed sounds of footsteps running in the hall. She looked around the room. *Good grief. It looked worse this morning than it had last night.* Feathers were everywhere. She tried to get up, but Vaughn was wrapped around her, with a leg thrown over hers and his arm holding her firmly against him.

"Vaughn." She nudged him with her rump. "I think someone just came in here."

He groaned and hugged her tighter. "It was probably Timothy, the man-servant assigned to me. Go back to sleep, love."

"It's morning. Don't you think we should get up?"

He huffed. "Don't you like the feel of me next to you?"

"Yes." She wiggled free of his hold, then rolled over, facing him. Vaughn was so adorable with his sleepy eyes and tousled hair. She snuggled against him, pillowing her head on his shoulder.

"Good." He sighed. "And men are not adorable," he murmured, sliding his leg over hers.

"Eavesdropping on my thoughts?" Rose smoothed her hand down Vaughn's back, and lightly pinched his adorable buns.

Their bedroom door flew open and banged against the wall. Vaughn rolled toward the door, shielding her nudity with his body from the intruder. "What!" He snarled at the intruder.

Rose squealed, gripped the sheet, and pulled it over her, knowing her face was red. It was bad enough a servant had caught them in bed together, but now someone else had barged in on them.

She peered over Vaughn's shoulders and groaned. Could this get any worse? Alan stood in the doorway, his eyes were wide, and his face pale. He looked as if he'd seen a ghost.

Alan's attention shifted to her and a smile formed on his lips. He shut the door behind him and held up his hand. "Give me a moment to compose myself."

Vaughn shrugged. His glowing eyes slowly returned to their pale cool green, and his fangs retracted.

"Father!" Royce's voice came from the other side of the door.

And yes it could get worse. Rose buried her face in Vaughn's shoulder. Now the whole family knew that she and Vaughn had done the horizontal tango.

Alan turned and barely opened the door. "Tell your mother everything is fine. Tell her it is better than fine." He closed the door and leaned against it, then pressed his fingertips together as he stared up at the ceiling. "When Timothy burst into my study, spouting gibberish about your room being sacked and blood-soaked sheets, I thought—never mind what I thought."

~ ~ ~

Vaughn wrapped his arms around Rose. He knew what Alan had thought. "You and Grandfather were right. I could never harm Rose."

Alan nodded. "I wish to see you both in my study in one hour to discuss your wedding. With luck, you will wed by evening." He turned and reached for the doorknob.

"Wedding?" Rose looked at Vaughn.

"There is no need if you do not wish it. I've already explained we are bound to each other."

"You have no choice," Alan said in a low voice.

"What am I to wear?" Rose muttered.

Alan chuckled. "I am sure Emma and Sara will be able to find something suitable for you. Even if it has to be the sheet you are wearing now." He opened the door, then closed it behind him.

Vaughn kissed Rose and fell against the bed with her in his arms. "No one argues with his lordship."

"You don't understand. I don't have a thing to wear right now. You tore my dress to shreds. Remember?"

He grinned. "How could I forget?"

"How will I get back to my room like this?"

He playfully nipped her shoulder. "Who said you were going anywhere?" He rolled on top of her, kissing her firmly.

She pushed against him. "Alan. He wants to see us both in one hour, remember?"

Vaughn lowered his lips to her neck. "Don't worry." He kissed a trail down between her breasts. "He cannot start lecturing us until we arrive."

She moaned and pushed harder against his shoulder. "But how do we get my clothes?"

Vaughn stopped his exploration and glanced up. "I will return you to your room safely and discreetly." His lips pulled into a thin line. "However, if what Alan said was true about Timothy I am sure we are already the latest topic of discussion."

Fear etched her lovely face. "Alan looked pleased enough. He seemed happy we're together, but what if Alan isn't? Maybe we should put this on hold until we find out what he wants."

"Rose, your fears are unwarranted. I have already explained to you, once my kind takes a mate, and a child conceived no one could come between them. No one can come between us. Not Alan, not the bloody queen herself."

"But—"

Vaughn placed his lips over hers, silencing her. *Alan wants to see us to discuss his plans for our wedding and to congratulate us on our child.* He sent his thoughts to Rose.

"Vaughn?" She leaned back. "I'm pregnant? Am I? How can you be sure? We only made love once." He cocked his brow and tilted his head staring at her. "Okay like six or seven times but still it's too early to tell."

He would never forget the way she looked at him. Her eyes shimmered with joy.

"I'm sure." His large hand pressed on her stomach. "Our child grows in you and eleven months will fill our home with joy."

"Eleven months?"

"That is the normal length of time until a Dhampir child is born." He chuckled. "Besides, it satisfies the old-biddies of society who count on their fingers."

"I think we should get dressed."

"Later." He trailed a line of kisses down her stomach. *After I pleasure you.*

Chapter Seventeen

Two hours later, Rose quickly rinsed away the lavender scented soap. She didn't have much time, they were already late, but she had to get the cobwebs from her hair. Vaughn had led her back to her room through the maze of hidden passageways. Unlike the ones Royce and she used to go back and forth to the gymnasium. These were dark, dusty, and thick with cobwebs. Vaughn told her the tunnels were Royce's favorite hiding place when he was a child and in trouble with his father. The house was full of secret passageways.

Her stomach tightened in anticipation. What did Alan want to say to them? He probably wanted to lecture them on their scandalous behavior.

She pushed back the heavy canvas shower curtain and met Vaughn's admiring gaze. "What are you doing in here?"

Vaughn smiled, revealing his fangs. His heated gaze perused her body as he shook open a towel. Tenderly he dried her. "Helping you dress."

Her cheeks burned under his intense gaze. How could she feel embarrassed around him, especially after last night?

"My thoughts exactly, but I do like to see you blush."

She took the towel from him and wrapped it around herself. "I don't know if I'll ever get used to you reading my thoughts."

He chuckled. "Then I will try not to listen so much."

"Thanks. On your way out, will you ring for Molly, please? I'm going to need her to help me dress."

Rose looked into the mirror and combed her fingers through her wet, tangled hair. "What I wouldn't give for a blow dryer right now."

"A what?" He tilted his head, furrowing his brows.

She was caught off guard by the sudden vibrancy of his voice and looked over at him.

Vaughn's puzzled expression amused her. "You wish me to blow you dry?"

"No." She bit her lip to keep from laughing at him. "A hairdryer is an electrical appliance. It's something every woman needs in the future to look good." She squeezed the excess water from her hair, then started towel drying it. "Trust me. I could use one now."

"You are beautiful. You do not need this hair blower."

She stopped drying her hair and glanced at Vaughn. His smile was strained, and tendrils of his emotions seeped into her. Sadness. "Vaughn? What's wrong?"

He wrinkled his brow. "Nothing."

"Liar." She went to him and cupped his face in her hands. "I feel something is bothering you. I feel your sadness. I take it this is part of the bond we now share?"

"When I was in your mind I saw so many wonderful things. I wish I could give you these things, but I cannot."

"I only need you."

He wrapped his arms around her, hugging her close. "I look forward to having you guide me through this new and fascinating century." His hand skimmed down her back.

"I do, too. I've already started to write down things in my journal, like what stocks to buy." She leaned back. "So much will happen. We will go through two world wars, a great depression, and inventions you can't even imagine, like the computer and the atom bombs. Man will walk on the moon. And the medical advances like—"

Vaughn placed his finger over her lips. "We will survive all that is to come. Together." He kissed her briefly. "As much as I like holding you, Alan is waiting."

Her stomach quivered at the thought. "You're right." She waved her hands at him, shooing him out. "Go on. I'll be ready shortly."

"I said I would help you dress. What do you wish to wear?"

"I don't need you gawking at me while I'm trying to dress. Please, ring for Molly."

"I do not gawk," he grumbled. "I admire." He opened the door and left the room.

"God, give me strength," Rose muttered as she slipped into her chemise, corset, and petticoat. Everything she'd learned about Twentieth Century in history, she would experience firsthand.

God had given her another chance at happiness with Vaughn and his family. She planned to make sure they were kept safe in the years to come. That is, once she survived this ordeal with Alan.

Rose opened the bathroom door and groaned. Vaughn was going through her wardrobe. "What are you doing?"

He closed the wardrobe and turned, holding a crisp white shirtwaist in one hand and a sage green corduroy skirt in the other. "You did not tell me what you wished to wear. Will these items do? I like you in green."

She gritted her teeth and counted to ten. Good grief Vaughn was a stubborn, one-track-minded-man. Why couldn't he do as she'd asked? "That's fine."

Beelzebub jumped from her bed, strolled over to her. The silly cat rubbed against her leg, purring as if trying to calm her.

She bent down and picked him up. "Good morning." She looked over at Vaughn. "Honestly, you don't have to do this. Why don't you go and get something to eat? I'll be down as soon as Molly helps me dress."

Vaughn placed the skirt on her bed, then held out her blouse. "It is only fair I help you, after all, you helped me this morning." He looked down at his feet. "But I don't see what was so funny about my socks, nor do I understand why you referred to me as a caddie."

She placed Beelzebub on the bed then slipped on her blouse. "I'm sorry, I shouldn't have laughed. You look

252

handsome in your knickers and argyles." She gave him her back. "Would you button me, please?"

"Apology accepted." He bent down, tilted his head, and kissed her cheek. "Your skirt, my lady." He slipped it over her head. His hands caressed her as he skimmed her skirt down her hips. "Perhaps I will also help you dress for tea."

"If you do, we won't make it for tea."

His lips turned up in a wolfish grin. "Or dinner." He motioned her to sit, then knelt before her.

Beelzebub jumped onto her lap.

She scratched him behind his ear. "Since you've been here, you haven't let me out of your sight. I'll bet last night you were having a fit, old boy." She smiled at Vaughn. "Thank you for bringing him with you. I never thought I could get attached to an animal."

"Do not thank me. I had nothing to do with that cat coming here." Vaughn took the buttonhook from the vanity. "That cat is attached to you. He was waiting inside the automobile the day I came after you. David did his best to toss the cat out, but he just darted back inside the vehicle."

Rose watched Vaughn's nimble fingers as he fastened her shoes. He'd dressed her as quickly as Molly would have and perhaps a little faster. "You've done this before."

"A time or two." When he'd finished hooking her shoes, he stood and took her hairbrush then began brushing her hair. He quickly had her hair properly coiffed in an upswept bun leaving a few curls brushing her neck.

"All finished, my love." Vaughn offered his hand. "See, you did not need your maid."

Twinges of jealousy twisted inside her. She knew Vaughn hadn't lived a monk's life. He'd even told her about his mistresses. Rose bit her lip. She'd no reason to feel this way, not now.

"Rose."

She looked up. Vaughn's eyes brimmed with tenderness.

"From the moment you walked into my life, you were the only woman for me, and you always will be the only woman who holds my heart." He kissed the tip of her nose.

"Reading my mind again?"

"Guilty." He lifted her hand to his lips. "You never have to doubt my love or worry I will have another. I will not."

He'd spoken these words, not in the heat of passion, but in the cold light of the morning.

Standing on tiptoe, she pressed her lips against his, then slowly covered his mouth. His lips parted and his tongue entwined with hers.

Her stomach grumbled, spoiling the moment.

Vaughn shook with a laugh and raised his mouth. "Perhaps we should stop by the breakfast room before we meet with Alan." His lips pulled in a sexy grin. "His lordship can wait."

"We don't have time, we're already over two hours late, and I don't want Alan any angrier than he is."

"What makes you think he is angry?" Vaughn opened the door for her, then led her down the hall.

Beelzebub followed them, playfully swatting at her hem.

"Even in my time, it's tacky for people who aren't married to be found in bed together. I don't think I will ever be able to look him in the eyes again."

"My love, you worry too much. The moment you gave me your blood in the carriage you became my mate. The wedding Alan spoke of is for appearances only."

"Well, I still won't be able to look him in the eyes for a while."

They stopped outside the door to the study. Loud laughs floated through the closed door.

"Ready?" Vaughn asked.

"No." Rose squeezed his hand as he opened the door to the study. It was worse than she'd expected. Every one of Vaughn's family was there. They all stopped their conversations and looked up as she and Vaughn entering the room.

Alan nodded at them, then peered at the grandfather clock against the wall. "Perhaps for your wedding gift a clock will do."

Vaughn just smiled.

Royce, Glen, and the Wolfe brothers stood by the balcony door, while Aileen and Sara sat with Emma on the sofa. Vaughn's grandfather sat on the chair beside them. So many people made the large study seem small.

Ian and Angelique MacPhee waited with their daughters, Caitlin, and Victoria. Rose made quick friends with them. Both were extremely sympathetic with Aileen over her dilemma with their father.

Rose smiled at Ian and Angelique. The smile Ian returned made him less intimidating.

Love, you have nothing to fear. Vaughn's words entered her mind.

Had he not held her hand so tightly, she would have turned around and bolted from the room.

Sara rushed over to them. "It pleases my heart to see the two of you finally together. The Creator planned for you both to be as one. The proof is the circumstances *Yeva* sent Rose to us." Sara took hold of Rose's hand, leading her across to where Emma and Aileen sat.

Vaughn followed. He bent and brushed a kiss to Emma's cheek. "Madam."

She smiled, and tears welled in her eyes. "When I first saw you, Rose, I thought you were Royce's chosen. It thrills my heart to know you are Vaughn's. If anyone deserves true love, it is him. So rare is it for their kind to find their rue mates."

Rose bit her lip. She hadn't imagined such a warm reception. She'd thought Alan would reprimand them.

Sara reached up and patted Vaughn's cheek. "You are lucky she decided to forgive you."

His cheeks reddened. "Yes, *Babushka*." He slipped his arm around Rose's waist. "I am fortunate."

"Rose," Emma asked. "Did you bring something you can use as a wedding dress?"

"I think I can find something." Rose was sure there was something among all the dresses Sara had ordered for her. Good grief, Rose had more clothes now than what she owned in her time. No. This was her time now.

Sara turned to Emma. "What time do we want the ceremony?"

Alan cleared his throat. "Ladies."

Emma waved her hand, dismissing him. "I have not spoken with Bishop North on the matter, but his wife suggested eleven o'clock tomorrow."

"Splendid," Sara said. "That would be perfect. We can serve a bridal brunch." She glanced at Rose. "You have several tea gowns which would be perfect for your wedding dress. We can go up to your room and look through them now if you wish. Oh, and Devon North will bring his camera. I so want a photograph of the day."

"I've already spoken with Mr. Peabody, our gardener. He says there are plenty of blooms in the greenhouse. We can go there after tea," Emma told Sara.

Rose was too shocked to offer objections to anything. The final knot in her stomach untied. She'd expected to be blasted, not bombarded with wedding plans.

Alan cleared his throat again, then spoke loudly, "Ladies, if you would please permit me a word with Rose. When I am finished, you may take her and do as you wish."

Sara's lips thinned, and her eyes turned a deep unholy red. "There was no need for you to raise your voice, son. None of us are hard of hearing."

"Forgive me, Mother. What I have to say will only take a moment." He turned and smiled warmly at Rose. "This is truly a joyous day. A day I am glad to see."

"Here, Here." Royce applauded. His cousins Glen and Tristan soon joined him.

"Aye," Ian said. "Fate has chosen *weel* for him." He looked across the room to Aileen. "Mayhaps fate will do the same for his sister."

Still in a dazed state, Rose gazed around the room. Warm smiles greeted her. She looked over, meeting Tristan's honey brown gaze.

He winked at her, then blew her a kiss. The rascal. God, Royce was such a bad influence on the boy.

Vaughn growled low in his throat and muttered something about an insolent pup.

Rose laughed.

Alan pulled her into his embrace, hugging her tightly. "Welcome to the family, my dear." He motioned to the burgundy wingbacked leather chair in front of his desk. "Please, sit."

Deep, loving warmth flowed through her.

Beelzebub jumped into the chair before she could sit, so she lifted him onto her lap.

Vaughn stood beside her, resting his hand on her shoulder. His thumb lightly stroked over the marks he'd made in her neck, sending shivers of pleasure straight to her core and she tightened her thighs. Damn every time he touched those marks it made her hornier than a cat in heat.

Alan leaned against his desk with his arms loosely crossed over his chest. "Bishop North has agreed to stay and perform the ceremony tomorrow. I would have preferred to have it today, but Bishop North will not be able to provide the license until then." Alan cleared his throat and looked pointedly at her.

Rose's stomach did a full flip and tightened again. Here it comes. He would blast her for her unladylike behavior with all of Vaughn's family as witnesses.

Holding onto Beelzebub for comfort, she tilted her chin up and boldly met Alan's pale blue eyes. She wasn't ashamed. She loved Vaughn and if things had been different, had she trusted him sooner, they would have made love months ago.

Alan's eyes were not angry, but gentle and understanding.

"Last night, Rose, your life changed," he said in a calm, low voice.

Here it comes. Rose braced herself for Alan's lecture.

Alan glanced over at Royce, then back to her. "I believe someone has already given you our family history. It pleases me you have accepted us for what we are, but our secret must remain that. A secret."

"I would never betray any of you. I couldn't."

"We know. You are one of us, and as such, certain aspects of your life must change. You will not be able to live in one place more than ten or so years. Your children may have special abilities that will prevent them from playing or attending schools with human children until they are properly trained." He glanced over at Tristan. "One would not want their child shifting into a pup during lessons." Alan chuckled, shaking his head. "Humans who do not know of us will start to wonder why you are never ill or show signs of aging. Because we are different, few humans know of us, and even fewer of them are permitted into our inner circle."

"I understand all of this."

Alan shook his head. "Do you? Do you understand you must cut all ties with your family and any human friends you have? They will not understand these changes in you. You must say goodbye to everything in your past."

She squashed the urge to laugh. She'd already done that. Rose smiled up at Vaughn, then at Alan. "The only family I have is Vaughn and the people in this room."

A rush of air escaped several mouths as if each had been holding his breath waiting for her answer. Even Vaughn.

Royce came over to them and slapped Vaughn on the back. "You have a rare beauty here, my brother."

"I know. Thank you."

258

Royce bent down and brushed a kiss to her cheek. "If he gives you any grief, let me know, and I shall come and referee your bouts." He grinned at her and winked.

Rose stood. "I don't think you have to worry."

"And I was so looking forward to it."

Vaughn laughed.

Aileen wrapped her arm around Vaughn's waist. "Enough of this silliness, Royce, you enjoy making Vaughn daft."

"That I do."

Vaughn grumbled, "And I enjoy bashing him." He turned to Rose. "Shall we get you something to eat? I do not want you fainting on me."

"I won't. I promise."

"You have not eaten?" Royce asked, with mock surprise. He raised an eyebrow, and his lips twitched as he tried to look serious. "What have you two been doing all this time? We have been gathered here, waiting for your arrival for over two hours." His eyes darted to the clock. "Make that three hours. Father is right. You do need a clock."

Rose looped her arm through Vaughn's and met Royce's mischievous gaze. "You mustn't blame Vaughn. Our tardiness was entirely my fault. I'm a slow dresser."

Vaughn placed her hand in Aileen's. "Take Rose into the breakfast room and let her eat before you and the other women take over her day." He bent down and placed a kiss firmly on Rose's lips. "I will see you later. I promise."

Aileen led Rose from the room. "I did not see any white tea gowns in your wardrobe. You know white is the fashionable color for weddings."

Rose glanced over her shoulder at Vaughn. By the look on his face, he wasn't too pleased with Royce. She wondered what they were discussing

"Rose," Aileen called, tugging on her arm. "Are you listening to me?"

"I'm sorry, Aileen. What were you saying?"

"I was only saying that I did not think you had any white gowns."

"I've been married before. I don't need to wear white. I have a nice green—"

"You cannot get married in green, married in green, ashamed to be seen."

"All right, how about pink?"

"Oh heavens, no. Married in pink, your heart will sink."

Rose rolled her eyes. "So what color can I wear? How about gray?"

"Married in gray, your love will go far away."

That chilled her. "Then certainly not gray."

Aileen stopped in front of the breakfast room door. "Let me see." She began to move her lips and count off on her finger. "Blue."

"Blue?"

"Yes. Married in blue, your love is true. And you have to wear orange blossoms. I'm sure Aunt Emma has some in the greenhouse. I do hope so. We will have to ask Mr. Peabody when we tour them."

Good grief, Rose hadn't had this much trouble when she married Richard, and she'd had to deal with his mother. Rose's heart lurched just a bit. By being in the past, living with Vaughn here, and growing older with him, what had she done to change Richard's future? She wondered if Richard would marry someone else, perhaps this time live a long and happy life. She hoped so. It would be wonderful if that happened. "Why orange blossoms?"

"Because they're fashionable," Aileen said matter-of-factly and opened the door.

Aileen stopped suddenly.

A mixture of emotions slammed into Rose, anger, and fear. She glanced over at Aileen. Her face paled, and her eyes were wide.

She gripped Rose's hand so tight she thought her bones would break. "Good morning, Philip. I thought everyone had already had breakfast."

Philip? Rose hadn't noticed anyone. She searched the room, spotting Philip by the window, holding a teacup. The glare from the window made it hard to see him, but she did notice the scowl he shot at Aileen.

"How could I eat before I discovered what all the excitement was about this morning? I mean, with his lordship summoning all of the Lucard family into the study and the hushed whispering of the servants. I have to admit my curiosity was aroused beyond control."

Rose coughed to cover up her snicker. When is Philip's curiosity not always aroused out of control? She took a plate from the sideboard and considered the delicious food. The oranges, eggs, potatoes, and sliced honey glazed ham made her mouth watered.

"Mrs. Kelly." Philip sneered "It is my understand congratulations are in order. I hear you succeeded in *seducing* yourself a rich husband."

"Philip!" Aileen gasped.

Rose almost dropped her plate. Surely, she hadn't heard him correctly. "Excuse me?"

He looked at her with disgust. "It is only my opinion. However, being found in an honorable man's bed almost always guarantees a ring." He set his cup on the table, then sauntered away.

Aileen grabbed Rose's plate before it slipped from her hands. "How dare he say that?"

"Don't worry about it, Aileen. As far as I'm concerned, Philip can take his opinion and shove it up his—"

"Rose," Aileen gasped.

"Ascot."

Royce leaned against the doorframe. "Rosie, I must say you have a way with words."

"Oh, bite me."

Royce threw his head back and roared with laughter. "Now you offer."

She turned her back and poured herself a glass of milk.

Large hands rested on her shoulders. Instinctively she knew from their familiar weight that they belonged to Vaughn.

"What has you so upset, love?" Vaughn brushed a kiss to her cheek.

"It's nothing."

"Nothing?" Aileen said, then proceeded to tell him everything Philip had said. "And this morning, right before Alan called us into the study, Philip tried to kiss me. I slapped his face and shoved him from me."

Vaughn's eyes glowed, and his lips thinned. "Leave Philip to me."

Chapter Eighteen

Today he would wed Rose. Vaughn gazed down at his mate, sleeping soundly. He should be in happier spirits, but he worried about her safety. Last night a groomsman discovered a rifle hidden in the stable. Alan was positive it hadn't come from the estate. Why would anyone want to harm Rose? She wasn't from this time. Maybe the culprit was after Royce.

If Royce had been the intended target, then the killer was human and didn't know Royce was Dhampir. Bullets would not kill their kind, bullets only irritated. Vaughn rubbed his hands over his face as he paced her bedroom. He threw open the balcony doors and ambled out into the cold, early morning air. The horizon held a faint glow. Why was it taking so long to catch this murderous bastard?

Vaughn slammed his fist down onto the marble banister. "Bloody hell!" Whom had he angered? They did not seek his death. They sought vengeance on him by killing those he loved. His mind whirled while he stared at the rising sun. He should be thinking of his wedding instead of a killer, but he knew his foe hid among Alan's guests.

Vaughn turned and went back into the room. He stopped at the side of the bed and stared down at Rose. If anything happened to her, how would he go on? She was his life. He had to find this murdering beast.

He brushed her hair from her face. How he wished this nightmare would end. As soon as he caught this villain, Vaughn vowed he would take Rose on a wedding trip far from London. Perhaps they would travel for a year. He'd take her to Egypt, the Far East, and India.

Rose rolled onto her side. The sheet slipped from her, exposing her beautiful breasts.

Just the sight of her made him want her again. He pulled the sheet up, covering her.

263

In an hour or so, Sara and Emma would be waking Rose to prepare her for the wedding. She needed her rest. He'd kept her up most of the night, making love to her. He cupped himself as he walked into the bathroom. He needed to finish dressing before he found himself buried deep inside her again.

Once dressed, he patted Beelzebub then brushed a light kiss across Rose's cheek.

Her eyes fluttered open. "Why are you up so early?"

"To prevent another scandalous morning."

When she sat, the sheet slipped to her waist. "I don't get it."

His eyes moved from her sleepy expression to her lush chest. "Sara, Emma, and Angelique will be here shortly to help you dress."

"But I have Molly to help me." Rose covered her mouth as she yawned.

"It is a tradition for the mated women from both families to assist the bride on this day. I believe it started as a way to explain to the young woman what went on in the marriage bed, and to inform her of any habits her future mate might have."

"Oh, well, in that case, I'll be sure to take notes."

He laughed. He finally understood one of Rose's unique phrases. "I believe Mum told you everything about me last night, including a few things I wish she had not."

"Mum? That's the first time I've heard you refer to Emma that way."

The word had slipped from his mouth without his realizing it. "I have called Emma mum in my heart and mind for so long." His throat tightened. "She can never replace my mother, but Emma filled the emptiness caused by my mother's death."

Rose slid from the bed. She didn't bother with her robe and plodded toward him. He groaned, taking in her lush body. Rose stepped close to him, pressing her nude self against him, and wrapping her arms around his neck. She would truly kill him before he had a chance to marry her.

"Emma loves you tremendously." Rose pressed her lips to his.

"I know and I her."

"So why don't you tell her?"

He exhaled. He'd asked himself that very question many times. "When Alan brought her here, I was already a man, but in my heart, I was still the lost boy Alan found all those years ago. However, Emma knew that deep inside me I harbored anger that would not die. One day I found myself telling her things I had not told another soul. That day the anger left me." He tipped Rose's face up and brushed a kiss across her lips. "After that, I never really knew what to call her. Lady Lucard seemed too formal, too cold, and to call her Emma never seemed respectful enough." He shrugged. "I called her madam with my mouth and mum with my heart."

"I think it would make her happy if you told her this."

He shook his head. "It is too late."

"No, it's not. If you have a chance, tell her. Please for me."

"The other day Alan told me Emma thought of me as a son."

"Alan does, too."

Vaughn laughed. "Alan? I think not. A charge, perhaps, maybe even a friend, but not a son."

"I won't argue, but I know I'm right."

"Do you?"

"Yes. I can see the pride in Alan's eyes when he looks at you."

A knot formed in Vaughn's throat and his eyes stung. He hugged Rose to him, resting his chin on her head. "I think my adopted family is quite fond of you, as well." He tilted his head so he could see her beautiful face. "The proof of which is the way they conspired, plotted and schemed to prevent me from speaking to you. What was it *Babushka* said last night?" He had to laugh, remembering the expression on Rose's face when they'd discovered the family had plotted to bring them together. "They wanted me to chase you until you caught me."

Rose leaned back. "Yeah, well, I'm kind of fond of them, too." She lifted herself on her tiptoes. She kissed his chin, then sighed. "Vaughn?"

He knew that tone. "What, my Love?"

"Is it possible for me to feel another Dhampir's emotions?"

"Why do you ask?"

"Yesterday morning when Aileen and I entered the breakfast room, I thought I felt hers. How can that be? I haven't given her my blood."

"Aileen is my sister. You feel her emotions because she and I share blood."

"That makes sense. Will I be able to feel Sara's and the rest of the Lucards?"

He nodded. "I have shared blood with all of my adoptive family. After the ceremony, you will feel their joy and their sadness, but you will not be able to hear their thoughts as clearly as you can mine."

She bit her lip and lowered her eyes. "Because of the drinking of the blood?"

Her thoughts flooded his mind, and he had to laugh. She pictured his family lining up to bite her. "You were not listening when I explained the ceremony to you."

She jerked her head up at him. "I was, too. You said Bishop North would hand me a glass of wine mixed with your blood and I will take a sip, then hand the glass to you. You did not tell me how everyone else would drink my blood."

"The glass contains a few drops of my family's blood. Drops of your blood and mine will be added during the ceremony."

She cringed. "So I will be drinking. . ." She lowered her eyes and turned her head.

"Sweetheart, it is not too late to have a regular wedding. You need not go through this for me."

"But I want to." She turned back to him. "Vaughn, I won't forget the look in your eyes when you told me of your sister's wedding, nor will I forget the smile on your face when I asked if we could have such a ceremony. I can do this. I can take a sip of wine. It is only a sip, right?"

He lifted Rose up, hugging her, then kissing her eyes, cheek, and finally her lips. *Yes, love, only a sip.*

He eased Rose down the front of him. Her naked body had aroused him to the point he wanted to bend her over and take her again. Instead, he tightened his arms around her. "Emma was right you are special."

Rose grinned. "You know she wants us to return for Christmas. Do you think we can?"

"Of course, I wouldn't think of having Christmas anywhere but here."

They had talked of weddings and wedding trips but not spoken of such things as Christmas, a holiday he immensely enjoyed. Perhaps such things were not observed in her time as Rose's birthday—Oh what a fool he'd been. He'd forgotten the pain he'd caused Rose on her birthday. "My love, do you celebrate holidays and birthdays in your time as we do now? Please forgive me for the pain I caused you on your birthday."

Rose tenderly smiled at him. "That night has been forgiven and forgotten. Besides, my favorite holiday is Christmas. Even when I lived by myself, I would always put up my Christmas tree the day after Thanksgiving. I didn't care if the tree was a small Charlie Brown tree. I just loved looking at the lights." She grinned up at him. "I can't wait to experience my first Victorian Christmas. I bet it will even be a white one. Living in the south all my life, I never had a white Christmas."

"I enjoy Christmas, too." He covered her hand with his. He would have to find out more about this Charlie Brown tree. Perhaps it was a new species of evergreen from her time. "More than likely we will have a snowfall. Then we will go skating."

"No."

"Why?" He frowned.

"Can't skate."

"Then I will teach you."

She threw her arms around his neck.

He gazed into her sparkling eyes. *Bloody hell, I wish I could take her far from here, just the two of us. She deserves a wedding trip. But I have to catch a murderer.* Vaughn eased Rose's arms from around his neck. "Come Spring I will take you on a wedding trip. And next year we will celebrate your birthday the way we should have celebrated it."

The love shining in her eyes warmed him.

"You don't have to take me on a honeymoon. However, that isn't what's bothering you. Is it?"

"I will take you on a wedding trip, and nothing is bothering me?"

Her lovely mouth twisted into a frown. "You're not doing a good job of hiding your thoughts. You're thinking about the murderer. You have been all morning."

Vaughn hadn't thought Rose was so attuned to him. He should have blocked his thoughts from her, but he'd promised he wouldn't. "I think he is here."

Rose nodded. "That's why you and Royce disappeared last night."

"Yes. A servant found a rifle in the stables."

"You think the person who shot at Royce and I is also responsible for the murders?"

"It is my assumption."

"Do you have any clue as to his identity?"

"No."

Rose bit her lower lip. "We can eliminate a few suspects by where they were at the time we were riding." She tapped her chin with her index finger. "And we can—"

He swatted her backside.

"Ouch! That hurt." She glared at him, rubbing her buttocks.

"There is no we, as far as this goes," he told her firmly, liking the faint pink of her buttocks. But not as much as the scent of her arousal. Which gave him delicious ideas.

"Every great detective needs a side-kick. Holmes Watson and—"

"Rose! I will not have you putting yourself in danger."

Her eyes darkened, and her lips thinned.

Vaughn set her from him and studied her stubborn expression, a look he knew he would receive many times in their life together. "You are my mate and the mother of my child."

His pocket watch chimed, saving him from the argument near at hand. The women would be here shortly to dress Rose. "I'd best take my leave."

He tilted his head and covered her mouth with his.

Someone knocked, and he ended their kiss, then handed Rose her nightgown.

"I think we've been caught again." Rose giggled.

"I do believe so." He walked over to the door, then opened it. Emma frowned up at him.

"Off with you now," Emma said, stepping into the room, and pushing him out. The rest of the ladies followed Emma into the room.

"You're as bad as Ian." Angelique winked.

Sara tsked, shaking her head at him.

Emma glanced over her shoulder. "Go on, son. You have only two hours to get ready." She shut the door.

Son. The word rang in his mind as he stared at the closed door.

His spirits soared. Rose was right. It wasn't too late to tell Emma how he felt.

Whistling, Vaughn made his way to his room. He quickly bathed then changed into his gray morning coat.

Vaughn stared at the small burgundy box from his vanity. He hesitated before opening it. Inside rested three rings he remembered his parents wearing, an emerald and diamond ring, and two matching wedding bands. Human males, seldom if ever, wore wedding rings. Vaughn would honor this Dhampiric custom with pride.

How Alan found the rings in the burnt-out rubble of Vaughn's parents home, Vaughn did not know, but he was thankful.

Vaughn fingered the small gold band. He'd given the rings to Aileen on her hundredth birthday. Last night before dinner she'd given them back, insisting he and Rose use them for their wedding rings.

He shut his eyes and pictured his parents. They would have loved Rose.

Someone knocked, bringing his thoughts out of the past.

He opened his eyes and slid the box into his coat pocket. "Enter."

Philip stepped into the room. "Vaughn, a moment of your time."

Vaughn drew in a deep breath. He needed to speak with Philip about his pursuing Aileen, but this was not the time. "Can this wait?"

"You should not marry this woman."

His jubilant mood waned. "And why not?"

"She is human."

"A fact I am quite aware of."

Philip crossed his arms over his chest. "Humans cannot be trusted. They hunted us down like frightened deer when we should have been hunting them for their blood."

"We do not need to slaughter humans for their blood to survive. If you remember, not all humans betrayed us. Some even gave their lives to protect us. My grandmother was human as was yours."

"A part of my lineage I am not proud of."

"If that is how you feel, then I pity you."

"Do not. All human females are whores."

Vaughn shoved Philip against the wall. "Both my mate and my adopted mother are human. It would behoove you to remember this."

Philip broke Vaughn's hold. "I meant no disrespect to your women. Hear me out. We are destroying our race by mating with humans. Your blood and Aileen's is like mine. We have the purest blood for our generation. Both of your parents were Dhampir. I have asked Aileen to mate with me. She need not love me to produce a pure child."

"My sister has already found her true mate."

"Found, but not claimed. I plan to persuade Aileen to see things my way. After all, I only have the well-being of our people at heart. Caitlin and Victoria are both of age. Perhaps you should take one of them."

"Caitlin or Victoria?" He shivered. "They are like sisters to me. It would be like bedding Aileen. Even if our laws did not condemn such perversion, I would never think of such a thing."

"The Creator will not condemn you. They are not your blood."

"They may not be, but they are my sisters."

"Vaughn, we need to strengthen our bloodlines. It sickens me to think we are committing genocide by mating with the creatures of this world."

"Genocide? Dorjan, you use a word from our ancestral home? Do you wish to create our past world? A world neither of us ever knew. The only pure among us are the ancients such as Mishenka, Sara, their siblings, and of course his lordship."

"Exactly my point. Do you not see what we are doing to ourselves? The more we breed with humans, the weaker we become. Look at our lord. He took a human for a mate, and their offspring should have been drowned at birth. Royce is a weakling."

"I will not listen to any more of your rubbish. Royce is my brother. Rose is my mate." Vaughn glared at Philip. "Stay away from Aileen or deal with me." He left his room and made his way to the drawing room, leaving Philip behind.

Vaughn threw open the door. Royce sat on the couch with his arms behind his head, while Alan and Mishenka stood on the balcony.

Royce looked up. "Why such a sour look? Have you and Rose had a squabble?"

"No."

"Then what? You should be joyous."

"Dorjan." Vaughn slammed the door.

Alan turned and stepped into the room. His expression hardened. "I regret inviting him here. He has hounded Aileen like a love-sick pup." He glanced at Mishenka. "Is Philip Aileen's destined mate?"

"Thank the Creator he is not." Mishenka took his pipe from his mouth and came over to Vaughn. "Aileen's mate is here. And we all know who he is. Don't we?" An evil smile curved Mishenka's lips. "Ah, the Creator has a wicked sense of humor." He laughed.

Vaughn's anger left. Yes, *She* did. Mishenka had hated Ian MacPhee almost as much as Ian hated the Campbells. "I do not think we have to worry about Philip anymore. I have told him to stay away from Aileen." He shuddered. "He has bizarre ideas about not taking humans as mates."

Mishenka held up his hand. "Let us speak of more pleasant matters. How did you persuade Rose to have a traditional ceremony?"

Vaughn grinned, remembering their conversation last night. Once he'd informed her, the good Bishop was Dhampir. Rose had wanted a traditional Dhampir ceremony. "It was her idea, Grandfather."

Mishenka raised his eyebrows. "Did you tell her about the blood?"

"Yes, Grandfather." Vaughn chuckled to himself, then took the burgundy box from his coat pocket, and handed it to Alan.

Alan offered his arm to Vaughn. "Are you ready?"

Despite the sudden weakness in his legs Vaughn nodded and walked from the room with Alan.

Royce and the rest of the male family members, along with the few guests followed.

Vaughn noticed Philip wasn't among the guests. At least the man wasn't a hypocrite.

The large doors leading into the ballroom opened. In the center of the room, Bishop North stood in front of a small table. A silver goblet sat on the table.

Vaughn gazed across the room, and his breath caught. Rose was beautiful. She wore a light blue gown with a high neck and long sheer sleeves. She'd pulled her hair on top of her head, allowing a few loose curls to frame her face.

It pleased him to see Emma standing on Rose's right, where his mother would have stood. Sara took the place of Rose's mother. Behind them, he saw Aileen. She winked at him.

He nearly laughed, seeing Beelzebub sitting at Rose's feet as if the bloody cat was a member of the wedding party.

~ ~ ~

Rose stared across the ballroom at Vaughn. The look of love shining in his eyes made him appear extremely handsome in his morning coat and pinstriped trousers.

When his eyes met hers, a warm euphoria engulfed her. This was right. She belonged in this time with him.

Bishop North motioned them into the room.

As Sara and Emma led Rose to the center of the room, Alan and Mishenka led Vaughn. They stopped in front of the table facing each other.

Vaughn had explained the ceremony was a joining of families.

273

Bishop North opened the book he held. "Do you, Mishenka and Sara Lucard of the line Lucard, claim this woman to your line as your daughter? And do you, Alan, and Emma Lucard of the line Lucard, claim this man to your line as your son?"

"We do," they said in unison.

"Then join their blood with yours." Bishop North handed Sara a white napkin.

Sara unfolded the napkin, revealing a silver knife. She smiled at Rose, taking her hand, and drawing the blade across her palm. Then Sara handed Alan the silver knife, and he drew the blade across Vaughn's palm.

Rose stared at the blood welling in her hand. Surprisingly, the cut had not hurt.

Bishop North lifted the goblet from the table, then took Rose's hand, held it over the goblet, and allowed her blood to drip into the wine. He then did the same with Vaughn's hand. Bishop North then placed Rose's bloody hand in Vaughn's. "As the blood of these two joins that already within the chalice, so do they join these families."

Bishop North looked at Mishenka. "Do you now give Rose as mate and sole mother of all children to Vaughn, born to the line Madoc, from now until the end of time?"

"We do," Sara and Mishenka, responded.

"Do you Alan and Emma Lucard of the line Lucard accept this woman as the true and only mate for your son, Vaughn Madoc?"

"We do," they said.

Alan removed a box from his pocket and opened it. Smiling, he took Rose's hand in his and slid two rings onto her finger, an emerald and diamond ring, and a gold band. He bent toward her and kissed her on her cheek, then gave the box to Mishenka.

He removed a large ring from the box, then slid the ring on Vaughn's finger.

Bishop North lifted the goblet from the table and held it above his head. "This vessel holds the essence of life. It will bind you to all who drink of it. Drink and become one." He handed the goblet to Alan. "Woman was created from man to be his partner and mate."

Alan took a sip, then held the goblet as Emma drank, she then passed the goblet to Mishenka.

Bishop North glanced at Vaughn. "Our God made woman to be protected by her mate and to be cherished by him. She is the vessel of life and the mother of his children."

After Sara drank from the goblet, Bishop North handed it to Rose. "Women were given a strong heart and strength to suffer the pain of childbirth. She was given compassion to understand and support her mate in time of need. Drink and join his family."

Rose stared at the dark liquid, then glanced up at Vaughn. Love filled his eyes, and all of her anxiousness vanished. She took a sip.

Vaughn's gaze met Rose's when he took the goblet from her. He drank the remaining liquid before he handed the chalice back to Bishop North.

"You are now husband and wife," Bishop North said, handing Vaughn a quill pen to sign the wedding register.

A round of cheers went up behind them.

Someone wrapped his arms around her, turning her.

"Royce," she greeted him.

He lifted her and firmly kissed her on the lips. "I don't get bashed for kissing you today." He winked, then set her feet back on the ground.

Vaughn's arms protectively circled her waist. "Mine," he growled at Royce.

Mishenka hugged them both. "Congratulations, my boy," he said, patting Vaughn on the back. "You have done my old heart good." He tenderly brushed a kiss across Rose's cheek. "And you, my girl, will bring new life into this family."

She gazed up into Mishenka's moist eyes.

Mishenka beamed and slid his hands down her arms. "I believe your child will be as strong as his father and his father before him. Who knows, he may even have the power of the DuMond line just as Vaughn's mother had."

Aileen ran up to them. "Dear sister, I can call you that now. You are my sister and my dearest friend. I could not have asked for more."

"Congratulations," someone said.

The joy and love Rose felt from Vaughn's family overcame her, flooded her mind and heart. Her head whirled as if she were drunk. She gripped Vaughn's hand to steady herself.

"Rose?"

She touched her forehead and blinked her eyes. So many emotions and whispers of thoughts rushed through her mind. "I'm fine."

"You lie."

She elbowed him. "I'm fine," she whispered behind a forced smile.

He chuckled. "It will pass, I promise."

A servant opened the large doors and announced brunch being served. Soft music floated from the room.

After the photographer took their wedding photos, including one where Rose demanded they smile, Vaughn led her into the dining room. Several people offered toasts in their honor during the meal. It seemed each time she lifted the fork to her lips someone new was offering up a toast.

Vaughn nudged her and pointed to Aileen slipping out the side door. "It appears my sister is sneaking out to meet David," he whispered.

"I could do with some fresh air myself."

"Are you feeling dizzy again?" He stood, helping her to her feet.

"A little." She took his arm. "There are so many different emotions, and thoughts swirling around in my mind that I can't separate them out from mine. It's giving me a headache."

"You will grow accustomed to your new senses. Take a deep breath and concentrate only on my thoughts."

She did. "I think I now understand how my computer must feel when I overload its system."

Vaughn raised an eyebrow and frowned at her. "I look forward to the day I fully understand all that you speak of." He led her through the open balcony doors and down the steps to the garden. "Are you happy living in this time?" he asked, staring into her eyes.

"Very much so, because I have you."

The farther they strolled from the house, the more serene her mind became until she could only hear her thoughts and Vaughn's. "You're right. I can't tell whose thoughts slip into my mind, only yours and I think Aileen's. Everyone else's thoughts are faint whispers."

"With time, you will ignore them." He folded her hand over his arm.

A cool November wind blew.

Rose shivered. "It looks like rain."

"We should go back inside."

"Not yet." She wasn't ready for the onslaught of emotions she knew waited for her.

Vaughn slid his jacket off and draped it over her shoulders. "Then this should keep you warm."

The wind blew harder, rustling the few leaves left on the trees.

Rose snuggled against him. "Let's go to the conservatory. It'll be warmer there."

"Vaughn," Royce called.

Vaughn rolled his eyes, then smiled at her. "Go ahead. I'll be there shortly."

Rose pulled Vaughn's coat tight across her chest and glanced up at the sky. Dark clouds loomed on the horizon.

She reached for the conservatory door as a shiver of panic gripped her. Storms had never frightened her before, so why did she feel so scared and helpless?

Rose pulled open the door as Aileen's screams mingled with the wind.

Chapter Nineteen

Rose flung open the conservatory door. Aileen was struggling with a man on the floor. Rose pushed the paralyzing fears from her mind and grabbed a shovel leaning against the wall. She swung at Aileen's attacker. "Get off her!"

The blow knocked the man from Aileen. He whirled around. His fangs glistened with blood, and his red eyes blazed with hatred.

"Philip," she gasped and gripped the shovel. "You son-of-a—"

He snarled and sprang toward her, knocking her backward. As she fell, she used the shovel still in her hand as leverage, flipping Philip off and behind her. Rose turned, but before she could prepare for his next attack, Philip was on her. He pinned her to her back, his hands grabbing her throat squeezing, choking her life from her.

Rose had to break free. She had to fight back. She would not let him win. Remembering her self-defense class, with all the strength Rose had she went for his eyes.

"Rose!" Vaughn shouted from behind her.

Philip screamed, and he released her throat, covering his face with his hands. He still straddled her hips. She dug her nails into his face again. Blood and fluid gushed from his right eye. She'd gouged her thumb into Philip's eye once more.

Vaughn's intense range filled Rose as he yanked Philip from her. He slammed against a table, sending clay pots crashing to the floor.

Rose scrambled to her feet in time to see Vaughn and Philip tumble backward through the glass door. She balled her fists, digging her nails into her palms, forcing Vaughn's emotions to the back of her mind. Aileen needed her.

Tears welled in Rose's eyes as Aileen's shame replaced Vaughn's rage.

So many thoughts pounded Rose's mind. It was as if she stood in the middle of the electronics department with every television and radio tuned to a different station. All the noise gave her a white-light migraine. She had to get a grip on her emotions. Otherwise, she wouldn't be any help to her mate and her sister. Rose gritted her teeth, determined to make herself immune to all other feelings but her own. She shoved all emotions from her mind.

Aileen's soft sobs broke through Rose's thoughts. She hurried to Aileen and knelt beside her. Aileen lay on her side, with her knees drawn up and dress shoved to her waist. Aileen's undergarments were ripped from her and tossed aside.

Rose reached her hand out, noticing her blood-drenched fingers. She wiped Philip's blood on her dress. She didn't want that bastard's blood on her skin or Aileen's. Rose tenderly brushed Aileen's hair away from her neck, noticing the wounds in Aileen's throat. "Aileen, do you need blood?"

Aileen vigorously shook her head and cried, blood-tinged tears streamed down her cheeks.

Rose pulled Aileen's tattered bodice together, then smoothed her skirt down over her legs. "Hush, I've got you. You're safe now." She shrugged Vaughn's coat off and covered Aileen.

"Phillip followed me," Aileen exclaimed. "I told him no. He just laughed, then he. . ." Aileen buried her face against Rose and cried.

Rose held Aileen, gritted her teeth, wishing for fangs. She'd love to rip that asshat's throat out. How dare that bastard do this to sweet Aileen? If it were up to Rose, she'd bring Philip back to life after Vaughn killed him, so that she could kill Philip again. Maybe even three or four times.

The far conservatory door flew opened. Rose covered Aileen's body with hers and looked up as David ran toward them.

"Aileen, dear God." David knelt beside them, pulling took Aileen into his embrace, meeting Rose's gaze. "Did he?"

Rose shook her head. "I don't know."

Aileen shoved from David. She wrapped her arms around herself, and rocked back and forth, avoiding his eyes. "He did not take me. If it hadn't been for Rose, Philip would have. He was too strong."

"Aileen," David said softly.

She leaned closer to Rose. "How can you look at me, knowing what Philip tried to do? I must have done something to cause this, to make him think I desired him. To make him think. . ."

David drew Aileen back to him, framed her face, and forced her to look at him. "Aileen *Nic a' Phì*, you did nothing wrong. Do not make Philip's evil your fault. Philip's evil is his."

She closed her eyes and shook her head. "But I must have...," her voice broke.

"Aileen, listen to me. You are the other half of my heart. I love you."

"But—"

David placed his finger against her lips. "I will say this one more time. This was not your fault. I love you."

"David, you forgive me." Aileen fell into his arms.

"My love, there is nothing to forgive. It is I who should beg your forgiveness, for not being here to protect you."

Rose stood and wiped her tears. Aileen was safe with David.

Rose had to find Vaughn. His rage still roared in the back of her mind. She turned and met the angry glare of Ian MacPhee. He filled the doorway. His jaw clenched tight, the muscles twitching. She glanced over her shoulder at David and Aileen, then back to Ian. So not good.

His hands hung limply at his side as he beheld Aileen. "*Ma* daughter—," his voice broke, and he cleared his throat. He took a step toward Aileen and stopped. Tears welled in his eyes. "Campbell, carry *ma* daughter *inta* the house. Her wounds need tending."

David stood, scooping Aileen up into his arms. "What of the bastard who did this? He needs to pay."

A grim smile crossed Ian's lips. "The blood rage is upon Vaughn. Tha' *deil* who did this is gettin' what he deserves." Ian motioned to the far door. "We can take ma child this way and avoid the crowd out front."

Rose rushed outside, pushing her way past Tristan and his brothers. A drizzling rain fell, and thunder rumbled in the distance. Someone grabbed her upper arm, yanking her back from the two men fighting.

"Stay back. Your thoughts and fears will distract Vaughn," Emma said.

Rose stared at Vaughn. His eyes glowed with the same anger she remembered seeing the night in the alley. She couldn't watch. She turned, scanning the crowd. Alan and Royce stood closest to Vaughn, cheering him on, while several male servants stood back, making bets.

Battle rage pounded inside Vaughn's head. He rolled, pinning Philip to the ground. "Damn you, Dorjan! I'll see you in Hell."

Despite not wanting to watch the fight, Rose could not help turning her attention to the battle.

"You think?" Philip sneered, jabbing his claws into Vaughn's side, and pushing him off.

Rose screamed. Blood soaked Vaughn's shirt.

"You've grown weak, living as a human." Philip scrambled to his feet.

Vaughn grabbed Philip by the throat with one hand and brought his other down across Philip's face. "Who's weak? My mate claimed your eye." Vaughn tightened his grip.

Philip thrust his free hand toward Vaughn's heart. "You'll be easier to kill than Wilcox."

Vaughn knocked Philip's hand away, bringing his clawed hand across Philip's face once again. "Wilcox? It was you?"

"Who do you think?" Philip whispered. He broke free of Vaughn's hold and jumped out of Vaughn's reach. "I killed him." He lunged for Rose.

To shocked by Philip's admission to move, she stared at him. She should have seen the signs. He was a braggart and cruel to animals.

"Rose!" Vaughn shouted and lunged at Philip, who dodged away from Vaughn.

Emma shoved Rose, pushing her to the ground.

Rose pushed to her hands and knees, finally making it to her feet. Philip held Emma in front of him, his clawed hand grasping her slender neck, red crescent shapes formed on her throat around his claws, and her blood trickled down her neck.

"Dorjan let her go, and I'll be merciful," Alan said, stepping toward them. His eyes glowed, his nails were black claws, and his fangs extended. Rose noticed Alan's brow, where small horns had erupted. She gasped as his massive black wings fluttered behind him. The man resembled the drawings she'd seen in books of demons. No, gargoyles—protectors.

"Merciful? Is that what you called it when you slaughtered my father, brothers, and the men of my clan?"

"Let my mother go!" Royce roared, running toward Philip.

"Come closer, and I'll rip out her throat," Philip hissed.

Vaughn grabbed Royce, pulling him back. "He killed Wilcox. He'll kill her as well."

"What do you want, Dorjan?" Vaughn demanded.

"Revenge."

"Why? I never harmed any of your family."

"Liar! I saw you tear my father's beating heart from his chest. My mother died three days later of grief. You murdered her, as well."

~ ~ ~

Vaughn stared at Emma. Fear showed on her face and tears welled in her eyes. Memories of his mother's screams pounded his brain. He would not let Emma suffer the same fate. He would free her, but to do so without harming her would take a level head. Anger would only bring her harm.

Rose's fears washed over him. She blamed herself for Philip capturing Emma.

Briefly, he made eye contact with Rose. *Do not worry, Love. We will not let anything happen to Emma.* He turned his full attention to Philip.

Vaughn tried to remember whom he'd killed that way. He sent his thoughts to Alan. *I know not what Dorjan is speaking. I tore the hearts from those who murdered my parents. However, they were Dietrich's men.*

Alan nodded. *It is possible Dorjan is not Philip's name.* "Who are you?"

Tristan and his brothers circled behind Philip.

"Call off your dogs," Philip warned.

The muscles in Alan's jaw twitched, and he glanced toward the Wolfe brothers. They moved back and away from Philip.

Alan eased closer to Philip. "Who are you?"

"Dietrich!"

Emma screamed and dropped to the ground. Blood spurted from her neck.

"Mother!" Vaughn lunged toward Emma, catching her in his arms and covering her wound with his mouth. He had to stop the bleeding, or he'd lose her. He knelt as Alan held his mate's hand. His face contorted with fear.

In his peripheral vision, he watched as Philip changed into a wolf and made his escape. Vaughn would worry about Philip later. Now, all that mattered was his mother.

Tristan and his brothers tore from their clothing and changed into their wolfen-forms, giving chase. Tristan didn't wait for his brothers, as he took off after Philip.

Royce knelt beside his mother, taking her hand in his, blood-tinged tears ran down his cheeks.

Vaughn lifted his mouth and sat back on his heels. He gently passed Emma to Alan. The wounds in Emma's throat were healing, but the amount of blood loss was great.

Alan cradled Emma's head on his lap. He bit into his wrist and pressed it against her mouth, gently massaging her throat.

Rose placed her hand on Vaughn's shoulder, giving him strength. "Is she going to be all right?"

He reached up, covering Rose's hand. He prayed Emma would be. He could not bear to lose her. He should not have hesitated in killing Philip, but Vaughn wanted Philip to suffer for what he did to Aileen.

"What can I do?" Rose asked, kneeling beside Vaughn.

He shook his head. "Nothing." However, he could do something. He could finish what he'd started. "I'm going after Philip." He stood and started toward the stables.

"Son," Alan called. "There will be time later to hunt Philip."

Now was not the time to argue. So many strong emotions ate at him. Hate for Philip and fear for his mother's life. Emma was so very pale.

Royce held Emma's hand, keeping his gaze intently on her face.

Vaughn gripped Royce's shoulder, feeling his pain, sharing his fear.

Emma's eyelids fluttered open, and Vaughn's heart eased. She smiled, squeezing Royce's hand, then turned her head and smiled at Alan. "My love," she whispered.

"Mum," Royce's voice cracked. He turned his face from her. His body shook as he let his tears stream down his cheeks.

Alan kissed Emma as he lifted her in his arms. He nodded toward Royce and Vaughn. "Let's get your mother into the house."

~ ~ ~

Vaughn closed the door to Aileen's room. She'd finally fallen asleep. He smiled at Rose, hoping to ease her fears. "David will make her a good husband."

"Yes, he will." Rose laced her fingers with Vaughn's and leaned against him. "Where did David, Glen, and your Uncle go?"

"Where I should be, out hunting Philip down. Blast it all! I don't understand why Alan insisted I remain here. Neither Ian nor Glen will be a match for Philip and certainly not David."

"Don't forget Quaid and Morgan are also hunting Philip." Rose slid her arm around his waist. "I'm sure Alan has good reasons. How's Royce holding up?"

"I'm doing fine, Rose," Royce said, walking up behind them. He gripped Vaughn's shoulder. "If Uncle Ian and Glen do not return soon, I say you, and I go after them. I want a piece of Philip myself."

"I agree. How is Emma?"

"She is still so very pale, but *Babushka* is giving Mum blood." The muscles in Royce's jaw twitched, but he didn't hide his tears. "I felt like such a coward. I couldn't do anything when I saw her fall. I just stood there."

Rose hugged him. "No one thinks you were a coward. You were in shock, Royce."

He looked up and wiped the tears from his cheek, then pointed to Vaughn's injury. "You've lost a lot of blood." Royce motioned to their room. "Come. Let me tend to your need."

Vaughn's fangs lengthened at the thought. The hunger had been gnawing at him. He glanced at Rose. She knew what he was, but he didn't want her to see him feed, not now when their love was still fresh. He didn't want her to see him as the monster of lore. "Thank you for your offer, but it looks worse than it is."

Rose narrowed her eyes. "Vaughn Madoc," she hissed through clenched teeth. "I feel your pain, and I don't know how you've stood it for this long. If you don't let Royce help you, then let me." She tilted her head, revealing the vein throbbing below the surface.

He nodded to Royce, as he opened the door to their room. Vaughn paused and glanced at his stubborn wife. "Rose, Aileen needs you."

~ ~ ~

Rose stared at Vaughn before turning and walking down the hall to Aileen's room. There was no reason for him to be embarrassed. She knew he needed blood to heal, and she'd bet Aileen didn't need her. She was probably still in a healing sleep.

Rose knocked lightly on the door. Receiving no answer, she slowly opened it and drew in a deep breath. She knew it. This was a ploy by Vaughn. Aileen slept peacefully.

"Do you need something, Rose?" Angelique asked. She sat on the chair near the bed.

"No. I was checking on Aileen. Can I get you anything?"

"Not unless you can get me that bastard's head."

"I'd have to get in line."

Angelique smiled. "Aileen told her father what you did, taking on a male and having the strength to wound him was extremely brave. Still, Philip may have killed you."

"The thought of Philip killing me, never entered my mind. Aileen is my sister. I couldn't let him hurt her. It galls the hell out of me. Philip has probably crawled under a rock somewhere waiting for his eye to grow back. I wish I had grabbed the pitchfork instead of the damn shovel."

"The bastard's eye will not grow back."

"May I ask a question?" Angelique nodded. "David referred to Aileen as *Nic a' Phì*. What does that mean? I'm curious."

"It means the daughter of the MacPhee," Angelique replied. "And you'll be pleased to know Aileen and David will wed as soon as she is strong enough and the banns read." She smiled. "Thus says the MacPhee."

287

"I'm glad. Aileen and David love each other very much." Rose pulled the door closed, then returned to the room she shared with Vaughn.

Vaughn lifted his mouth from Royce's wrist as she entered.

She crossed the room and smiled at Royce. "Thank you." She wiped the blood from Vaughn's mouth and brushed a kiss to his cheek. "Angelique told me Aileen and David would be married as soon as she is well enough."

~ ~ ~

Vaughn met Rose's gaze. He saw only understanding and love. "I figured they would when I saw David and Ian in her room and not trying to kill each other."

Royce strode toward the open door. "I don't know about you two, but I'm not standing around here, doing nothing anymore."

"It's been three hours since the Wolfes went after Philip. They should have returned with some news by now." Vaughn walked out onto the balcony and stared across the meadow. "Unless they were Philip's allies." He'd underestimated Philip, something he wouldn't do a second time.

"Vaughn!" Rose gasped. "How can you say that?"

He understood her shock, felt her anger wash over him. She liked the Wolfe brothers, but the facts were there. "They can shift just as Philip."

"You did not just say that," Rose replied.

Royce shook his head. "I know our cousins. They would not betray the family."

"You're right. Bloody hell, I sound as bigoted as Phillip." Vaughn scrubbed his hands over his face. "Forgive me my stupidity. I'm frustrated and lashing out at our family. I have fought alongside both Morgan and Quaid." He sighed. "I can't stand around any longer doing nothing. What do you say we go after Ian and Glen, just in case they need our help?"

"No, you will not!" Alan stood in the open doorway, his eyes red with anger, but his horns no longer visible. "Emma and I fear for your safety. You will remain here."

Vaughn clenched his hand. Alan didn't trust him. "I underestimated Philip once. I will not permit it to happen again."

"Vaughn is right," Royce agreed. "We should be hunting the bastard instead of sitting here on our hands."

Alan's eyes flicked. "Both of you listen well. Your mother needs you here. She needs all of us." Alan turned his angry glare to Vaughn. "You still think as a fledgling. Perhaps Philip wants you to chase him? Has it occurred to you he may have men waiting for you to go after him so he can return and butcher our women!"

"I hadn't thought of that." Vaughn looked away. He'd underestimated Philip again. His gaze fell to Rose. Today was her wedding day. Her dress was tattered and bloodstained. "I have made many blunders in my life, but none as bad as the one I made today. I hesitated in killing Philip, and because of it, Emma suffered. Her injuries are entirely my fault."

"No, Vaughn, what happened today started long before you were born." Alan placed his hand on Vaughn's shoulders and glanced at Rose. "Let's go down to the parlor and wait for Ian's return."

As they walked down the steps, Ian burst through the door carrying Tristan's naked body. His side had a huge gaping gash. His head hung limply over Ian's arm. The gaping wound in Tristan's throat could have been a killing wound.

The guilt of his earlier words weighted on Vaughn as he stared at Tristan's wound. "All of this because of Philip's revenge." Vaughn's anger became a scalding fury, burning at his soul. "Tristan is a boy, a child. Damn Dorjan to hell!"

"Let's get him to bed." Rose dropped Vaughn's hand and hurried back up the stairs. He felt her worry for the boy, her anger for what Philip had done to the pup.

Vaughn turned to follow Rose as David and Glen entered, closely followed by Morgan and Quaid, both bloodied and naked. They were both fierce warriors.

"What happened?" Alan demanded of Quaid.

"Tristan broke away from us. He said he knew of a path that would cut Philip off. By the time we reached them, Philip and six others had Tristan down. If it had not been for you sending Ian and his sons after us, I fear we would not be here." Quaid met Vaughn's gaze. "We've seen to Tee's blood need. His body just needs to heal."

They followed Ian into the room. A moan slipped from Tristan as Ian placed him on the bed. "'Twas a *sarry* sight we found." Ian shook his head. "Philip and two other Dhampir escaped. We took care of the others. Two were humans."

Alan narrowed his eyes. "What do you mean by were?"

Ian grinned, then slapped Alan on the back. "Now, *brither* what do you think I mean? These lads needed blood after seeing to their brother's needs." He pointed to Quaid and Morgan. "I'm *sarry* tha' we weren't able to kill all of them."

Alan rubbed his hands over his face. "I thought the clan feuds were over."

Morgan and Quaid stood near Tristan's bed, licking their wounds, and keeping an eye on their younger brother, watching every moved Rose made. The fur rippled over their bodies with each moan and whimper that Tristan made. Quaid's upper lip quivered with a snarl.

Sara strolled into the room, followed closely behind by a male servant. Harry, Vaughn believed the boy's name to be. "Quaid, Morgan, go clean up and put on clothing. We'll tend to the boy. And do not argue with me. Go." Sara motioned to the door while studying Tristan's battered body. Her lips pulled thin. "I have a good mind to skin him alive once he recovers. Impish pup, making me worry." Vaughn noticed the moisture shimmering in Sara's eyes. The whelp had wormed his way into her heart, as well.

Rose and Sara washed Tristan's battered body. The wounds weren't as angry as when he first arrived. What had that whelp been thinking?

A faint moan slipped from Tristan. "Shh, I've got you. You're safe." Rose whispered, quieting him.

Vaughn watched her briefly, then backed from the room and closed the door.

Mishenka stood in the hall. "I've called a meeting. The others are in the study."

Alan had groomed Vaughn as the Enforcer from the moment Alan wrapped his wings around Vaughn's shoulders. He was the one who ensured justice was carried out, the one who ensured their people upheld the laws. Vaughn didn't have to attend 'the meeting,' he knew the task before him, and he would happily execute. Philip would die.

Vaughn pushed open the heavy oak door and entered the study. He met the gazes of the men who had attended his wedding a few hours ago. Their earlier smiles replaced with grim expressions.

Alan stood in the center of the room. "You are all aware of what happened. Philip is to be killed on sight. Anyone aiding him will die as well. I will not risk the destruction of our race because of the ill-will of one individual. We will stop Dietrich. He now calls himself Dorjan."

"Dietrich?" The name echoed in the room.

Mishenka held up his hands. "Listen to me. Dietrich happened because I refused to kill the mates and young of my enemies. My compassion proved to be a mistake."

Vaughn respected Mishenka too much to permit the man to shoulder the blame. "No, Mishenka, this is not your fault. I'm the one who first sought revenge."

Mishenka pierced him with his cold eyes. "This started long before you were born, Vaughn. Raoul and his elite guard believed each clan had to stay to themselves. He did not believe in inter-mating. He also believed humans were only food. His purist beliefs were never made so clear to me than

291

the night he dragged Sara from our bed. Dietrich held me while Raoul ran his sword through her. Though I saved her life, we lost the child she carried."

Nausea rose in Vaughn's throat. He'd not heard this story before.

"Sara's only crime was she came from another clan. She was DuMond, as was your mother, Kimberly." Mishenka pointed at Vaughn. "Your grandfather, Ibon, was my dearest friend and Raoul's younger brother. Ibon led the rebellion against Raoul and the Dietrich clan."

The last piece fell into place. "Philip continues the clan wars. It has to end. Too many innocent people have died while our race is dwindling to near extinction."

Alan nodded and glanced behind Vaughn.

Vaughn turned. Rose and Sara stood at the back wall. The look in Rose's eyes told him she'd heard.

"Your Lordship," one of the men said, as he went down on one knee. "My house is loyal to the line Lucard."

The others in the room also went down on their knees, each swearing their fidelity.

Alan cleared his throat. "Dietrich." He shook his head. "Dorjan has followers who will suffer the same fate." He hesitated, and his jaw twitched. "As well as their families."

"No!" Vaughn would gladly kill Philip and those who followed him, but the thought of killing innocents sickened Vaughn. He turned and left the room, ushering Rose out with him.

He stopped, then framed her face in his hands, and kissed her, briefly. "When I return to London you will remain here or with Mishenka and Sara."

"No."

Chapter Twenty

Rose paused in her writing. She glanced at her wedding photo with Vaughn. She giggled remembering the expression on the photographer's face when she told everyone to smile. She didn't care if it wasn't *fashionable,* she wanted everyone to look happy and not like they were sucking on lemons.

Rose then stared out the parlor window. The soft glow of the streetlights reflected the snow as it gently fell, blanketing the ground. A cold December wind whistled in the tree branches. She shivered at the sound and turned back to her writing, thankful for the warm fire in the fireplace.

Beelzebub placed his paw on her hand. His tail swished across her journal. She gently moved him aside and glanced at her writing. Her journal had provided a welcome escape from the chaotic activities of the past six weeks. She wondered if things would ever calm down, perhaps after Christmas.

David and Aileen were wed and lived at his estate. Tristan had recovered and was back at Eton, while his brothers searched the continent for Philip. All of the leads in England had grown cold. Mishenka and Alan believed Philip was hiding somewhere in Europe or possibly the States. However, America was too uncivilized for Philip. Vaughn disagreed with them all. He strongly believed Philip was still somewhere in London.

She turned the page, wondering how Vaughn had convinced Alan not to punish all of the Dorjan clan. Philip and his followers would be the only ones punished. No harm would come to their mates or children.

Warm hands rested on her shoulders, and Rose leaned back against Vaughn. She tilted her face up. "Hey, lover."

He grinned. "Writing in your journal, I see." He slid the book from under Beelzebub, then flipped through the pages. "I see you only have a few empty pages. I will purchase you another journal on my way home."

She turned in her seat. "Where are you going? Mrs. Brown is preparing tea."

"Andrew has informed me Inspector Hughes rang. He left word for me to meet him." Vaughn bent down and kissed her lips. "I should be home for dinner."

"Be careful. Until Philip's captured I'm going to worry."

"I know, love. I've informed Andrew not to answer the door to anyone until I return."

She rolled her eyes. "I'll be all right."

"I wish you had stayed at Wyvern house."

She didn't miss the acid tone of his voice. This was one argument that would end, now. Rose stood and tilted her face up to his. "I married you, for better or worse."

"Those were not our vows," he snapped.

She wrapped her arms around his waist. "You're right. They weren't. But my place is at your side, not hiding somewhere worrying myself sick about you."

He sighed and rested his chin on top of her head. "I know Philip's motives. He wants to take from me everyone I care about, just as he feels I did to him." Vaughn tenderly framed her face. "He knows my love for you and will stop at nothing to take you from me."

"Oh, please! Philip won't take me from you. We'll catch him. I know we will."

"We?" A faint smiled curved Vaughn's lips, and he shook his head. "Until *we* do, I will worry." His gaze lowered to her waist and his smile widened. "Soon I will be buying you more dresses."

"Why?"

He laughed then he quickly kissed her lips. "Your waist is getting thicker."

Vaughn reached over and patted Beelzebub. "Take care of our lady." He then kissed her again, passionately. "I won't be late."

Rose watched as Vaughn left. Biting her lip, she looked away. A deep uneasiness crept over her. "I'm being silly, Beelzebub. There is nothing for me to worry about." She patted the cat's head. "Come on, let's go find a nice cheerful book to read."

Rose ran her hand over the spines of books. "Shakespeare, Poe, Dickens, I don't feel like reading any of these." She walked over to the far wall to try her luck there. One of these days, she planned to rearrange his books.

Across the room, a shiny object rested on a shelf. Rose picked it up and held the small knife in her hand, trying to remember where she'd seen it before. Her hands gripped the knife tightly as she remembered it was the knife Royce had at the picnic. It was also the very knife Vaughn had handed to her before she was catapulted back in time.

Anxiety rushed through her as she stared at the object she held. It was the knife Vaughn had used in her time to pry the paneling that had sealed the room. "This is silly, Beelzebub. This small knife had nothing to do with my time travel." But, for some reason, she wondered if maybe it had.

Penny's screams had Rose rushing from the room and into the hall.

Rose screamed at the sight before her. Philip stood over Andrew's still and bloody body.

Philip laughed, glaring up at her. Blood smeared his face, and he wore an eye patch over his right eye. "Scream all you want. There's no one to save you." He started up the stairs, keeping his gaze on Rose.

She backed away from the steps. A flood of memories flashed through her mind, and she remembered him. He was the man at the hotel the night Simon told her about his brother embezzling from the company. "Dear God."

Rose turned and ran back into the study, slamming the door, then bolted it. She tried to push the desk, but it was too heavy to budge.

The door shook as Philip pounded on it. "Whore! You're only delaying the inevitable," he shouted. "I think I will rip out that bastard you carry, then your heart."

Rose ran into the library as Philip broke through the door. She tried to shut the library door, but Philip shoved it open with such force it threw her across the room.

Philip blocked her only way out.

Beelzebub hissed and sprang at Philip, clawing his face.

Rose saw her chance and ran toward the opening.

Philip threw Beelzebub against the wall and lunged at her. He grabbed her around the throat, choking her. "You're harder to kill than a cat with nine lives. But I'll succeed this time," Philip hissed.

Rose fell back against the bookshelf. Out of the corner of her eye, she spotted the small decorative knife. She grabbed it and thrust it into Philip's chest.

Shock crossed his face as he stumbled back.

Rose broke free of his hold and ran for the door, but Philip grabbed her again. A scream tore from her as his claws dug deep into her shoulder.

She rammed her elbow into his gut and attempted to throw him to the floor, but Philip was too much for her. He countered each move she made.

Philip pulled the knife from his chest and leered at her. "Perhaps I will cut your pretty face." He drew the blade slowly across her cheek, cutting her deep. She wouldn't scream. She wouldn't give him the satisfaction.

Gritting her teeth to the pain, Rose twisted and pulled until she stood in the doorway between the study and the library. She brought her knee up, catching him in the groin. He flinched but still held her tight. Philip sliced her face again.

Rose jerked and grabbed his wrist, trying to wrestle the knife from him.

The lights brightened, and the room seemed to tilt. Philips' eyes grew wide, and his grip on her wrist slackened.

Suddenly someone forcibly yanked her backward. The room exploded in a kaleidoscope of colored lights. Unable to move, Rose stood frozen, staring at Philip. The longer she stared at him, the smaller he became as if he were moving farther away from her. He was shouting something, but she couldn't make out what he was screaming.

~ ~ ~

Vaughn ran up the walk to his home. His heart pounded wildly as Rose's fears overtook him. Through the bond, they shared he knew she was in danger.

The front door hung open on its hinges. Penny sat on the floor of the entry, sobbing and cradling Andrew's lifeless body.

He had to get to Rose. Vaughn rushed past and took to the stairs.

Penny shouted, "'E's dead, Sir. My Andrew is dead."

Vaughn rushed into his study and grabbed Rose, yanking her free from Philip's clutches.

The second Philip's hand slipped from Rose the room exploded with a burst of bright light. Vaughn shielded his eyes and blindly reached for Rose again. He blinked his eyes, clearing his vision. "Rose!"

She didn't answer. His heart broke. He could no longer sense her. Rose was gone. His Rose was gone.

Philip's eyes went wide, his mouth hung open, and he backed away. "What sort of trickery is this," he whispered. Philip backed toward the window. Before Vaughn could stop him, Philip jumped through, shattering the glass.

Vaughn followed. Philip wouldn't get away this time.

The instant Philip landed he changed into his wolf form and ran off into the night. Vaughn was quick on Philip's heels. He would not escape.

Philip's wolf darted beneath carriages and ran down streets. He cut through an alley leading to the market. Vaughn rounded the corner and stopped. The market was crowded at this hour. Bloody hell, he'd lost Philip in the midst of the people. He'd failed.

Philip had succeeded in eluding him, but he couldn't hide forever.

Vaughn's tears blurred his vision as he trudged into his house. "Rose!" He called, knowing she wouldn't answer. "Please, *Yeva*, I pray my Rose has returned to her time and is not lost somewhere strange to her. Please keep her safe until I can find her." He dropped to his knees and roared with the rage and pain in his heart. A part of his soul had been severed. He bowed his head, gasping for breath. He had to gain control of his emotions. He could not mourn, not now, not when others depended on him.

Drawing in a deep breath, Vaughn set about the task of contacting Allen, notifying the authorities of Andrew's death, and having Mrs. Brown comfort and console Penny.

In the wee hours of the night, Vaughn stood on the balcony, Beelzebub in his arms. The misery consuming him was so great that he wept.

The days turned into weeks, months, then years. Without his Rose, the only thing that kept him going was his promise to her he'd find her again. Every night he read her journal. The words brought her closer. He made sure Sara and Mishenka were not in Russia during the revolution. Vaughn saw to it his friends and family were relocated to America before Hitler came into power. All along he hoped and prayed what he did didn't interfere with finding Rose again.

He served in the first, then the second World Wars. He took passage on the Titanic in hopes of preventing it's sinking. He also flew in the Hindenburg, even though Rose told him to stay away from the airship. The temptation was too great.

He made money in the stock market, taking Rose's advice, and investing in several companies as they started. He'd watched in awe with the world as man stepped on the moon. Through all of this, Rose was with him in his heart.

~ ~ ~

The blinding light spun around Rose like a twister, engulfing her with sounds and emotions. She heard voices, muted and loud at the same time. Her head ached with the pounding of music, radio, and news broadcasts.

The chaos stopped, and she fell back against a solid form.

Rose turned, looking up at Vaughn. "Philip is behind me!"

"It's all right. You're safe. I've got you."

Why was he so calm? "Vaughn! Philip is right behind me," she all but shouted at him. Then looked over her shoulder and gasped. Her heart pounded in her chest, and she slowly looked back at Vaughn. He wore a sage green shirt and low slung tight jeans instead of a white lawn shirt, vest, and trousers.

Shaking her head at what she was seeing, Rose backed away. This wasn't right. The room was all wrong. "No, no. I have to go back." She turned, shuddering inwardly at the knowledge she'd returned to her time. The dark, dusty, and empty library gave silent proof she had indeed returned.

"Rose, please." Vaughn placed his hands on her shoulders.

Outside, lightning flashed, then thunder rumbled in the distance.

Confused and needing time to compose herself, she looked around the dim and dusty room. Rain streaked the dirty windows from which only minutes ago she'd watched the falling snow. Tears stung her eyes while she stared again at the dark and empty doorway. Trembling, she glanced down at herself. She still wore the dark green flannel wrapper Penny had dressed her in this afternoon for tea.

Rose stumbled toward the library door. She had to go back. Her Vaughn needed her.

"Rose," Vaughn called, tenderly turning her to face him. "Please, I love you. I have missed you so much. I can't live another second without you."

She wanted to believe, to hope the man standing before her was her Vaughn. Which Vaughn did she love? Did she love the one of the past or the one standing in front of her here and now? Were they truly the same? She gazed up into his love-filled eyes. "How long have I've been gone? What day is it?"

He slowly shook his head. "Not long. I don't think you were gone more than a few seconds from this time."

She ran her hand over her dress and gazed up at him. "Look at me. I lived with you for almost half a year. I had to have been gone longer."

"Rose, I didn't have time to make it to the steps when I heard your screams. I ran back in here and saw you in the past struggling with Philip. He was pulling you through the doorway. I lost you once. I wouldn't lose you again. I grabbed you and yanked you back into this room. Back to me."

"I really went back in time, and everything truly did happen, didn't it?"

He nodded. "I've waited, hoped, and dreamed I would find the place in time where I could hold you again." Vaughn ran the pad of his thumb along her cheek. "Let me heal you," he said as he lowered his lips to her cheek. Brushing light kisses along the cuts Philip inflicted on her. Vaughn whispered. "I love you so much."

Her heart sang. A cry of relief slipped from her lips. "You've waited for me all this time? You still love me?" she asked, falling into his open arms.

"With all my heart," he murmured against her ear as he swept her up and carried her from the room. "I'll never let you go again."

Rose rested her head against his broad shoulders and thrilled in the knowledge he still loved her, and they were together. "You planned all of this. Didn't you?"

Vaughn didn't answer as he carried her from the house. He used his powers and willed the passenger door open and slid her into the seat. Blood coated his hands from her wounds. "Why didn't you tell me you had other injuries?"

The concern in his voice warmed her. "Just scratches."

"Are you sure?" He arched his brow.

"Yes." Her mind spun, and dizziness assaulted her. Odd. The connection they'd shared was weak, but slowly growing stronger.

"Very well." Vaughn shut the car door. He ran around the front of the car, then slid behind the wheel and closed his door. He turned to her, framed her face with his hands, and sealed his mouth over hers.

Rose parted her lips, and Vaughn's tongue delved deep into her mouth. His tongue teased, and danced with her, stroking the passion she had for him. God, she loved this man. Vaughn broke off his kiss and pressed his forehead to hers. His heavy breathing matched hers.

He pressed another kiss to her lips before he sat back in his seat. Tears glistened in his eyes, and he blinked them away. "When I saw you again at the restaurant, I wanted to grab you and kiss you, but I couldn't. I couldn't do anything that would risk our being together. I've waited so long. So very, very long."

Rose looked at her hands and twisted her wedding band around her finger. A hundred years was a long time. "You've told me you love me, but am I still your wife?" Bravely, she faced him.

"Yes. Until the end of time," The faint tremor in Vaughn's voice and the love in his eyes spoke louder than his words.

"Then take me home." Rose reached over and covered his hand with hers.

He smiled and started the engine.

They drove only a few blocks before Vaughn turned down a narrow drive and stopped in front of a stately old home.

"We're here." He killed the engine but didn't move to get out of the car.

They sat silently as a light drizzle fell. Vaughn's apprehension surged through their growing connection. Rose waited. After a long while, Vaughn let out an audible breath. "You asked if I'd planned all of this. The answer is yes, but I had help from you."

"From me? How? Did I come to you in your dreams?"

"Not exactly. You see, every night I read your journal. It was the only thing I had of yours. I knew when you were born. I felt it. My heart began beating again that day."

"But—"

He held up his hand. "Let me finish. You wrote about everything. I knew the day your parents died. I was there. I tried my hardest to prevent their accident, as well as that of Richards, but failed, both times."

Emotions she couldn't comprehend engulfed her. "You tried to prevent my parents' deaths and Richard's?" Tears burnt her eyes. "Why? If you had succeeded, then I'd still be married to Richard, wouldn't have traveled into the past. We wouldn't be together."

Vaughn sat like a statue, staring out the front windshield, the muscles in his jaw ticked. "I love you so much, Rose, I couldn't bear watching you suffer their loss. Even though I knew what I was risking, I didn't want you to suffer. After I failed to save Richard, I realized I could not fight fate, a lesson I should have learned several years before. I had to allow your life's events to unfold. I don't know why I couldn't save your parents' lives or Richard's life. Maybe because these events had already happened, because you already lived this part of your life. I don't know. Maybe it's because I couldn't fight fate." Vaughn laced his fingers with hers, and she drew comfort from him. "So I stayed in the shadows, loving you from afar and ensuring your safety until it was time."

Rose stared at the man beside her and realization struck her. "It was you. That's how Simon had the money to give everyone severance pay. You were the person he was meeting. That's why he wanted me to take on your house freelance."

Vaughn nodded as a boyish smile curved his lips. "Guilty."

Rose leaned over and quickly kissed his lips and winced. Perhaps her shoulder was more than a scratch.

"Let's get you inside," Vaughn said as he exited the car. He opened her door and helped her, shaking his head. "I am an ass for not tending to your *scratches* sooner."

"No, you're not. My wounds are not serious. Besides, you saw to the cuts on my face." She ran her finger down the side of her face where Philip had sliced her cheek. Call her vain, but she hoped she would not have a scar.

Vaughn's eyes glowed, a sure sign of his anger. "You should never have been hurt. I should have never left the house that night. Inspector Hughes never called. It was Philip. It was all Philip."

"I want to know everything," she told him.

Vaughn nodded and opened the door "After I see to you, I will tell you everything." He then escorted her into the house. The lights instantly came on.

"Still doing your light trick, I see." She laughed.

"That wasn't me." He chuckled and shut the door. "I have the lights set on a motion detector." Vaughn then pointed down the hall. "This way."

Despite Vaughn's laugh, his apprehension continued to seep into her. Vaughn had told her he loved her, had waited for her, had planned everything so they could be together, but time could change a person. A hundred years was a long time. "Vaughn?"

He slid his arm around her waist. "Come on. I want to have a look at your shoulder."

She followed him down the narrow hall and into a small bathroom. It contained only a sink and a toilet.

He lowered the toilet lid. "Have a seat." Vaughn pulled opened a drawer. "I have a pair of snips somewhere. Ah, found them." He pulled out a pair of scissors. His hands trembled as he cut her dress.

"Good, the bleeding has stopped, and you've started to heal." Vaughn reached over and wetted a washcloth under the faucet. "Your face will not scar, but I'm afraid where Philip clawed you on your back will." Carefully he washed her wounds.

She couldn't take this not knowing any longer. Rose closed her eyes. Perhaps Vaughn had found another love and was torn between the two of them. That would explain the white band on his finger and the turmoil she felt from him. "Vaughn?"

"Yes."

"What is her name?"

He paused in his treatment of her wound. "Whose name?"

"I've been gone a long time, over a hundred years." Tears stung Rose's eyes. "You can tell me if you've found someone else. I'll understand." How she got the words past the lump in her throat, she'd never know. Her heart crumbled. To have Vaughn again in her life, only to lose him—the thought was unbearable.

The washcloth slipped from his hand. "There is no one else. In all this time there has never been anyone. My heart and body have belonged only to you. Only you."

"In over a hundred years you've never…"

"Since the moment you vanished, I've not had the desire."

"Then why are you acting so distant?" She didn't understand his sudden change in behavior toward her. Sudden? No, not sudden, she'd been away from him for over a hundred years. To her, it had only been a matter of moments.

"Oh, God, Rose." Vaughn dropped to his knees and wrapped his arms around her waist, pressing his cheek against her chest. He hugged her tightly as if drawing strength from her.

She held him and waited. Her hand smoothed down his back, then up again, offering him all the comfort he needed.

"The moment you vanished I knew I'd lost you. The only thing keeping me alive was the fact I knew someday I would find you." He leaned back, meeting her gaze. "I'm terrified you will not love the man I have become."

Chapter Twenty-one

Vaughn knelt on the washroom floor, staring up into Rose's eyes. Could she love who he was now? In the past hundred years, he'd hardened his heart and had committed some heinous acts, many heinous acts for God, country, King, and Queen. For over a hundred years he'd been faithful to Rose and kept to himself. His only true companions were her journal and Beelzebub. For over a hundred years he'd hunted Philip and Dorjan's followers, enforcing clan justice. How could Rose still love him once she discovered how many he'd killed? "I'm not the same man you fell in love with so very long ago. You must believe me when I tell you there has never been anyone else. I love you, Rose, with all my heart. I could never betray your love."

Keeping his gaze locked on her eyes, he opened his mind to her and held his breath, waiting for her response. Rose's fingers lightly caressed the white band circling his finger where his wedding ring had been. He pulled the gold chain from under his T-shirt. "I took this off just before I went into your office the other day. It was the first time it has been off my finger since our wedding." He slipped the necklace from around his neck and placed his wedding band in her hand.

The disbelief on her face slowly faded, and she slid the ring back on his finger. "You'll never be alone again."

His lips smothered her words. Rose's hands slid up his chest and around his neck. Her lips parted for him, and he kissed her with all his heart. He ended his kiss and rested his forehead against hers and tenderly stroked her cheek. "Why don't you rest a bit? You look a little pale."

"I'm fine." She let out a long breath. Her eyes smoldered with a passion he'd spent countless nights, dreaming of seeing once more. "I'm pale because of the many times I could have

306

lost you." A mischievous spark lit her eyes. "The Hindenburg? After I unequivocally told you no?"

Vaughn shook his head and stood. He had his Rose back. He would not spoil this time with an argument about the risks he'd taken. "Your shoulder wound is nothing more than a bad scratch now. But in your condition, you should rest." He gently kissed Rose as he lifted her in his arms, then carried her across the hall into their bedroom. He ended their kiss as he placed her on the bed.

Rose took his hand and covered her stomach with it. "At least our child will be born in a modern hospital."

His child grew inside his wife. Vaughn held his hand on Rose's flat stomach. He'd hoped and prayed for her safe return, having both Rose and his child back was more than he could have dreamed. His years of loneliness had been rewarded.

Beelzebub padded into the room and nonchalantly jumped onto the bed. He sniffed Rose's hand, and Vaughn swore he saw the cat smile.

"It's about time you came out and said hello."

The cat purred and rubbed its head against her hand.

Rose's fingers threaded through the cat's fur. "His markings are identical to Beelzebub's."

"That's because he *is* Beelzebub. He's missed you as much as I have."

She lifted the cat in her arms and hugged him, burying her face in his fur. "I can't believe he's still alive. After all this time?"

"Believe it. I'm going to bring in the luggage. Oh, I thought you would want this." He reached across and pulled open the drawer to the nightstand, then removed an old but familiar white box, now dingy with age. "Percy finally got this charged." Vaughn handed her the phone that over a century ago had amazed him. "You stay put." He brushed a chaste kiss to her forehead.

Vaughn quickly grabbed her luggage and carried it back inside. Their bed was empty. "Rose, are you all right?"

She didn't reply.

"Rose!" Panic surged in him. "Rose." He exhaled, hearing the water running. She was in the shower and not catapulted back to the iron age. He knocked on the bathroom door.

"Come in."

He opened the door, and his breath caught as his gaze roamed over her naked body standing in the shower.

Rose looked up from shaving her legs. "I hope you don't mind, but I felt like Sasquatch with all the hair on my legs." She grinned. Her leg was propped up on the shower seat, giving him a wonderful view of her pink pussy.

Vaughn felt the stirrings of lust. His cock throbbed and pressed against the zipper of his jeans. Damn, just looking at her nude body was enough to make him come.

"Water's fine, come on in."

That was all he needed to hear. He quickly shed his clothing then slid open the shower door. He wanted Rose. It'd been so very long since he'd held her, made love to her but he didn't want to renew his claim on her in a shower.

Rose stepped to him, wrapping her arm around his waist while she slid her other hand down his stomach until her fingers circled his cock.

"Rose."

She cupped his balls, gently fondling him. "Hmm...?"

"Love, you can't." His brain forced him to say, but his cock wished he's shut up. He hardened against her hip. "You're hurt. You've had a traumatic experience."

"I want you."

He took a step back from her. "Turn around and let me wash your back."

Rose did as he asked, but it didn't escape him how straight her back went or the fact she'd crossed her arms. He bet she even gnawed on her lower lip.

He lathered up the washcloth then gently began to wash away the dried blood. Philip's claw marks were faint pink lines.

In a day or two, they would be only faint white lines, barely noticeable by any human.

"Rose, I'm sorry I didn't protect you from Philip."

"No more talking." She turned and dropped to her knees in front of him and took him in her hands. "Let me show you, that you still belong to me. For me, I was only gone a matter of moments, but for you..."

Oh, bloody hell, Rose took him into her mouth. Her plump lips wrapped around the head of his cock. She slid down his dick, her tongue teasing the underside of his shaft as she took more of him.

Rose slid up and down his cock, sucking him until the head struck the back of her throat. Then she sucked and hummed as she slid up and down. Bloody hell! His knees nearly buckled. He'd wanted to claim her again in their bed, not in the shower.

"Rose," he growled out.

She looked up through her lashes while her talented tongue teased him and her fingers fondled him.

"Love." He wasn't sure what he wanted to say. The demon who shared his soul wanted him to shut up.

Rose began a rhythm, sliding up and down his shaft while her hands fondled his balls. She squeezed the base of his length, and he groaned. Rose removed her mouth from him, and he whimpered at the loss.

"I want you to come. I want to swallow you down." Water sprayed her face, and he reached behind him, shutting off the shower.

"Rose—"

Her mouth slid down him, and she squeezed him again as she hummed, shutting off his words and his brain.

Rose increased her pace drawing him closer. Vaughn's cock pulsed and twitched. Rose sucked harder, hollowing out her cheeks. Then her finger slipped behind his balls and tapped that sensitive patch of skin.

His breath caught, and he lost the battle. He roared with his release, his hands fisting her hair. His ecstasy rolled through him, and he bucked his hips.

Rose's lips sealed around his cock at his base, and she swallowed all of him.

Finally, his release ebbed, and his flaccid cock slipped from her mouth. She licked her lips and tilted her head back.

Rose gazed up at him, and her hazel eyes shimmered with the satisfaction of a woman who'd just rocked her man's world. She turned her head. "Mine!" And bit the inside of his thigh, then placed a chaste kiss on the abused skin.

The effect of her bite had his dick fully hard and ready to go again.

Vaughn bent and scooped Rose up into his arms. His sudden action tore a squeal from her.

Dripping with water, he strode from the shower and dropped a laughing Rose in the middle of their bed. She was beautiful and all his. Her breasts were fuller, and her stomach slightly rounder with their child than she'd been only an hour ago when they landed in England.

Their child. He didn't want to harm the baby.

"Oh, no, you don't." Rose locked her ankles around his legs and her arms around his neck. "I need your cock to fill me. I want your fangs in my throat. I need you to claim me again."

With her words, he lunged forward, sliding into Rose's warm sheath, filling her completely. He'd wanted to make love to her slowly, to relearn her body, but that wasn't what Rose wanted. She thrust her hips up meeting his downward motion. He pounded Rose's body as she peppered kisses along his jaw, cheek and finally settling on his neck where it met his shoulder. She nipped the tender flesh nearly causing him to lose control.

Roses inner muscles clamped down on him as she bit his throat. His release tore from him as his fangs sank deep into her neck, her blood filling his mouth just as his blood filled Rose's. She'd bitten him. She'd claimed him.

After a few seconds, or an hour, or a day, he didn't know how long he'd lay spent on top of her, Vaughn rolled from Rose. Her eyes were closed, and a smile pulled at her lips. He'd loved his lady well.

He'd tend to her while she slept. Vaughn strode into the tiny bathroom catching his reflection in the mirror. He leaned closer to the mirror and ran his fingers over the marks in his throat. His mate marks. Rose had marked him. After a hundred years he finally carried her marks.

He wondered. Vaughn glanced at his inner thigh. A smile spread across his lips, and he knew he looked like a grinning fool as he returned to their bedroom.

Rose looked up, and tears shimmered in her eyes. "Vaughn."

"Rose? What is it?"

She shook her head. "Philip did kill Andrew. I saw Andrew at the foot of the stairs. I'd hoped."

"Even if I had been there, I would not have been able to save him." Vaughn pulled her into his arms. He held her as she'd cried. To Rose, Andrew had just died.

When her sobs turned to hiccups, he tenderly dried Rose's tears. "Penny gave birth to a son, who she named after Andrew. Their great-grand-son works for Royce."

"Is he as kind and sweet as Andrew?"

"Percy is like no other." There was no way Vaughn could describe the man. Rose would have to meet him.

He jerked when Rose's fingers lightly gaze over his shoulder, tickling him. "So, what's the story of this tattoo on your shoulder?" Hmm.

He glanced at the red rose with a blood drop falling from a petal. "To this day I can't remember too much about the night I got it. It was after World War One. I was with Royce."

"Why doesn't that surprise me?"

"If you want it removed, I will."

"No. I like it." She rolled to her side. "I want to snuggle."

He stretched out beside her and pulled her tightly to him. "I've dreamed of this for so long."

She sighed and rested her head on his shoulder. "I can't believe the many times I could have lost you," Rose countered. "And the Titanic! Seriously? Vaughn, why?" Despite her angry tone, he did not miss the smile in Rose's eyes.

"I could not allow the loss of so many innocent lives. I thought if I were on that cursive ship, I could warn the captain. But like I could not prevent the deaths of your parents or of Richard, my attempt to prevent the sinking were for not. If any good came from this, I did manage to save the lives of a few. Perhaps fate intended for me to be on that ship." He shrugged. "We may never know."

"Was the inside of the ship as grand as depicted in the movie?"

"No. Grander."

Rose snuggled closer to him. She slipped her leg between his and rested her head on his chest. "Tell me about everyone. I want to know about Royce and Aileen."

"Aileen and David have four sons. No daughters. Ryder, their oldest has been working with the family. He's a good kid and looks like his father. Glen and Victoria are still unmated as is Royce, however. Royce does have a mate."

"He does!" Rose bolted upright. "Why hasn't he claimed her yet?"

"He will, in good time. Caitlin was mated a little over a year ago. Her mate, Raven, is an American, like you."

"Raven's a girl's name." Rose arched her brow.

"Raven was a detective. *He* works with Glen and Scotland Yard."

"What else?" Rose yawned.

"Alan is considering stepping down as head of the Clans. Royce has taken over most of the Clan business already. Of course, as long as Mishenka has breath in his lungs, he will always control the clan. The old man can't help his meddling."

"What about Tristan and that bunch." Rose's eyes fluttered closed, and she nuzzled his chest.

"Quaid is the Clan's Healer. Morgan runs the financial aspects for most of us. As for Tristan, he finally graduated even with Royce's influence."

Rose's even breathing teased Vaughn's chest. He pressed a kiss to her crown and closed his eyes. He'd tell her about the rest of the family later.

~ ~ ~

Three days later the sun glared through the windscreen. Vaughn pushed his sunglasses up, as he glanced over at Rose sleeping in the passenger seat. He had taken his love shopping yesterday. The clothes she brought along with her no longer fit her waist. The first time he'd met her, he'd dressed her in the latest fashions. He'd teased her about having to dress her all over again.

After their shopping excursion, he'd sprang his surprise on her. Rose squealed so loud when he'd told her they were going to Wyvern house everyone in the café stared at them. He loved his Rose.

Rose was so excited about their trip today she had not slept much last night. He'd lost count of the many times she left their bed to check on something or another, making sure she'd not forgotten anything.

Since her return, Rose had called Denny and let him know she was staying in England for a while. Vaughn chuckled when he overheard her telling the older man she'd fallen in love with Vaughn.

He and Rose video called Alan and Emma. It had taken several hours of explaining everything to finally get them to understand what had happened all those years ago. When Emma informed Rose that Sara and Mishenka were in Japan, and wouldn't be back for several weeks, it had upset Rose, but she knew she'd see them soon. Rose was nearly heartbroken to find out Aileen, and her family were on holiday and wouldn't be back for several days. Rose was looking forward to seeing Aileen again.

Vaughn covered Rose's hand with his and mentally patted himself on the back. He'd not told her Alan had arranged for Mishenka and *Babushka* to be at Wyvern house when they arrived, or that Aileen and her family would be arriving tomorrow.

Another surprise for his Rose. Alan planned a celebration like no other. Rose was back. His heart pounded as if it would burst from his chest.

Vaughn glanced in the rearview mirror again. The same silver Mercedes-Benz had been following them for the last twenty minutes, keeping the same distance. Vaughn pressed the accelerator. The other car sped up as well. "Bloody hell! Rose, wake up."

Her eyes fluttered open. "Are we there yet?"

"No. Do you know how to use a pistol?"

"Ah . . . yeah, why?"

"There's one in the glove box. Get it out." He glanced in the mirror again. "The clip is there, too."

~ ~ ~

Rose opened the glove box and removed the gun. She stared at the pistol, briefly before taking it out. The worried tone in Vaughn's voice caused every alarm in her to go off. Rose inserted the clip, racked the slide, chambering a round. "What did you do, take this from some Nazi officer?"

Not answering her, Vaughn pressed a button on the steering wheel. "Ring Alan." The phone rang, then someone answered. Rose did not recognize the voice.

"Percy, we're ten minutes from the house and being tailed." He disconnected then glanced over at her.

In the three days she'd been back, their connection had grown stronger. She knew Vaughn worried over her safety. The tick in his jaw was enough of a tell she didn't need to read Vaughn's mind.

Rose forced a smile, trying to show him she wasn't fearful. "Perhaps it's just a tourist." Her hands clutched tight. Rose turned in her seat and peered out the rear window.

The car behind them sped up to pass.

"Get down!" Vaughn pushed her toward the floorboard.

The rear window shattered and Vaughn swerved, running off the road and into a ditch. The car jerked to a sudden stop.

"Are you all right?" he asked.

"Shaken, that's all." Terrified, but she wasn't about to tell him that, though she figured he already knew. She could feel his anger, and fear for her safety.

Vaughn opened his door. "Whatever happens next, stay down and," He picked up the gun on the floor of the car. "aim for his heart." He locked, then slammed the door, not glancing back at her.

Despite his order to stay down, she peeked over the seat and gasped. Philip sat in the car behind them, glaring through the windshield. Every muscle in her stiffened with dread.

Philip emerged, slapping the flat of an ax across his hand as he approached. "I must say I've been looking forward to this day." He gestured at her. "Don't worry, Vaughn. Your whore will join you shortly."

Rose swallowed hard while she forced her fear from her mind. Vaughn was unarmed. Her attention locked on the double-bladed ax in Philip's hand.

Vaughn straightened. "I see you're still full of yourself."

A motorcycle cut across the meadow, then came to a stop next to Philip's car. The rider dismounted.

Her heart hammered and her breath came out in a gasp as she gripped the pistol. Philip was armed, and he had backup as well. She glared at the new intruder. From here she had a damn good shot at him.

"Stay out of this," Vaughn ordered.

His outburst puzzled her. Surely, Vaughn wasn't speaking to her.

The biker held up his hands and backed away, then circled until he stood near her door. He removed his helmet and looked in at her. The tall, dark, broad-chested man gave her a reassuring smile, before turning to watch Vaughn.

She recognized those honey golden eyes. "Tristan." His name came on a breath, bringing some relief.

Her sense of relief was short lived as panic overcame her. Philip lunged at Vaughn, swinging the ax at his throat. The tip of the ax must have nicked Vaughn as a line of red blood stained his shirt.

Vaughn jumped back, delivering a roundhouse kick to Philip's midsection. Philip recovered, turned, lunged, and swung the ax again. Vaughn ducked and tackled Philip. They rolled down the bank and vanished from her sight.

Rose peeked around the seat, trying to see what was happening. She had to know what was going on. She unlocked and tried to open the door. Tristan leaned against it and shook his head.

Her heart lifted when Vaughn stood. He picked up Philip, lifted him, then slammed him to the ground. Philip tried to get to his feet, but Vaughn kicked him, knocking him to the ground again. He rolled, and Vaughn lunged after Philip. His car blocked her view. Rose tried again to get out of the car. She pushed on the door, but couldn't budge it "Tristan, let me out."

The irritating boy, ah man, shook his head, keeping his attention on the fight before him.

The blade of the ax appeared above Philip's car. Who held the weapon? The ax fell, and she screamed.

After what seemed like hours, Vaughn stood, then glanced over his shoulder at her. His shoulders raised and lowered with each deep breath he took.

Rose shoved on the car door. This time Tristan let her out.

"Rosie, stop," Tristan ordered.

Ignoring Tristan, Rose ran toward Vaughn, but Tristan grabbed her around the waist and pulled her back against him, then took the gun from her hand.

"We wouldn't want you to shoot your mate, now would we?" Tristan gazed down at her with his warm honey colored eyes. "Rosie, stay here for a few more minutes. You don't want to see this."

"Let me go!" She pushed from him and ran to Vaughn. Rose froze, seeing Philip's headless corpse sprawled on the ground, with a gaping hole torn in his chest. His heart lay next to his lifeless body, and his head rested feet away, his one eye, open, staring at them. "Oh, God." She turned away and covered her eyes.

Vaughn pulled off his blood-covered shirt. He wiped the blood from his hands before drawing her into his embrace. "Shh." He rained kisses over her hair, forehead, and finally her lips. "Shh. It's over. Philip is dead," he said between kisses.

Rose stepped back and looked him over. "You're bleeding."

"No more than a scratch." Vaughn glanced down at his chest, then shrugged. "Most of it's not my blood."

When a car came toward them, Rose stepped behind him. "Vaughn?"

"It's all right, Love. They're on our side." He breathed deeply and smiled at her.

The car pulled next to them, and the window lowered.

"Well, it's about bloody damn time you showed up," Vaughn said.

The driver winked at her. "As if you needed us."

She couldn't believe her eyes. It was like seeing Andrew's ghost. He had the same dimple and, other than his Technicolor-hair, the gentleman looked just like Andrew. "Oh, God," she whispered.

The passenger door opened and Royce stood from the car. He came over to them, keeping his intent gaze on her. "Rose! It is you." He swung her up in his arms and brushed a kiss to her cheek before setting her down. "I couldn't believe it when Vaughn and you called us, telling us you'd returned. I still can't believe my eyes." Royce ran his hands down the length of her arms, grinning like a fool. "It's you. It's truly you."

"Yes, Royce, it's me." She tried not to look at Philip's body. She wanted him stopped. Wanted him dead. But wanting and seeing are two different things. "Can we stand somewhere else?"

Royce looked at Philip's headless body, then up at Vaughn. "You did jolly well without us. A little bit of overkill don't you think, ole man? Head and heart?"

"Rose didn't need to witness this," Vaughn stated flatly, glaring at Tristan.

He shrugged. "I told Rose to wait. Not my fault she's still as stubborn as ever." Tristan motioned toward Philips body. "Didn't take as long as I thought."

Without thinking, she glanced at Philip's lifeless body, only to see his empty clothes. His body had turned to dust. "What? What happened to him?" She stared up at Vaughn.

"I explained it to you before. When we die, our bodies turn to ash. The older we are, the faster the process."

She remembered him telling of watching his enemies turning to ash, but she never thought he'd literally meant their bodies turn to ash and crumbled to dust. Rose wrapped her arms around him and buried her face in his chest. Her body shuddered at the thought that it could have been him.

Royce turned to his driver. "Percy, take Vaughn and Rose home. Tristan and I will tidy up things here."

"Very good, sir."

"Percy," Vaughn called to Royce's driver. "I'd like you to meet Rose, my mate."

"At your service, my lady." He bowed.

"Rose," Vaughn said. "This is Percy. He is Royce's valet."

"Babysitter," he whispered and winked at her as he brought her hand to his lips. "Andrew was my great-grandfather." His bright eyes offered the same friendship as Andrew's had. "Let's get you home. From what I've heard, you've had a rough go of it lately." He gave her hand to Vaughn, then strutted over to their car. Percy peered inside, then turned. "Where the bloody hell is that devilish feline of yours?"

"At the vet's," Vaughn replied, opening the car door, and helping her inside. Vaughn slid in, closing the door.

Tears welled in Rose's eyes, and she trembled. In the last three days, she'd lived two lifetimes, lost, and found her true love, all the while being hunted by a madman. Her body shook uncontrollably. What if there were more like Philip watching and waiting?

Vaughn took her in his arms and held her until she'd stopped crying. "Then we will deal with them. Philip is gone."

"Reading my mind?" She swiped at her tears with the back of her hand.

He smiled sheepishly at her. "I couldn't help it."

Percy started the engine and pulled onto the road. Ten minutes later, he stopped in front of Wyvern house. It looked the same.

The front door opened and Sara, Mishenka, Alan, and Emma rushed out. Mishenka opened Vaughn's door while Alan opened Rose's.

Alan pulled Rose in to his embrace. "It's you! It's you! My God, you're back. Not that we doubted Vaughn, but seeing you, touching you."

"Alan," Emma came to his side. "Let the child breathe. She's been through enough without you squeezing her to death."

He eased his hold and gazed down at Rose. "Inside, both of you." He grinned at Vaughn. "Come on, son. You look like hell."

~ ~ ~

Rose chewed her lower lip and held Vaughn's hand tight, waiting for Alan's response. He accepted her time travel as fact and not that she'd been kidnapped. When she'd vanished Sara concocted the ruse of Philip kidnapping Rose to cover up her time travel. With Vaughn so distraught, it was easy for the other family members to believe this to be so. Alan had the Wolfes to even searched all of America for her. It was over. Philip was dead, and she and Vaughn were together again. She was home.

Alan sat still. His ice blue gaze perused her, and his lips pulled thin.

Rose couldn't take the silence any longer. She glanced around the drawing room noting the changes. Other than the lighter color of paint, it looked the same. The same beautiful furnishings she remembered were now antiques. She glanced up at Vaughn. *Do you know what Alan is thinking?*

Nope. Vaughn leaned down and gently pressed his lips to her temple.

The dead silence grated on Rose's nerves. Why wouldn't Alan say something? Even Mishenka and Sara sat tightlipped.

Loud laughter broke the silence as Royce and Tristan entered. They smelled of gas and smoke.

Tristan came over to her. His honey-brown eyes seemed to twinkle. "Damn, it's good to have you back, Rosie. Where the hell, have you been?"

"I went through a doorway and traveled through time."

"Say what?" Tristan's mouth hung open. "You're joking, right?"

Mishenka shook his head. "Sara knew all along and kept it from us. Rose went back in time, where she met Vaughn, then somehow her fight with Philip caused her to return to her time. Which is now."

Sara patted Mishenka's hand. "I didn't want to risk our Rose not returning. I could not tell you what happened. And Vaughn..." Sara's voice trail. "We all knew the grief he endured."

Tristan raised his brow. "I don't believe it. Rose, you're sitting right before my eyes, and I still can't believe it."

Royce stood behind him. "I couldn't believe it either, but Vaughn convinced me last night. Don't worry, Tristan, by the time Aileen and her brood arrive tomorrow. I'm sure you'll be convinced, as well."

Rose grinned. "Aileen is coming? I can't wait to see her."

Vaughn glared at Royce. "It was to be a surprise."

"Oh bugger it! No one told me it was a bloody secret." Royce tossed something to Vaughn.

Vaughn caught it. "Philip's eye patch?" He tossed it back to Royce. "Burn it."

Alan folded his hands together and brought them to his lips. He sighed. "And you can torch that cursed house as well."

Rose looked from Alan to Vaughn. She and Vaughn had this argument last night. As silly as it was, she'd fallen in love with that house and was looking forward to restoring it, but Vaughn wouldn't budge. He didn't want to risk losing her or their child. However, he would permit her to salvage all she could, with one stipulation, nothing from the library.

Alan lowered his hands and pinned her with his icy blue gaze. When he spoke, his voice was soft and unthreatening but left no room for argument. "I will not have my grandchild or you, for that matter, walking through that hellish room and being ripped from this family again."

Vaughn held up his hand. "You need not worry. We've already discussed it. The house will be destroyed, and the lot turned into a park."

"Good. You can purchase another home, one not so far away."

"Father, Rose, and I will be returning to the States. She made a promise to start her own restoration business and give the people she'd worked with jobs."

Alan's eye's welled, and a smile stretched across his lips, reaching the corners of his eyes. "That's the first time you've called me that."

"Called you what?" Vaughn asked.

"Father."

Vaughn placed his hand over his heart. "But not the first time I felt it here. You are my Father, and soon you'll be my child's Grandpa."

Alan grinned. "Perhaps my grandson will be a flyer."

"Who knows? Maybe *she* will," Rose said.

Epilogue

Eighteen months later Rose stopped her jeep in front of a rundown Victorian home. Vaughn was waiting for her. He tapped his watch and shook his head as she opened her car door.

Rose opened the back door. "Come on, Kimberly, Daddy has been waiting long enough," she said, lifting her daughter from the car seat.

"What took you so long? I was getting worried," Vaughn asked, taking his daughter from Rose.

"I couldn't find Beelzebub, and you know how I hate leaving him out at the apartment when we're not there. Then somebody needed changing."

Vaughn slid his free arm around Rose. "Well, what do you think of the outside? The house sits on twenty acres. Denny and your crew have already given her a look over. The inside will need some work, however. Before we go in, I'm warning you. The previous owners liked the ultra-modern look."

Rose shivered at the thought and glanced up at the old painted lady. In its heyday, the house would have been the showplace of the town. When Vaughn said he'd found her dream home, he wasn't kidding. "Is it open? Can we have a look inside?"

"Sure, the realtor left it opened for us."

They entered and strolled from room to room. Rose made notes of the changes that would need to be made. "The first thing I'm doing is tearing down this horrible wallpaper. This house deserves to be restored to its original splendor."

Vaughn grinned at her. "So you like the house?"

"I don't like the damage those idiots did." Wonderful warmth came over her. Rose glanced around the living room and walked into another room. With each step, she knew she belonged. "We'll be able to use the lighting and the stove from the old house."

Vaughn laughed. "Come on, let me show you the upstairs."

She liked the well-lit hallway. She knew Beelzebub would love the two large windows at either end of the landing. Rose passed the master bedroom, turned, and looked again. She could have sworn she saw someone. Rose walked into the empty room. Perhaps it was only a shadow. "Why so cheap? Are there any hidden rooms, disappearing owners, skeletons in closets?"

~ ~ ~

Vaughn stopped making faces at Kimberly and glanced at Rose. He might as well tell her the truth. "No missing rooms, but the neighbors said the place is haunted."

Rose's face paled. "Haunted?"

"Now, Rose, from what I understand only the previous owners had problems."

"Ghost or no ghost, I love it." She leaned against him. "It feels like home. What do you think?"

Vaughn glanced around the room. He held his daughter in one arm and his wife with the other. The past year and a half had been the happiest of his life, thus far. He woke every morning with a smile because of Rose and Kimberly. "I think the house is perfect. It has plenty of rooms for when mum, dad, and everyone else come to visit. And we are far enough from the neighbors so Kimberly, and I can practice her flying."

Rose turned in his arms. Her hazel eyes sparkled with joy. "She hasn't even learned to walk yet, and you told me you didn't learn to fly until you were much older."

"I was a slow learner." His joy bubbled up inside him, and he lifted Rose with his other arm while still holding Kimberly. "Let's buy it."

A warm breeze gently blew through the room, and Kimberly cooed, kicking her feet.

Don't miss Crimson Hearts, book two in the Crimson Series!

A 200-year-old Dhampir, a human detective, and a serial killer.

Crimson Hearts

Chapter One

"Love, personally, I'd throw him to the floor, have him a time or two, then bite him."

Caitlin nearly dropped the phone. "Mother! I can't do that to Raven."

"Sure you can. Trust me. Men love it. How do you think I got your father?"

"Father rescued you from being burnt at a stake."

"Details, details, details, besides, we are not talking about your father and me. We are discussing you and Raven. You're not getting any younger, so when are you going to act?"

Caitlin tapped a pencil on her desk and stared at her reflection in the office window. A successful, award-winning journalist, she was still intimidated by her mother. Caitlin loved talking to her mum, but the same question always came up. When would she claim Raven O'Brien as her soul mate? "I don't know. These things take time, Mum. I can't just go up to him and say hey, you're the other half of my soul, my one true mate. Let's get married."

"Why not?"

"So how's Victoria?" She tried to change the subject. "I haven't heard a word from my wayward sister in over a month. And by the way, she isn't mated, either."

"Don't you worry about your sister? I'm working on her, as well. She's fine. At least she was when she came home two weeks ago. For some strange reason, she had to cut her holiday short. Now, don't you believe it's time you claimed this man?"

Caitlin groaned. Thank God her mother was on the other side of the Atlantic Ocean. Otherwise, she'd be here harassing poor Raven.

"You've known him for two years." Her mother wouldn't let it go. "What's the holdup? Caitlin, are you listening to me?"

"Yes, I'm listening. I haven't told him about myself yet. Raven is a no-nonsense detective. If he can't see it, smell it, or taste it, it isn't real. I have to find the right time to tell him."

"Love, there isn't a right time to tell someone that you are, for no other word, a vampire. No matter if we call ourselves Dhampir, Vampyr, Vurvulak, or Day-walker, the meanings are all the same.

We are Vampires."

A movement caught her attention. Caitlin looked up as Raven strolled down the dark and empty aisle between the office desks.

He smiled and sat on the edge of her desk. He plopped a copy of the afternoon edition of The Herald in front of her. The paper opened to her story.

"I'll be with you in a sec." She smiled. "Mum, I've got to get back to work."

"Hi, Mom," Raven said as he loosened his tie. Then he undid the first two buttons of his shirt.

Even wearing a rumpled suit and sporting a five o'clock shadow, he made her heart beat faster.

"Tell him," her mother urged.

Smiling up at him, she said, "Mum says hi."

"I did not."

"Got to go. Love you, Mum." She hung up and leaned back in her chair. No wonder Vicky always cut her holidays short.

Caitlin gazed up into Raven's black, unfathomable eyes. She could spend eternity staring into those dark pools. She licked her dry lips. "What brings you here, Detective?"

He motioned to the paper. "The guys and I just wanted to thank you. It means a lot to us, having someone in the press on our side." He chuckled as he scanned the article again. "I even sent a copy to my folks in Chicago."

"No problem. I know you're doing all you can to catch this creep."

"I stopped by your house, but your roommate said you were still here. I frightened her."

"How?"

"I knocked on your door. Inky was grooming himself on your porch, since I know Stacy doesn't permit him outside I opened the door to put him inside. Stacey screamed so loudly. I think she broke my eardrum."

Caitlin covered her mouth, stifling her laugh. "It's not funny. Stacey has been uneasy lately.

Everyone in town has."

"She also told me to tell you to hurry home." He pointed to the wall clock. "It's after six. You were supposed to be off today."

"I was. I treated myself to a spa treatment, and then I came in to work on this story. I had to.

Anne Thomason makes the third victim killed by this maniac in eighteen months. And his sixth total. He's stretching his time between victims." Her throat tightened.

Biography

Georgiana Fields

Born in coastal North Carolina, Georgiana Fields spent her summers on the Atlantic Coast, where she developed a love for the ocean, nature, and coastal ghost stories and legends. As a child, she used to love listening to her aunts tell and retell stories and legends surrounding New Bern, N.C., and other coastal towns.

She married her high school sweetheart and moved to Georgia where she worked for the American Red Cross as a Medical Technologist.

Georgiana currently resides in North Georgia with her husband, two dogs, and two cats.

While she loves nature, horseback riding, and scary movies, she currently spends most of her time writing paranormal romance and suspense, where strong women, sometimes don't know their own strength.

Connect with Georgiana here:

https://www.facebook.com/AuthorGeorgianaFields

https://www.instagram.com/fieldsgeorgiana/

https://twitter.com/georgianafields

http://georgianafields.com/

http://amazon.com/author/georgianafields/

https://www.goodreads.com/AuthorGeorgianaFields

Made in the USA
Columbia, SC
21 August 2019